THEY EAT PUPPIES, DON'T THEY?

THEY EAT PUPPIES, DON'T THEY?

A NOVEL

CHRISTOPHER BUCKLEY

TWELVE

NEW YORK • BOSTON

Twelve
Hachette Book Group
237 Park Avenue
New York, NY 10017

www.HachetteBookGroup.com

Printed in the United States of America

RRD-C

First Edition: May 2012

Twelve is an imprint of Grand Central Publishing.

The Twelve name and logo are trademarks of Hachette Book Group, Inc.

The Hachette Speakers Bureau provides a wide range of authors for speaking events.
To find out more, go to www.hachettespeakersbureau.com or call (866) 376-6591.

The publisher is not responsible for websites (or their content)
that are not owned by the publisher.

10   9   8   7   6   5   4   3   2   1

Library of Congress Cataloging-in-Publication Data

Buckley, Christopher, 1952–

They eat puppies, don't they? / Christopher Buckley. — 1st ed.

p. cm.

ISBN 978-0-446-54097-1 (regular edition)—ISBN 978-1-4555-1347-5 (large print
edition)   1. United States—Foreign relations—China—Fiction.   2. China—Foreign
relations—United States—Fiction.   3. Political fiction.   I. Title.

PS3552.U3394T53 2012

813'.54—dc23

2011042436

For Katy

PLAYERS

WASHINGTON

Walter "Bird" McIntyre, defense lobbyist, would-be novelist

Myndi, his wife, an equestrienne

Bewks, his brother, feckless but amiable Civil War "living
  historian"

Chick Devlin, CEO, aerospace giant Groepping-Sprunt

Angel Templeton, directrix, Institute for Continuing
  Conflict, Washington, D.C., headquarters of interventionist
  Oreo-Con movement

Rogers P. Fancock, exhausted, put-upon director, National
  Security Council, the White House

Barney Strecker, profane, risk-taking deputy director for
  operations, CIA

President, United States of America

Winnie Chang, chair, U.S.-China Co-Dependency
  Council

Lev Melnikov, founder, chairman, and CEO, Internet giant
  EPIC

Chris Matthews, taciturn TV-talk-show host

BEIJING

Fa Mengyao, mild-mannered, tormented president, People's
  Republic of China; general secretary, Chinese Communist
  Party

Gang, his loyal longtime aide

Lo Guowei, scary, sexually aggressive minister of state security, PRC

Han, constipated, bellicose general; minister of national defense, PRC

Politburo Standing Committee, CCP, various members, names too complicated to list

Zhang, retired admiral, People's Liberation Navy; former minister of state security; mentor to Fa

Sun-tzu, long-dead but very much alive military theoretician and strategist

As to the escape of the Dalai Lama from Tibet, if we had been in your place, we would not have let him escape. It would be better if he were in a coffin.

—Nikita Khrushchev to Mao Zedong, 1959

Hold out baits to entice the enemy. Feign disorder, and crush him.

—Sun-tzu

Om mani padme hum.

—Chenrezig

THEY EAT PUPPIES, DON'T THEY?

PROLOGUE

Dumbo

The senator from the great state of New York had been droning on for over five minutes; droning about drones.

Bird McIntyre sat in the first row behind his boss, the recipient
of the senatorial cataract of words. He scribbled a note on a piece of
paper and passed it forward.

Chick Devlin glanced at the note. He let the senator continue for
several more mind-numbing minutes so as not to appear prompted
by Bird's note. Finally, seizing on an ellipsis, he leaned forward
into the microphone across the green-baize-covered table and said,
"Senator, pardon my French, but isn't the whole *point* to scare the
shit out of them?"

The committee collectively stiffened. One senator laughed. Several smiled or suppressed smiles; some pretended not to be amused;
some were actually not amused. Not that it mattered: This was a
closed hearing, no cameras or media in attendance.

"If I may, Senator," continued Devlin, chief executive officer
of the aerospace giant Groepping-Sprunt, "the idea that a predator drone should be unobtrusive, some speck in the sky, so as not to
alarm the general public..." He smiled and shook his head. "Forgive

I

my asking, but who the heck wrote the specs for *that* paradigm? Look here, we're talking about a part of the world where one-third of the so-called general public are in their kitchens making IEDs to kill American soldiers. Another third are on the Internet recruiting suicide bombers. And the last third are on cell phones planning the next 9/11. These are the people we don't want to *alarm*?" He sat back in his chair, shaking his head in puzzlement. "Or am I missing something here?"

"Mr. *Devlin*," said the senator, straining a bit obviously for the satanic homonym, "we are talking about a predator drone the size of a commercial airliner. Of a jumbo jet. A drone, by the way, that may or may not"—she jabbed an accusatory finger in the direction of the neat, blue-uniformed air force general sitting beside Devlin—"be nuclear-capable. I say 'may or may not' because I can't seem to get a straight answer from the air force."

The general leaned into his microphone to protest but was waved away by the senator before he could achieve takeoff.

"So I'm asking *you*, Mr. Devlin: What kind of signal does this send to the world? That the United States would launch these huge, unpiloted—"

"Sentinels."

"Sentinels? *Sentinels?* Come on, Mr. Devlin, these are killing machines. Not even H. G. Wells could have come up with something like this. Read your own specs. No, on second thought, allow me."

The senator put on her bifocals and read aloud: "'Hellfire missiles, Beelzebub Gatling gun. Seven thousand rounds per second. Depleted-uranium armor-piercing projectiles. CBUs.' CBUs—that would be cluster bombs—"

"Senator," Devlin cut in, "Groepping-Sprunt did not make the world we live in. Groepping-Sprunt—if I may, ma'am—does not make U.S. foreign policy. That we leave to such distinguished public servants as yourself. What we do make are systems to help America cope with the challenges of the world we inhabit."

"Please don't interrupt me, Mr. Devlin," the senator shot back, returning to her reading material. "What about this so-called Adaptable Payload Package? 'Adaptable Payload Package.' There's an ambiguous term if ever I heard one. No wonder it's got General Wheary there talking out of both sides of his mouth."

"Senator, if I might—" General Wheary tried again.

"No, General. You had your chance. Now I'm asking Mr. Devlin—for the last time—what kind of signal does it send to the world that we would deploy such an awful symbol, such a device—a device by the way you have the gall to designate 'Dumbo.' Dumbo!" she snorted. "Dumbo! This, sir, is a creature from hell."

"Senator, with respect," Devlin said, "the platform is designated MQ-9B. Dumbo is merely a . . ."

Bird McIntyre nodded thoughtfully, as if he were hearing the name Dumbo for the first time. In fact, the name was his suggestion. If the idea is to make a breathtakingly large and lethal killing machine (as the senator would say) sound less lethal, what better name than Disney's cuddly pachyderm? Bird had considered "Cuddles," but that seemed a bit much.

". . . a nickname," Devlin continued, "like, say, 'Dragon Lady' for the U-2 spy plane or BUFF, 'Big Ugly Fat Fellow,' for the B-52 bomber. Military vehicles all have nicknames. But as to your question—what kind of signal does it send? I would say the answer is—a serious signal. A very serious signal. If I for one were a member of the Taliban or Al-Qaeda or some other sworn enemy of freedom and the American Way, and I looked up from the table in my IED lab and saw Dumbo—if you prefer, the MQ-9B—blotting out the sun and preparing to obliterate me and introduce me to Allah, I believe I might just consider taking up another line of work."

A murmur went through the committee.

Bird nodded, well pleased by his ventriloquism. Devlin's speech was almost word for word from Bird's briefing book—Tab "R."

Groepping-Sprunt was Bird McIntyre's largest account. And the Dumbo contract was a biggie—$3.4 billion worth of appropriations. Bird had worked furiously on the public-awareness campaign. For the past several weeks, every TV watcher in the Greater Washington, D.C., Area, every newspaper or magazine reader, bus-stop passerby, Internet browser, sports spectator, and subway rider—all their eyeballs and ears had been assailed by messages showing Dumbo— MQ-9B—aloft, soaring through serene blue air high above the piney mountains of the California Sierra Nevada, looking for all the world like a great big friendly flying toy that might have dropped out of Santa's sleigh. Bird had proposed painting the fuselage in a soothing shade of teal. Beneath the photo were these words:

DUMBO: CAN AMERICA AFFORD NOT TO DEPLOY HER?

The problem was money. The appropriations climate on Capitol Hill these days was brutal. The Pentagon was drowning in health-care costs, administration costs, war costs. Cutback time. They were even pensioning off admirals and generals. Not since the end of the Cold War had so many military been given the heave-ho: an aggregate of over three hundred stars so far.

Meanwhile, defense lobbyists were scrambling. In happier times, getting approval for a Dumbo-type program would have consisted of a couple of meetings, a few pro forma committee hearings, handshakes all round, and off to an early lunch. Now? Sisyphus had it easier.

On top of the "funding factor" (Washington-speak for "appalling cost overruns"), Bird and Groepping-Sprunt were up against a bit of a "perception problem" (Washington-speak for "reality"). Dumbo, MQ-9B, Fifth Horseman of the Apocalypse—whatever—was stark evidence that somewhere along the line Uncle Sam had quietly morphed into Global Big Brother. With wings. The proud American eagle now clutched in one talon the traditional martial arrows, in the other a remote control.

Perhaps, Senator, you'd prefer that we conduct war the old-fashioned way—having our boys blown up by roadside bombs while trying to instill Jeffersonian democracy door-to-door. "Hello? *Excuse us, sorry to bust in on you like this, but we're the United States military, and we're here to read you the Bill of Rights. You wouldn't be harboring any terrorists in here, would you? You're not? Fantastic! Would you care for some sugarless gum?*"

Bird jerked himself out of the reverie. He was exhausted. He told himself sternly, *Do not fall asleep in a Senate hearing!*

Uh-oh. The senator from the great state of—*damn*—Wisconsin, where approximately zero Dumbo components were manufactured, was now preparing to fire his own Hellfire missiles at Chick.

"What has it come to..." he began.

Bird suppressed a groan. He'd begged—begged—Chick to buy some Wisconsin-made components—anything—for Dumbo. *Tell him you'll install an on-board Wisconsin dairy cow. Or dead cows. Why not? Didn't they catapult diseased animals over the walls during sieges back in the Middle Ages?*

"...that the United States should resort to such"—he was shaking his head—"dreadful weapons as these?"

Bird thought, *What has it come to, Senator? You really want to know? I'll tell you: This. It has* come *to—this. Our country is going broke. No, is already* broke. *And you know what? Everyone out there in this big, wide, nasty world is still trying to kill us. Or maybe word of this hasn't yet reached Wisconsin? By the way, do you use oil in Wisconsin? You know, the kind we get from all those horrible countries in the Middle East? Or are you getting all your electricity from some other source? Wind? Solar? Methane from flatulent cows?*

Bird had anticipated this and had provided a primed hand grenade for Chick to toss back into the senator's lap. It was in Tab "S," highlighted in orange. Unlike some clients, Chick did his homework, bless him.

"Well, Senator," Devlin said with just the right air of embarrassment, "frankly, when it comes to protecting our country, I for one would rather spend a dollar than an American life."

Bird mentally high-fived. *Yesss.*

The committee voted 12–7 against funding the MQ-9B.

THAT NIGHT, AFTER AN EPIC number of drinks with Chick at the Bomb Bay Club, a favorite Washington haunt of defense contractors, Bird managed to crawl into a cab and make it back to his apartment across the river. Instead of collapsing into bed, he drunkenly banged out a highly misspelled, indignant statement on behalf of Groepping-Sprunt, wishing Wisconsin National Guard units serving in Iraq and Afghanistan "good luck over there—because your [*sic*] sure going to need it."

Bird awoke the next morning with a Hiroshima-level hangover and the cold, prickly-sweat fear that he had hit Send before collapsing into the arms of Morpheus.

He dragged himself to his computer and with pounding heart checked the Sent folder.

Not there.

It was in the Drafts folder. *Thank you, God.*

He deleted it, swallowed a heroic quantity of ibupropfen—kidney damage was an acceptable risk—and, like a mortally wounded raccoon, crawled back to bed, where he lay with poached tongue and throbbing skull, staring at the ceiling.

Somewhere above in the empyrean, Dumbo, answer to America's twenty-first-century security needs, flapped his wings one last time and tumbled, Icarus-like, from the sky.

CHAPTER I

BIRD

A n unearthly sound—clarions, shrieking—summoned Bird from the land of the undead.

Gummily, his eyes opened.

The hellish sound continued.

As his wounded brain clawed its way back to consciousness, it dawned on him that it was his cell phone. The ringtone—opening bars of "Ride of the Valkyries"—announced his wife.

"Unh." Valkyrie hooves pounded on his cerebellum.

"Well, *you* sound good."

Myndi's voice was an unhappy fusion of Gidget and marine drill sergeant. He looked at his watch. Not yet 7:00 a.m.; she'd have been up since four-thirty, training.

"Went out with... Chick... after... the..." It emerged a croak, the words forming letter by letter, syllable by syllable, Morse tappings from the radio room of a sinking vessel. "... vote. We... lost."

"I saw," she said in a scoldy tone, as if to suggest that Bird obviously hadn't put his all into it. She added, "I suppose this is going to have an effect on the stock price?"

He thought, *Yes, darling. It will in all likelihood have an* effect *on the stock price.*

"Walter," she said—Myndi refused to call him "Bird," hated the name—"we need to talk." Surely the unhappiest words in any marriage. *We need to talk.*

"We are," Bird observed.

"Why don't you have some coffee, darling. I need you to process."

Process. How she loved that word.

"I'm processing. What?"

"I'll call you back in ten minutes. Make it fifteen. That'll give you time for a nice hot shower." She hung up, doubtless having activated her stopwatch.

Walter "Bird" McIntyre blinked his eyelids at the ceiling. It looked down on him with disdain.

He rose unsteadily and confronted the full, blazing glare of the morning sun through the floor-to-ceiling glass panels. He shrank like a vampire caught out past the dawn.

Bird called his condo the "Military-Industrial Duplex." A flippant nickname, to be sure. It was in Rosslyn, Virginia, on the once-Confederate side of the Potomac River. The compensation for the unfashionable zip code was a truly spectacular view of the nation's capital. This time of year, the sun rose directly behind the great dome of the Capitol Building, casting a long, patriotic shadow across the Mall—America's front yard. Myndi, seeing the view for the first time, sniffed, "It's nice, darling, but a bit of a cliché."

Coffee. Must. Have.

At least, he reflected with what little self-congratulation he could muster in his debased state, he hadn't yet reached the point where he needed a snort of booze to get himself going again in the morning.

His computer screen was on. He remembered the (thankfully) unsent e-mail with a shudder of relief and mechanically went about the rituals of caffeination, acting as his own combo barista/EMT.

THEY EAT PUPPIES, DON'T THEY?

The Valkyries shrieked anew. Apparently his fifteen minutes had elapsed. *For God's sake...*

Myndi had been unamused to learn the ringtone he'd chosen to announce her calls. *Really, darling. Passive-aggressive, are we?*

He decided—manfully, mutinously—not to answer. He smiled defiantly. Whatever she had in store for him this morning, it could wait until his system had been injected with piping-hot Kenyan stimulant.

He wondered idly, what could it be this time? Another termite-rotted column? Peckfuss the caretaker drunk again?

He didn't care. He would call back. Yes. *Muahahaha!* He would... pretend he'd been in the shower.

He poured his coffee and sat before the laptop, pressed the buttons to launch the cybergenies of news.

Post: SENATE KILLS DUMBO
Times: SUPERDRONE DIES IN SENATE COMMITTEE

Bird wondered how Chick's hangover was coming along. Or whether he had even made it back to his hotel. Was he lying facedown in the Reflecting Pool across from the Lincoln Memorial, dead, another casualty of the appropriations process? It was a distinct possibility. Chick had defiantly switched to tequila at some point after 1:00 a.m. Always a smart move at the tail end of a long evening of drinking.

Bird maneuvered the cursor to the desktop folder marked ARM .EXFIL. He clicked open CHAP.17 and read a few paragraphs as the Valkyries shrieked anew.

"Brace for impact!" Turk shouted above the high-pitched scream of the failing engines.

Bird considered. He inserted *through gritted teeth* after *shouted.* Yes. Better. But then he wondered: can one in fact shout through gritted teeth? Bird gritted his teeth and tried to shout "Brace for impact!" but it came out sounding vaguely autistic.

The ARM.EXFIL folder contained the latest in the McIntyre oeuvre, his current novel in progress, titled *The Armageddon Exfiltration*. This was the third in his Armageddon trilogy. The first two novels—which had not succeeded in finding a publisher—were *The Armageddon Infiltration* and *The Armageddon Immolation*.

It was the literary output of nearly a decade now. He'd started when he went to work right out of college at a Washington public-relations firm specializing in the defense industry. During the day he wrote copy and press releases urging Congress to pony up for the latest and shiniest military hardware. But the nights belonged to him. He banged away on novels full of manly men with names like Turk and Rufus, of terrible yet really cool weapons, of beautiful but deadly women with names like Tatiana and Jade, who could be neither trusted nor resisted. Heady stuff.

He treated his girlfriends to readings over glasses of wine.

The mushroom cloud rose like an evil plume of mycological smoke over the Mall in Washington. The presidential helicopter, Marine One, yawed frantically as its pilot, Major Buck "Turk" McMaster, grappled furiously with the collective stick—

" 'Yawed frantically'?" the girlfriend interrupted. "What's that?"

Bird would smile. Women just didn't get the technology, did they? But then Bird had to admit that he didn't get the women writers. Danielle Steel, Jane Austen, that sort.

"It's when a plane does like this." Bird demonstrated, rotating a flat palm around an imaginary vertical axis.

"Isn't it a helicopter?"

"Same principle."

" 'Yawed frantically.' Okay, but it sounds weird."

"It's a technical term, Claire."

"What's 'mycological smoke'?"

"A mushroom cloud. 'Mycological'? Adjective from mushroom?"

Claire shrugged. "Okay."

"What's the matter with it?"

"No, it's fine. It's lovely."

Bird put down the manuscript. "Claire. It's not supposed to be 'lovely.' There's nothing 'lovely' about a twenty-five-kiloton thermonuclear device that's just detonated in the Jefferson Memorial."

"No, I guess not."

"They have to get the president to the airborne command center. Every second is—"

Claire yawned, frantically. "I could go for sushi."

Again the Valkyries shrieked.

"Hello, Myn."

"*Walter. I've been calling.*"

"Sorry. Just vomiting up blood."

"What?"

"I was in the shower. You said you needed my brain to work. So it can process. Okay. We are go for neuron function. On one. Three, two, one. Initiate neuron function. Whazzup?"

"It's Lucky Strike."

Oh, God . . .

Myndi launched into what Bird estimated would be a three-, maybe four-minute disquisition. He didn't want to listen to any of it, but he understood that to interrupt an equine medical diagnosis would open him to a charge of indifference in the first degree. He let his head tilt back at a stoical angle.

"So Dr. Dickerson said I absolutely have to stay off her until the tendon is fully healed. Walter? Walter, are you listening to any of this?"

Tendon. That word. How Bird hated that word. It had cost him tens—perhaps even hundreds of thousands of dollars over the years. There were other equine anatomical terms that made him shudder: *scapulohumeral joint, fetlock joint, coffin bone*—but he reserved a special odium for *tendon.*

"Really, it comes down to a moral issue."

Bird had been fantasizing about dog-food factories and the excellent work they do.

"Whoa, Myn. Did you say 'moral issue'?"

"Yes. If I keep riding her instead of giving the tendon time to heal...Walter, am I not getting through to you? If the tendon goes..." Was that a *gasp* he heard? "...I don't even want to think about that."

"Myn." Bird sighed. "This is not a good time."

"Do you want me to call you back?"

"No, sweetheart. I'm talking about...You saw the news this morning?"

"Walter. The speed competitions are six weeks away." Pause. "All right—so what do *you* think I should do?"

Bird massaged his left temple. "I take it you've already priced a...replacement...animal?"

"It's a *horse*, Walter. Sam"—another word that always induced a shudder: her trainer; or rather enabler—"says there's a superb nine-year-old filly over at Dollarsmith."

"Don't tell me. Is this one related to Seabiscuit, too?"

"If she were, Walter, she certainly wouldn't be going for such a bargain price. The bloodlines are stunning. The House of Windsor doesn't have bloodlines like this."

Bloodlines. Noun, plural: 1. qualities likely to bankrupt. 2. hideously expensive genetic tendencies.

"Myn."

"Yes, darling?"

"How much is this nag going to cost me?"

"Well, as I say, with those bloodlines—"

"*Myn.*"

"Two twenty-five?"

A new pain presented—as doctors would say—behind Bird's eyeballs.

"But we'll need to move fast," Myn added. "Sam says the Kuwaiti ambassador was over there the other day sniffing around."

Despite his pain, Bird found the image of a Kuwaiti ambassador "sniffing around stables" grimly amusing.

"Baby. Mercy. Please."

"Walter," she said sternly, "I assure you I'm not any happier than you about this."

"But surely it's possible I'm more unhappy about it than you."

"What? Oh, never mind. Look—we agreed when I decided to try out for the team that we were going to do this together."

This, it occurred to him, was Myn's concept of 'together': She'd compete for a place on the U.S. Equestrian Team and he would write checks.

"I know we did, darling. But what *we* didn't know when *we* embarked, *together*, on *our* quest for equestrian excellence was that the stock market would dive like a submarine, taking the economy with it, and defense spending. Defense spending? You remember, the thing that makes our standard of living possible? I am looking out the window. I see defense lobbyists all over town, leaping from buildings. Myn? Oh, *Myn*-di?"

Silence. He knew it well. Betokening The Gathering Storm.

Finally, "So your answer is no?"

He could see her now: pacing back and forth across the tack room in jodhpurs, mice and other small animals scurrying in terror, sawdust flying. In the distance a whinny of tendinitis-related pain coming from the stricken Lucky Strike. "Lucky"? Ha. Myndi would have unbunned her honey-colored hair, causing it to tumble over her shoulders. She was beautiful. A figure unruined by parturition. Didn't want children—"not just yet, darling," a demurral now in its, what, eighth year? Pregnancy would mean months out of the saddle. Bird was okay with the arrangement. He had to grant: the sex *was* pretty great. One day in the dentist's office, browsing the latest unnecessary bulletin about Prince Charles and Camilla Parker-Bowles, Bird read that the Duchess of Cornwall—"like many women who love to ride"—was great in the sack. Who knew?

What point was there in struggling?

"Have Sam call me," Bird said. The left side of his brain immediately signaled, *Dude. You're already broke, and you just okayed a quarter million dollars' worth of new hoof? Are you out of your mind? Wimp! Pussy! Fool!*

"Thank you," Myn said, a bit formally, Bird thought. Maybe she didn't want to sound too appreciative when really all he was doing was living up to his side of the bargain. Right?

It was a bit late to try to salvage the remains of his manhood, so he said, "I don't know if the bank's going to go for it. I wouldn't if I were the bank."

"Things will turn around, darling," Myn said. "They always do. And you're brilliant at what you do."

"All right. But I get Lucky Strike."

"Why would you want Lucky Strike?" she asked suspiciously.

"For the barbecue this weekend."

"What?"

"Aren't we having Blake and Lou Ann over on Saturday for a barbecue? At this rate, we can't afford beef. They say horse meat's tasty, but you have to cook it slowly."

"Really, Walter. That's in appalling taste."

But her tone was playful, frisky. And why not—she'd just scored a new horse.

"Call Sam, darling," she said. "I have to go deal with Peckfuss. There's an awful smell coming from the woods. And you have to do something about his teeth. I just can't bear to look at him anymore. It's revolting."

"Whoa. Choose: new horse or Peckfuss's dentition."

"See you Friday. Oh—don't forget the sump pump. They're holding it for me at Strosniders."

So now Bird had his to-do list for the rest of the week: (1) Borrow $225,000. (2) Pick up sump pump for the basement, which had now been flooding since, oh, 1845. (3) Peckfuss's dentition. All the elements of a terrific weekend.

Myn had always wanted a place in the country. The real estate agent who'd sold it to them had said, perhaps even truthfully, that Sheridan's troops had looted it and tried to burn it down.

"And do you know, it was the *slaves* who saved it!"

Bird thought, *Oh, really?* This was the third house in the area they'd been shown that had allegedly been saved by devoted darkies. He wondered—it was surely a logical question: Why would slaves risk their lives to save the Massa's house? *Oh, never mind.* The agents also delighted in pointing out scorch marks, supposedly mementos of General Sheridan's slave-thwarted arsons.

It was a lovely old house, though, on 110 acres and at the end of a long, winding oak-lined driveway. Stables, barn, willow trees, trout stream—source of much of the flooding.

The original name was Upton. After a few years of paying bills, Bird renamed it Upkeep. When his mother's Alzheimer's progressed to the critical point, he moved her in—not in the least to Myndi's liking. One night Mother was found wandering the hallways in her peignoir, holding a lit candelabra.

"Sort of perfect, in a Southern-gothic kind of way, don't you think?" Bird said, trying to put a good face on it. When Myndi didn't bite, he added, "Or is it just another cliché?"

"Walter. She's going to burn the place down. With us in it. You have to do something."

The caretaker, Peckfuss, volunteered his daughter, Belle, to keep nocturnal vigil over Mother. Bird felt sorry for Belle. She had five children, each of whom, insofar as he could tell, had been sired by a different migrant worker. Belle's amplitude—she weighed in at about three hundred pounds—put a strain on the ancient staircase. At night Bird and Myndi would listen, holding their breath, as the staircase groaned beneath Belle's avoirdupois. Bird playfully proposed to Myndi an arrangement whereby Belle could be winched up to the third floor with block and tackle. But dear, sweet, kind Belle was an ideal companion. She'd sit by Mother's bed through the night, consuming frozen cakes, watching reality-TV shows. Her favorite was a showcase piece of American programming imbecility called *1,000 Stupid Ways to Die*. One night Bird found them both watching an episode that re-created the demise of a man who had sought to conceal from the police a canister of pepper gas—in his lower colon. Mother was riveted. Bird thought sadly of the days when Mother read to him and his younger brother, Bewks, from *The Wind in the Willows*. When her condition deteriorated further, the impecunious Bewks moved in to help. Bird loved Bewks. Bewks's great passion was "living history," the term preferred by its practitioners to "reenacting" or "dressing up in period military costumes and playing war."

As it happened, Bewks's period was the Civil War. His specific adopted persona was that of a Confederate colonel of cavalry. Nutty as it all was, Bird conceded that Bewks cut a neat, dashing figure as he clumped along the porch in his cavalry boots, tunic, and saber. He styled his hair long, after the windblown look of George Armstrong Custer, hero of Gettysburg and Little Big Horn.

How Mother's brain processed Bewks's 19th-century appearance, Bird could only guess. For her part, Myn found him "odd." But Bewks knew his way around a stable and was a bit of a horse whisperer himself, so he and Myn could talk about tendons. Myndi was far too smart to let condescension get in the way of convenience.

Sitting on the porch of a summer evening with an old-fashioned in hand, watching the sun set over the Shenandoah and turn the fields purple, Bird reflected on his fortune: a trophy wife, candelabra-wielding mother, staircase-threatening caregiver, saber-wielding brother, dentally and mentally challenged caretaker, crumbling house, money-sucking mortgage, dwindling bank account.

If he was not from these parts himself, Bird felt at such halcyon moments that he was at least a reasonable facsimile of a Southern gentleman. He smiled at the thought that just the other day an impersonal letter had arrived notifying him that Upkeep's mortgage was now held by a bank in Shanghai. So if he wasn't an authentic Southerner, he was at least an authentic American, which is to say, in hock up to his eyeballs to the Chinese.

CHAPTER 2

TAURUS

Bird emerged from the chill interior of Groepping-Sprunt's corporate jet into the Turkish-steam-bath heat of Alabama.

For the umpteenth time, he wished Al Groepping and Willard Sprunt had built their first rockets in a more temperate clime. Years of visits to corporate headquarters in Missile Gap had taught Bird to limit his outdoor exposure to sprints between air-conditioned spaces. But it wasn't the heat that was troubling him most just now.

Yesterday there had arrived from Chick Devlin a terse e-mail summons slugged URGENT. Bird knew that layoffs would follow the Dumbo shoot-down. Was his own head on the chopping block? Losing Groepping as a client would be ... well, disastrous.

Chick was not his usual grinning self. He barely looked up from his desk when Bird entered. Bird braced to hear, *Sorry, pal, but this isn't going to be easy . . .*

"Coffee?" Chick said, mustering a brief, perfunctory grin. "I swear I'm still hungover from last week. Why in the name of all that is holy and good did you let me start drinking tequila at that time of night?"

"I tried to stop you," Bird said, "but you seemed intent on suicide."

18

"Felt like roadkill. So guess who I just got off the phone with? Lev Melnikov. Man, oh, man, is he one pissed-off Russian."

Melnikov was chief executive officer and chairman of the Internet giant EPIC. And he had recently thrown a tantrum of (indeed) epic proportions over China's censorship and hacking of his operations there. In a retaliatory snit, he'd pulled EPIC out of the country.

"I imagine he would be a tad displeased," Bird said. "It's not every day you lose two or three hundred million customers."

"Weird thing is how personally he's taking it. That's unlike him. Lev's a nerd. Nerds don't get emotional."

"You're a nerd," Bird said. "You get emotional."

Chick grinned. "Only about our stock price. Hell, Lev Melnikov's got more money than God. But you got to remember about Lev—he grew up in Soviet Russia. He doesn't like getting jerked around by a bunch of Commies."

"Commies." Bird smiled. "Ah, for the good old days of the Cold War. Course, I'm way too young to remember all that. More your era."

"Lev was about thirteen or fourteen when he and his folks got out. But he remembers what it was like, growing up scared, waiting to hear that three a.m. knock on the door, KGB hauling your daddy off to the gulag."

"And now he's an American citizen worth twenty billion dollars. The only midnight knock on his door he needs to worry about is the IRS. Tell him to chill. Buy a football team. That'll take his mind off Chinese *Commies*." Bird set his coffee cup down on the glass with a clunk. "Okay, I guess that's enough small talk. So, why did you drag my sorry ass down here to this swamp? Give it to me straight up. Am I getting the boot?"

Chick sighed. "Bird, I had to lay off three hundred people this morning."

"I don't like to hear that, Chick."

"Three hundred people. Three hundred, times all their families.

So many lives. You run the nums. I may be an engineer, but let me tell you, today my heart is hurting."

"I know it is," Bird said. *Chick, pull the trigger. Put me out of my misery here.*

"Dumbo," Chick mused. "What a beautiful weapons platform. Want to talk about lives? How many *lives* would Dumbo have saved?"

"Don't go there, Chick. Don't. We did what we could. There wasn't one thing more we could've done. Short of getting up from that table and strangling a few key senators."

Chick leaned forward across the glass coffee table. "You know, it's too bad *they* weren't in charge of Union army appropriations during the War of Northern Aggression. We'd have won."

"Chick," Bird said, "you grew up in Pennsylvania. You went to MIT. You're not Southern any more than I am. You explained to me some time ago why you do the Southern-patois thing, to get along down here and all that. But is it really necessary to call it the 'War of Northern Aggression' when you're talking to me?"

Chick shrugged. "Habit, I guess. Sort of seeps into the wetware. Marcia's always getting on me about it."

"Whatever. Long as you don't start telling me what a great actor John Wilkes Booth was." *Meanwhile,* Bird thought, *please get to the point? Am I being fired?*

"At the rate we're going, we'll be fighting our enemies with slingshots. Rocks. Clubs. God almighty."

"I know," Bird said sympathetically. "Makes you want to curl up in the fetal position."

Chick said, "Got something for you, Birdman."

Bird's buttock muscles unclenched. Had the moment of danger passed? "I'm right here."

"It's big."

"I love big."

"Can't tell you a whole hell of a lot about it."

Bird made a face. "Don't tell me that, Chick. Don't tell me that."

"No, listen to me, now. This thing's more sensitive than a stripper's nipple. As of right now, there aren't more than a half dozen people on the planet know about it. Including you-know-who." You-know-who was Chick-speak for the president of the United States.

"What am I going to do?" Bird said. "Post it on Facebook? Tweet? How long have I been working for you?"

The answer was six years, ever since Bird got Chick's attention with his campaign for Groepping's HX-72 stealth helicopter: "Under the Radar but on Top of the Situation."

"I can tell you this much," Chick said. "Once this baby's up and running and online, the American people are going to sleep a lot more soundly."

Bird waited for more.

"Really?" he said finally. "A new sleeping pill. I had no idea Groepping was in the pharmaceutical business. Why didn't I get that memo?"

Chick sighed. "All right." He lowered his voice to a whisper. "It's about China."

Bird stared.

"That's all you're going to get out of me," Chick said. "Waterboard me. Go ahead. You won't get any more out of me."

"China," Bird said. "Americans will sleep better. Well, that narrows it. Okay. So, what exactly is it you want me to do with this cornucopia of information? Want me to get cranking on a press release? 'Groepping-Sprunt Announces Top Secret Initiative to Help Americans Sleep Better. Has Something to Do with China' "?

"Damn it, Bird. Okay, but this is all you're going to get out of me. Don't you dare ask me for more. The project's code name is Taurus."

"Taurus. Taurus as in bull?"

Chick looked at him earnestly. "This is the real deal, Birdman. I'm talking Manhattan Project stuff. Twenty-second century. This thing'd give the Lord himself a case of the shits."

Bird was impressed by Chick's intensity. "Guess I'll have to take it on faith. But could you give me *some* guidance here?"

"I was getting to that. We've got to loosen things up with Appropriations. But if you so much as say the word *China* on Capitol Hill, they start running for cover. They're more nervous about China than a long-tailed cat in a room full of rocking chairs."

"Well," Bird said, "China *is* more or less financing our economy. Not that I don't hate them much as the next person. Commie swine."

"I'm thinking," Chick said, "that maybe it's time to put the 'Red' back in Red China."

"Red China," Bird mused aloud. "It's been a while since we called it that, hasn't it?"

"Last time I checked, their flag was flaming Communist red. Yes, I believe the time has come to educate the great big dumb American public—God love them—to educate them about the..."—Chick paused, as if searching for just the right word—"the peril we as a nation face from a nation of one point three billion foreigners."

Bird stared.

Chick said, "Wasn't it Charles de Gaulle who said, 'China is a big country, full of Chinese'?"

"If he didn't, he should have," Bird said, not entirely sure where this was going.

"Bird, we need to educate the American people as to the true nature of the threat we face. If we can do that, then those limp dicks and fainting hearts and imbeciles in the United States Congress—God love *them*—will follow."

Bird nodded thoughtfully. *What the hell was Chick talking about?* He said, "Is there a particular threat that you had in mind? Or is it more just...the principle of the thing?"

Chick shrugged. "That's where you come in, Bird. You've always had a genius for putting your finger on the nub of a situation. What about world domination? I don't suppose I want to live in a world dominated by the heirs of Mao Zedong."

"World domination," Bird said. "Yes, that is sort of a grim prospect, isn't it?"

Chick patted Bird on the knee. "There. We're on the same page."

"Chick," Bird said. "Just so's I'm clear here—are you wanting me to go rustle you up some anti-China sentiment?"

Chick smiled. "You have a way with words, my friend. Guess that's why we pay you so damn much." He rose. "I like you, Birdman. With you I never feel like I have to dance around a thing. The way I do with so many of you Washington types."

You Washington types. Bird thought, *What a compliment.*

"That's nice of you to say, Chick. Nice of you to say."

"A practical matter," Chick said. "I'm thinking it might look better if you weren't on our payroll."

Bird said, "Not sure if I'm still with you there, General."

"Once you start spraying 'China Sucks!' graffiti on that Great Wall of theirs, it might look funny if we're still your client. Helen Keller could connect those dots."

"Not that I don't love our military-industrial complex on its merits," Bird said, "but are you proposing that I whip up all this anti-Chinese fervor for you pro bono? Because those are the saddest two words in the English language."

"*Pro bono* is Latin." Chick smiled.

"So is '*Et tu, Brute.*'"

"*Dulce et decorum est pro patria mori.* You know what that means? 'How sweet it is to die for one's country.'"

"A fine sentiment," Bird said. "Now, don't get me wrong. I love my country. I love Groepping-Sprunt. I love you—in a heterosexual way. If I were of the gay persuasion, I have no doubt that I would be attracted to you physically. I would want you to be my civil partner and for us to adopt an African orphan. But I have a roof that leaks, a barn that leaks, and mouths to feed. Oh, and did I mention the new horse that my wife informs me she cannot live without? Do you know anything about tendons? Has Groepping considered getting into *that* market? Because never mind drones—there is a real killing waiting to be made in horse tendons."

"Bird. Re-lax. Wasn't suggesting that you work without compensation. I know how it is. I know you've got your own antebellum Tara out there in horse country. How is that fine-looking wife of yours? She *is* a stunner. She ought to be on the cover of one of those magazines like *Town & Country*. She really going for the gold? That is impressive, truly."

"She's going for my gold," Bird said. "What's left of it."

"You be sure to give her my best. That brother of yours—he still dressing up like Stonewall Jackson?"

"It's more of a modified Custer. But yes, Bewks is still doing his living history. And helping out with Mother. That would be the Mother with Alzheimer's? You're catching my subtle drift, here, Chief?"

"Loud and clear." Chick chuckled. "I read you five by five. Don't you worry. We will make you whole. More than whole."

"I was an English major," Bird said. "You being the science guy, tell me, is it mathematically possible to make someone more than whole? Isn't whole a hundred percent?"

Chick gave a dismissive wave. "We'll set up some foundation. That way you'll be technically working for it." He smiled. "Instead of the old military-industrial complex, God bless it."

"So long as it's kosher, legally," Bird said. "They're sending my type off to jail about every fifteen minutes now. 'Lobbyist Gets Five Years' doesn't even make the front page anymore. It's back there with the crossword puzzle and the certified-preowned-car ads."

"Legal is good." Chick slapped Bird on the shoulder. "I'm for legal. All right now, Birdman, you get yourself back to Gomorrah-on-the-Potomac and open me up a can of whoop-ass on Beijing. I want to see angry crowds outside their embassy. Flags burning. Signs. 'No more Tiananmens! Hands Off Taiwan!' 'Tibet for the Tibetans!' I want..." Chick's voice trailed off. His face had taken on a strange, dreamy look.

"Nice speech," Bird said. "Reminds me of that Leni Riefenstahl movie about the Nuremberg rally. Good old fashioned patriotism."

"Okay. So I get a little carried away when it comes to our national security."

"Have you tried Xanax?"

"Your country is depending on you, Birdman."

A FEW DAYS LATER, back at his office in D.C., Bird sent out two press releases.

The first announced that after many excellent and productive years together, McIntyre Strategies and Groepping-Sprunt had amicably decided to "pursue exciting new challenges." The second said that Bird was forming a foundation called Pan-Pacific Solutions, "focusing on national security and Far Eastern issues." It seemed a vague enough description.

This done, Bird holed up in the Military-Industrial Duplex and immersed himself in a crash course on China. He bulldozed—and dozed—through books and periodicals, went online, read scholarly monographs by eminent Sinologists. Surely somewhere in all this he would find the key to the—what was the word Chick used?—*threat*. Yes. The unnerving specter that would cause America to snap-to out of its coma of complacency and tremble.

Surely there was something. But . . . what?

After days of eyeball-glazing study and Googling, the new Red Menace was proving elusive.

Not that China wasn't potentially scary. Or even already scary. The Communist Party controlled every aspect of life. It made Big Brother look like Beaver Cleaver. It was implacable, ruthless. The government lost no sleep driving tanks over students and Tibetan monks. It tortured and executed tens of thousands of "serious criminals" a year. It cozied up to and played patty-cake with some of the vilest regimes on earth—Zimbabwe, North Korea, Sudan, Iran,

Venezuela; poured millions of tons of ozone-devouring chemicals into the atmosphere; guzzled oil by the billions of barrels, all while remaining serenely indifferent to world opinion. But apart from a few forlorn Falun Gong protesters outside Chinese embassies or self-immolating Tibetan monks, where was the outrage?

As for world domination? Well, to be sure, China was clearly intent on becoming *daguo* (a new word in Bird's vocabulary), a "great power." But it was going about achieving this goal in a relatively quiet, deliberate, and businesslike way. It was hard, really, to put any kind of definite *face* on China. The old Soviet Union, with its squat, warty leaders banging their shoes on the UN podium and threatening thermonuclear extinction, all those vodka-swollen, porcine faces squinting from under sable hats atop Lenin's Tomb as nuclear missiles rolled by like floats in a parade from hell—those Commies at least *looked* scary. But on the rare occasion when the nine members of China's Politburo Standing Committee, the men who ruled 1.3 billion people—one-fifth of the world's population—lined up for a group photo, they looked like a delegation of identical, overpaid dentists. This was no reflexive racist stereotyping. Bird actually read that they all dyed their pompadours the identical shade of black. (Individual grooming statements were, apparently, not the rage among the party elite.) They *wanted* all to look alike; in a way, a statement of ultimate egalitarianism. After days of studying photographs of the individual Politburo members, Bird still could barely tell one from another; though the one in charge of state security did at least look like a malevolent overpaid dentist.

Further confounding Bird's attempt to locate the envenomed needle in this immense haystack was the fact that America had gotten itself a serious China habit. It couldn't buy enough Chinese goods, sell Chinese banks enough Treasury bills. Absent some really serious provocation, the U.S. government was in no position to tsk-tsk or wag its finger at Beijing over Taiwan or Tibet. As for human rights, forget it. A nonstarter.

ONE NIGHT TOWARD THE END of Bird's weeklong cram, eyes veinous with fatigue, central nervous system fizzing like a downed power line from caffeine and MSG (Chinese takeout—why not?), Bird laid down his books and decided—enough. He showered, went out and bought a juicy red New York steak and a seventy-five-dollar bottle of fat, fleshy burgundy, and took the night off.

He grilled his steak and drank his wine and turned on the TV. *Boring In* was on—Washington's thoughtful weekly show about policy and policy makers, perfect to watch with one eye. On any given Friday, its guests consisted of a former member of the Council of Economic Advisers and a current assistant deputy undersecretary of something, mumbling knowledgeably at each other about Argentine wheat-import quotas. The show could just as well be called *Boring*, but Bird had a soft spot for it. He had been invited on once, and it had considerably raised his public profile. The guest opposite him that night was a formerly famous movie actor who had become virulently antimilitary after playing the role of a morally demented submarine captain who uses pods of innocent whales as targets for torpedo practice.

The actor, a voluble sort of the type who refers to distinguished U.S. officials as "mass murderers" or "serial killers," became so enraged by Bird's well-reasoned defense of the defense industry that he called him "an evil pig" and expressed the hope that Bird would die from a "morphine-resistant form of cancer." Bird merely smiled and replied, "I guess we'll have to put you down as 'Undecided, leaning against.'" This drove the actor into a spittle-flecked frenzy of four-letter invective. Lively stuff by the standards of *Boring In*, certainly. *Washingtonian* magazine included Bird that year in its annual list of "Washington's Ten Least Despicable Lobbyists."

He forked another lovely morsel of steak into his mouth.

So who was on *Boring* tonight? Angel Templeton. Well, now. She was worth watching with both eyes.

CHAPTER 3

ANGEL

Tall, blond, buff, leggy, miniskirted: Angel Templeton was hardly your typical Washington think-tank policy wonk.

For the cover of her most recent book, *The Case for Preemptive War: Taking the "Re-" Out of Retaliation*, she posed in a red, white, and blue latex dominatrix outfit. With riding crop. But if readers purchased the book for this reason alone, then the joke was on them, for it itself was a thoughtfully-argued, well-researched, and extravagantly footnoted argument for vigorous, indeed, continuous, U.S. military intervention throughout the world.

Ms. Templeton held a Ph.D. from the Johns Hopkins School of Advanced International Studies, had worked on the staff of the National Security Council, and had served as deputy director of policy planning at the Pentagon. A lustrous résumé, to be sure. She was currently chair of the prestigious, if controversial, Institute for Continuing Conflict. If her flair for publicity raised eyebrows at the Council on Foreign Relations or among the Nobel laureates sipping bouillon at the Cosmos Club, it brought her regular appearances on TV, considerable sales, and five-figure speaking fees.

Tonight on *Boring In*, Angel's opposite number was a Princeton professor famous for having written a book comparing America to Rome (as in *"Decline and Fall"*). He was not enjoying himself, for Angel was playfully tromping all over his elegant references to Livy and Tacitus with her Jimmy Choo shoes.

"You know," she said with a coy, embarrassed smile, as if to suggest she was only being polite in not mentioning that the professor had been caught engaging in unnatural sex acts with manatees, "it's nice you've found yourself a cushy penthouse apartment up there in the old ivory tower, where you can grind out books about what a crummy, second-rate nation our country is."

The professor glared at Angel with owlish contempt. "That's not what my book says. Not at *all* what my—"

"I see," she interrupted, "that you decided to save money on a fact-checker."

"What are you implying?"

"Not implying anything." Angel smiled. "I'm stating for a fact—oops, the F-word again!—that the only thing you managed to get correct in the entire book was the semicolon on page four seventy-three."

"This is—"

"But it doesn't really matter. It's not like anyone's actually going to read it. It's really a pseudointellectual coffee-table ornament. A way of telling your guests, 'I hate America, too.'"

"I didn't come on this show to listen to insults."

"Oh, come on, Professor," she said kittenishly. "I'm not insulting you. I'm simply pointing out that the central message of your book is that America can no longer afford to defend itself against its enemies. So we might as well just throw in the towel."

"That is a *complete* perversion of my argument."

"Some would say that the real perversion is your idea that America is finito as a world power. Look, I'm sure it may play with the dewy-eyed freshmen in the cushy groves of academe but here in the real world—and I'm sorry to be the one to break this to you—great nations don't just roll over and play dead. They fight."

"You obviously didn't read my book."

"No, I actually did," Angel said with a laugh, "but I had to keep my feet in a bucket of ice water. I know that academic prose is supposed to be boring, but hats off to you. You've taken it to a whole new level."

THE INSTITUTE FOR CONTINUING CONFLICT is on Massachusetts Avenue, off Dupont Circle in a house that appropriately enough was once the residence of Theodore Roosevelt, who as secretary of the navy did so much to usher in the dawn of American imperialism. The building's nickname among those who worked in it was "Casa Belli."

Standing in the marble lobby, waiting for Angel's assistant to collect him, Bird studied the inscription above the gracefully curved grand staircase, chiseled into marble and leafed in bright gold.

> *Extremism in the defense of liberty is no vice.*
> —Barry Goldwater

Bird felt nervous. He had met Angel Templeton a few times on the cocktail circuit. He found her intimidating. Well, she *was* intimidating. Angel's legend was well known around town. During her tour of duty at the Pentagon, she had been romantically involved with two generals and an admiral. The admiral was on the staff of the Joint Chiefs. Mrs. Admiral was less than thrilled to learn about the affair and made a scene that resulted in the admiral's being reassigned to sea duty. Angel had never married. She was the single mother of an eight-year-old son named—Barry. Despite her reputation as a man-eater, Angel was by all accounts a devoted mother, a regular at parent-teacher conferences.

Bird studied the contents of a glass case in the lobby, books by ICC resident scholars and fellows: *The Case For Permanent War.*

Retreat, Hell: Assertiveness in U.S. Foreign Policy, 1812 to 2003. Give War a Chance. Pax Americana: You Got a Problem with That? Double Stuff: The Rise of the Oreo-Con Movement. How America Can Keep from Becoming France—and Why It Must.

The Institute for Continuing Conflict was headquarters for the so-called Oreo-Cons—"Hard on the outside, soft on the inside." Hard because they were unapologetic advocates of American military muscle. Soft because their domestic politics were for the most part laissez-faire; Oreo-Cons didn't really care what presidents and the Congress did so long as they kept the Pentagon and the armed forces well funded and engaged abroad, preferably in hand-to-hand combat.

Oreo-Con critics, of whom there were no small number, thought them a shifty and largely self-satisfied bunch. Oreo-Cons had the uncanny knack of distancing themselves from failure. When one of their foreign interventions backfired, it was always someone else's fault. *The idea was sound. It was the execution that was flawed.* For a group that had gotten America into one tar pit of a quagmire after another, Oreo-Cons were awfully blithe. Not for them, dwelling on disasters. No. Pass the ammo, pass the hors d'oeuvres, and on to the next calamity! Their current agitation was for a preemptive strike on Iran's nuclear facilities, preferably with nuclear weapons. Slam dunk!

"Mr. McIntyre?"

Bird turned.

"Mike Burka. I work with Ms. Templeton."

Bird was expecting a secretary. This Burka fellow looked like an active-duty Navy SEAL in mufti. His neck must have been the diameter of a young redwood tree; the eyes were steely cool and appraising. Wouldn't want to be on his bad side. Bird followed him up the marble staircase.

"We have a pretty busy schedule today," Burka said, "but we have you slotted in for twenty minutes. You're lucky. Christiane Amanpour only got ten."

"I'll try not to waste Ms. Templeton's time," Bird said as they passed by Barry Goldwater's clarion call.

"She may have to take a call from Dr. Kissinger. If she does, I will come in and escort you out of the office. I will then bring you back into the office after her call with Dr. Kissinger is completed. Her time with Dr. Kissinger will not be deducted from your twenty."

Bird nodded. "As a matter of fact, I'm expecting a call myself."

Burka looked at him uncertainly. "Oh?"

"The Dalai Lama. But I don't mind if Ms. Templeton remains in the room while His Holiness and I talk. We usually converse in Tibetan."

Burka's pupils narrowed to laser pointers. His expression said, *Normally I'd crush your windpipe, but I'm in a good mood and I don't want to get blood on my shirt cuffs.*

They walked through an outer office with four busy secretaries. Bird was ushered into The Presence.

Angel Templeton rose from behind a black-glass and stainless-steel desk.

"Bird McIntyre." She beamed, extending a hand. "I've heard so much about you. Sit. Please. I don't mean to gush, but Groepping-Sprunt is my absolute favorite aerospace defense contractor."

"Really? Well."

"The upgrade package you did on TACSAT-4? In a word? Oh. My. God. And the FALCONSAT-26 real-time imaging during the run-up to Pakistan? I can't even discuss it. Brilliant. Would you care for coffee? Tea? Red Bull? Adderall?"

"Uh, no thank you." Bird flushed. "But I'll be sure to pass that along to my former colleagues at Groepping."

"Former?"

"Yes. All very amicable, of course. It's just that I've decided to go in a new direction. In fact, that's what brings me here."

"I shudder to think where we'd be if it weren't for companies like Groepping-Sprunt." She laughed. "Throwing spears at our enemies. Pouring boiling oil on them. What those brain-dead, spineless jellyfish up there"—she hooked a thumb in the direction of Capitol Hill—"did to the MQ-9B...Jesus wept. Chick Devlin did an amazing job."

"But that was a closed hearing."

"I read the transcript."

"I am impressed."

"Mr. McIntyre, do I look like someone who gets her news from the *Washington Post*? This is in no way a criticism, okay? But if it had been me testifying, I'd have told those senators, 'Okay, not interested in saving American lives over there? Then how about every body bag that comes back from there we stack outside your office door?'"

Bird laughed nervously. *What does this woman sprinkle on her breakfast granola? Gunpowder? Powdered C-4?*

He found himself staring at her stockinged legs, which seemed as long as the Washington Monument. He looked up, embarrassed, and saw that she was smiling.

"It's all right. I enjoy it when men notice my legs, as long as they're attractive. The men, that is. I know the legs are. Okay, Mr. McIntyre, enough persiflage. What's this visit *really* about?"

"Well," Bird said, "as I mentioned on the phone—"

"I know what you said on the phone."

"I'm not quite sure I follow."

"Don't you think I do my homework?"

"Ms. Templeton—"

"Angel. It was originally Angela, but I dropped the final *a*. Too girlie. Go on." She looked at her watch. "I don't mean to rush you. It's just that I'm expecting a call from Henry. Kissinger."

"Yes. So your Sergeant Rambo informed me."

"Mike? He was with the team that..."

"What?"

"That got bin Laden. And please do *not* tell him I told you that.

33

I'm really not into the whole bodyguard scene, but we get death threats here. Pain in the butt. Had to evacuate the building twice this month. Really, it would be simpler to have our offices in a bunker somewhere out in Virginia, but I'm not into chain restaurants. Are you all right, Mr. McIntyre?"

"Fine," Bird said. "Just…"

"Would you like a soothing beverage? Chai tea? A hot towel? We have an on-premise Thai masseuse. She used to do King Pramashembatawabb. A miracle worker. I get these knots. Right here. Feel."

"Why don't I just come to the point?"

"Enough foreplay?"

"China," Bird said. "I'm here about China."

"China? Well." Angel laughed softly as if at a private joke. "China. Have you seen the latest figures on their naval-fleet buildup? They just added five new *Luhu*-class guided-missile destroyers. And what do we suppose they're planning to do with those? I shouldn't really be discussing it, but a little birdie tells me they managed to hack into a U.S. Navy server and download the *entire* TR-46-2 program. They're *such* pirates. Don't you just hate them? The good news is stealing keeps them dumb. God forbid they should actually figure out how to make something by themselves."

Bird affected an impressed look, though he had no idea what the TR-46-2 was.

"I read your piece in the *Wall Street Journal* last month," he said, "where you called for expelling them from the UN Security Council unless they cut off aid to North Korea. Powerful stuff."

Angel shrugged. "Am I the only person in this town who's tired of hearing that the twenty-first century is going to be 'the Chinese Century'? Could someone tell me—please—why America, the greatest country in history, only gets one century? And by the way, who decided this was going to be *their* century? Some thumb-sucking professor at Yale? Please."

"It's so refreshing to hear that."

"All we do is kowtow to those people. Did you see what our secretary of commerce said over there last week? I almost barfed."

"Deplorable." Bird nodded.

"But what can you expect? We made them the real Bank of America. What are we going to do? Ask them—nicely—'Please play fair'? 'Please stop with the intellectual-property thievery'? 'Please don't arm Iran'? 'Please don't destroy the environment'? 'Please don't invade Taiwan'? Meanwhile those nutless squirrels—pygmies, all of them—on Capitol Hill are gutting the defense budget."

"Angel," Bird said, "that's why I'm here."

She looked at him. "How can I help?"

"I head up a foundation called Pan-Pacific Solutions. My board feels that it's time—past time—that we focus the country's attention on the Chinese situation. Specifically, on the... the..."

"Threat?"

"Yes! The threat."

Angel laughed softly. "Oh. ICC has been focusing on that for years. But I'll tell you—frankly, it's a tough sell in this environment. Americans just don't seem to care"—she sighed heavily—"they should. I could show you contingency plans we helped draw up for the ROC—"

"ROC?"

"Republic of China. Taiwan?"

"Of course."

"Plans for a post-invasion environment."

"Oh," Bird said, "sounds dire."

"You have no idea."

"So," Bird said, "do you think we might work together on this?"

Angel leaned back in her chair. "It's worth exploring. Absolutely. Now, Pan-Pacific Solutions. I'm not familiar with them. They're based...?"

"Virginia. Right across the river."

"I'd want to do some due diligence."

"Naturally. But I might as well tell you upfront that my board prefers to keep a low profile. I'd be surprised if you found much at all about us. But I can tell you this. We're patriotic Americans. And we have deep pockets. Money is not an issue."

Angel chuckled. "Money is only an issue when there isn't any. Oops—plagiarism alert. I *may* be quoting Oscar Wilde there. But tell me—you still have good relations with the folks at Groepping?"

"Thick as thieves. I mean, best of friends."

Angel said in a coquettish tone, "So what can you tell me about Taurus?"

Bird's eyes widened. "Taurus? What's that?"

"Bird. I don't live in a cave."

Bird shifted in his seat. "You have me at a disadvantage, I'm afraid."

"Good."

"It's highly classified."

"Do I look like a virgin?"

"Oh, no. I mean...sorry." Bird blushed.

"Oh, relax. So Taurus. Does it have a ring in its nose? Horns? Does it snort and run over drunk tourists in Pamplona? What kind of bull are we talking about?"

"Well," Bird said in a conspiratorial tone, "I can tell you this much—it's pretty darn scary."

"I love scary."

Bird glanced around her room. "Office clean?"

"Swept twice weekly."

He took a breath. *Think, man!* Finally he said, "Well, seeing as how you have TS clearance...But I'd want your assurance that we're speaking in total confidentiality."

Angel rolled her eyes.

"It..." Bird's mind raced. "Essentially, it's about rearranging molecules."

Angel stared. "Molecules."

Bird leaned forward and whispered, "I may just have put both our lives in danger by telling you that."

Why did that line sound familiar? He suddenly remembered where he had heard it: in the middle novel of his Armageddon trilogy—scene where Major Buck "Turk" McMaster reveals to Chief Warrant Officer Beatrice "Bouncing Betty" O'Toole the location of the muon bomb that he's just planted beneath the presidential palace in Tehran.

Bird said in a grave voice, "I won't pretend that I understand the science. But it involves subatomic particles. Muons."

"Must be the next-gen neutron weapon," Angel mused. "Remember the good old neutron bomb—destroys people, not property? Moscow denounced it as 'the perfect capitalist weapon.'"

"Well," Bird said, "I'm—was—just on the marketing side."

"Muons," Angel murmured. "Muons. Well, well, well."

"You will be discreet?"

"You never have to worry about that with me, Mr. McIntyre," she said sternly.

"Of course, the idea is not to have to deploy it. It's all about deterrence."

Angel smiled. "We're not really into deterrence at ICC."

"That's right. I read your book. *Taking the 'Re-' Out of Retaliation.* Bracing stuff."

"Well, as we say around here, an ounce of preemption is worth a pound of enriched uranium. Isn't *that* the height of vanity—quoting yourself?"

"I look forward to working with you," Bird said.

Angel's intercom announced, "Dr. Templeton, I have Dr. Kissinger on the line."

"Tell him I'll call back."

CHAPTER 4

UPKEEP

Bird found himself whistling on the drive out late Friday afternoon. He kept to the back roads, now that Washington could proudly boast of having the nation's second-worst traffic.

He was speeding. The meeting with Angel Templeton had left him with a strange feeling of exhilaration. He felt the way he did when the writing was really going great guns. It occurred to him that Taurus—whatever the hell it was—had the makings of a darn good novel. After dinner tonight he'd sit down at the old laptop and bang out a few pages. He made a mental note to move the muon-bomb scene from volume two to volume three. Yes. And to build a new subplot around it. Talk about going out with a bang. Good stuff!

He looked at the speedometer. *Whoa. Slow down.*

"*You* look cheery," Myndi said with an air of mild annoyance as he came in and planted a kiss on her cheek.

"Great day. Excellent day." He kissed her again. "How's with you?"

Myndi exhaled a lungful of built-up weltschmerz. "Walter, you have to talk to Peckfuss. He makes no sense. None. I can't get him to focus on that ghastly smell. Half the time I can't even understand what he's saying. Those *teeth*." She shuddered.

Bird sniffed the air. "I can't smell a thing. Other than your perfume. Rrrrr."

"It comes and goes. Trust me. From the woods by the swamp. I'm not about to venture down there this time of year, with all the snakes. Peckfuss did manage to convey that he'd killed a water moccasin there the other day. You'd better wear those high-top boots, the reinforced ones."

"*I'm* not going down there," Bird said. "Getting snakebit isn't my idea of a fun Friday night. But thank you for suggesting it."

"Then you'll have to talk to Peckfuss. Either he's back on the sauce or he's gone totally demented. Speaking of which, your mother—"

"Myn. Not nice."

"*Joking.* Did we lose Mr. Sense of Humor? But I think the time has come that we had The Conversation."

"What conversation?"

"Don't be obtuse, Walter."

"I'm not booting Mother out of the house. End of conversation."

"You're not *here* half the time. I'm left to cope."

Bird laughed. "*You're* not here half the time. Look, babe, it's Friday night. I've had a rough week. I want drink. I want food." He put his arms around her. "I want . . . *you.* Rrrruff."

"I have an early day tomorrow."

"Then we better get started."

In this area Bird had no complaints. Myn might be a bit of an ice queen, but she could still set the bedsheets on fire. Could it be . . . the horse thing? Bird was increasingly bedeviled by images of making love to the Duchess of Cornwall. He wished he hadn't come across that article in the dentist's office.

Afterward Myn set about making dinner. Bird made himself an old-fashioned and went out on the front porch, his perch. Heart and other organs at peace, he looked out over his corner of the universe.

It was a perfect early-summer evening. Dragonflies hovered about. It seemed improbable that this same landscape had been the scene of so much misery and devastation a century and a half ago.

As he was thinking these very thoughts, he spotted a figure on horseback approaching. He saw the outline of the hat, the sword. Bird watched his brother with fond bemusement. Absurd, yes, but there was a charm to it. Except for his shiny German car parked in front, the scene before him could have been a tableau from the 1860s.

Bewks drew up on his horse, removed his hat, grinned at his brother on the porch, and saluted. "Compliments of General Lee."

Bird returned the salute. "You're too late," he said. "Sheridan's men have come and gone. They set fire to the house, ravished the womenfolk, stole the silver. Fortunately, our devoted slaves put out the fire."

Bewks dismounted, removed his cavalry gloves, and slapped them against his thighs, causing micro dust storms to rise up. "They leave any liquor?"

"They drank all the Montrachet."

"Damn Yankees," Bewks said. "They do love that white burgundy."

"War is hell. I believe they left some whiskey. Go pour yourself a snort, then come tell me some lies. And make them entertaining. I had a rough week."

Bewks returned with his drink, unbuckled his saber, and sat next to his brother.

"Long day out there. Gettysburg's coming up, July first. We've got work to do."

The two brothers sat silently, taking in the evening. Fireflies blinking on and off, fairies with flashlights.

"Don't take this the wrong way," Bird said, "but do you and the boys ever reflect on the fact that you're fighting on the slavery side?"

"Now, big brother, you know it wasn't all about that."

"Oh? What was it about? Remind me."

"Yankee soldier's talking to a captured butternut. Asks him, 'Why do you hate us so, Johnny Reb?' Reb says, 'Because this is our land. And you're on it.'"

Bird took a slug of his drink. "We're Yankees, you and I. And here we are. On it."

Bewks shrugged. "You got me there."

They watched the shadows lengthen.

Bird said, "Myn says there's some kind of horrible smell coming from down by the swamp. Know anything about that?"

"It's in the nature of swamps to smell."

"She says it's some chemical kind of smell. Is Peckfuss okay? He's not operating a meth lab down there, is he?"

"Peckfuss hasn't been quote/unquote okay since the day he was born."

"I know. But Myn says he seems kind of excitable lately. Edgy."

"Suspect he took another tumble off the old wagon. You got to feel for the guy."

"Bewks," Bird said. "I do more than 'feel' for him. I support him. I clothe and feed him. I could find a more capable caretaker at the state asylum for the brain-impaired."

"By the way, Belle busted a riser on the staircase."

Bird sighed. "That girl has *got* to shed some weight."

"Tell me about it. She's going to bring down that whole staircase."

"She's still the only person Mother doesn't snarl at. I'll look in after dinner. How's Mother been?"

"She wanted me to drive her to the polling booth the other day."

"In June?"

"So she could vote. For Eisenhower."

Bird reflected. "That's Alzheimer's for you. She was a Stevenson girl."

Bewks lowered his voice. "I don't think Myndi is very content with the present arrangement."

"I know."

"I heard her talking on the phone. I wasn't eavesdropping. I was just getting something from the kitchen. But it sounded like she was talking to someone about a *home*."

"I'm not sending her away, Bewks. Not going to institutionalize her."

"Wasn't suggesting anything of the sort. Just pointing out to you that your wife is not exactly in a state of equilibrium with respect to the existing situation."

"Well, my wife can go—"

"Go where?"

Myndi was standing behind them, arms folded.

"Darling!" Bird said with spastic merriment. "I was telling Bewks how you can go over any-height fence on that horse of yours. In any kind of terrain. Jumping..."

"Really?" Myndi said coolly. "How complimentary of you. *Darling*."

"Is dinner ready? I could eat a horse. Bewks, want to join us?"

"No!" Bewks said quickly, leaping to his feet. "Got to get Chancellor settled in for the night. Thanks anyway. Myn."

Bird and Myndi ate a quiet dinner.

Finally Bird said, "Darling?"

Myndi looked up from her arugula with grapefruit and pine nuts. "What." No question mark. Just what.

"I'm an asshole."

"Why? For telling your brother what a wonderful jumper I am?"

"Myn."

"No, Walter," she said, dabbing her mouth with a napkin. "I really don't know what I'm supposed to say at this point."

"I was just feeling protective about Mother."

Myndi put down her fork and knife. She was on the verge of tears. "I try, Walter, you know. I really do try."

"I know you do, baby. You're—"

"It's not easy, running this house."

"I know, baby."

"When we talked about living in the country, I didn't think I was going to end up in a trailer park."

"The garden looks great."

"I don't do the gardening."

"I know, but you do such a wonderful job of supervising all those nice Mexicans."

"I'm under a great deal of stress right now. I'm *this* close to qualifying. I have to focus."

"I'm so proud of you. How's the new horse doing?" Bird thought, *No tendon jokes.* "Is it all working out all right? Horsewise?"

"She's no Lucky Strike."

How was he supposed to respond to that wee note of discontent? *Two hundred and twenty-five thousand dollars and she's "no Lucky Strike"? Well, great. Wonderful. Couldn't be more delighted.* "Sorry to hear that."

"Sam seems to think she's coming along," Myndi said, "but I don't know. I have my doubts. I'm doing my best. I can't do more than my best."

"I bet you're doing just—"

"Belle destroyed the staircase."

"Bewks mentioned. I did wonder why there's all that yellow crime-scene tape across the bottom."

"I got the estimate. Eighteen thousand."

Bird stared. "Eighteen thousand? For a riser?"

"Walter, the entire staircase is about to come down. It wasn't built to be a footpath for elephants."

Bird sighed. "Okay. I'll deal with it in the morning."

"She's up there now. Probably watching another reality show starring cretins. It can't be healthy for your mother. Not that she notices. Walter, I simply can't go on like this. It's getting to me."

"Can we talk about it in the morning?"

"It's a very big deal, this competition. If I make the team, I go to China."

"China? What's happening in China?"

"Oh, Walter, I told you about this months ago. You never *listen*."

"Sorry, babe. I know. Mind like a sieve. Tell me again?"

"The Tang Cup. Tang as in Tang dynasty. The famous terra-cotta horses?"

"Is that where they got the name for the orange-flavored powdered beverage?"

"The Tang dynasty was a hugely important era for horse development in China. The Beijing government decided to celebrate it by holding a gymkhana in August. In Xi'an. It was the capital during the Tang era. It's going to be a huge international equestrian event. Teams from all over. It's a big, big deal. And if I make the team, I go. I'll be representing our country."

Bird's mind raced. "Gosh," he said, somewhat ambiguously.

"You don't sound very excited about it."

"No. No, I am. China. China is...big. Definitely. Didn't de Gaulle call it a 'big country. Full of Chinese'?"

"What are you talking about?"

"Nothing, really."

"You do *want* me to succeed, don't you?"

"Of course I do, darling. It's just that..."

"What?"

"Well, I mean...their record on human rights. Tiananmen Square. Taiwan. Tibet. You know..."

"What does all that have to do with the Tang Cup?"

"Nothing, I suppose," Bird said, sounding retreat. "I suppose it's all about reaching out. Hands across the ocean. Global..."

Myndi dumped the dishes into the sink with petulant efficiency and stomped off. Bird reflected that his wife had developed the unique ability of stomping in stocking feet.

He loaded the dishwasher.

Did it have to be China? He'd have to maintain a very low profile. That was probably doable. Angel would be the one on the front lines, leading the public charge.

He took the back stairs up to Mother's room. Belle was sitting beside her, both of them bathed in television light. Bird avoided looking at the screen.

"Hey there, Mr. Mac," Belle said pleasantly. The front of her smock was littered with nacho scree. "Ma, look who's here. It's Mr. Walter. Your son."

"Walter who?"

Bird tried to give his mother a kiss.

"Don't you touch me!"

"Mother, it's me. Walter."

"I don't care who you are. You get away from me. I've got a gun."

"I just wanted to tell you good night. I love you."

"Where is it? Where's my gun? Did you take my gun?"

"Bewks has your gun, Mother. Remember? He's getting it fixed?"

"Bewks? What kind of name is *Bewks*?"

"Now, Ma," Belle intervened, "why you being so snickety at Mr. Walter? He's your son."

"Where's my gun? You give me my gun. I'm going to shoot him through the head."

"You hush, Ma," Belle said in a commanding voice. "You don't hush, I'll turn off the television. You know I will."

"Good night, Mother," Bird said. "I love you."

"You come back here, I'll shoot you dead. Where is my gun?"

Bird descended by the back stairs, which also seemed to be creaking ominously.

He went into the den and poured himself a stiff nightcap, sat down, and flipped open his laptop. The screen came alight to the Yahoo! home page. He hesitated a moment, then typed, "Alzheimer homes Rappahannock County Virginia." He was about to hit Enter when, amid the other headlines on the home page, he saw this one: DALAI LAMA "HEALTH EPISODE" FORCES CANCELLATION OF MEETING WITH POPE.

Bird stayed up until after 2:00 a.m., clicking and surfing.

Myn was long gone by the time he awoke at eight. He reached Angel on her cell phone at her son's soccer game.

"Hold on," Angel said. "Barry, sweetie! Stay with the *ball! Stay with the ball! The ball! Kick it! Kick the ball! Barry! Kick THE BALL!*"

CHAPTER 5

THIS IS OUR EUREKA MOMENT

Angel refused—refused absolutely—to meet with Bird over the weekend. Apparently she had a rule about weekends being devoted exclusively to the eight-year-old Barry Goldwater Templeton.

It was Monday morning now, and Bird and Angel were in a car on the way to a TV studio. Her bodyguard, Mike, was at the wheel. A briefing book was open on Angel's lap. She was scanning the pages at an urgent tempo.

Bird scribbled on a piece of paper and handed it to her: CONFIDENTIAL. RAMBO OK?

Angel scribbled. OF COURSE.

Bird spoke just above a whisper.

"According to the latest reports, he's still in the hospital in Rome. They're saying he's okay. That it was some stomach bug. Bad clam, Roman tap water, whatever. They're doing tests."

"Uh-huh," Angel said, not looking up from her briefing book.

Bird said, "Hello, hello, is there anybody *in* there?"

Angel gave him a frosty look. "I can multitask, you know."

"I'm saying, this could be a gift. A gift from the gods of spin."

"It's a stomach bug," Angel said, returning to her book. "What's the 'gift'?"

"They're canceling a visit with the pope because of an upset tummy? Really? They couldn't give him Pepto-Bismol or Imodium?"

Angel sighed. "Do you imagine, for one second, that His Holiness the Dalai Lama, spiritual leader to twenty million people, is going to risk throwing up—or worse—on His Holiness the pope, spiritual leader to one billion?"

"I *understand* all that," Bird said. "But suppose a rumor got started that it wasn't a tummy bug. That they tried to poison him?"

"Who?"

"Could you pay attention for two seconds, please? The *Chinese.*"

"Why would they do that?"

Bird groaned. "You're supposed to be the foreign policy guru here. In 1959, after China invaded and took over Tibet, the Panchen Lama—the number-two lama, vice-lama, backup lama, whatever—returned to Tibet. Bad move. He gave a speech about what assholes the Chinese were for taking over Tibet. *Very* bad move. Five days later he's dead. Of a"—Bird made quotation marks with his fingers—" 'heart attack.' So the Chinese have some street cred when it comes to offing lamas."

"That was 1959," Angel said.

"So? Are you telling me that totalitarian governments no longer go in for assassination? Look at the Russians. They're poisoning people every two minutes! That poor son of a bitch ex-KGB guy—Litvinenko—the one they got in London? Polonium-210 in his tea? He ended up *melting.* Nas-ty."

"What are you proposing? That we start a rumor that Beijing tried to kill the Dalai Lama on his way into a meeting with the pope?"

"Yes. Exactly."

"And what are we offering by way of evidence?"

Bird grinned. "Who needs evidence when you've got the Internet?"

"So we post it on your Facebook page that the evil Chinese tried to poison him. And you expect that to lead the evening news?"

"There are a few details to work out." Bird leaned into Angel. He could smell her perfume. "Friday I stayed up until the roosters started, doing research. The Dalai Lama is the one thing having to do with China that Americans actually care about. Human rights? *Zzzzz.* Terrible working conditions in Chinese factories? *Zzzzz.* Where's my iPad? Global warming? *Zzzzzz.* Taiwan? Wasn't that some novel by James Clavell? *Zzzzzz.* When's the last time you heard anyone say, 'We really must go to war with China over Taiwan'? But the Dalai Lama? Americans *love* the guy. The whole world loves him. What's not to love? He's a seventy-five-year-old sweetie pie with glasses, plus the sandals and the saffron robe and the hugging and the mandalas and the peace and harmony and the reincarnation and nirvana. All that. We can't get enough of him. If the American public were told that those rotten Commie swine in Beijing were"—Bird lowered his voice—"putting...whatever, arsenic, radioactive pellets, in his yak butter, you don't think that would cause a little firestorm out there in public-opinion land?"

Angel took off her glasses and looked out the window pensively. "Getting the story planted isn't the problem," she said. "The Lama people will pooh-pooh it, though. I'm not an expert on Tibetan Buddhism, but I'm guessing they're not about spinning fake assassination attempts."

"That's the beauty of it!" Bird said. "Of *course* they'll deny it. Why? Because they're all about peace and forgiveness and turning the other cheek. Meanwhile—world opinion in a furor! And Beijing?" Bird smiled. "Beijing gets to put out statement after statement saying, 'We did not poison the Dalai Lama!' Angel. It's a slam dunk."

Angel shuddered. "Don't use that expression. Please."

"All right. A home run."

She put her eyeglasses back on. "You might have something."

Bird threw up his hands in exasperation. "I bring you E equals mc-squared and you tell me, 'You might have something'? Angel, this is our eureka moment. Move over, Archimedes."

"We'll discuss. Look, I have to concentrate. I'm walking into a gang bang."

Friday, in the course of a call-in radio interview about her article in *Neo-Com* magazine, "Nuke Iran Now," Angel had referred to the head of Mothers Against Military Action (MAMA) as a "headline-hungry harridan." Now she was on her way to a TV studio to expand on her comment, which had triggered a tsunami of indignation.

Burka had informed her that they were anticipating hundreds of furious protesters outside the studio. Some were planning to pelt Angel with their sons' and daughters' Purple Heart medals—truly a photo op from hell. Extra security had been laid on. They were to enter the studio via the basement entrance.

"You know you're doing your job," Angel observed, "when they have to bring you in through the basement."

Bird let her concentrate on the briefing book while he turned over scenarios in his mind.

"Radioactive pellets . . . in the rice bowl," he murmured. "Radio-active pellets. Rice bowl. Fabulous juxtaposition."

Angel said, without looking up, "Not to rain on your parade, but if you eat radioactivity, you die. Horribly."

"So?"

"But he's not going to turn into a lava lamp and glow in the dark and melt, is he? He's not going to die. So what's the point of announcing that they put radium in his tapioca?"

"They tried, but the pellets . . . expired. Or he ate from a different rice bowl. But they'll keep trying."

"Needs work."

"No. It should be *herbal*. Yes. Yes. Of course. The Chinese are all about herbal. They wrote the book on herbal. We just need to find out what's the best death herb. I bet they've got some killer stuff, don't you? Bat wing. Tiger claw. Tiger *penis*."

"Bird. Please. I need to read this."

Bird gripped Angel's arm. *"Panda."*

"What are you talking about?"

"They took a death enzyme from a dead panda's...liver. That's it. They killed a panda. It's a twofer. Americans are crazy about pandas. Every time the one at the National Zoo gets a head cold, the TV networks go on a deathwatch. 'This just in from the National Zoo. Ping-Ping's temperature is up to a hundred and two! The president has asked all Americans to join in prayer.' Yes. The rotten swine killed a panda—a baby panda—and extracted the death enzyme. In order to poison the Dalai Lama." Bird fell back against the car seat in a swoon of creative exhaustion.

"That's sick," Angel said.

"But good sick."

"Oh, *God*."

"What?"

"Her father. Damn it."

"Whose father?"

"The harridan's." Angel sighed heavily. "He was wounded at Iwo Jima. Well, that's just *great*."

"Why *did* you call her a harridan anyway?"

"Because she's undermining the war effort. Do I really need to explain this to you?"

Bird shrugged. "She seems like a nice person. You can hardly blame her for being upset about losing her son."

"She's an opportunist. She's making a killing on the lecture circuit."

Bird looked at Angel. "Could I suggest that you *not* say that on TV?"

"She's getting twenty-five grand a pop!"

"Can't you just say that the harridan comment was taken out of context and move on?"

"Apologize? I'm not about to apologize to some grandstanding professional mourner—"

"Just say it's an emotional issue and we all get a little excited—blah, blah, blah. Her son died in a great cause—blah, blah, blah. In, out. And on to Beijing!"

"*She* started it."

"Angel. You called her an opportunist for protesting against the war. I'd say you started it."

"'Never, ever, ever, ever give in.' Winston Churchill."

"Fine. Call her a whatever. While you're at it, why not reach across the desk and bitch-slap her? Look, Angel, we need to move on this while our boy's still in that hospital in Rome. Before long, he'll be up and out and making huggy with the pope." Bird paused. "We could say that they were trying to knock off both of them. The Dalai and the pope. Um. The Chinese hate Catholics, you know. They're always tossing some poor bishop into prison for hearing confessions or handing out a Communion."

The car turned a corner. Angel groaned. It was indeed an impressive crowd. Including mounted police.

"Cops on horseback," Bird said. "You go, girl."

Burka accelerated around the corner and pulled up at the entrance to the basement ramp. A half dozen security guards and police stood by, looking nervous.

"Templeton?" said a guard with a clipboard.

Burka nodded.

"Go on in. We're trying to keep this entrance clear, but there's a lot of angry folks here."

Angel had her compact open and was applying lipstick. She snapped it shut.

"Welcome to the Angel Templeton Experience," she said.

Two hours later she and Bird were back at the Institute for Continuing Conflict. Angel was a bit pale, even beneath the TV makeup that she still had on. She reached into the refrigerator under the wet bar and pulled out a frosted bottle of vodka, filled two glasses halfway, handed one to Bird.

"For the record, I don't usually drink this time of day," she said.

"You did fine," Bird said. He sipped his vodka. "Do they normally have that many guards *inside* the studio?"

Angel drained her glass. "*Ohh.* I got really blotto once with the head of Finnish Air Defense. God, Finns can drink. Well, I said what I had to say."

"You did. And I must say, it took guts to call her a 'paid mourner.' I don't think I've ever seen Chris Matthews at an actual loss for words."

Angel shook her head. She looked defeated.

"Maybe you should lie down," Bird said.

"I've been through a lot worse than that. So you think this poison thing is the way to go?"

"You know the saying, 'You can fool some of the people some of the time—and those are the ones you need to concentrate on'? Yeah, I think it's worth a shot."

"Let me talk to my peeps. Obviously, it can't originate from here." She considered a moment. "India."

"India?"

"The Indian media will run anything. I've been feeding them stuff for years. Once it's appeared in a newspaper there, then it gets requoted and you're off and running."

Bird smiled. "I feel I'm in the presence of greatness."

"Greatness is easy." Angel grunted. "Removing bloodstains is hard."

"Oh. Do you...have to do that often?"

"Barry gets nosebleeds. The pediatrician says he'll grow out of them. I was up all night with him. Poor baby. It's scary for him, you know. You want to just hug them and say, 'There, there, sweetie. It'll be okay. Momma's here.'"

Bird was confused. *One minute she's bashing Private Ryan's mother, the next she's on the verge of tears about her little boy's nosebleeds.*

He felt a stirring. She looked very attractive today, softer than her usual self. Feminine, without the show-off miniskirted legs and cleavage.

The stirring increased. *Uh-oh,* he thought, and issued a mental cease-and-desist order to the testosterone-generating zone. *Emergency shutdown!*

Bird had never cheated on Myndi—well, okay, except for that one scotch-drenched night in Seoul with the woman from the helicopter company. And even if he was tempted by Angel—okay, he *was* tempted—but even so, he knew perfectly well he was no match for Angel Templeton. She made the man-eating lions of Tsavo look like hamsters. She'd chew him up and spit him out in little balls of gristle.

"Well," he said, rising from his chair, "I'll let you get back to work."

Oh, damn. Awk-ward.

He swiveled to adjust his trousers.

Embarrassing. Bird felt the blood rushing into his face. At least blushing was drawing it away from other parts.

He saw from Angel's bemused, faintly contemptuous look that she'd noticed. And that she was not in the least interested.

IT WAS HARDLY the first spontaneous erectile *hommage* that Angel had been tendered. She was an old hand, indeed had been fending off overexcited, panting males for many years. The current fendee was—of all people—Tibor Fanon, one of the ICC's resident scholars, a brilliant but extremely high-maintenance Hungarian émigré.

He'd started sending her inappropriate e-mails. As if she could be attracted to a man thirty years her senior, fifty pounds overweight, with nicotine-stained teeth and badgerlike thickets of ear hair. The very thought of this slobbery Magyar cybergroping her...She'd have to do something about it before the annual ICC retreat next month at the Greenbrier. The prospect of him trying to play footsie with her under the conference table in the midst of a session on U.S. naval strategy in the Strait of Hormuz was...yucko.

Ever since her time at the Pentagon, Angel had made it a rule never (again) to have in-house affairs. That resolution came to her one day there when she overheard one secretary gossiping with another and using what was—apparently—Angel's Pentagon nickname: "Silo." *Silo! Mortifying!*

Now, looking at the crimson-faced Bird as he tried to conceal his woody...Angel thought, *Oh, please.*

Not that he wasn't cute. But she had another rule: no lobbyists. Anyway, Bird was married. Angel had done her due diligence. He and the wife lived in some sort of semi-grand house out in Horseburg, Virginia. The wife was a Muffy. A looker, but right out of *Town & Country*. Probably wore white gloves during sex.

Angel could do way better than Bird McIntyre. She'd come close, oh so close—most recently with that deputy secretary of defense, the big venture capitalist from California. Lots of zeros in that portfolio. Billions. The bastard had promised, sworn—*four times*—that he was going to divorce his wife and marry Angel. Then what happens? Wifey gets cancer. *Great.* But then he tells her he can't very well leave the bitch now—how would that look? Dumping her while she's hooked up to chemo bags and taking off with... *Silo*? He's going to run for governor someday. *Be patient,* he says. *Let nature take its course. The docs say six months, tops.* Then what happens? The bitch recovers! *Total* remission! And by the way, how come her hair never fell out from chemotherapy? Now she's back lunching every day at Café Milano. *Wolfing* down food with the girls.

"Sorry, what did you say?" Angel said.

"I said why don't I let you get to work."

"Oh. Yes. No e-mails."

"No, absolutely," Bird said. E-mails were the new herpes: You were never rid of them.

"No cell phones."

Bird nodded. "Strictly landline."

They were staring at each other.

"Okay, then," Bird said.

"Okay. See you."

"Bye."

"Bye."

TWO DAYS LATER the *Delhi Beast* ran a front-page article below the fold:

WAS HIS HOLINESS DALAI LAMA
POISONED BY CHINESE AGENTS?

Any discerning reader of the article, whose "sources" consisted of anonymous "insiders," would instantly conclude that the answer was, "Almost certainly not." But people read the *Delhi Beast* for entertainment, not news.

The moment after the story went up on thedelhibeast.com, Bird and Angel threw themselves into work, ensuring that the item would spider its way throughout cyberspace like a rapidly metastasizing tumor. Within hours, world media was abuzz.

Three days later one of the American television networks couldn't resist and did a two-and-a-half-minute story on it. The tone was somewhat skeptical. There were comments by a gastroenterologist, a former CIA operative (a "consultant" to the network, which is to say, "paid"). The story duly quoted the indignant denial issued by

Xinhua, the official Chinese news agency, but in such a way as to make it sound defiantly mendacious. The segment ended on a note of seething outrage, supplied by Hollywood actor and Dalai Lama acolyte Branford Dane, wagging a finger at the camera.

"I have a few words for the Chinese government in Beijing," he said, "The whole world is watching."

CHAPTER 6

Cool Limpidity

F a Mengyao, president of the People's Republic of China and general secretary of the Chinese Communist Party, sat in his office in Zhongnanhai, the leafy, walled enclave north of Tiananmen Square, studying the disturbing report that lay before him on his desk. It was not yet 7:00 a.m., but already he was smoking his fifth cigarette of the day. He rebuked himself. He must cut down—truly.

Comrade President Fa was of the *disidai*, the fourth generation of Chinese leaders after Mao Zedong. He was sixty-three years old but could pass for a man of forty. (Mengyao translates roughly as "superior handsomeness," a name that had occasioned much teasing during his school days.) If his looks were not—to be honest—quite of movie-star quality, Fa was certainly handsome enough, a soft-faced man of mild aspect, who might have spent his entire life inside an office, dealing with nothing more urgent than memoranda and having to lift nothing heavier than a stapler.

His mind was a marvel to the party leadership and most of the other eight members of the Politburo Standing Committee. Total coal production in Guangxi province between 1996 and 2001? Fa

58

could recite the entire column of figures right off the top of his head. His temperament was equable. No one—even his family—had ever heard him raise his voice. The Guards Division, who undertook the security of top party officials, assigned him the code name Ku Gingche: "Cool Limpidity." Fa joked to his wife that he would have preferred a more impressive name, such as "Genghis" or "Terrible Immensity." But either of those would have been an ill fit for Fa Mengyao, who regarded his high position with humbled awe.

He held no grudges and made it his business to get along with everyone. (Although not every member of the Standing Committee reciprocated.) He shied from fanfare and was a paradigm of self-effacement, a quality greatly favored by the party. On public occasions when his presence front and center was required, he comported himself with reticence and demureness. One party wag went so far as to dub him "The Invisible Man." This was not much of an exaggeration, for a secret study undertaken by the Central Committee revealed that about 70 percent of the Chinese people did not recognize his photograph. Fa was not entirely displeased when informed of this fact. He derived satisfaction enough from knowing that he was, indisputably, one of the most powerful men in the world, nominal leader of one-fifth of its population. Leader, of course, in consultation with the party—the real and true leader of the People's Republic of China.

On this particular morning, however, Fa Mengyao felt neither cool nor limpid as he read the disturbing top-secret paper before him. It had come in overnight, from the head of Guoanbu, the Ministry of State Security (MSS).

Fa read:

Begin. Story originated in Indian newspaper DELHI BEAST, notorious purveyor of unreliable and often hostile news. Six and Ten Bureaus analyzing. Xinhua has issued formal denial and denunciation. Embassy Washington monitoring American media. Embassy

*Washington reports US State Department briefers actively down-
playing story. Six Bureau Washington reports US intelligence agency
involvement "unlikely" but is pursuing. US and world media continuing to play up story. Propaganda Office linking story to Falun
Gong and White Lotus elements. End.*

The door opened. Gang, his personal assistant of more than
twenty years.

"Comrade President. Minister Lo has arrived."

"Thank you, Gang. Please show him in."

Fa stubbed out his cigarette in the ashtray. Why, he chided himself, had he filled his office with cigarette fumes right before meeting with the minister of state security? Not that Minister Lo Guowei
would care an apricot whether or not Fa smoked. However, President
Fa *had* recently unveiled—and with considerable fanfare—his "Four
Improvements" campaign. The Fourth Improvement, following the
first three—pollution, carpooling, and reporting tax evaders—was
"Honor One's Body and the Party by Ceasing to Smoke!" And Fa
knew that Lo Guowei would derive mischievous pleasure from telling his colleagues at the ministry that the president was undertaking
the Fourth Improvement with less than total commitment.

Lo Guowei, whose given name meant "may the country be pre-
served," was the most feared person in China, something of an accomplishment in a country of 1.3 billion. In this capacity he was chief
policeman, jailer, interrogator, and keeper of state secrets. Fa exercised
a certain caution in his dealings with Lo, for one reason above all: Lo
had orchestrated the downfall of the previous minister of state security, Admiral Zhang. Years before, Zhang had taken an interest in the
promising young deputy Fa Mengyao and had been a mentor to him
as Fa rose through party ranks. Fa retained great affection for the old
man and despite his ouster had kept in touch—a fact he did not adver-
tise to Lo. Zhang, a man of quiet wisdom and deep humor, privately
referred to Lo's ascent as "The Great Leap Backward."

There was this, too: Lo had forged a close relationship with General Han, minister of national defense, China's top military man. The coarse and untutored Han did not go out of his way to disguise his disdain for Fa, whom he regarded as soft. (In truth, General Han regarded everyone who had not endured actual combat as "soft.") When Fa was made president and general secretary, it was Han who saw to it that Fa was not also given the chairmanship of the Central Military Commission along with his other titles. "Let Comrade Fa first demonstrate his mettle before being given stewardship of our military." It was said that Han had even gone so far as to tell a fellow member of the Politburo Standing Committee that Fa had demonstrated "more tin than steel" in recent dealings with the criminal regime in Taiwan and the rebellious elements in the Tibet Autonomous Region, where Fa himself had spent three years as provincial committee secretary and should therefore *know* better.

For these reasons Fa felt it prudent to maintain good, if somewhat formal, relations with the ministers of state security and national defense.

Minister Lo Guowei entered. Fa rose, as was his custom when greeting anyone, whatever his or her rank or position, and came around his desk, smiling, hand extended.

"Comrade Minister," he said heartily. "Welcome."

"Comrade President."

"Well, look at you. Have you lost weight? You look thin. Too thin!"

Lo Guowei was a heavyset man and therefore not immune to this flattery, especially when the converse was in fact the case. He was a man of well-known appetites.

Lo patted his stomach dismissively. "My wife feeds me too much and too well." He pointed at Fa's ashtray and grinned. "This is why I, *too*, have not yet taken up the Fourth Improvement."

Fa held up his hands in mock surrender. "Did I not say to myself this morning, 'Foolish fellow, do not smoke until *after*

Minister Lo has come and gone'? So now you have me. Please, Comrade, sit."

Lo settled into the overstuffed armchair, a decorative relic of the era of Sino-Soviet entente.

"You've read the report?"

"I have." Fa frowned. "An unpleasant business. Who is behind this?" He added, "The Americans?"

Lo shrugged. "We don't know—yet. The Americans are usually more subtle with agitprop of this type. Ah, don't worry. We'll get to the bottom of it soon enough. I assure you, great efforts are being expended."

"I have no doubt of that." Fa nodded. "If only all our ministries were as diligent as yours—I could take every day off and go fishing."

Lo had served as chief of Six Bureau (Counterintelligence) in Washington, D.C., for several years. There he had distinguished himself with high-level recruitments, including CIA and State Department. Back in Beijing he had been promoted to head of Four Bureau—Technology, an area in which he took keen interest. It was under his direction that the American Internet company EPIC had been successfully hacked and compromised, resulting in its Russian-born chief, Melnikov, petulantly withdrawing his operations from China. As far as Lo was concerned, this was good riddance. He despised Russians almost as much as he did Taiwanese, Tibetans, and Americans.

Some months earlier a listening device had been found in Fa's limousine. What embarrassment! There were urgent meetings, scurryings-about, finger-pointings, and sackings. But under Minister Lo's calm and resolute direction, Four Bureau concluded that the device was of a type used by the Russians, which almost certainly meant that it had been planted by the Americans, in the hope of implicating Moscow.

Upon being informed of this, Fa asked Lo, "But how is it that the Americans were able to plant this thing in my vehicle?"

Lo, always on the lookout for any slight or rebuke, read this as, *How is it that your ministry is not able to keep my own car safe from busy American fingers?*

Lo coolly reminded Fa that it was he—not MSS—who had spontaneously invited the visiting American secretary of state to ride in the presidential limousine from their meeting at Zhongnanhai to the Great Hall of the People.

Fa accepted responsibility but said, "Comrade, are you saying that *she* planted this thing—herself? The secretary of state?"

Lo shrugged and smiled. "How else are we to conclude, Comrade? No more giving rides to hitchhiking American secretaries of state."

"I'll say this," Lo offered. "If this Lotus poisoning business *does* turn out to be American disinformation, it is a grave provocation. We'll have to respond."

Lo lit a cigarette. Fa decided to have one himself—his sixth of the day. *Oh, dear.*

"To be sure," Fa said. "Of course I have every confidence in you and the ministry."

The two men smoked in silence awhile.

Fa said, "Let me ask you, Comrade—do you have any theory as to why such a story should appear now? At this particular moment? In the event it was the Americans, could this be connected with my visit to Washington next month?"

"Mischief makers are like spiders. Weaving, weaving, always weaving. Not to let the Americans off the hook, but my guess? That this originated from Dharamsala." Home, that is, to the exiled Dalai Lama.

Fa nodded. "It was after all an Indian newspaper. What can you tell me about the incident in Rome?" He always took care with Lo to frame his questions as polite *requests* that Lo could decline to go into for reasons of security.

Lo hesitated, to show he was being courteous in vouchsafing

such confidential information. "Do you want to know everything, Comrade, or just enough?"

"Tell me what you want me to know," Fa said, "and that will be 'just enough'."

"We were lucky. As it happened, we had people in place at that hospital." He paused. "It's the one where they take the popes."

"Ah. But that doesn't sound like luck to me." Fa smiled indulgently. "That I would call vigilant intelligence work."

Lo feigned modesty. "When they brought him in, he was coughing and having respiratory difficulties. Fever, diarrhea, wheezing. They're doing a lot of tests on him. I'm informed that one possibility is something called Katayama fever."

"This sounds Japanese."

"I'm no specialist in infectious disease. It's some form of schistosomiasis. You get it from walking barefoot in lakes. From snail shit."

"Oh," Fa said, wincing. "Unpleasant."

Lo continued. "We'll have full access to the test results. Soon we shall have a *wealth* of information about every medical aspect of the Dung Lotus. That would be a nice bit of Buddhism, wouldn't it, if it turns out the Dung Lotus got sick from walking in snail dung." Lo laughed heartily at his joke.

The crude nickname—Dung Lotus—always gave Fa pause, but he was careful to disguise his discomfort. Jetsun Jamphel Ngawang Lobsang Yeshe Tenzin Gyatso, His Holiness the fourteenth Dalai Lama, was called by many names: The Presence, Absolute Wisdom, Ocean, Holder of the White Lotus. Within the organs of China's State Security, however, he was the Dung Lotus.

Fa was not strictly speaking "soft" on the Tibetans, as General Han—and Minister Lo, too—thought him to be. As party boss in Lhasa, Fa had presided over the putting down of a half dozen or more uprisings. He had personally signed the execution orders for 679 Tibetans, a third of them women. And then the nightmares began.

In this way: On one occasion a lama was being executed by firing squad, a burst of 7.62-millimeter automatic-rifle fire to the back of the skull. Standard procedure. Gang related to Fa that the lama had gone to his death cursing. "Isn't that a bit unusual, for a lama?" Fa asked. Moreover, the man had personally cursed Provincial Committee Secretary Fa Mengyao, by name. Indeed, he had shouted out loudly as he was dragged by soldiers to the mud wall, *"Fa Mengyao! Phai.sha.za.mkhan!"*

Fa's knowledge of the Tibetan language was rudimentary. Gang seemed uncomfortable.

"So, Gang? What was he saying?"

"A traditional Tibetan curse, apparently, Comrade Provincial Secretary. I'm told that it means..."

"Oh, come, come, Gang."

"He was saying that you are an eater of your father's flesh. Something to that effect."

Fa forced a dry, nervous laugh. "Not a very *Buddhist* sentiment, I must say."

But the curse clung to his mind. That night he had the first dream.

Fa was hungrily eating dumplings from a large bowl. But the dumplings began to take on a strange taste—a truly awful taste. Peering into the bowl, he saw with horror the face of his late, much-beloved father staring up at him. Fa awoke with a cry, drenched in cold sweat. The almost identical dream came to him night after night, until the thought of going to bed struck terror.

"What *is* it?" Fa's wife said after the fifth or sixth nightmare.

"Nothing." Fa shuddered. "Something I ate." He could not bring himself to share the details, even with Madam Fa.

He began to take more time reviewing the death sentences. Many of them he commuted, or even overturned outright. To some he granted clemency—if lengthy sentences in verminous prison cells could be considered clemency.

The nightmares persisted. Fa began to give speeches on the need for "harmonious convergence." This raised a few party eyebrows back in Beijing. But his moderation toward the Tibetans did usher in a period of relative calm in the "Autonomous Region." The uprisings ceased. The remainder of Fa's tenure as party boss in Lhasa was uneventful but productive. Under his supervision the party's main goal in Tibet was achieved: the immigration of hundreds of thousands of ethnic Han Chinese. Within twenty, thirty years, ethnic Chinese would outnumber the native Tibetan population and the integration of Tibet into Great China would be complete. The Tibetans understood this, and in the past the arrival of large numbers of Han had often provided the spark of unrest. Under Fa's leadership this was avoided. Fa was promoted upon his return to the capital.

Only two minor incidents marred his remaining time in Tibet. Susceptible to the region's extreme altitude, Fa had fainted one evening in the middle of a speech he was giving on the theme that "total unquestioning obedience to the party is the truest path to freedom." On another occasion, also a speech, this one on the theme of "resisting with diligent and patriotic strenuousness those who proclaim the so-called superiority of Japanese-manufactured televisions," he was suddenly stricken with altitude sickness and vomited over the podium into the laps of a high-ranking delegation from Zimbabwe, China's most devoted and faithful ally in Africa. Unpleasant.

"When," Fa said to Lo, "do you anticipate having the results of these medical tests?"

"Soon enough," Lo said. "Some of them take time. Maybe it will just turn out to be food poisoning. We're told that he ate some vermicelli dish with clams." Lo laughed. "He was a vegetarian for a time, but he took up eating meat and fish because he decided he needed the protein. Situational Buddhism! Maybe the clam was an insufficiently reincarnated blowfish."

Fa regarded Lo's expression of contempt. Lo hated the Dalai Lama with more than just professional passion. He hated all religions but reserved a special loathing for Tibetan Buddhism. Fa had been present at a dinner once when Lo had held forth at great length about the "theocratic gangsterism" of Tibet under the lamas before China "liberated" the country in 1950, a year after the glorious success of Chairman Mao's Great Revolution.

Lo chuckled darkly. "Or maybe it was a mushroom—a mushroom with doubtful karma!"

Fa rose. "I thank you profusely, Comrade, for your always excellent work. China's security is truly safe in your capable hands. Do keep me informed."

The two men shook.

As they walked to the door, Lo said, "Don't spend your time worrying about this one, Comrade. The media will chew on it like dogs for a while and then move on to the next bone. It's no great matter."

"Perhaps not. Still, it is troubling."

"How so?"

"To stand accused of such things when they are not true."

"Bah," Lo said. "He's an old man. He'll be dead soon enough, of something."

"To tell the truth"—Fa smiled, putting a hand on Lo's shoulder and pointing at the overflowing ashtray—"*we* may be dead sooner!"

Lo gave a polite laugh.

Fa said, "Tell your wife that she is making me jealous."

"Jealous? Why?"

Fa made a show of looking about as if someone might be listening. He whispered into Lo's ear, "Between ourselves, Comrade. I think you are getting better meals at home than I."

Lo smiled and nodded. "Well, that we can do something about. If you will do us the honor, come with Madam Fa to our house. I'll have Daiyu make us her special dish."

"My mouth already waters. What is the dish?"

"Dumplings."

Fa felt a prickle of cold sweat along his hairline. He swallowed dryly and forced a smile. "Wonderful," he said.

"In that case it will happen. I will see to it."

Fa went to his desk and immediately lit his seventh cigarette of the day. The lighter's flame trembled in his hand.

He rose and paced, away from the window so the guards in the courtyard below wouldn't see. His mind reeled.

Dumplings. Was it possible that Lo knew about the nightmares? But how could he know? Fa had shared it only with the person who was closest to him, whose devotion and loyalty were beyond question—Gang.

CHAPTER 7

Muons?

The story had gone cold. It was four days now since any mention of it in the media.

Bird and Angel confronted the most likely reason—namely, that His Holiness the Dalai Lama had been discharged from the hospital, smiling and in the very pinkest of health. Not merely pink: vibrantly, *vibratingly* alive, positively thrumming with well-being and serenity.

His meeting with His Other Holiness had been rescheduled. Photographs of "Their Holinesses" were everywhere, two elderly divines embracing, smiling, patting each other—practically groping!— a pair of beatific old sweetie pies, one in red Prada loafers, the other in Bata sandals.

"Look at him," Bird said morosely to Angel. "Like he's about to run the New York City Marathon."

According to the statement issued by the Rome hospital, His Holiness—that is, the one in sandals—"may have been" the victim of a bad clam in a serving of *linguine alle vongole*. A terrible embarrassment for his Vatican hosts. Severed monsignorial heads were rumored to be "bouncing down the Bernini staircase like so many marbles."

69

The hospital also noted that there had been "a slight shadow" in His Holiness's lung but that it "was not seen again" on a subsequent X-ray—a fact possibly consistent with a diagnosis of schistosomiasis. Out of cultural nicety, the hospital was reluctant to announce that the Dalai Lama had "worms."

As for the poisoning rumor, this had been officially dismissed as, variously, "absurd," "ridiculous," and a "canard." Various governments—especially those friendly to China—had gone so far as to rebuke the world media for "shameless sensationalism."

"Over and out," Angel said. "Well, we gave it a shot."

"It's not a total loss."

"How do you figure that?"

Bird tapped on the keyboard. "Google 'Dalai Lama,' 'poison,' and 'China' and you get . . . four and a half million matches. I'm not declaring total victory, but it's something."

"Give it up, Bird. Look, there are a hundred and one reasons to go after China. Let's not put all our eggs in one basket. I'll tell you what we ought to be focusing on."

"Panda genocide?"

"Will you forget the pandas? Intellectual-property theft. Industrial espionage."

"Intellectual-property theft. You really think that's going to get Americans rushing into the streets with torches and pitchforks?"

"Okay, what about their massive naval buildup. Did you read General Han's speech last week at the WuShen Boat Works?"

"No, I missed that somehow."

"Talk about a wake-up call."

"General Han," Bird said. "Remind me, which one is he?"

"I keep forgetting—you know nothing."

"Okay. Let me rephrase. Who—the hell—is General Han?"

"Head of Zhonghua Renmin Gongheguo Guofangbu."

"Stupid of me."

"The minister of national defense, dum-dum. Head soldier. And one very tough SOB. He spent two years during the Cultural Revolution in a five-by-five-foot cell and came out *grinning*. From what I'm hearing, he and Lo Guowei are bonding tighter than epoxy." Angel looked at Bird. "Please tell me I don't have to explain who Lo Guowei is."

"Wait, I know this one. Secret-police guy?"

"Check out the big brain on you. My Politburo-watcher buddies say those are the two to watch."

"All well and fine," Bird said. "But I still don't see the American public staying up into the wee hours Googling 'Lo Guowei' and 'General Han.' With all respect to your superb skills at manipulating public opinion—PR is where I *live*. We need something a little more juicy than inside-Politburo baseball. We need red meat."

"Is it my fault the Dalai Lama didn't die? If you feel that strongly about it, why don't we just bump him off ourselves?"

Bird stared. "You're saying that with a slightly-too-straight face."

Angel shrugged. "I know people. Mike Burka could put together a team like that."

"Angel. Be serious."

"I'm always serious. Do you have any idea how many out-of-work military guys are out there right now reading classified ads? Special-ops guys? Seasoned people."

"Stop."

"Special Forces, Delta, CIA—"

"Angel. I don't want to hear this."

"I'm just saying it wouldn't be all that hard."

"Thank you, Mary Poppins. Got it. Can we move on?"

"Do you realize the Pentagon has cashiered over two hundred two-, three-, and four-stars? Generals, admirals. Never mind the colonels and commanders."

"The panda population in Shaanxi province is down forty-six percent," Bird said. "Coincidence or—"

"I know a lot of those guys," Angel continued. "Your heart goes out to them. They feel betrayed. And why shouldn't they? You give your life to your country, put your ass on the line. And suddenly—bam—you're out on the street wondering if your medals will buy you a cup of coffee. I said this at the time: Winning the Cold War was the worst thing we could have done. The absolute worst."

"Angel," Bird said. "It's 2012. Wake up. Smell the latte."

"I'll tell you something else. Right now the situation in the U.S. military is exactly where it was with the Iraqi army in '03."

"What are you talking about?"

"After we liberated Iraq—what did we do? Disbanded their army. Smart move. I argued against that until I was blue in the face. And what happened? We ended up with four hundred thousand pissed-off, highly armed, out-of-work, sexually frustrated, mustachioed alpha males. All wanting payback. But who listens?"

"Are you actually comparing U.S. military retirees—with their pensions and benefits, the GI Bill, all the extras—to Saddam Hussein's army?"

"I'm *saying* there are a lot of pissed-off vets out there. Remember the Bonus Marchers in '32? Hoover had to order MacArthur to open fire on those poor bastards. You think something like that couldn't happen again?"

"Honestly? No. Not in a trillion years. And you're making me nervous with this talk."

"Too bad," Angel said. "I thought you wanted to play in the major leagues."

"No," Bird said. "I'm just another K Street hustler trying to make a buck." Bird stood up, this time woodyless. "I'll call you later. We'll think of something."

Angel started to laugh. "Did you really think I was being serious?"

"You have a weird sense of humor," Bird said. "The sign in your lobby does say 'Extremism in the defense of liberty is no vice.'"

"Oh, my God!"

"What?"

"Barry!"

"Goldwater?"

"I was supposed to pick him up at four-fifteen."

Angel whipped out her cell. "Barry? Hi, sweetheart! It's Mommykins...I know. I know. Mommy is *such* a bad person. She was supposed to be there half an hour ago! Bad Mommy. Is Yolanda there, honey?...Oh, thank God. Put Yolanda on...Yolanda?...Sí, sí, yo mistako-biggo. Enormo. Siento, siento. Yo be casa in veinte minutos. Put Barry back teléfono. Gracias, gracias, gracias...Barry, honey? Mommy's on her way, baby. I wuv oo, my widdle pumpkin-schmumpkin."

ON THE SIDEWALK Bird found himself thoroughly confused. Angel was a maze of contradictions. One minute she was fantasizing about hiring a hit team of disgruntled American vets to assassinate the Dalai Lama. The next she's making goo-goo talk with her eight-year-old.

His cell went off. This ringtone was the voice of Houston's Mission Control: *"Three, two, one, we have ignition."*

"Birdman," Chick Devlin said. "How they hanging?"

"About thirty-two inches off the ground. How are yours hanging?"

"Hey, you following this crazy story about the Chinese trying to bump off the Dalai Lama?"

"Am I..." Bird started to laugh. "Did you just ask me if I'm *following* it?"

There was a pause. "Holy shit. You mean—"

"On cell, Chick."

"Oh. Right. Right," Chick said excitedly. "Well, goddamn. Goddamn, goddamn! How about that? Call on the landline soon as you can. Boy, those Chinese. Guess they play for keeps, huh?"

"Yeah," Bird said. "Tough customers."

Chick sounded gleeful. "It's an outrage. I hear he's a peach, the Dalai Lama. I've always been attracted to the whole Buddhism deal."

"Maybe you should name a new nuclear missile after him. I'm sure he'd be honored."

"You call me on that landline soon as you get to the office."

Bird continued on toward his office on K Street. His clothes were dampening in the heat, which was rising off the pavement in nearly visible thermal layers. He wondered how much he should tell Chick. Chick was obviously thrilled, but the story had gone dead. Old spidered hits on Google were diminishing returns. He could always tell Chick about Angel's idea of going down to the American Legion and rustling up a hit team.

Assassination. Intrigue. Secret phone calls. Bird felt like a character in one of his novels. He rather liked the feeling. He considered. What would Buck "Turk" McMaster do in this situation? The answer was—play it cool. Frosty.

Bird had barely sat down at the desk when the phone rang. Chick.

"You son of a bitch," Chick said. "You son of a bitch. You evil genius."

"I feel your joy," Bird said. "But don't go wetting your pants just yet. In case you hadn't noticed, our saffron-robed friend has fully recovered. He's bouncing around, hugging the pope, and giving speeches on the environment. I wouldn't be surprised if next photo we see he's shooting hoops with the Harlem Globetrotters or banging a tambourine onstage with Bono."

"Be a shame to lose the initiative, Bird."

"I'm shakin' it, boss, I'm shakin' it."

"Well, *keep* shaking it. I got a bull down here who's snorting to be let out of the pen."

"Oh, yes. How is that bull of yours?" Bird said.

Chick lowered his voice. "We ought not to be talking about this, Bird. Even on a landline."

"You brought it up. Oh, and by the way, my colleague, the very fetching Angel Templeton, knows all *about* your bull."

Bird heard a sharp intake of air over the line.

"That can't be," Chick said. "That just couldn't be."

"Asked me flat-out what I knew about it. By name. The T-word."

"Holy..." Chick spluttered. "Damn. There is just no such thing anymore as a secret. You didn't tell her anything, did you?"

"What could I tell her? You haven't told *me* squat. Me, your faithful servant of how many years?"

"Lord God," Chick muttered.

Bird decided to make Chick suffer for being so hush-hush about Taurus. He said, "According to her, word on the street is it's all about muons."

"Muons?" Chick said. *"Muons?"*

"They're subatomic particles."

"I'm a physicist! I damn well *know* what a muon is."

"No need to get huffy." Bird was immensely enjoying this.

Chick was spluttering. "Did you say 'word on the street'? You mean to tell me people are talking about this? All over Washington, D.C.?"

"That was the impression she gave me. Yes."

"This is bad, Bird. Very bad. This just couldn't *be* worse." He sighed. "There's a leak."

"Call a plumber. It worked for Nixon."

"Damn it, Bird, this is serious."

"Hey—don't shoot the messenger."

"All right. Not your fault. Angel Templeton, she's one of the good guys, right? I mean, she's on our side, correct?"

"Oh, huge fan of Groepping. Loved the upgrade package on TACSAT-4."

"Yeah? Maybe we ought to get her down here, give her the ten-dollar tour. Put her on the Vomit Comet." Groepping's 757, used to acquaint trainee pilots and astronauts in the physiological joys of weightlessness.

"I'm sure she'd love nothing more than to spend an afternoon puking up breakfast in a zero-g environment."

Chick said, "You stay on this Dalai Lama thing. And you *definitely* let me know if you hear any more about people walking round yapping about Taurus. Muons. That town of yours drives me up a wall, Birdman. A wall."

"President Kennedy called it 'a city of southern efficiency and northern charm.'"

"I don't know about that."

Bird thought, in all the years he had worked for Chick, never had he heard him quite so rattled. Taurus must be quite the bull.

CHAPTER 8

The Humanitarian Thing to Do

"Comrade President, Minister Lo has arrived."

"Show him in, Gang."

Lo had requested the meeting. A matter of "the highest urgency." Fa had an uneasy feeling in the stomach.

The two men greeted each other with wonted collegiality but dispensed with pleasantries. Lo took from a crimson leather attaché a single piece of paper and laid it on the president's desk. "Only I and four people have seen this document."

Fa took a breath and read the first line:

Results of Medical Testing on Subject 7255.

"Seven-two-five-five?"

"The Tibetan."

Fa made note of Lo's oddly neutral terminology. Was this not the occasion for the usual Dung Lotus remarks?

He read to the bottom of the page, swallowed, removed his eyeglasses, and rubbed the bridge of his nose. "You say that only ourselves have seen this?" Fa said at length. "But surely the Italian doctors are aware?"

Lo shook his head. "No. Our people at the hospital in Rome switched the blood and urine. And the chest X-ray."

"Switched—with other people's?"

"It was to our advantage to know more, Comrade, and for others to know less."

"But the bad clam that he ate. What was—"

"Someone else ate the bad clam, Comrade. An American tourist named Winchell. From Portola Valley. In California."

Fa was impressed—truly—by the competence of Lo's people. A cigarette. He must have a cigarette.

Lo was already holding out an opened flip-top pack of Marlboros. He had acquired the taste for them during his tour of duty in America. His nickname at the ministry, used by very few people, was "Cowboy."

Fa exhaled smoke, nerves steadying from nicotine. "But the Tibetan's people—*they* have no knowledge of this?"

"None," Lo said. "This we know for certain."

"But how could this be? Surely he has had physical exams in the past. Wouldn't they have picked up . . . ?"

"He's had medical problems. Gallbladder infection. Pinched nerve. Dysentery. Routine things. Something like this, you would have to be looking for specifically. It must have developed since his last checkup. Maybe physical health isn't your top priority if you believe you're going to be reincarnated." Lo tapped his cigarette ash. "We have people in his circle. And we know that no one's aware of this. If this diagnosis is correct—and there's no reason to think that it is not—there will be another episode, another collapse. But we don't know when, or where it will occur. And when it comes, we may not have the same access to him that we had in Rome." Lo sat back in the heavy armchair. "When they do more tests on him, then they'll know."

Fa reread the paper on his desk. He said the strange long word aloud: "Pheochromocytoma." He read on: "A tumor of the sympathetic nervous system, arising from the adrenal glands, manufacturing an excess of epinephrine."

"Cancer," Lo said, lighting another cigarette. "It's spread to the lung." He extended the pack of Marlboros toward the president.

"No, thank you," Fa said. He sat back in his chair. "Well, I suppose this will solve our Tibetan problem."

Lo nodded pensively and pursed his lips. "It solves one problem, Comrade. But it creates another. A serious one."

"The succession? But we already have the next Dalai Lama picked out."

"Yes, yes, but that's not the problem."

"Explain."

"According to our medical people, he's got maybe two months. Plenty of time to create trouble."

"Specifically?"

Lo said with just a slight air of condescension, "I assumed you knew. Once he learns that he's dying, he's sure to petition to be allowed to return to Tibet."

"Yes." Fa nodded. "In all likelihood, yes."

"And that cannot be allowed."

Lo caught the look on Fa's face. He added, "Of course, Comrade President, that is not my decision. I'm only a servant of the party. I'll make my recommendation and report as usual to the State Council. But I hardly need to point out to you that the council, as well as we in the Standing Committee, would never permit such a thing." He added, as if to insert a note of levity, "I don't suppose I need to tell you what our good General Han would say to such an idea."

After the last uprising in Tibet, General Han had publicly expressed his desire to "grease the treads of our tanks with the guts of five hundred lamas." Quite the flair for public statements, General Han.

Fa's mind worked over the problem as Lo continued.

"As you're aware," Lo said heavily, "the funeral protocol for Dalai Lamas is called stupa burial. The corpse is dried and entombed. So not only do you have the problem of his returning there to die and spending his remaining days stirring up anti-China hatred. But we're then left with the relic. And relics"—he shook his head slowly— "relics are always problematic. You have the shrine. Then come the worshippers. Pilgrimages. Do we want a Vatican or a Kaaba or a Jerusalem in our backyard? I think not."

"No," Fa said. "Certainly."

Lo leaned forward, a look of playfulness on his face. "So here's the immediate problem: It's announced that he's dying. He petitions for return. We refuse—as we must. But what then? Our enemies use it against us. How callous is China—refusing the dying request of this *wonderful person*? See?"

"Doubtless there would be unpleasantness. But in the end it's back to business. Look what happened after '89."

"Ah." Lo smiled. "But why not *avoid* all that?"

"I don't follow you, Comrade Minister. Tell me plainly what is on your mind."

"Suppose," Lo said, "the Dung Lotus were to die *before* it is discovered that he's got this pheochroma…this cancer tumor?"

"How 'before'?"

"Well, Comrade." Lo shrugged. "There are all sorts of ways."

Fa blinked. "You mean, kill him?"

"If you want to put it that way."

Lo spoke as if he were discussing something as prosaic as a recipe for cake. "There are so many ways, Comrade. Dozens. We have an entire division for this. Thirteen Bureau. It could be made to appear like a heart attack. Some other natural cause. The chemicals these days are *so* advanced." He smiled with an air of proud professionalism. "Unlike the Russians, I prefer not to leave my fingerprints all over the body. But that's the Russians for you. They *wanted* everyone to know they'd killed Litvinenko. That's why they used polonium," he said dismissively. "That's not our way."

Fa was straining to remain composed. He tried to imagine they were discussing a budgetary matter. His stomach was in knots.

"Such a step," he said at length, "surely, an... enormity."

Lo stubbed out his cigarette. "Considering the alternative, I would call it a lesser enormity."

Time. Need time, Fa thought. He said mildly, "I have no authority to rule on such a matter. It's for the Standing Committee, in consultation with the State Council. Yes. Such a thing would be for the party to decide."

"Comrade President. Comrade General Secretary. With all respect to the State Council, the Standing Committee, and our great party, there's no time for endless meetings. Any moment now the old boy is going to collapse, and when he does, they'll find out what he's got, and then it will be too late. He's already a dead man. All we would be doing is to hurry things along a bit. For the good of China. If you think about it, we'd be helping him. Relieving him of suffering. Really, Comrade." Lo smiled. "If you think about it, it's the humanitarian thing to do."

"Perhaps. Nonetheless, Comrade, a decision of this magnitude calls for at least some meetings. We are Communists, after all."

Lo looked about the large office, as if he were a tourist admiring a historic space. "This was the Great Helmsman's office?"

"Yes," Fa said cautiously. "This was Chairman Mao's office."

"And now you are chairman. So, lead us. Not every decision, Comrade, consists of neat columns of numbers on paper."

"Thank you for your report, Comrade," Fa said a bit stiffly. "I will consider this." He added, "In the meantime no action is to be taken. I trust that is clearly understood?"

Lo stared at the president. "Of course, Comrade."

He left without proposing a date when President and Madam Fa might come to his home to sample Madam Lo's dumplings.

CHAPTER 9

THE GATHERING STORM

*T*humpathumpathumpathumpa...

Bird was on the treadmill at Abs Fab, a fitness center near his office. His routine was to run until the sweat drenched his shirt to below the sternum.

He channel-surfed as he ran, eyes glazing through nonpremium channels: an infomercial about how to get rich selling a new type of "precious" gem called Exquisium; a "Breaking News" report about a warehouse fire in Lincoln, Nebraska; an interview with a model he had never heard of, promoting nutrition in a country he wasn't quite sure he'd heard of; a report on steroid use among golfers. Golfers on steroids? Why not? Everyone else in sports was on them. On C-SPAN, an author he had definitely never heard of was promoting a book he was certain he wouldn't read, much less buy. The Cooking Channel. *The World at War.* Dive-bombing Stukas. *Eeeeeeeee-boom.* The Home Improvement Channel. How to get out even the stubbornest grout mold. It was enough to make one yearn for the good old days of three networks, plus the station you needed the funny round antenna to get.

Bird checked his shirt. Damp to the pecs. Almost...

Cartoons. Soap opera. A suspiciously handsome young doctor was telling a suspiciously healthy-looking woman hooked up to tubes and wires: "*We did everything we could. But we won't know until we get the report back from Path.*" An 800 number: Operators were standing by, operators who cared—really cared—about your debt problems, ready to consolidate all of it into single, convenient monthly payments. A rerun of *Friends.* That preposterous-looking bounty hunter with the hair and the tattoos; his even more preposterous family, lying in wait to ambush a stoned nineteen-year-old who had obviously neglected to consolidate all his debt into one single, convenient monthly—

The crawl at the bottom of the screen announced:

REPORT: DALAI LAMA COLLAPSES
DURING MEETING WITH PRINCE CHARLES

Whoa.

Bird punched the red emergency Stop button on the treadmill and stood on the suddenly inert rubber belt, sweat trickling into his ears, soaking the earbuds of his headphones.

He dressed without showering and, as soon as he hit the sidewalk, phoned Angel on her cell.

He could barely hear for the background noise. "Where *are* you?"

"Chuck E. Cheese. Can't talk. Sweetie, not on Melissa's dress. No, Charley. Charley, please don't do that with your french fries. Charley. Take the french fry out of Brendan's nose, please. I'm not going to ask you again."

"Angel. Forget the french fry in Brendan's nose. *We're back in business.*"

"What do you mean?"

"We are back in business. Guess who just keeled over during a meeting with the Prince of Wales?"

"Who?"

"The Dalai Lama, dum-dum."

Silence.

"Isn't that great? Now you don't have to hire your friends to finish him off!"

Silence.

"Hello? Angel?"

Her voice was one degree above freezing. "I have no idea who this is or what you're talking about."

"It's Bird. Ditch the ankle-biters. Get to a TV. I'll meet you at your office in an hour. We're back in business!"

"You must have the wrong number."

Angel hung up.

Bird thought, *What was* that *about?*

A FEW HOURS LATER, he was in the Military-Industrial Duplex, watching TV news with one eye and tapping away on his laptop, mining cyberspace for every nugget about the Dalai Lama's collapse at Clarence House. This is what he knew so far:

His Holiness had been having a private discussion with His Royal Highness when he collapsed. He had coughed up blood. Some bitchy British commentator had said, "An hour with Prince Charles could make anyone bring up blood." God save the prince.

For some reason they'd taken His Holiness to the Hospital for Tropical Diseases. A team of eminent physicians headed by Sir Eldryd Perry and Professor David Moore were in charge. Not much information yet. "Hemoptysis" was apparently medical-speak for coughing up blood. There was some thought it might have to do with "worms."

A crowd had gathered outside the hospital and was growing by the minute. Flowers were being laid, so many that Mortimer Street was now impassable. Candles. Dr. Moore emerged briefly to speak to the crowd. His Holiness was "conscious and resting comfortably."

He thanked everyone for their prayers and apologized to Prince Charles for "leaving him in such a rude manner."

The lobby phone rang.

"Buzz me in," Angel said.

Bird opened the door. Angel burst in—literally, shoving Bird to one side in the hallway. Her face was flushed. She wheeled on him.

"Idiot!" she exploded. " 'We're back in business'? On a *cell* you tell me this?"

"I . . . thought you'd want to know."

" 'Now you don't have to hire your friends'—your *friends*—'to finish him off'? I can't believe you said that. Why not just tweet it?"

"Sorry. I was excited. But isn't it amazing news?"

" 'Sorry'? You mean like in, 'Ah, well, never mind'?"

"*As* in."

"No. No grammar lessons today. My God. What a moron."

"What's the problem? Do you know for a fact that your cell phone is tapped?" Bird went to the glass wall and looked down. "I don't see police or FBI cars pulling up. Oops, is that a sniper team I see?"

"It's a cell phone, nitwit. Do you know what a cell call consists of? Little digital signals, twittering through the air like so many butterflies. Do you know where I was when you called me? In northern Virginia. Do you have any idea how many U.S. intelligence agencies are in northern Virginia? More or less *all* of them. Listening. To the little digital butterflies flitting through the air. God . . ."

Angel hurled her purse onto the floor. It made a hard, metallic sound, causing Bird to consider the possibility that there was a gun in there. While he didn't think that she'd actually shoot him, a pistol-whipping was at this point not beyond the realm of possibility.

"Do you realize," she fumed, "that you may just have put both our lives in danger?"

Bird thought, *Wait a minute.* He held up his hands. "I'm sorry.

Truly. Pinkie swear." He held out his pinkie finger. "Would it help if I chopped it off? The way they do in the Japanese gangster movies?"

Angel was still glowering, arms folded across her lovely chest.

"But before we chop off the pinkie, how about a drink?" Bird went to the freezer and pulled out a bottle of vodka. He half-filled a highball glass and handed it to her.

"So did Charley remove the french fry from Brendan's nose?"

Angel looked out the floor-to-ceiling glass at the view of the Mall with its gleaming, illuminated memorials.

"Nice view," she said.

"Do you like it? My wife thinks it's a cliché."

"Your wife? She's not... *here*, is she?"

"Oh, no. She almost never comes. We have a place out in Virginia. She's an equestrienne. A rider?"

"I know what an equestrienne is, Bird."

"She's pretty serious. Competing for a slot on the U.S. team. Apparently there's this big competition coming up in..." Bird paused. He had enough female trouble right now without telling Angel about his Myndi–Tang Cup problem.

Angel returned to the spectacular view of the Mall. "I saw her picture in *Washington Life*. Some horse thing. Middleburg. Upperburg. She *is* pretty."

"Oh, yes."

"Why don't you have children?"

"She... What with the riding and all. It would mean... But we're definitely planning to. Kids are great. Do they all stick french fries up each other's nose?"

"Relax," Angel said.

"Sorry?"

"You're babbling. Relax. I didn't come here to have sex with you."

"No, I didn't think you did, from that entrance. I was more expecting that you might shoot me."

"I considered having sex with you. Then you pulled that cell phone stunt and revealed yourself to be a complete retard. And that's one of my rules. I don't sleep with retards."

"Very sensible," Bird nodded, taking another sip of vodka.

Angel finished her drink and set it down on the glass tabletop with a loud rap. "I'm going now. Home. To the man in my life."

"Oh? Are you—"

"Barry. My son."

"Oh, *Barry.* Well, great."

"I read to him. Every night."

"That's nice. Mother used to read to me and my brother. It's very bonding. What are you reading him?"

"The Gathering Storm."

"Is that...Dr. Seuss?"

"Volume one of Winston Churchill's memoir of World War II."

"Oh, that *Gathering Storm.* Well. Gosh. How old is Barry?"

"Eight."

"Eight? And reading Winston Churchill."

"He's extremely precocious."

"When I was eight, I could barely keep up with Ferdinand the Bull. Churchill. World War II. Impressive."

"His teacher thinks I'm strange. But by the time this kid is ten, he'll know more history than the rest of his class put together. This kid is going to be a freshman at Harvard by age sixteen."

"Does he get nightmares or anything, reading about Hitler and Stalin and...I don't think I'd even *heard* about World War II until I was ten."

"Sleeps like a baby, straight through. Wakes up smiling. My widdle koala bear. We split a Valium. Half for Momma, half for Barrykins."

"You give him—Valium?"

"Not *all* the time."

"You should write a book on child rearing. You'd get on the talk shows."

"I'm already on them." Angel gathered up her purse. "Okay," she said. "So as you said—over the *cell*—we're back in business. My office, ten o'clock."

She paused on her way out. Looked out onto the Mall.

"By the way. That's not a cliché," she said. "That's America."

BIRD TOSSED AND TURNED. Finally around two, he took a pill. Why not? Barry did.

CHAPTER 10

I Don't Think We're in Afghanistan Anymore, Toto

Shouldn't we hold off on the poison until we at least hear what it is he's actually got?" Angel demanded.

They were in the newly organized "war room" at the ICC, a windowless and, Angel assured Bird, electronically impenetrable space. Staffers sat in cubicles beneath plaques: DL, BEIJING, LHASA, USGOV, MEDICAL, DISINFO, BUDDHA, MEDIA, INTEL.

Angel had handpicked them from among the crème de la crème of the Oreo-Cons. She had made them sign scary legal documents swearing them to eternal secrecy. But it was an easy sell. Promote conflict with China? Oreo-Cons *lived* for this sort of thing! The rest of the ICC staff was given a cover story that their absent colleagues had been pulled off regular duty for a rush-rush, hush-hush North Korea post-invasion scenario presentation for the Pentagon.

The Oreo-Cons were pumped. China was the Big One. As one of them said, "I don't think we're in Afghanistan anymore, Toto."

Bird pecked away at his keyboard.

"No sense in not being ready," he said to Angel. He summoned the staffer beneath the MEDICAL sign, a sallow-faced young man named Twent. "Anything on the panda enzyme?"

"No," sighed Twent, in a way to suggest that he had been asked this one too many times.

"When do you—"

"I'm *working* on it."

"Still fixated on the pandas, Bird?" Angel said. "Micromanaging much? What's wrong with arsenic? Or cyanide?"

"Arsenic?" Bird said. "Arsenic leaves traces a blind pathologist could detect. Look, do you mind? We're working."

"Or your basic phosphate esters," Angel pressed. "Malathion, parathion..."

"Angel," Bird said sharply. "Could we leave this to the professionals?"

"Are you suggesting that I'm unfamiliar with this? For your information, Chemical Ali, when I was at the Pentagon, I dealt with this stuff practically on a daily basis."

"All I'm suggesting, O Wicked Witch of the West, is that you let your *own* expert, Dr. Twent here, do his job. He happens to have a master's degree in biochemical warfare from the Naval War College."

"I still think you're gilding the lily with this panda stuff. And BTW, it's *my* ass out there on TV, not yours."

"It's 'painting the lily,'" Bird said. "*Everyone* gets that wrong."

"I'll make a note of it. Look, I'm not going to ruin my credibility just because you're obsessed with bumping him off with essence of panda. This isn't one of your unpublished novels."

Bird looked up. "Well. *That* was bitchy."

Only last week, Bird had presented Angel with handsome, leather-bound printouts of the Armageddon trilogy. Bird noticed that they remained on her desk exactly where she'd put them after thanking him somewhat perfunctorily.

"I didn't mean it that way," Angel said.

"For your information, there's a difference between 'unpublished' and 'unpublishable.' J. K. Rowling's first Harry Potter book got turned down. Now she's richer than the queen of England."

"Meaning what, exactly?"

"Why don't you go prep for your showdown with the Dragon Lady?" Bird said. "I hear she's good. Might give you a run for your money."

Angel snorted. "Bitch is going down in two rounds."

Staffers stared.

"Why don't you call her a 'war profiteer' like you did to Private Ryan's mom?" Bird returned to his computer. "And you're worried about your 'credibility'? That's a laugh."

"If you actually *find* the elusive panda enzyme," Angel said, "why don't you test it on yourself first?"

"See you next Tuesday!" Bird called out after her.

Without turning, Angel continued on her way and flipped Bird the bird.

Bird soothed his offended literary sensibility with the knowledge that he was now quietly at work on a fourth novel. His Armageddon trilogy was now a tetralogy in progress. Bird felt confident about this one. It was a much more mature work than the previous three. Its working title was *The Armageddon Revalidation*. The hero, Buck "Turk" McMaster, had been handed another against-all-odds assignment by the desk-hugging, soft-faced politicians in Washington—rescuing the Grand Xama of Nibbut, a once-proud, theocratic kingdom that had been invaded and cruelly crushed by its neighbor, Mantagolia. Good stuff, *far* above the genre of mere thriller writing. This, Bird sensed, truly aspired to the level of Literature.

The code name for Turk's mission improbable was Red Bull. Bird had contemplated calling it Taurus but feared that Chick Devlin might have an embolism. He wondered if there might be some copyright problem with the energy-drink manufacturer? Surely not. They should be flattered; anyway, he wasn't about to give up a great name like that without a formal legal demand. His agent would handle all that. This reminded him: He needed to get an agent. The last one had stopped returning his phone calls.

He was making excellent progress. Already up to chapter 10. Turk had just completed a stunning HALO (high altitude, low opening) parachute drop into Nibbut's harsh and unforgiving mountainous terrain, a muon bomb strapped to his back. But no sooner had he landed than he was being pursued by his old nemesis, Colonel Zong. Clearly there had been another leak out of Washington. The perfidy of those pusillanimous politicians! Once again Turk had been betrayed by the very people who had sent him off to certain death. He would deal with *them* in due course. Bird couldn't wait to get back to his laptop.

He emerged from the war room and stretched. He was exhausted. He would need more Adderall if he was going to get another chapter done tonight. Terrific stuff, Adderall: The writing just *flowed*.

He checked his cell messages. There were a half dozen voice mails, five of them from Myndi. Angel was right about one thing: The war room was electronically impenetrable. He listened to the messages. Myndi's voice grew more frantic with each call.

"Hi, darling," he said when he called her back.

"Walter. Where on earth have you been? I've been trying to reach you all afternoon!"

"I'm afraid I can't say, darling."

"What do you mean?"

"Highly classified project. I'm working off campus. Undisclosed location, hardened rooms. Can't get cell calls."

"Hardened? Never mind. Do you want to know why I was calling? Or do you not care?"

Bird sighed. "Of course I care."

Her tone lightened. "Guess what?"

"You're pregnant?"

"Walter," she said, reverting to her prior tone, "you know perfectly well I couldn't be pregnant."

"Okay. Give up."

"I made the team!"

"Oh, that's great. Let's celebrate. Drive in. I'll get us a table at Café Milano."

"Couldn't possibly. Way too much to do. But now, darling, now that I'm on the team, I'm going to need another mount. In fact, Sam is insisting on two more."

"Myn. You can't be serious."

"Walter, I just made the U.S. Equestrian Team. Do you have *any* concept what this means?"

"Beyond costing me another arm and a leg? At this rate I'm going to be a quadruple amputee."

"That is so . . . I can't believe you said that."

"Myn, could we just have a conversation about this instead of another jousting tournament?"

"I call you up to share the best thing that's ever happened to me and you make *amputee* jokes?"

"Whoa."

"Don't say 'Whoa'! You *know* I hate that!"

Bird yearned to be back in the electronically impenetrable war room.

"And please don't sigh," she said. "You know I hate that, too."

"Myn. I'm thrilled you made the team. I'm proud that you, my own girl, will represent our country in—"

"The People's Republic of China. I am so . . . *humbled*, Walter."

"Yes, darling, and my heart, too, is truly full. But speaking as the chief financial officer of Mr. and Mrs. Walter McIntyre, Inc., I have a legitimate, even pressing concern when you call me up and ask me to go another half million dollars into debt so that you can buy two more horses."

Silence.

"Myn? Hello?"

"Harry Brinkerhoff has offered to help."

Brinkerhoff was a hedgefunder, a fellow member of the Hoof and Woof Club. More Myndi's friend than Bird's. Nice enough guy. He owned more horses than the U.S. Cavalry during the Indian Wars. He flew them around the world in a specially outfitted Boeing 757. A flying stable. Bird was as capitalist as the next person, but Brinkerhoff's airborne stable—lushly featured in a recent issue of *Plutocrat* magazine—was of perhaps questionable taste at a time when the unemployment rate was above 10 percent. Brinkerhoff was in the midst of getting a divorce from wife number three—or four. Number two—three?—was a cousin of the sultan of Brunei.

"Walter? Walter, speak to me."

"I don't think it's appropriate to accept a gift of that magnitude."

"Darling." Myndi laughed. "For Harry, this would be a *rounding error.*"

"Still."

"He's patriotic. He's *so* excited about this. The Tang Cup! He's going to fly us all over there in the plane. Is that wonderful? He wants to help us bring home the gold!"

"So you've already... are you saying this is a done deal? Before even discussing it with me?"

"It was completely spontaneous. We ran into each other last week at the club. He said he'd be happy to help if I made the team. It was *en passant.*"

"A half million bucks? That's a lot of *en passant.*"

"If it helps your pride, darling, he'll make it a loan. You can pay him back."

"A loan? From the First Bank of Harry?"

"You know, this is just not good enough. Here I am, trying to make it easy for you, and all you can focus on is money."

"We'll talk about it this weekend."

"I'm not here this weekend."

"Why?"

"Walter. I do wish you'd listen sometimes. We discussed this three weeks ago. I'm in Saratoga Springs."

"Whatever. But I won't have you accepting money from some—"

"Some *what*?"

"From some guy who flies horses around in a plane!"

"It's not your decision, Walter."

"What the hell is that supposed to mean?"

"Competing at the international level has been my dream since I was four years old. I'm not about to let you screw that up for me ... Walter ... I'm talking to you, Walter. Walter?"

Bird was in the middle of a reverie, a most unpleasant one. It was a year from now. They were at the club. People were congratulating Myndi—and Harry—for "bringing home the gold." He saw himself, looking on, the Impecunious Bystander-Husband. People were whispering, pointing. Knowing side glances. *Isn't it wonderful that Myndi and Harry have become such good friends?*

He took twice his normal dose of Adderall that night and cranked on chapter 10. In the middle of the desperate firefight between Turk and Colonel Zong's men, he suddenly stopped typing. Today was the first time he'd hung up on Myndi. He wondered: Did this represent progress?

CHAPTER 11

HAVE WE GONE OVER TO THE DARK SIDE?

A s head of the U.S.-China Co-Dependency Council, Winnie
Chang wielded considerable influence in the nation's capital.
Indeed, her position made her de facto China's top nongovernmental representative in the United States.

The council's mission statement was straightforward: "To promote commerce, mutual understanding, and harmonious relations between the People's Republic of China and the United States." (Translation: We've got you Americans by the short ones, but let's pretend we're friends.)

Winnie was not without critics. Anti-China hard-liners regarded her as just a high-level flunky and called her insulting names like "Beijing Betty." But even they conceded, if grudgingly, that she cut an attractive figure. In photographs the man standing next to her was often the U.S. president, the commerce secretary, or a significant senator; no matter who, any male in the vicinity of Winnie Chang was almost always smiling or laughing and transparently thinking that it would be even nicer to have some private time with her.

She was a player in Washington society. The "Co-Dep"—as the council was called—spent heavily on local institutions: the Kennedy

Center, the Washington National Opera, the Folger Theatre and Shakespeare Library, hospitals, museums, and the tonier diseases. Her residence in the "fashionable" (i.e., expensive) Kalorama neighborhood was the scene of lavish, A-list parties. *Washington Life* had put her on the cover, wearing a gorgeous, sleek red silk cheongsam dress, above the predictable but not-inaccurate headline CHINA DOLL.

An important aspect of her job, aside from promoting harmony and mutual understanding, was appearing on television and radio and writing thoughtful op-ed articles for the newspapers, explaining away Beijing's latest effrontery or outrage, whether saber-rattling at Taiwan or the appalling number of female newborns being found in Chinese dumpsters. Winnie didn't always win the argument, but she always made it with style. When the attack dogs of the right went after her, snarling and snapping, she responded with a lightness of touch that made their fury seem disproportionate or even pathetic. Winnie personified the Chinese proverb that says, "You cannot prevent birds from dropping on you, but you can prevent them from building nests in your hair."

Winnie was chatting pleasantly with the makeup lady when Angel appeared in the doorway.

The intern escorting Angel immediately realized her mistake, but too late. Ice was already formed on the makeup mirror. The two women sat in Antarctic silence as the cosmeticians hastily completed their ministrations with the intensity of emergency medical workers at the scene of an accident.

"Angel Templeton, welcome," said the host of the show *Hardball*, Chris Matthews. "You've been making some pretty tough accusations lately. Let me ask you—do you have any real, *actual* evidence that China tried to poison the Dalai Lama?"

"I wish I didn't, Chris," Angel said sadly, "but the evidence will soon see the light of day. Meanwhile we at the Institute for Continuing Conflict are praying night and day for His Holiness's recovery.

We're also formally requesting that the U.S. Treasury Department provide Secret Service protection for the Dalai Lama. We have information that Beijing is going to make another attempt on his life. It seems they are desperate to silence this good man."

"Winnie Chang, head of the U.S.-China Co-Dependency Council, thanks for coming on *Hardball*. Before we get into this, I've got to ask you. Are you really a *spy*? *National Review* magazine recently called you 'China's top spook.' Are you?"

Winnie beamed. "Well, Chris, all I can say to that is, if I am a spy, I must be a very bad one, since all these people are calling me one."

"That's good. So what about Ms. Templeton's allegations, that your supposed *masters* over there in Beijing, your *controllers*"— Matthews was laughing— "are trying to *assassinate* the Dalai Lama? What do you say to that?"

Winnie laughed along. "I'm not sure what to say, Chris. Honestly, I think Ms. Templeton, who is obviously a clever person, is trying to use this to raise money for her institute, which openly promotes global conflict. She makes the late Senator Joseph McCarthy sound like Little Bo Peep."

Angel snorted. The battle was joined.

"You know, Chris," she said, "that's really a mouthful, coming from someone who makes her living flacking for a totalitarian regime that among other things executes fifteen thousand people a year and throws thousands more into dungeons for so much as complaining about garbage collection."

"But what do you *really* think about China?" Matthews said with a laugh. "Okay. But come on, answer the question. You say you've got evidence. Where is it? And why would China be trying to assassinate someone who's—what?—seventy-six years old? How much longer can he have to live anyway?"

"You have to understand the totalitarian mind-set, Chris," Angel said. "The psychology—pathology, if you will—of evil. It just can't tolerate criticism. It's a kind of narcissistic injury. But this isn't about strategy. This is about revenge. And of course China can't wait to install its own puppet Dalai Lama when this one goes."

Winnie Chang shook her head sadly and smiled. "There, you see, Chris? You asked Ms. Templeton for evidence, and all she has to offer are more reckless and baseless accusations. It makes me want to say to her, sincerely, dear lady, you are not making *sense*. You seem to know about narcissistic injury. Perhaps you should seek professional help?"

Angel laughed. "I'm crazy? Oh, that's good. Wow." She turned to the grinning Matthews, who was thinking, *What a great show.* "As you know, Chris, another characteristic of totalitarian regimes is to accuse anyone who disagrees with them of being mentally ill. So they can throw them into quote/unquote psychiatric hospitals and inject them with psychotropic drugs until they hurl themselves out the window. Speaking of which, I see another miserable worker in Guangdong hurled herself off the roof yesterday. What's the death total for that factory now? Must be in the dozens."

"Hold on, hold on," Matthews interjected. "Are we getting off the topic here?"

"No." Winnie smiled. "I think we are very much on the topic— namely, Ms. Templeton's unfortunate mental breakdown."

"Thank you, Madame Chang," Angel said, "but really, I don't think I need to listen to that kind of hoo-hah from someone in the pay of a regime whose idea of street cleaning is driving tanks over students."

Winnie's smile was hard as porcelain.

"Yes, Chris, here we have the obligatory reference to the events in Tiananmen Square. When was that? My heavens. It is so long ago I cannot remember exactly—1989? It would seem that Ms. Templeton is unaware that no one who was in charge then is in charge now. But for Ms. Templeton, this is what would be called an inconvenient truth."

Angel laughed again. "I get it. I get it. It's ancient history! Like the Great Leap Forward, when Mao starved to death—you're a student of history, Chris, how many millions was it? Twenty? Thirty million of his own people?"

"Wait a minute, wait a minute," Matthews said, "both of you. We're not *debating* Chairman Mao! We're talking about the Dalai *Lama!*"

"You're right, Chris," Winnie said. "Therefore I will not bring up the Kent State massacre."

"Kent *State!*" Angel said. "Kent *State?* Oh, my God, Chris, did you hear that? She's comparing Kent State to Tiananmen Square! Freeze this moment, everyone. You heard it here first, America."

"All right, let me ask you, straight out," Matthews said to Angel. "You've got it in for China. Can we stipulate that?"

"I don't hate China," Angel sniffed. "I'm just not that into Communist dictatorships."

"This is from an article you wrote two months ago in the *National Review.* Quote: 'There are one point three billion reasons to be afraid—very afraid—of China today. They have the highest execution rate in the world. They're the biggest industrial polluters on the planet. They throw their dissidents into gulags, run over students with tanks, cozy up to loathsome regimes like North Korea, Iran, Venezuela, Zimbabwe. They're building up their navy, cornering the world market on essential minerals. They unleashed epidemic SARS on the world and then—oops, forgot to tell the World Health Organization about it. And if *that's* not enough to keep you awake at night, let's not forget—they eat puppies, don't they?'"

Matthews shook his head. " 'One point three billion reasons?' 'They eat puppies, don't they?' And you're saying you don't *hate* China? Really? I'm not feeling a lot of *love* here for China."

Angel shrugged. "I don't know if they have cooking shows on TV over there, Chris. But if they do, I'll bet you a *renmimbi*—whatever that is in real money—there's a chef giving lessons on how to chop up Pekingese for stir-fry. What does dog taste like anyway, Ms. Chang? Let me guess—chicken?"

"I really wouldn't know."

"Don't go away," Chris Matthews said. "You're watching *Hardball*."

"So?" Angel said to Bird, back in the war room.

"A fine piece of bitchery," Bird said. "I think it's probably safe to say you won't be getting a visa for the People's Republic anytime soon. But if they do let you in? I wouldn't go too close to the edge of the Great Wall."

The TV was turned to CNN.

"Anything on Saffron Man?" Angel said. "Why are they taking so long on this?"

"They said they're expecting an announcement 'any minute now.' Which means if you go to the bathroom, you'll miss it."

Angel sipped her coffee. "They've been saying that for days. I realize British medicine is hopeless and socialized, but there must be *one* doctor over there who can read an MRI. Or do they not have MRI machines in England?"

Bird yawned. "Who knows. Maybe Dalai's people are holding it up. It's possible that Buddhists have a slightly less urgent sense of time than the rest of us."

Angel looked at Bird. "You look kind of raggedy. Did you not sleep last night?"

Bird yawned again. "I got so stimulated watching you insult Ms. Chang on *Hardball* that I couldn't sleep." In fact, Bird had been up until 4:00 a.m., banging away on the novel. He was up to chapter 14 already. "Maybe Barry would lend me half a Valium."

"Really funny," Angel said.

The TV screen flashed: LIVE—ANNOUNCEMENT ON DALAI LAMA MEDICAL CONDITION.

"Here we go," Bird said. "Ten bucks says it's his ticker."

"Brain. Fifty bucks."

"You're on." Bird paused. "Listen to us. Have we gone over to the dark side?"

"Never left it."

"Angel, could I ask you a personal question?"

"What?"

"Have you ever been in love?"

"Oh, please."

"No, really. I'm curious. I want to know. I have no agenda."

"'What's love got to do with it? What's love but a secondhand erosion?'"

"With all respect to Tina Turner, you're avoiding the question."

"What's it to you?"

"I'm trying to figure out how your brain got wired the way it did. This is not a criticism. It's an interesting brain. Frightening, but interesting."

"You haven't seen the half of my brain."

Bird smiled. "Your name. Angel. That should have been my clue. So you and Satan, how long have you been working together?"

"Shh," Angel said as two white-gowned doctors approached a podium bristling with microphones. "Showtime."

CHAPTER 12

BIGGER THAN ANNE FRANK

U ntil now, the word *pheochromocytoma* had been familiar only to
    endocrinologists, oncologists, and those unfortunate enough
to be afflicted by one. Within hours of the announcement, most
TV screens on the planet were filled with a white-coated medical
authority gravely discussing the subject.

Bird had been staring at various screens and monitors all morning, barely moving or speaking.

Angel clicked over in high heels. When he didn't look up, she
leaned over and rapped him softly on the head with her knuckles.
"Hello? Anyone home?"

"Poor guy," Bird murmured. "Gee whiz."

"Yo, Debbie Downer. Enough with the black crepe. Time to
saddle up and move out."

"Not now, Angel. Just leave it."

"What's with you anyway? Did JFK just get shot again?"

"Do you *mind*?"

"I don't believe it. You've gone squishy. I should have known."

Bird swiveled in his chair. "Would it kill you to allow me a moment
of sympathy here for His Holiness? He has a pheochromocytoma."

"He's the Dalai Lama. He'll *reincarnate.*"

Bird turned back to his computer. "I've read so much about him. I feel like I know him. Such a good and decent man."

Angel groaned. She shouted across the war room, "Heads up! Got a weeper here!" Staffers popped up from their cubicles, like prairie dogs. "Somebody get a mop!"

"You know, Angel," Bird said, "you really can be a total—"

"See you next Tuesday? No argument. So are you going to sit there making puddles or get up off your fanny and help your good and decent friend?"

"Oh, so now you're all about helping?"

"This may be too complicated for you to grasp, but walk with me for a second. Saffron Man—"

"Would you please stop calling him that?"

"Excuse me. His *Holiness* has spent his entire life trying to get even with the bastards who seized and subjugated his country. With me so far? Good boy. All his life, all his efforts, all his work—at least when he's not levitating or making mandalas and whatever else it is they do—"

"They don't levitate, Angel. They meditate."

"Whatever. Okay. So he's got the Big C. Pheochromosayonara. You're missing the big picture. Don't you see? We just fell into a huge tub of butter."

"Angel. The man is dying. The Dalai Lama, one of the most revered personages on the planet."

"Will you *stop* with the *revered* and the *decent*? I stipulate he's a nice guy. A sweetheart. A lama among lamas. I'm down with all that. I'm saying let's give his death meaning. Bird, listen to me. We have it in our power—in our hot little hands—to make him the biggest martyr since Anne Frank. Bigger than Anne Frank. Do I have to hire a skywriting plane to explain this to you? We've got the bastards by their red testicles. All we have to do now is *yank.*"

Bird thought, *She's right. Scary, but right.*

"Okay, I'm in."

Angel patted him on the head. "There's my bravest boy. Now, go get with Dr. Death over there and rustle me up some credible pathogens." She added in her best Slim Pickens imitation, "Time to get this thing on the hump. We got some *lyin'* to do!"

She walked off, heels clicking. Turned, wagged a finger. "Bird?"

"Hm?"

"No pandas. Promise Momma?"

"Yeah, yeah."

Bird conferred with Dr. Twent. "Speak to me."

Twent took off his glasses and leaned back in his chair.

"Pheochromocytomas. Essentially, tumors of the sympathetic nervous system. They present when the adrenal glands produce an excess of epinephrine. Typically—"

"Jeremy," Bird said wearily, "I've spent the last four hours listening to at least two dozen pheochromocytoma experts on TV. At this point, there is not much that I *don't* know about pheochromocytomas. What I need from you is, What could our friends in Beijing have put in his yogurt that could have *caused* the pheochromocytoma in the first place?"

Twent frowned. "Nothing."

"Not the answer I was hoping for."

"Pheos aren't caused by poison," Twent explained wearily. "Generally they're associated with genetic abnormalities and—"

"No, no, no, no. Genetic abnormalities do me no good. I need you to think outside the box."

Twent said sullenly, "This is science."

"Could you make it a little science fictiony? I'm not asking for a Ph.D. dissertation."

Twent considered. "Theoretically? They could have given him something that might have exacerbated an existing pheo."

Bird smiled. "Now we're cooking. Excellent. Continue. I'm in awe."

"That's it."

"Okay. Then that would presuppose that they *knew* he had the pheo in the first place?"

"Well, yes. Obviously."

"But how would the Chinese know that? Are we suggesting that they slipped into his Rome hospital room in the middle of the night dressed like ninjas, threw him into a sack, and shoved him into an MRI machine, then put him back in bed and left—with the MRI readout?"

"They wouldn't need an MRI. They could tell from his urine."

"Yeah? Tell me more."

"They'd have collected his urine for twenty-four hours. Mind you, they were looking for worm eggs. But if they'd checked his urine for metanephrines and catecholamines, they'd have found levels indicative of a pheo." Twent looked puzzled. He said, "What I *don't* understand, given the time frame, is why didn't the doctors in Rome find it?"

Bird considered. "So...they...*switched* his pee with someone else's." He shrugged. "Why not?"

"Highly unlikely," Twent said. "This is a top hospital. It's where they take popes. They're not going to be sloppy with Dalai Lama urine. They were thorough. Remember they did an X-ray and said there's a shadow on it. And then they did another and said it was gone. Consistent with worms. Or a bad clam."

"Let's stay with the switched pee. I'm running hypotheticals here."

"Well, it's an absurd hypothetical," Twent sniffed. "But I forgot you write *thriller*-type novels."

"I happen to be a novelist, yes," Bird said. "I wouldn't really call my genre the thriller type."

"Are you published?"

"I'm waiting until I finish the last in the series. Then I'll probably bring them all out at once. It's a tetralogy."

"A what?"

"Tetralogy. Four novels."

"Isn't that called a quartet?"

"Can we get back to business, here? Okay. So let's say the Chinese had a mole in the hospital. And they switched out the Dalai's wee-wee with someone's—someone who was in for a bad clam. Not that far-fetched."

"To a *novelist*, maybe."

Bird continued. "And so the Chinese knew that he was sick. From the Rome episode. That he had a pheo. But no one *else* knew. You said you can give someone who has a pheo something to exacerbate it? To make the pheo go wacko or whatever they do?"

"Theoretically. Yes. Any number of things could do it. Certain toxins. Cheese."

"Cheese?" Bird said. "Really?"

"Sure. Cheese is full of tyramine. That would light up a pheo. Symptoms would include palpitations, profuse sweating, abdominal pain, cardiac enlargement, retinal hemorrhage." Twent turned to his computer and studied the screen. "Some of those symptoms *are* in fact consistent with what he had when they brought him in to the hospital in London."

Bird considered. "We can't go claiming that they tried to assassinate him with Stilton. I mean"—he sighed—"cheese? How's that going to sound? Death by cheese?"

"There are other triggers," Twent said. "Amphetamines."

"*Okay.*" Bird brightened. "Now you're talking, professor. Speed. Definite improvement on cheese."

The sound of high heels heralded Angel's return.

"You boys are moving in geologic time. What do you have for me?"

Bird and Twent explained.

Angel winced. "I'd really prefer not to be out there talking about the Dalai Lama's *urine*."

"But it's the plausible scenario," Bird said.

"This isn't one of your novels, Bird."

Bird blew. "What *is* it with you people? Is being a novelist considered some kind of *disability?*"

"Wait," Angel said. "Forget poison. Forget pee. We don't need that anymore. Don't you see? He's *dying.*"

"So?"

A witchy smile came over her face. "Think it through. How does it play out?"

"Well," Bird said, "presumably, they fly him to the U.S. for treatment. Cleveland is the top place, apparently. Or Sloan-Kettering."

Angel said impatiently, "Yeah, yeah, but what's that going to accomplish? Buy him a few more months, maybe? According to the reports, he's toast, right?"

"That's the—yes, basically. It's not curable."

Angel tut-tutted. "You boys are being very slow today."

"Okay," Bird said. "According to traditional Tibetan custom, first they have to consult with the Nechung Oracle. Then the search begins for the new reincarnation of the living Buddha. Then—"

"You know," Angel said, "sometimes it's a real drag being the smartest person in the room. Never *mind* all that. *He's going to want to go home to die. Home? Tibet?*"

"That would... ah," Bird said. "Yes. Right."

"And what's Beijing going to say about that?"

"Whatever the Chinese is for 'Forget it.'"

"Precisely. The bastards won't even let the poor guy come home to die in peace." Angel rubbed her hands together. "Boys, we just got dealt a royal flush." She kissed Bird and Twent on the foreheads and walked off. She shouted back at them, "I'd have sex with you, but I don't sleep with the help."

"Mom sounds happy," Twent said.

Bird regretted losing the poison scenario, especially after all that research. But he could always use it in the novel.

CHAPTER 13

Comrade Fa's Great Secret

"E veryone is present, Comrade President," Gang announced, opening the door to the secure conference room beneath Zhongnanhai.

The president of the People's Republic of China entered. He nodded a collective greeting to the eight other members of the Politburo Standing Committee. It was not an occasion for hand-shakes and pleasantries.

Two men did not return President Fa's nod: Minister Lo and General Han. Lo did not bother to look up from the papers in front of him. General Han regarded Fa as he usually did, with an atti-tude of condescension verging on contempt. Fa had made several concerted attempts at establishing cordiality with the general; Han disdained these baits like an old, fatted carp, serene and indifferent, lord of his own pool. He affected an air of simplicity and gruff-ness, the uncomplicated proletarian warrior, unswervingly loyal to the people and the party. On closer inspection Fa found this per-sona not entirely convincing. Han was oddly conversant about such recondite areas of expertise as French wine, moray eels, and Fabergé eggs. He could quote—at somewhat tiring length—entire routines (in Chinese) by the 1950s American comic pair Dean Martin and Jerry Lewis. He admitted to a confidant later on that it was reciting these, rather than the 427 thoughts of Chairman Mao, that had kept him from going insane inside that suffocating prison cell during the Cultural Revolution. Like many Chinese who suffered terribly throughout that upheaval, he was still capable of a cognitively dissonant reverence for the man who had orchestrated such mass misery. Still the good soldier. Han had commanded a regiment of PLA infantry during China's punitive 1979 invasion of North Vietnam and a decade later led another sanguinary corrective exercise, in Tiananmen Square. The rumor, never uttered above a whisper, was that Han's own son, with whom he had a troubled relationship, was one of the demonstrators, never again heard from.

So Han had earned his hardness. Fa respected that but it did not altogether compensate for his pathological hatred of outsiders. In this, perhaps, Han was a disciple of Wei Yuan, the nineteenth-century Confucian mandarin who enunciated the policy still (quietly) adduced by China's leadership: "Let barbarians fight barbarians."

Fa noticed with a pang that ashtrays had not been set out on the table. "Comrade Minister Lo," he said, "why don't you begin?"

Lo leaned forward and spoke in a dirgelike tone. "As the members of the committee are now aware, there was an opportunity some weeks ago to avoid the situation now upon us. But that opportunity was"—he glanced at President Fa—"not taken."

Fa's jaw muscles clenched. He'd expected something like this. Gang had warned him. There had been much whispering and murmuring in the corridors of Zhongnanhai and party headquarters. Indeed, a torrent of whispers—a veritable gale, Gang reported: President Fa was showing "lack of steel" in the matter of the Dung Lotus.

The phrase "lack of steel" was no mild rebuke. Half the members of the Standing Committee—and indeed many among the party leadership—were metallurgical engineers by training. Moreover,

Gang reported, Minister Lo had reportedly made comments "of a personal nature" about President Fa during a meeting of the Executive Committee of the State Council.

Then there was this unpleasantness: a pun on the president's name was making its way through the Central Committee, causing sniggers. *Fa*—"to send forth." *Fan*—"mortal." *Comrade President Fan.*

Finally there was the article in *Liberation Army Daily*, the official newspaper of the PLA. Headline:

GENERAL HAN WARMLY PRAISES MINISTER LO
FOR DISPLAYING VIGOROUS FIRMNESS IN
COUNTERING TIBETAN GANGSTERISM

Outrageous! Fa thought. You could hear the sound of Han's tank battalions warming their engines. A crisis in Tibet would give him all the excuse he needed for a grand culling of "gangster elements."

So on this morning, Comrade President Fa was in no mood for pouting and theatrics.

"Comrade Minister Lo," he interjected. "Shall we move forward, or are we going to spend all day talking about the past?"

Heads turned. Mouths opened. Lo stared. General Han's eyes narrowed.

Lo said sullenly, "Our information is that they're going to move him to Cleveland. Ohio. USA."

"Is that all you have for us?" Fa said.

"The medical evaluation there will take between forty-eight and seventy-two hours."

"But is it not already established that this is a terminal illness?"

"I informed you of *that* fact, Comrade, ten days ago."

General Han chortled. "Maybe with all these prayers being said for him, there will be a miraculous recovery!"

Some laughed along. Han gave Lo a comradely glance and said, "Pity we didn't act when we had the chance."

Vice President Peng Changpu said, "Is it too late to put into effect what Comrade Lo proposed?" Peng's nickname was "The Barometer": always the first in the room to sense a change in the weather.

Lo sighed heavily to signal that it was too painful for him to relive President Fa's tragic act of timidity. "The moment of opportunity has come and gone, Comrade. The moment he lands in America, he will be under the protection of their Secret Service."

Han wagged his finger. " 'The clever combatant imposes his will on the enemy. He does not allow the enemy's will to be imposed on him.' "

Nods, murmurs.

Fa had wondered when Han would start quoting Sun-tzu. At least it was preferable to another endless Martin and Lewis recitation.

Fa smiled blandly at Han and said, " 'No leader should put his troops into the field merely to gratify his own spleen. No leader should fight a battle simply out of pique.' " He skipped over the middle bit. " 'Hence the enlightened leader is heedful, and the good leader full of caution.' "

Veins appeared on Han's neck. Lo came to his aid with his own contribution from *The Art of War*.

" 'Making no mistakes,' " he said, " 'is what establishes the certainty of victory, for it means conquering an enemy that is already defeated.' "

Han grunted approval, as if to suggest that this conclusive apothegm had been on the tip of his own tongue.

Fa smiled. "What a truly learned committee we are, Comrades. Does anyone else care to share a favorite line from Sun-tzu?"

Several members laughed.

Fa turned to Xi Renshu, chairman of the Standing Committee of the National People's Congress. Xi was an avid consensus seeker. He could find the middle ground on the side of a cliff.

"Comrade Xi, assuming they petition to return, what would your recommendation be?"

"Assuming?" Lo grunted.

Fa ignored him

Xi frowned and said, "I'm not sure I understand, Comrade General Secretary. "Surely there's no question of permitting him to return?" Xi glanced about the table in confirmation of the rightness of his perplexity.

"Very well," Fa said, "let me clarify. Suppose we allowed him back?"

The air in the room turned to aspic. No one moved.

Xi, to whom this stupefying proposition had been addressed, stared at the president with open mouth.

Lo finally broke the silence. "With all due respect, Comrade, you're thinking on your knees."

There was an intake of breath around the table.

Fa said coolly, "You're the one who's been lecturing us about lost opportunities, Comrade. Very well, here's an opportunity. Shall we not even consider it?"

General Han said, "It's madness."

"Thank you for your diagnosis, Comrade General," Fa said. Turning to the others, he said, "Comrades. There are two paths here. One whereby we wait for them to petition and then refuse. And endure the storm. Two, we seize the initiative and invite the Lotus in. But under certain conditions, of course, yes. Minister Lo and General Han can surely keep him in an iron cocoon once he's in Lhasa. We should have no concerns on that score. Let us then ask ourselves, What do we lose by this? And also ask, What might we *gain*? Respect. Admiration. They will say, 'China is confident. China does not fear old, dying men and their ridiculous fantasies about reincarnation. China is generous. China is bighearted. Truly, China is great."

No one spoke or moved. The silence was total.

Minister Lo began to laugh. Louder and louder. He gripped his belly, as if it might explode.

The members of the Politburo Standing Committee stared at one another. No one seemed to know what to do. Lo continued until finally, gasping for breath and wiping the tears from his eyes, he brought his hand palm down upon the table with such a clap that Executive Deputy Premier Wu Shen jerked upright in his seat.

"Well, Comrades," Lo said, dabbing at his eyes, "now we know Comrade Fa's great secret! He wants a Nobel Peace Prize!"

BACK IN HIS OFFICE after the meeting, Fa loosened his tie, something he rarely did. His shirt was damp with perspiration. He lit a cigarette, inhaled deeply, and stared into space. He felt more tired than he had ever been.

After collecting his thoughts, he buzzed for Gang, who, as was his practice, had listened in to the meeting through an earpiece.

"Well?"

Gang said, "Had you intended to propose that, about inviting him back to Tibet?"

Fa smiled at his aide. Gang knew him so well. "Since you ask, no. It *came* to me, you might say."

Gang nodded. "That was my impression. Unlike you, Comrade."

"Yes. I don't seem to be myself lately."

"Do you truly think this is the wise way to proceed?"

Fa considered. " 'To win one hundred victories in one hundred battles is not the supreme excellence. To subdue the enemy without fighting is the supreme excellence.' "

Gang said, "Sun-tzu is certainly getting a workout today."

"It's not without risk. I understand that well enough. Believe me. Do you think they'll go for it?"

Gang shook his head. "No. Han wouldn't permit it. Nor Lo.

And they've been busy cultivating the others. Especially the ones with vulnerabilities."

"Yes. Han's probably telling everyone, 'Can you imagine if we had made Fa chairman of the Central Military Commission?' And Lo will be out for blood. I overruled him, and that his pride cannot bear." Fa smiled. "Perhaps if I went to Cleveland, Ohio, and personally strangled the Lotus in his hospital bed."

"It would be a start."

"Gang?"

"Yes, Comrade President?"

"Do you think…I don't know enough about this form of cancer, but do you think it's possible that Lo's agents somehow…*gave* it to him?"

"I've learned as much as I can about it," Gang said. "Nothing that I have read persuades me that it is something you can cause in someone. But this is not my worry now. My worry is for you. Lo and Han are out there now. Calling you 'Fa, Lotus Lover.'"

"In that case get my plane. We're off to Cleveland. We can see the Rock and Roll Hall of Fame after we kill him."

But Gang saw the look of pain and fear beneath it. He knew the signs. He said gently, "The nightmare, Comrade—it's back?"

"Not yet."

Fa lit a cigarette and was about to tell Gang, "Call Admiral Zhang," then hesitated. He scribbled the characters on a piece of paper and handed it to Gang. Gang read it and looked up, nodded, and left Cool Limpidity to the silence of his thoughts.

CHAPTER 14

WHAT WAS THE NAME OF THAT MOVIE?

Bird would have killed not to have to go out for dinner at the Hoof and Woof on this particular Saturday night. (Or on any Saturday night, for that matter.) He was beat, beyond exhausted.

He'd gotten back to Upkeep late Friday night, weary from a long week of fomenting Sinophobia by day and banging away at volume four of his Armageddon tetralogy—quartet, whatever. All he wanted to do tonight was get into his pj's, pour himself a mind-numbing bourbon, and reread what he'd written. But such pleasures were not on the agenda for tonight. No.

As he and Myndi dressed, Bird uttered the plea of many an American husband: "Say, how about we stay in tonight?" But he knew this would be a nonstarter. Tonight was Myn's victory lap, her first night at the club since she'd made the team. And despite his annoyance over having to shell out additional hundreds of thousands for a couple of new nags, Bird felt that she deserved a round of applause. She'd worked hard for this. She was getting some nice recognition, too. *EQ*, the glossy bible of Horse World, was doing a big feature on her, sending a photographer—and stylist—out to Upkeep. How about that?

Bird felt a mix of fondness and amusement as he watched Myn try on different bits of jewelry. She couldn't seem to make up her mind tonight.

"What about *these?*"

"Great," he said.

"Walter." Myndi sighed. "It's not helpful when you say 'Great' to everything."

"I liked the first earrings. I liked the second pair. The third made me want to bang my head against the wall for joy. I like the ones you have on now, too. But if you'd prefer, I'll just say, 'Boy, do *those* suck.' "

She sat in front of the mirror, fussing with her hair. "I *never* should have agreed to EQ. I'm only doing it for Sam."

"Your trainer? Not sure I get that."

"It's such nice recognition for him. I couldn't care less. By the way, they're coming Wednesday. It's an all-day thing. It would be nice if you were here, darling, for once. People are beginning to won-der."

"Won-der? About what?"

"Our marriage. Zip me."

"Well," Bird said, "if it's our marriage you're worried about, I say let's stay in tonight and make whoopee till the cows come home. I'll open a bottle of that '82. Come on. Whaddaya say? Ruff!"

"You're not planning to wear that cummerbund and tie? Oh, Walter, please. They look like something you'd get at Wal-Mart. These are people with taste."

"No, darling, they're people with money."

"Well, they don't wear cummerbunds and bow ties with *missiles* on them."

The cummerbund and tie were last year's Christmas present from Chick Devlin.

"We're sitting at Harry's table."

"Oh, joy," Bird lied.

"I don't know why you've decided not to like him. He likes you well enough."

"Well enough? You mean, the minimum permissible amount?"

"Walter. If you're going to ruin the evening before it's begun..."

They drove in silence to the club, where Myndi was received as a local heroine.

"You must be so *proud!*" people said to Bird. Over and over. He was proud. Genuinely. He just didn't like people demanding that he confirm the fact for them.

Harry found Bird in a corner, where, after yet another *you-must-be-so-proud* remark, he had taken refuge. He sat with his vodka and tonic—his third—flipping through the pages of a coffee-table book about famous steeplechase horses with names like Lord Cardigan and Geronimo.

"Wally! There you are!"

Harry had at some point decided to call Bird "Wally," a name no one else called him and one he particularly detested. Bird retaliated by calling Harry "Hank."

"Hello, Hank."

"Been looking all over for you!"

"Well"—Bird smiled—"here I am."

"I just wanted to say thanks."

"For what?"

"For being such a great sport."

"I'm not really much of a sport. Little tennis every now and then."

"No. About Myn's horses. I'm thrilled that she's letting me do this for her."

The air went out of Bird. It had been such a crazy week that he'd forgotten to call the bank about extending the line of credit. Had Myn proceeded without telling him?

"We had to move fast," Harry said. Bird's fingers tightened around his vodka and tonic. Harry winked at him. "But I guess I know a thing or two about horse-trading. If we'd gotten there any later, those horses would be on their way by now to Prince Waznar's stables in Kentucky. Guess we showed *him,* huh?"

Bird flushed.

"Well," Harry said, giving him a whack on the shoulder blade, "you must just be so damn proud of her. Ben! You son of a gun, where the heck you been keeping yourself? Jill! You look like a million euros! Oops—I meant Swiss francs!"

The sound of braying jocularity buffetted Bird's ears. He escaped to the bar to self-administer more vodka. En route he spotted Myn and pulled her by the elbow away from her circle of worshippers.

"Harry just told me that I was a real sport. For letting him buy you the horses."

"Darling, I was going to tell you. We had to move quickly. I tried calling, but you were at your 'undisclosed location,' making the world safe for the arms race. You were supposed to speak to the bank? Remember?"

She adjusted his missile-themed bow tie. "It's actually starting to grow on me. What kind of missile is it, exactly? Are we using it against anyone at the moment?"

The VanderSomethings were approaching.

"Myndi! Congratulations! We are just so proud of you! Walter, are you proud of this girl or what?"

Dinner was served.

While the others filed in, Bird repaired again to the bar to refuel. This was his...what...fifth? Sixth?

Myndi was seated next to—surprise—Harry. Bird was seated next to—surprise—the wife of the Saudi defense attaché. As they took their places, Myn whispered, "Harry thought she might be useful to you. Show her your cummerbund and tie."

Bird tried to make conversation with Mrs. al-Hazim, but it was slow sledding. She had no interest in Bird, correctly sensing that he was not a billionaire. After valiant conversational forays, all he managed to extract from her was the riveting information that she found Washington "nicer than New York."

He felt light-headed. He realized he hadn't touched his food.

"I know what you mean," Bird said to Mrs. al-Hazim. He leaned in and winked at her. "Not as many *Jews*."

Mrs. al-Hazim stared.

"I was speaking of the New York *traffic*," Mrs. al-Hazim said stiffly, pivoting forty-five degrees to her right and not addressing another word to Bird for the rest of the dinner. Bird seized on his liberation by repairing to the bar for a sixth—seventh?—V and T.

Myndi and Harry and the others were laughing and chatting away. It dawned on Bird that the current Mrs. Brinkerhoff was not present. Then he remembered that she was in the process of becoming the formerly current Mrs. Brinkerhoff.

The conversation turned to the naming of horses. It seemed that Myndi had given Harry the right of naming the two new nags. Well, why not? Harry, in an expansive mood, was inviting suggestions from the table.

"Rappahannock."

"Traveler."

"Terpsichore."

"Yes We Can."

Bird dinged his glass with his fork. "Wawaza name of that movie...?" His tongue had turned into a dead flounder. Myndi shot him a look of frigid horror.

"You know," Bird continued, "the one where the kid blinds the horses and sets fire to the barn? And they all burn up? Great movie. *Loved* that movie."

Conversation came to a screeching halt. Everyone stared. Bird went on. "Hell of a movie. Seen that movie, Hank? You're a horshperson. Wait—whoa, everyone. I got it! *Equush!*"

"I'VE NEVER—EVER—BEEN so mortified in all my life," Myndi said as she drove, fingers wrapped around the steering wheel in a death grip.

"Shperfectly good name," Bird announced from the backseat, where he had assumed a horizontal posture. *"Equush."*

"You're *stinking.*"

Bird began to hum "The William Tell Overture." "Da-da dum, da-da dum, da-da dum-dum-*duuuuum . . .*"

"Walter! Stop that! Stop it right now!"

"Da-da dum, dum duuuuuuum . . . da . . . dum."

BIRD AWOKE, STILL IN THE BACKSEAT, still in evening clothes, to light and the twittering of fowl. His head hurt.

He lumbered into the kitchen in a zombielike manner, a pathetic creature in search of ibuprofen. Myn was sitting at the table with her coffee. She looked beautiful in blouse, riding pants, and boots.

"Morning," Bird said. Maybe she'd forgotten everything.

"Did you just say 'Morning' to me?"

Bird tried to focus on his wristwatch. "Is it afternoon already? Must have been some party."

"Walter, you have a drinking problem. I've done the research for you. There's an AA meeting at ten o'clock—ten *this* a.m.—at the Unitarian church in Downers Corner. The information is on this piece of paper here. I'm making it a condition of your remaining in the house that you attend."

She left. Boots on tile to a slammed screen door.

BEWKS FOUND HIS BROTHER in a rocker on the porch, still in evening clothes, holding a bag of frozen peas to his forehead.

"Late evening last night, big brother?"

Bird groaned.

"Didn't know you aristocrats partied so hard. Would have come along if I'd known."

"Sit," Bird said, "and pray let thy speech fall quietly from thy tongue."

"You and the missus going through a rough patch?"

"Why do you ask?" Bird said, eyes closed.

"No reason. Well, she did kind of seem to be trying to run me over in her car just now."

"Bewks," Bird said, "is my wife having an affair?"

Bewks shrugged. "Not to my knowledge. She seems kind of focused on the riding. That's great she made the team. You must be proud."

Bird moaned.

Bewks said, "I haven't seen any yoga instructors or anyone tippy-toeing out the back door or nothing, if that's what you mean."

"He wouldn't need to tippy-toe. He's got his own plane. A 757."

"Well," Bewks said, "if you're going to screw around, might as well be someone with a 757."

"He flies his horses around in it. They get massages."

"Hell, in that case, I'll have an affair with him."

The two brothers sat in silence.

"I'm sorry for you," Bewks said. "But sounds like you won't have to pay alimony."

"Have you considered a career as a grief counselor? My head..."

Dragonflies hovered above the fields in the summer heat. From the shaded edge of the pond came the foghorn moan of bullfrogs.

"How's the Civil War going?" Bird said. "Any progress?"

"We kicked butt last weekend over at Culpeper. But it's uphill, really."

"Bewks," Bird said, "this is in no way a criticism but have you ever been tempted to say screw it and get a job?"

"Been there, done that. I don't honestly see the attraction in it. Hey, you been following this whole Dalai Lama thing?"

Bird opened his eyes slightly. "Sort of. Why?"

"I was watching that Penelope Kent on TV last night."

"Penelope Kent? The woman's a nutjob."

"I know, Bewks said, "but she is kind of fun to listen to. She's got a tongue on her like a komodo dragon."

"If I were a komodo dragon and I saw Penelope Kent coming," Bird said, "I would crawl in the opposite direction. Fast. I can't believe she was actually governor of a state."

"Well, Penelope Kent says it's a one-hundred-percent-certain fact those Chinese gave him this phemo cancer he's got. Man, do those Chinese play *rough*."

Bird looked sideways at his brother. He felt—what did Joyce call it?—"agenbite of inwit." The prick of remorse. It's one thing to lie to the world, but to your baby brother?

Bird said, "Bewks, how would a nitwit like Penelope Kent know the first thing about that?"

"I don't know. But she says the United States government is sitting on the evidence but is afraid to come forward with it on account of it'd piss the Chinese off and they'll stop lending us all that money."

"Well, that's fine, but if I were you, I'd ask Penelope Kent to show you some actual proof. She's just looking to drive up her speaking fees." Bird muttered, "This country. It's going to hell."

"Maybe. But it's a human tragedy what those Chinese have done to that poor country."

"What country?"

"Tibet."

"Oh. Well, I suppose they had their reasons."

"Whose side you on, anyway?" Bewks said. "They've pretty much destroyed it, you know."

"I know, Bewks."

"I was watching that Chris Matthews show the other night," Bewks said. "He had that woman on, Angel Templeton. Heard of her?"

"Slightly. We met. Once."

"Man oh man is she a *fox*. There's another woman with a

tongue on her. I wouldn't want to get on the wrong side of it. No, sir."

"You seem to be watching a lot of television these days."

"I like to keep up. Living out here in the country as I do. And spending most of my time, as it were, back in the nineteenth century. Anyway, Angel Templeton says now that the Dalai Lama is dying, the least the Chinese could do is let him go back home to Tibet, where he can die in peace. She was on with some woman named Winnie or Minnie Chang. Chong. I can't make sense of their names. Boy, they were going at it like a couple of Vegas mud wrestlers. Hammer and *tong*." Bewks chuckled. "Chris Matthews looked like he'd died and gone to heaven."

"Sorry I missed it. I was busy ruining Myndi's big night out."

"Winnie Chang, Chong, whatever," Bewks said. "*She's* some kind of hot, too."

"Bewks. If it's hot women you want, why not just watch the Hooters Channel?"

"I like them with brains, you know," Bewks said. "Anyway, Winnie says it's all a bunch of lies cooked up by Angel Templeton. She says the United States government ought to file an official protest at the United Nations in New York City."

"Yeah, *that'll* put the fear of God into the Chinese."

Bewks rocked back and forth. "It's certainly an interesting situation. It was on the news this morning that China's putting on some kind of massive naval exercise. Calling Admiral Perry!"

"That was Japan, Bewks. It'll all get sorted out in the end."

"Oh," Bewks said, "almost forgot what I stopped by to tell you in the first place. I went over to Peckfuss's coupla days ago to yell at him about not fixing the fence in the high field. Man, there were some *strange* characters there with him."

"That's news?"

"I'm not talking about your standard trailer trash from Peckfuss's normal social circle. These people looked like they'd just got out of *prison*. Escaped. And still *ought* to be in prison. One of them had a .357 lying there on the passenger seat of his truck. I said to him, 'Is that thing loaded?' He gave me this look. I thought he was going to pick it up and demonstrate."

Bird groaned. "Are you telling me that my caretaker—the father of our mother's companion—is consorting with armed criminals?"

"Well, they didn't look to me like Mormon missionaries," Bewks sniffed. "Unless the Mormons have decided to take a whole new approach. Something's going on. And I wouldn't be surprised if it turned out to have something to do with that smell."

Bird raised himself from his rocker of pain. "Just what I need right now—ATF agents busting down my doors. All right. I'll speak to him."

"Oh, by the way, Belle's pregnant again."

"Again? Oh, for crying out loud. Who is it this time?"

"I don't know," Bewks said, "but I sure hope it isn't the guy with the .357, 'cause if it is, that is going to be one *horrible*-looking child."

Bird decided that the only thing to do was to go to bed.

MYNDI RETURNED about three o'clock, looking beautiful, wind-blown and simmering.

"Did you go to the meeting?" she demanded.

"Yes," Bird lied.

"How did you get there?" she said suspiciously. "Your car hasn't moved."

"How do you know? Did you check the odometer?"

"All right, then," she said, sounding unconvinced. "And how did it go?"

"Great," Bird said. "Very nice people."

"Did you tell them you're an alcoholic?"

"Um–hm."

"And? Walter, do I really have to drag every word out of you? What did they say?"

"They said if I was going to drink six vodkas, I should at least eat something."

"They told you . . . *that?*"

"They also suggested I switch to beer. Beer is more filling than vodka or bourbon, so you drink less. Very sensible."

"What kind of AA meeting *was* this?"

"It's a four-step program instead of the normal twelve-step. Apparently there's been some new thinking about alcoholism. Suits me. Wasn't really looking forward to going totally cold turkey."

He propped himself up on his elbows and smiled at his wife. "You look good, babe. Wanna play horsey?"

Myndi sat down on the side of the bed. "Walter, look at me."

"I am, darling. And you're so beautiful my eyeballs hurt. Of course, that could be the hangover."

"Tell me the truth. Did you go to the meeting?"

"You first," Bird said. "You screwing Harry?"

Myndi jumped to her feet. "That is a *despicable* thing to say!"

She stomped out of the bedroom. Myn was doing a lot of stomping these days, Bird reflected. No wonder the staircase was in such bad shape.

CHAPTER 15

The Things Henry Tells Me

I hear you and Dragon Lady went at it again the other night," Bird said. "You two are getting better ratings than Friday-night wrestling."

"Yes. Nature red in tooth and claw. I gather you missed it?" Angel said, sounding a bit miffed.

"I was otherwise engaged, destroying my marriage. But I made good progress."

"Oh? All is not quiet on the Virginia front?"

"I got a little tanked at dinner. It was at that club of hers. I just don't have much conversation in me about horses. And what conversation about them I did have they didn't seem to like much. Myn was on edge to begin with. All keyed up on account of..." Bird decided again not to mention the Tang Cup. "These horse competitions. It's pretty intense pressure. She made the U.S. team. Impressive."

"Indeed." Angel yawned. "Just got word they're going to make the announcement at noon. And then"—she rubbed her hands together—"we move from DefCon Three to DefCon Two. I remember the first time I was in the War Room—the real one, the

NMCC, at the Pentagon. The electricity. You could touch it. How's our ad hoc committee coming along?"

"It's coming. I'm getting some good names."

"Show me."

Bird punched a few keys and brought up the list on his computer. Angel read over his shoulder. She scrunched up her face.

"Jason Stang?" she said. "Who the hell is he?"

"Movie actor. The one with the aikido moves? *Ankles of Death. The Dragon Will See You Now.*"

Angel stared.

"I take it you don't get out to the movies much," Bird said. "Google him. He's revered in the American–Tibetan Buddhist community. According to his official bio, he's the tenth reincarnation of Rampong Jingjampo."

Angel did not appear impressed.

"I'm telling you, he's huge."

Angel's eyes ran down the list. "I haven't heard of half these people. I thought you were going to get some religious biggies. We need to get some ecumenical rage going. What about the archbishop of Canterbury?"

"I've got a call in to his person."

"What about the U.S. Catholic bishops? This ought to be a low-hanging fruit for them."

"I spoke to their monsignor. He said they're sympathetic, but they can't be on the committee. They'd prefer to work behind the scenes."

"The way Jesus did?"

Bird shrugged. "He said it's tough enough in China as it is, being Catholic. They're shutting down churches all the time, throwing priests into jail. They don't need this."

"Pussies," Angel muttered. "What about Jews? You promised me major Jews. Where's Elie Wiesel? Why isn't *he* on the list?"

"He's out of town. He has to make a lot of paid speeches since getting fleeced by Madoff. I've got a call in to him. I got Norman Podhoretz."

"Norman Podhoretz? *That's* your definition of a major Jew? Please."

"Then call your pal Henry Kissinger. He's the biggest Jew since Moses."

Angel laughed. "Henry? For an anti-*China* committee? Dream on. Speaking of whom..." Angel glanced about and lowered her voice. "I had forty-five minutes on the phone with him yesterday."

"Oh?" Bird said. "Did he ask about me?"

"Oh, my God, Bird, the stuff that's going on over there. Henry is *so* plugged in."

"He must be thrilled by your recent contributions to Sino-U.S. relations."

"Are you kidding? He's *furious!*" Angel smiled coyly. "But he loves me. He can't help himself. I'm his bad-girl protégée. The things he tells me. He knows everyone over there. They worship the ground he walks on. There is major caca going down in Beijing. *Major.*"

"Like what?"

"I really can't say."

"'Don't tell me that. I'm up to my walnuts in this."

"He trusts me. He's like an uncle. I can't betray his confidence."

"So now I'm a security risk? Who told you about Taurus anyway? And muons?"

Angel hesitated. "All right, but this is in *the lake*."

"Yeah, yeah."

"There's this big split in the Standing Committee. Over whether to let Saffron Man come home. The Standing Committee? With me?"

"*Yes.*" Bird rolled his eyes. "The Politburo Standing Committee. The nine who rule China. Want me to name them? Dopey, Grumpy, Sneezy—"

Angel lowered her voice to a whisper. "Han, the general, the defense minister, and Lo, the security minister, are hard-core Lama haters. If it were up to them, they'd pave Tibet and put up a parking lot. But Henry says there are others on the Standing Committee who think this could be an opportunity to score points at the UN by letting Saffron Man back in. Meanwhile Fa—the president—word is he doesn't know whether to crap or go crazy. Remember, they didn't make him chairman of the Central Military Commission. It would be like the U.S. president wasn't in charge of the Pentagon. Tricky. So he's got to watch it, or General Han could fire an RPG up his ass. Han and Lo think Fa's gone totally squish on Tibet. Why, exactly, no one can quite figure out. When Fa was party boss in Lhasa, the firing squads were working overtime. Then he lightened up a bit and managed to get things calmed down." She chuckled. "The poor guy barfed in the middle of some speech he was giving. Altitude sickness. Projectile-vomited over the podium into the laps of the delegation from Zimbabwe. What I'd give to have been there. Anyway, Henry says things could get ugly over there. Very, very ugly." She grinned. "Wouldn't *that* just be terrible?"

"Is terrible desirable?"

Angel said almost tenderly, "Dear sweet Bird, we've got to work on your strategic thinking. I'll give you some books to read. Listen to Momma. So there's a power struggle going among the nine guys who rule China. You've got your hawks and your ducks. Assuming Henry is right—and on China, Henry is *always* right—Fa is leading the ducks. Which is logical, because Fa is all about harmony. His nickname is 'Iced Tea' or 'Cool Tranquillity,' or something like that. Wants everyone to get along. So there's the Big Picture. Now, more important—what's in this for us? You tell me. Why have we been doing everything we've been doing?"

Bird said, "Well, I think I know why *you're* doing it. This is your idea of fun. Why am I doing it? As I explained, the foundation I represent wants to show the world the"—Bird sounded tired all of a sudden—"true nature of the threat. And all that."

"You sound like you're reading off cue cards. Okay, pay attention to Momma. Fa. Harmony. Smiles. Looks like a dentist. Imagine him surrounded by grandchildren, dandling them on his knee. How do we make our case that China is Public Enemy Number One when the top guy looks and sounds like a guest on Sesame Street? He can't get through a sentence without saying 'harmony' and 'mutual understanding' and 'panglobalism' and 'interconnectivity' and all that cuddly yap. But General Han—he's like an actual reincarnation of Genghis Khan, only this time No More Mr. Nice Khan. And Lo? Sca-ry. If they shove Fa out the door and take over, then Americans will see the real face of China. The one with *fangs*. And it's going to scare the shit out of them." Angel smiled. "And our job will become so much easier. Questions?" She checked her watch. "God, I'm late."

"Just so I'm clear," Bird said. "We don't actually want a war with China. Right?"

"Well"—Angel smiled—"I'm not sure I'd go *that* far."

"Oh, Angel."

"Calm down. Not a full-scale war. But I wouldn't say no to a little naval bang-bang in the Taiwan Strait. A little wingtip-to-wingtip in disputed airspace? Incidents like that can be so clarifying."

Bird stared.

"Sweetheart," Angel said, tousling his hair. "Sometimes I think your way of flirting with me is pretending to be obtuse. But assuming you really are obtuse, don't you see? There's a larger purpose here. If our country, the greatest country in the world—in the history of the world—is going to remain strong, we've got to wean ourselves off that big yellow tit."

"Which tit?"

"The Central Bank of China tit. But because we can't get our act together, we go on suckling and running up all this debt. Which we're passing along to the next generation. You don't have children because—excuse me for saying this—it would interfere with Mrs. McIntyre's dressage practice. I, however, do have a child. And someday, if we go on this way, my little Barry will go to the ATM machine and it'll say, 'Would you like to continue in Mandarin or in Cantonese?' I'm not going to let that happen. This country is going to come to its senses about China if I have to smash every dish in the cupboard."

She stood up, and as she did, her miniskirt rose rather too high. She blushed, suddenly girlish, tugging down the hem.

"Oops, wardrobe malfunction."

Just then her bodyguards entered the war room: Burka and the two new guys.

"I know," she said. "I'm *calamitously* late."

Angel had been getting more and more death threats because of her increasingly high media profile. Two more myrmidons had been added to her security entourage: unsmiling, crew-cut cinder blocks with dark glasses, earpieces, and webbed vests that bulged. They clinked when they walked.

"Delta," she explained to Bird. "Expensive. But this is not an area where you skimp."

"Do you think they'd like to come over some night for hot chocolate and charades?"

Bird himself was trying to maintain as low a profile as possible. It would hardly do if Groepping-Sprunt's allegedly "former" top lobbyist were unmasked as Angel's co–China-baiter. And his "foundation," Pan-Pacific Solutions, existed only on paper. Any investigative reporter ten minutes out of J school would connect the dots. And there was an even more pressing reason for Bird to keep his China profile horizontal. Things on the home front were tricky enough without having Myndi learn that her husband was spending his days spinning lies about the country that was hosting the Tang Cup

International Equestrian Competition, for the high moral purpose of lubricating some mysterious weapons system through Congress.

But keeping a low profile was getting harder. The Dalai Lama was now on U.S. soil, in Cleveland, and hot news. In a few hours, the world was going to be told whether he had a mortal illness. And with Angel leading the charge, media interest was intense. The sidewalk in front of the Institute for Continuing Conflict had become a bivouac of satellite vans and stand-ups. Bird was reduced to sneaking in and out of the ICC via the basement. At this rate they'd have to start smuggling him in and out disguised as a pizza deliveryman. Exciting as it all was, he chafed at the indignity of having to slink through an underground entryway next to a dumpster that reeked of sour garbage. He consoled himself with the thought that it was good research for the novel, which was going very well indeed.

CHAPTER 16

We're Looking for a Saffron Revolution

Truly, it had been an exhausting day. Too weary to wait up to hear the announcement, Fa retired at eleven. Gang would wake him.

He was asleep within minutes of his head touching the pillow. Asleep, but not soundly, for the grim phantasm had been resummoned from the synaptic abyss. Once again Cool Limpidity tossed and turned on a bed damp with sweat, staring into a steaming bowl of dumplings, each bearing the grotesque, distinct visage of his father, him of blessed memory.

The president of the People's Republic awoke with a gasp. Madam Fa was away in Shenzhen, opening a new maternity hospital, part of the new propaganda office campaign to counter the unfortunate publicity occasioned by the large number of newborn female infants being found in China's garbage.

Fa could feel his heart pounding in his chest. He wiped the perspiration from his face with the sleeve of his pajama top, poured a glass of ice water from the thermos on his beside table, and gulped down the cool water.

He turned on the light and saw the time. One-fifteen. He contemplated a sleeping pill. *Must get a grip.* His heart was beating even faster now—like a drum. Surely this was not healthy. The dreadfulness of the nightmare had made him forget entirely about the business going on halfway around the world. At that very moment...

...At a podium in the auditorium of the Duncan-Neuhauser Institute in Cleveland stood a Dr. Daniel Coit, identified at the bottom of a million television screens as

WORLD'S TOP PHEOCHROMOCYTOMA EXPERT

It fell to the pleasant-faced, white-coated Dr. Coit to convey the grave news that His Holiness the Dalai Lama's condition was "inoperable" and "end-stage." He avoided the words *fatal* and *terminal* and *he's toast.*

Back on the other side of the globe, President Fa arrived at the decision that he *would* take a pill. Perhaps even two pills. A good thing Madam Fa was not here; she would have forbidden him the second pill.

As he was unscrewing the cap on the bottle, a soft knock on the door announced the presence of the faithful Gang. The knock reminded Fa of the events transpiring in Ohio, USA. He saw from Gang's expression what the news was.

"How long?"

"The doctor who made the announcement tried to make it sound like a bad head cold," Gang said. "Cheerfulness—the great American passion. Always they want to be *cheerful.* A month, maybe. There's no treatment for it. Even in Cleveland, Ohio, USA."

The two men looked at each other and nodded. On cue, Gang said in a slightly louder voice, "So our Minister Lo was right after all?"

"Yes," Fa replied evenly, following the script. "And I was wrong. China is fortunate to have a man like Lo. A true servant of the party. I should never have questioned his instincts."

Fa enunciated this pabulum with as much enthusiasm as he could muster in the middle of the night, his nerves still jangly from the nightmare. He made a face at Gang as if to say, *Enough of that.*

Gang looked at his boss with concern. He saw how rattled he was. "Comrade, are you...*well?*"

Fa stared at the floor.

Gang knew straightaway. "It's back?"

Fa nodded. "Yes. The indigestion is back."

"Let me send for Physician Hu," Gang said. Physician Hu looked after the party elite. He was an excellent doctor—Harvard trained. Thoroughly modern, yet also an ardent herbalist.

"What can Hu do?" Fa said. "For something like this?"

Fa and Gang had kept the nightmare a secret. Little good could come if it were known by State Security. MSS kept a vigilant eye on all the medical files. If the leadership had been aware that their rising star Fa suffered from bizarre night terrors—Well, no, that would not do. Calmness and equanimity—conscious and otherwise—were the qualities prized in the top echelons of the CCP.

Fa had even kept the dream and the lama's curse from his own wife. Why trouble her with superstition and witchery? Lacking the real explanation for her husband's troubled sleep, Madam Fa put it down to an incident from his childhood, when at age eight Fa had eaten a bad shrimp dumpling and endured a traumatic episode of food poisoning.

As for telling Physician Hu about the nightmares—it was out of the question. There was danger enough without handing Lo Guo-wei information that the leader of the nation and the party, the president of China, was convinced that an evil spell had been cast on him by a hysterical Tibetan monk being dragged off to the firing squad.

Gang said, "I only thought...perhaps one of his soothing teas, to help with the indigestion."

"Soothing," Fa snorted. "Yes, I could use some soothing." Petulantly, impulsively, he reached for the cigarette case. He lit one and inhaled deeply. He held out the case to Gang. Gang had been practicing the Fourth Improvement even before it had been formulated as state policy, but he took one out of companionship. The president lit it for him. Gang pretended to inhale.

"In view of the news, then, shall I convene the committee, Comrade President?"

"Yes. Nine o'clock." He took another long pull on the cigarette— it *was* soothing—and exhaled. He smiled. "No, best make it eight. If I wait until nine, they'll say, 'Aha, President Fa thinks his *sleep* is more important than this!'"

"Very well. Eight o'clock. Oh, Comrade President, I almost forgot. That report you asked me for?"

"Report?"

"From the Guizhou Provincial Environmental Protection Bureau. Regarding the leak from the lithium plant in Zunyi into Lake Lengung?"

"Ah," Fa said, picking up the cue. "Yes, yes. I want very much to see that. Terrible business. Show me."

Gang removed from his jacket a folded piece of paper and handed it to Fa. Fa opened it and read.

It was in Gang's handwriting. Gang never used a computer for matters of strict confidentiality. Anything typed on a computer in Zhongnanhai—even in the presidential secretariat, *especially* in the presidential secretariat—mirrored on a screen at MSS. No, such notes as these—not that there had been any quite like this one— Gang took care to write in light pencil, on a single sheet of paper atop a hard, nonimpressionable surface.

Fa read.

Have established contact with Shihong...

"Shihong" was their code name for Admiral Zhang, Fa's old mentor, Lo's predecessor as minister of state security. Zhang had chosen the name himself, which translated as "Mankind Is Red." "Protective coloring!" Zhang explained. Zhang was an unrepentant maker of puns, many of them truly awful. He loved practical jokes as well. If these characteristics seemed unusual in someone of his profession, it helped to remember that before he took over State Security, he'd been a sailor. And sailors... are, well, sailors.

Fa read on:

Extends warmest personal wishes and expresses keenest enthusiasm in this endeavor. Proposes as operational code name "CHANGPU." Approve?

Changpu. "Flourishing vine."

Fa thought, *Dear Zhang—he cannot help himself. Well, why not "flourishing vine"?* Fa nodded at Gang and continued to read.

Shihong confirms that he remains under continuous MSS surveillance—on personal orders Lo. Therefore proposes the following: that a request be made to Deputy Commercial Minister Xu Finma (I can arrange this myself) that Shihong be added to a delegation departing Shanghai this Thursday for San Diego USA to attend an int'l fisheries conference. (Rationale: Shihong's prior navy role and involvement in sea treaty negotiation.) Shihong confident this will not raise alarms MSS. In San Diego, Shihong will establish contact with Beluga. Shihong has maintained cordial relations with Beluga. Shihong estimates chance of Beluga agreeing to the plan at 70 percent.

Fa nodded.

In event Beluga is agreeable to plan, Shihong and he will implement and execute CHANGPU. In event Shihong and Beluga deem

*Shihong continued presence USA vital, Shihong will contrive illness
requiring hospitalization. (Has means to effect this.)*
    Approve?

Fa folded the piece of paper and handed it back to Gang. He
nodded.

Gang lit a match and held it to the paper, then dropped it flaming
into the wastebasket. He took the wastebasket into the presidential
bathroom and flushed the ashes down the toilet.

"I must say, Gang, a most disturbing report," Fa said. "Let us
hope that the provincial environmental deputies are up to this.
One's heart breaks for the poor fishermen."

"What about the *fish*?" Gang said. "Not that there are any left.
Well, Comrade President, try to get some sleep. It will be a busy
morning, I think."

BUSIER, AS IT TURNED OUT, than either Fa or Gang might have
supposed.

Minister Lo and General Han arrived wearing their gravest
expressions, as if China had been fiercely attacked by enemy forces
in the middle of the night.

President Fa opened the meeting by stifling a yawn, not from
boredom but from the sleeping pill that he finally took at 4:00 a.m.
after hours of fruitless pillow thrashing over the fear that sleep would
bring back the dream. He took care to begin with a bit of flattery
that he had to force up his gorge centimeter by centimeter.

"Comrades," he said, "our Comrade Minister Lo is to be most
warmly congratulated. The information that he provided at the
beginning of this unfortunate business has now been verified. His
performance and that of his ministry have been exemplary. If only
this could be made widely known, so that all China would realize

what a true party servant it has in him." Fa paused. "Let us show our appreciation."

The room filled with the sound of soft hands clapping and murmurs of "Yes, well done, well done." All this, Lo accepted without expression. His face put Fa in mind of the strange stone creatures on Easter Island, those low-browed totems of hewn volcanic rock, persistently enigmatic despite the explanations for them by archaeologists and anthropologists: absurd perhaps, yet still terrifying. General Han, sitting beside Lo, had on his best totemic-warrior face, but it was more terra-cotta than rock: reddish, grimacing, the face of a man simultaneously sharpening his sword and straining at stool.

"So, Comrades," Fa said. "Now it's a matter of time, perhaps very little time, until we will be hearing from the Dung Lotus." That bit of tactical terminology also required a deliberate shove up the gullet. Eyebrows rose around the table.

He continued, "As you all know, I have expressed my opinion on how we should proceed. Now I ask for your wise counsel, adding only this caution: If we are to seize the initiative, it would be best not to delay."

The discussion went around the table for a half hour. It was clear that Lo and Han had been lobbying and arm-twisting. Two of the committee members made such identically worded speeches against Fa's proposal that he was at pains to suppress amusement. Some others, however, seemed to incline toward Fa.

Lo said nothing. Then, clearing his throat, he said everything.

"With your permission I should like to share something with the committee," he said. "But I must ask for your assurance that this remain inside this room."

Fa stiffened. *Well now, what's this?* He said in a pleasant tone, "Comrade, we are all here in the service of the party. I think we can be trusted."

"This is a transcript," Lo said, "of a meeting that took place"—he looked at his watch—"about five hours ago, in Dharamsala."

Fa thought, *Five hours ago? How very timely.*

"There were two participants in the meeting. The first speaker—with the committee's indulgence, I would prefer not to identify him. He is in the Dung Lotus's innermost circle. What's more, he is Dung Lotus's principal liaison with the criminal elements and agitators in Lhasa and the autonomous region. He is in the employ of the American CIA. This is a relationship that has been going on now for over a decade. Let us call him Hong. Wild Goose.

"The second speaker is his CIA control officer. That is, the one to whom he makes his reports. Not a bad field officer. Indeed, a man of some skill. But"—Lo smiled—"perhaps not quite as good as he *thinks* he is. Why don't we call him...what's a good American name? Mike. Yes, let us call him Mike. Shall I read?"

Fa, who had been listening to this with mounting anger, nodded tightly. As if reading the president's thoughts, Lo said, "Naturally, Comrade President, I would have informed you of this first. But since you had already called the meeting, and given the late hour, I took the liberty of not disturbing your...dreams."

Fa forced a smile. *So you do have microphones in my bedroom, eh?* He consoled himself by reflecting that he and Gang had wisely taken precautions.

"Yes," Fa said. "We all need our sleep. I thank the minister for his courtesy. Proceed, then, with your...script."

"*Tran*script." Lo smiled. He read:

HONG: This is our moment.

MIKE: Hold on. Hold on. You need to give us time to get organized. That's critical. Otherwise we're just going to get a lot of people killed.

HONG: We are not concerned about that. What is death?

MIKE: Yeah, yeah, I know. I—we—understand all that. But, look, Washington doesn't want a bloodbath. Bloodbaths are nonproductive. Noble? Okay. Maybe. Fine. But it's not going to advance your cause. This is an opportunity to embarrass Beijing. Embarrass the crap out of them.

" 'Crap'?" inquired Minister Jen.

"Feces," Lo explained.

"Ah." Jen frowned.

Lo continued:

HONG: This is our chance to take back our country. That was stolen from us by these devils.

MIKE: I'm on your side. But be realistic. China's not going to hand you back Tibet. But this is an opportunity to make those bastards in Beijing look like what they are.

HONG: (Angry) They must allow the Lotus to return. If they refuse to let him back, there will be trouble.

MIKE: You want to toss a couple of PLA soldiers off the cliff of Potala Palace? If that makes you happy, be my guest. But Washington will not support civil war. If we see that, you're on your own. We walk away.

HONG: (Tone very angry) Yes, America has long record of walking away!

MIKE: Fuck you.

HONG: No, fuck you!

Lo looked up from his transcript and smiled. "Warm relations." The ministers laughed.

MIKE: Look, Jangpom—

Lo looked up again. "The transcript appears not to have been completely redacted. My apologies." He sniffed, "Certainly someone shall hear from me about that." He continued:

MIKE:—we're not looking for another Tiananmen. We're
looking for a Saffron Revolution, okay? Meanwhile, you
can take it from me that Washington is going to bring big
pressure, major pressure to let him come home. They're
going to bust chops.

" 'Chops'?" asked Minister Xu.

Lo said in a lofty, scholarly manner, as if interpreting a difficult
Confucian analect, "He is saying that the Americans are planning to
be very severe with us."

Fa could take no more of this. "Comrade Lo, I think we all have
the sense of this *transcript* of yours."

"One more paragraph. In my opinion it is worth hearing."

"As you wish," Fa said.

HONG: What is Washington doing? What pressures are they
making?

MIKE: You'll see. But you have to remember who we're dealing with here. We're dealing with the CCP. Asshole Central. The Chinese invented gunpowder. They invented the
compass. Paper. Printing. Hell, just about everything. But
they also invented the concept of not giving a fuck. And
that's what we're up against.

Lo took off his glasses. He smiled. "Well, Comrade Assholes.
There you are."

CHAPTER 17

Why Not Just Nudge the Thing Along a Bit?

"W alter, you *promised*."
"I know I did, baby. But things are crazy right now. We're crashing on this huge presentation. It's going gangbusters, but I'm getting about three hours' sleep a night."

Technically true. Bird was indeed staying up until all hours, pounding away at the novel, which—he reflected—might be a misallocation of priorities. But when you're hot, you're hot.

Turk's shoulder oozed crimson from the hole put through it by Colonel Zong's crack sniper, U Trang. He was leaking like a rusty crankcase but determined to complete the mission. Meanwhile, somewhere in the skies above him and the hellish, unforgiving terrain of Nibbut, "Bouncing" Betty O'Toole was standing sentinel over her warrior-lover at the controls of an AC-130 gunship capable of raining hell on Turk's relentless pursuers. Unbeknownst, however, to Turk, the lead foil wrap around the muon device in his knapsack had been torn open by the same bullet that had pierced his shoulder. Muon-gas emanations were seeping out of the knapsack—invisible to the naked eye but clear as neon to the tracking device deployed by Colonel Zong's wily

144

tech-wizard lieutenant, Ing Pao. Ing quipped to his superior with an evil smirk, "The American might just as well have put a police siren in his knapsack! Muahaha!"

"No, Ing," replied Zong, twiddling his highly oiled mustache. "Muon-ha-ha!"

Bird thought, *Great stuff.*

"Walter, are you listening?"

"Sorry, baby, someone was—what were you saying?"

"Do you have any idea what a distinction, what an honor it is to be featured in *EQ* magazine?"

Bird wanted to say, *Is it like getting the Nobel Prize for Horsemanship?* No, don't go there. "I do, baby. Really. I'm so proud of you."

Angel was gesticulating at Bird: *Get. Off. The. Phone.*

The announcement had just come in courtesy of Xinhua, the Chinese state news agency, a bright shiny gem of mendacity, brilliant even by Communist standards of propaganda. It was a mere two-line item, buried next to an announcement of rail-service interruption between Fuzhou and Xiamen:

Deputy Minister Nei Li Meng of the Sanitary Subcommittee of the Central Directorate for the Tibetan Autonomous Region has announced that the application of Tenzin Gyatso is denied for reasons of protection of the general public health.

This curious pronouncement was open to two interpretations: (1) The Dalai Lama's brain tumor might spread to the general population. (Who knew that brain tumors could be contagious? Doubtless, party medical researchers were working on a monograph about this amazing medical discovery.) A more likely interpretation was (2) that the Dalai Lama's physical presence in Tibet might lead to mayhem and unrest, thus endangering the aforementioned "public health."

Angel was trembling like a racehorse at the gate, champing to get out a statement expressing the institute's incredulity and outrage. And here was her in-house PR maestro, yapping with the horsey wife. *Get. Off. The. Pho-one!*

Bird gestured: *Two seconds.*

"I told them you'd be here," Myndi said. "They're expecting you. I gave them your suit size, shoe size, everything."

"Why would you do that?"

"Darling, they're assembling an entire *wardrobe* for you. They've gone to incredible trouble."

Bird paused. Had he heard correctly? "They're bringing... what?"

"Clothes, darling," Myndi said. "They sent me a PDF. You're going to look *smashing.*"

"Myn," Bird said, rubbing the bridge of his nose, "I haven't been on a horse for six years. Not since that one you told me was tame went psycho under me." Two months in traction. Bird's spine hadn't been right since.

"You don't have to get on a horse, sillykins. You do want to look nice, don't you?"

"Myn," Bird groaned. "I don't want to *be* in a horse magazine."

"Walter. I'm trying to include you in all this, and you're acting put out."

"You want me in costume? Okay. I'll borrow one of Bewks's Civil War uniforms. You can wear a hoop skirt. We'll rub shoe polish on Belle. She can be Mammy. That'll make a nice photo spread. They could call it 'Gone with the Bullshit.'"

"Fine. You want to look like a *slob* in the pages of the country's leading equestrian publication. Wear blue jeans for all I care. The ripped ones you love so dearly."

"No, because I won't *be* there. I'll be here tomorrow. Why will I be here? Let me tell you why. Because *here* is where I earn the money that buys the oats for those nags. But wait. What am I saying? I don't need to work, do I? We have our own personal banker now. The First Bank of Harry."

"That is so…"

"Myn, can we talk about this some other time? My country needs me."

"What are you doing anyway, that's so urgent? You've been acting weird for weeks. And I don't mean just your boozing."

"It's a defense program, Myn. It's what I do."

"You've never been like this. Are we about to be at war or something? I know I haven't been paying much attention to the news, but *someone* would have mentioned."

"Baby. We've been over this. I can't talk about it."

"Walter. Are you having an affair?"

"Myn. It's eleven a.m. Who has affairs at eleven a.m.?"

"Well, tell me *something*! I'm your wife! All you do is push me away."

"Baby, if I told you, I'd…be putting both our lives in danger."

There was a pause.

"That is about the dumbest thing I've ever heard."

"Really?" he said.

"Yes. It's the sort of thing you'd put in…in…"

"In what?"

"In one of your dumb *unpublished novels*!"

Bird ground enough enamel off his back molars to refinish a vintage bathtub. He was about to say something he knew he'd regret when Myndi spared him the trouble by hanging up. Bird slammed his phone down, a Pyrrhic, but satisfying, retaliation.

Angel looked on with an air of contemptuous bemusement. "I want to thank you," she said.

"For *what*?" Bird snapped.

"For making me *so-o* grateful I'm not married."

"Any White House reaction?"

"They're 'watching the situation,'" Angel said disdainfully. "Closely."

"That'll have Beijing quaking in its boots."

"They're *such* weenies, this administration. We should be dispatching carrier battle groups. Canceling military leave. Lofting bombers. Warming missiles. Patton, thou shouldn't be living at this hour."

Bird looked up at her. "Wordsworth? I'm impressed. I thought all you read was *Jane's Modern Weapons of Mass Destruction*." He swiveled in his chair and began to compose the institute's *J'accuse!* Then paused.

"Maybe we should give the White House just a little time to get its stuff together. You know they're meeting in the Sit Room right now."

"Uh-huh," Angel said, "picking lint out of their navels."

"GODDAMN IT," said Rogers P. Fancock, director of the National Security Council. "Really."

The expostulation was directed at the cosmos in general rather than at his aide, a budding young internationalist by the name of Bletchin.

"As if we didn't have enough on our plate," Fancock said. "Once, just once, it would be nice if someone came through that door bringing me something other than another goddamned horror story."

Was this a personal rebuke? Bletchin wondered.

Fancock scowled at the top-secret cable from the U.S. ambassador in Beijing alerting him to the development that had been announced on CNN twenty minutes before.

"Thanks for the warning," Fancock grumbled rhetorically, crumbling the cable into a ball and tossing it into the wastebasket.

"Shouldn't that go in the burn bag, sir?" Bletchin said. Every afternoon a Secret Service officer carrying a bag would come by and ask, "Classified trash?"

"Bletchin," Fancock said. "It was just on CNN, for God's sake."

"Yes, sir. Still, it is a top-secret cable."

"Why do we even have embassies at this point? Do you know why, Bletchin? So they can appoint their damned campaign finance director ambassador. I told him, 'He wants to be ambassador? All right, send him to the Bahamas. Bermuda. Namibia. The Seychelles.' And where does he send him? China. China! We need *professionals* out there, Bletchin. Not campaign fund-raisers. Hacks. That's all they are."

"Yes, sir."

Fancock scratched at his shin. Stress exacerbated his psoriasis. "So they're taking the position he's a public-health hazard, are they? What *Confucian* in their Propaganda Department came up with that beauty, do you suppose?"

"I spoke to Jud Davis at State," Bletchin said. "He thinks—"

"Actually, it's rather deft. Do you know why, Bletchin?"

Bletchin thought he did, actually, but sensed that it would be politic to let Director Fancock continue with the mentoring.

"It's code," Fancock sniffed. "That's what it is. Code. And do you know how it decrypts? *We don't give a hoot in Hades what you damned Americans think. So there!* And they don't. They truly don't. You can do business with the Chinese, Bletchin. I've done my fair share, God knows. But the moment they feel their back is against the wall? *Up* comes the drawbridge, and archers to the tower. They won't budge an inch on this. Game over. Will this make *our* job easier? Care to hazard a guess?"

"Shall I get Dr. Kissinger?" Bletchin's favorite thing in life was to place urgent calls to Henry Kissinger, especially at strange hours.

Fancock puffed out his cheeks like a blowfish. Beacon Hill fugu. "No," he said. "Let's save Henry for when no one's speaking to each other. Which day is coming as surely as tomorrow's dawn. Unless we get lucky and His Holiness pops off to the great beyond before plunging the entire world into chaos."

Fancock looked at his aide warily. *Probably making notes for his White House memoir.* "I'm only *venting*, Bletchin."

"Yes, sir."

"You have to vent around here or you'll go cuckoo. Extraordinary man, the Dalai Lama. Spent a bit of time with him. Serene sort. Quick upstairs and a good sense of humor. Likes an off-color story. Ghastly business, this phemotomo..."

"Pheochromocytoma."

"Yes, well, no picnic however you spell it. Suppose I ought to send a letter. Draft one, and make the tone personal."

"Yes, sir."

"Fondly I remember our visits together. Et cetera. Have Susan look them up in the log. Profited from his wisdom. So on. The president and First Lady join me, along with the entire nation. And so forth. Don't suppose there's any point in wishing him 'a speedy recovery.' Prayers. You might cast about for some appropriate Buddhist sentiment. And flowers, Bletchin. Fifty dollars ought to buy some decent flowers in Cleveland. Get it from the petty cash, not my personal account."

"Yes, sir."

Fancock's expression reverted to its default position of perpetual indignation: a man of superior intellect, breeding, and culture, marooned on an island of proles and incompetents in a shark-infested sea. And yet the Brahmin Code of Honor—what the French call noblesse oblige—dictated that one must soldier on. To those to whom much has been given and all that.

"Why?" Fancock said. "Tell me, *why* did they schedule a press conference *knowing* that this was coming? Really—that whole communications office is a disaster area. They ought to seal it off with yellow tape. Put up *cones*."

Bletchin nodded. Director Fancock inculcated in his protégés a lofty disdain for the media—*Foreign Affairs*, the *FT*, the *Economist*, and the other British publications excepted.

"We can't have him go out there and say that we're continuing to *watch* the situation. However 'closely.'"

Bletchin said, "Sir, Ambassador Ding's office called."

"Oh, joy. What do they want?"

"They're requesting a meeting."

"With the president? Absolutely not."

"No, sir. With yourself. They made it a formal 'urgent' request. He'd like to see you. Today."

"Tell them to imagine a snowball, surrounded by all the fires of the infernal regions."

"I told him you had a busy schedule. Still..."

"All right. But stall. Tell them...six o'clock. Now, before you do anything else—get Barney Strecker in here. Tell him I need to see him *tout de suite*. I don't care what he's doing or who he's doing it to. Quickly, Bletchin. What *is* it?"

"Shouldn't we put that request through Director Deakins?" Bletchin said, referring to Strecker's boss, head of CIA. "You know how he doesn't like it when we go directly—"

"Just do it, Bletchin. Look lively, man."

Bletchin scurried off to make the call.

Barney Strecker, deputy director for operations, CIA, pulled up at the West Wing less than an hour later, in his own car, trailed by two black SUVs full of bodyguards. The bodyguards had standing orders—signed by Strecker himself—to kill him rather than let him be taken hostage, if it came to that. As a young case officer, Strecker had spent three years shackled to a wall in a military prison in Rangoon and was resolved not to repeat the experience.

Bletchin always felt nervous around Strecker. He escorted him to the Situation Room with a minimum of small talk. Director Fancock was waiting, along with the assistant secretary of state for East Asian and Pacific affairs as well as various military personnel from the Office of the Joint Chiefs of Staff. Fancock had included State and Pentagon so that he'd be able to say that they had been consulted. He had no interest in their views on the matter and planned to get them out of the room as quickly as possible.

"Barn."

"Hello, Rog. Jim. Bud. Fred. Fellas."

Barney Strecker was a jovial sort, despite all he'd been through in life. Fifteen years in the Marine Corps, twenty at CIA. He was hefty in frame. When he plunked down in the chair, there was a whoosh of escaping air. As was his custom when the president was not present, he put his feet up on the Situation Room table, revealing black python-skin cowboy boots. Fancock shook his head. *Really, Barn.*

"Well, gents," Strecker said merrily, "bit of a pig's breakfast, isn't it?"

"Rather," Fancock said.

"Ding-Dong on his way over?"

The assistant secretary of state's eyes widened at Strecker's rendition of the name of the Chinese ambassador.

Fancock and Strecker had known each other for more than two decades. After leaving the Corps, Strecker had decided to get a master's degree in international relations. Dr. Fancock was his adviser. He liked to teach between government jobs. He enjoyed the company of bright young minds before whom he could hold forth uninterrupted for hours as they hung on every word. His seminar was "Exit Strategies in a Post-Hegemonic World." As the title implied, its emphasis was on how to extricate from foreign-policy disasters rather than create them in the first place. Most of his students were Bletchin types: twitchy Ivy Leaguers eager to rise to the top while steering clear of the grittier trenches in which people like Barney Strecker did their apprenticeships. Fancock and Strecker were from opposite worlds, but Fancock had taken a liking to the brash Mississippian, and over the years they'd maintained their improbable, asymmetrical friendship. It consisted of a kind of role-play in which each exaggerated his own traits: Fancock, patrician, urbane, aloof, censorious; Strecker, uncouth, incorrigible, outrageous. The template suited them. They knew each other's buttons and liked to press them.

"Ding-Dong?" said Fancock. "Yes, His Excellency the ambassador of the People's Republic has requested a meeting. Which is why I asked you here, along with Assistant Secretary Nadler and Admiral Goliatis and General Simms and the others. I thought it might be useful to have the benefit of your thinking. That is, *before* the ambassador arrives and administers me the Death by a Hundred Cuts."

Strecker grinned. "Want to have some fun with him?"

"Not today, Barney, no."

"Ask him about that sweet little bit of lychee he's got stashed up in New York."

Strecker winked at the assistant secretary of state. The military men were at pains to suppress their amusement.

"She's in their consular department," Strecker said, "but from what *I* hear, her real talent is—"

"Barn," Fancock interjected. *"Ça suffit."*

Strecker shrugged. "Only trying to help."

"As you're undoubtedly aware, the press secretary, in his wisdom, went ahead and scheduled a press conference for the president—tomorrow."

"Nice timing."

"Ours not to question why." Fancock sighed. He turned to the others and said, "Gentlemen, I hardly need to stress the confidentiality of this discussion. Are we recording?" he said to a Sit Room aide. "If so, shut the damned thing off." Fancock turned to Strecker. "Barn, who do we have in His Holiness's immediate circle? Close to the body."

"No one."

"No one?"

"Nope."

"Well, I must say that's disappointing."

"Oh, we tried. He's one Teflon cat. Nothing stuck."

"Are you referring to His Holiness?" said Fancock.

"Jetsun Jamphel Ngawang Lobsang Yeshe Tenzin Gyatso.

Impressive fellow. Straight shooter. Not like some of your other religious types. He's got this *aura*."

"Yes," Fancock said. "I've been in his company on multiple
occasions."

"The real deal. I know you Bostonians get all weak-kneed
around Kennedys. Well, this guy's got more charisma than that
whole Hyannis Port clan put together."

"Thank you for that cultural insight," Fancock said dryly. "Why
don't we stipulate that His Holiness is a person of considerable mag-
netism. So why *don't* we have a man on the inside?"

"Every time we turned one of his people, he knew. Right away.
He's got better antennae than a Martian. Well, he *is* the living Buddha, right? He finally sent us a message basically saying, 'Cut it out,
fellas. I got enough trouble as it is without them thinking I'm working with you guys.' So we backed off."

Fancock shook his head. "These billions we spend on the intelligence budget."

"Don't start, Rog. Don't you start on that. I got assets in presidential offices, palaces, and desert tents. I got people so high up
you'd need a proctoscope to find them. I'm saying it'd be easier to
flip one of the twelve apostles than get inside this cat's posse."

"Calm yourself, Barney. I wasn't slighting your professionalism.
I was only pointing out that I wish we had some sandals on the
ground in this case."

"MSS has people in his circle," Strecker said. "But that's because
His Holiness *wants* them there."

"Why?"

"Can keep an eye on them. Feed them a little something every
now and then to keep Beijing calm." He paused. "That so-called
poisoning incident last month in Rome?"

"Was that..."

"Hell, no. Why would they bother, now? He's in his mid-
seventies. How much longer does he have? But the whole thing has

kicked up some dirt, all right. Oh, yes. There are troubled skies over Zhongnanhai. If those walls could talk." He chuckled. "Actually, they *do*."

"What's going on?"

"Well," Strecker said, "they had themselves a very *lively* discussion at the last meeting of the Standing Committee over whether to let His Holiness back in. Looks like Lo and Han are gearing up to make a move against Fa. I hope he's got it in him to push back. A lot's at stake here."

"You don't think there's a coup coming, do you?"

"Far be it from me to instruct you on Chinese history," Strecker said, "but if I'm not mistaken, didn't the first peaceful transfer of power in China in four thousand years take place in—2002? We're not predicting a coup. Yet. But Lo and Han have gotten real buddy-buddy. *Brokeback Mountain*."

Fancock looked aghast. "You don't mean . . ."

"Just a metaphor, Rog. Just a metaphor." Strecker looked over at the assistant secretary of state. "I'm sure our good State Department is developing its own narrative about what's going on. But if Lo and Han are fixing to make a move, oh dear, oh dear. The thought of that country being run by those two makes me want to reach for the bottle. But you're the Harvard-educated geopolitical strategic thinker. I'm just an ex-jarhead trying to get through another day."

Fancock asked for comments around the table. He bided his time while the assistant secretary of state dismissed everything Strecker had said as baseless nonsense.

"Thank you, gentlemen. I'll present your views to the president." As they were leaving, he said casually, within earshot of the others, "Barn, walk me back to my office. I need to ask you about that business in Oman last last week."

He told Bletchin that they weren't to be disturbed and closed the door.

"Barn, why do you do that to State every time?"

"Everyone needs a hobby."

"What do we do? What the hell do we do?"

Strecker shifted in his seat. "Well, I know what *I'd* do."

"Well?"

"You won't like it."

"Just tell me."

"Ten cc's of potassium chloride."

Barney watched the expression on Fancock's face. It reminded him of the bronze bust in Fancock's home, of his ancestor, the one who'd hanged that poor Quaker woman in Boston back in 16-whenever, probably for suggesting it was all okay to put sugar on your porridge on the Sabbath.

"Barn," Fancock said, "for God's sake. What are you saying?"

"You asked."

"Are you suggesting that I go in there and tell the president, 'Let's just finish him off'?"

"I'm not suggesting that he announce it during his *press* conference."

Fancock was waving his hands as if trying to ward off a swarm of bees. "It's... You can't... It's not... We don't..."

"Rog. It would *solve* the problem."

Fancock collapsed back into his leather chair. "I'm glad I didn't ask you in front of the others. Judas Priest, Barney."

Strecker grinned. "Kinda wish you had. Just to see the look on Nadler."

"Assassinating a revered world spiritual leader...the Dalai Lama...in one of our own hospitals. In Cleveland."

"Now, don't go wetting your Brooks Brothers boxers. It's not what they teach at SAIS, and it may not be the most palatable course of action. But neither is having Tibet go up in flames. And having U.S.-China relations go gurgling down the toilet bowl. Look, Rog, he's *already* dying. You heard what the doctors said. Why not just... nudge the thing along a bit? Spare everyone a lot of Sturm und

Drang. When King George the Fifth was dying, his doctor gave him a shot of cocaine and morphine so his death'd make the morning edition of the newspapers. Not a bad way to go, really, when you think about it. We can make it painless if that's what's—"

"It's not the same thing, Barney! For God's sake!"

"No need to shout. There's no need to shout, Rog. We've just been served a big bowl of chickenshit. Agreed?"

Fancock nodded faintly, like a man with a pounding headache waiting for the aspirin to kick in.

"I'm saying we have the opportunity of turning chickenshit into chicken salad. *And,*" he added with a gleam in his eye, "make it look like Chinese cooking."

Fancock stared. "What are you saying?"

"Make it look like they did it."

"Accuse the Chinese of...killing him?"

"Walk with me, Rog. Suppose the hospital security cameras showed someone with one or two, say, distinct physical characteristics, wearing a white gown, slipping into his room. Right before His Holiness takes his last breath on this godforsaken planet. And say the autopsy report shows that he didn't die of this cancer thing? Now, *none* of this would come out in public. The hospital would notify the FBI. The FBI would report it to the attorney general. And the AG would report it to the Big Guy. And the Big Guy would tell his director of national security, the great Rogers P. Fancock, to get Ambassador Ding-Dong in here, chop-chop on the double, and explain what in the hell his country is thinking, assassinating the Dalai Lama in his Cleveland, Ohio, hospital bed.

"Now, Ding-Dong—once he's picked himself off the floor—will deny everything and denounce it as the pack of lies it in fact is. Vehemently. I would, too. But that doesn't matter. You reach across the table, slap him upside the head a couple of times, and say, 'You get out of my office, you lama-murdering scoundrel. You ought to be ashamed!'

"He'll scurry on back to his embassy and call Beijing in a sweat and say, 'What the hell's going on? They got evidence we killed him!' Beijing'll say, 'Hold on. We didn't kill him.' Let 'em deny it. Meanwhile, we put out word that MSS has gone rogue and is knocking off Dalai Lamas.

"The Big Guy calls Fa and says, 'This is a damn disgrace. You people ought to be ashamed of yourselves. We're not going public with it, but we're going to FedEx the remains to you and we want to be seeing a nice funeral for him in Lhasa.' Then hang up the phone.

"Now Fa, maybe he buys it, maybe he doesn't. But now he's got the excuse to call Lo in on the carpet—in front of the whole Standing Committee—and tear him a new one and say, 'Look what you've done. We're just lucky the White House isn't going public with it. You're fired. Gimme your ID badge and your BlackBerry.' Lo can deny it all he wants, but now the momentum's with Fa. It's his excuse to clean house. Fa stays in power. His Holiness gets a proper funeral on home soil, China looks magnanimous, everyone calms down. What do you say? Rog? Rog old buddy, you okay?"

CHAPTER 18

Isn't Momma Clever?

Y ou look cheerful," Bird said as Angel clickety-clicked in high heels toward his war room cubicle. Cheerful and quite fetching, Bird thought—all leg and cleavage today.

"Check out these nums," she said, whapping a newspaper onto Bird's desk. It was folded open to the headline:

U.S. PUBLIC APPROVAL OF CHINA PLUMMETS
FOLLOWING CHINA RULING ON DALAI LAMA

"'Plummets,'" Angel cooed. "Not 'dips,' not 'declines,' not 'falls.' 'Plummets.'"

Bird scanned the story. "Thirty points. That *is* a plummet."

"Did you hear Penelope Kent this morning?" Angel said. "She's called for a boycott of all Chinese goods. I love that woman. Well, let me rephrase. She's an idiot, but as Lenin would say, a useful idiot."

"Boycott?" Bird scoffed. "Good luck with that. Look around this room. These computers. Your BlackBerry. Your *three* BlackBerrys. The iPhone. That—if I may—rather revealing skirt. The shoes—"

159

"Italian," Angel said. "I have the sales slip. You think quality like this is made in China?"

"I still wouldn't hold your breath waiting for any boycott of Chinese goods. The U.S. economy would come to a screeching halt in ten minutes."

"Thank you, Captain Obvious. Come on, Bird, smell the roses. Take a bow. We did it. I'm not saying there isn't work to be done, but"—Angel lovingly caressed the newspaper—"indulge. Have a moment of wallow. Do you not feel just the teensiest bit proud?"

She was looking at him in a certain way. He wondered, *Is she flirting? What happened to I-don't-do-lobbyists?*

"I feel a warm tingling sensation all over," Bird said. "Who knows. A few more gallons of fuel on the fire and we might just have ourselves a shooting war. And then our work will be done. I see a Nobel in our futures. Maybe not the Peace Prize..."

"I'm on with Dragon Lady again tonight," Angel said. "Why don't you come along and hold my towel? I think it's going to be sweaty."

"It would be an honor to hold your towel," Bird said. "But I think I'll keep a low profile. You're kind of radioactive these days. I mean that as a compliment."

Angel held out her forearm. "Feel. *Hot.* Careful, babe, don't burn yourself."

True enough. Angel had made the cover of one of the newsweeklies: DUCK, BEIJING! ANGEL TEMPLETON'S GOT YOUR NUMBER!

Meanwhile it had not escaped Bird's attention that Angel had begun calling him "babe." Was this mimickry? She'd heard him calling Myndi that over the phone, usually in a pleading context. Or was she sending a signal? Bird couldn't tell. He was certainly attracted. But he told himself, *There be dragons there.*

"Much as I'd like to sit ringside and watch you beat up on Ms. Chang, I'd better pass. You're the star. I'm content to be the genius behind the curtain. I think the board of Pan-Pacific would prefer it that way."

Angel sat on Bird's desk, swiveled toward him, and crossed her legs. Those endless, stockinged legs. Her knees were inches from his chest. Bird didn't need braille to read this body language, though come to think of it, braille would be a nice way to read it. She was smiling at him.

Bird protectively crossed his legs. "Yes?" he said. "May I help you?"

"Pan-Pacific Solutions," Angel said. "We never really talked much about your *foundation*, did we?"

"You never asked."

"Don't ask, don't tell?"

"You didn't ask any questions on your way to the bank to cash our checks."

"No complaints there. I've enjoyed working with you, Bird. We've generated some amazing synergy."

Bird crossed his legs more tightly. "Well, great minds... You know..." He could smell her perfume. Why was Angel sitting on his desk like this? Why were her knees almost touching his chest? The legs. That skirt. *Stop staring at her thighs.*

"Pan-Pacific Solutions," Angel said in a melodic, querulous tone. "I finally decided I should do some due diligence. So I asked the boys to do a little checking. And it turns out there's really not a lot out there about Pan-Pacific Solutions. In fact, there's hardly anything. It was only incorporated a week or so before you and I met. One might *almost* suspect"—she smiled—"that it's a front."

"As I told you," Bird said, "my board consists of people who prefer to be low-key. Our motto is 'Under the Radar but on Top of the Situation.'" Bird hoped Angel wouldn't remember that was the slogan for Groepping's stealth helicopter.

"*I* think," Angel said, sounding like Marlene Dietrich, "that I would like to *meet* some of your board."

"Well." Bird laughed. "I'm *sure* they'd like to meet you. Especially after all the glowing things I've told them about you. However—"

"Aw," she said, switching from Dietrich to Barbara Stanwyck, "aren't you the peach?"

"No, no. Just like to give credit where credit is due."

"Did I mention that the *Times* is planning a story on us?"

"No, you didn't. That's . . . great."

"They have three reporters on it."

Bird thought, *Not great.*

"One of them is Luke Tierney."

Really not great.

Bird said, "Isn't he one of their top investigative reporters?"

"Oh, yes," Angel said. "Regular beaver. Chomp, chomp. He wanted to know all about Pan-Pacific Solutions. I was my usual shrinking-violet self. But he was persistent. I finally suggested he talk to you."

"Oh, I don't think that would be appropriate," Bird said. "I'm pretty sure my board wouldn't want to see my name in the *Times*. I'm not in this for the glory, you know."

"Well then," Angel said silkily, "what would you suggest? I don't think he's just going to drop it. You know those investigative types."

"Let me talk to my board," Bird said.

Angel was smiling at him. Bird thought, *Enjoying this, aren't you?*

"You do that," Angel purred. "You talk to your board."

Her fingers reached for his throat. Bird recoiled.

"Relax, Mr. Jumpy," she said, tenderly adjusting his necktie, sliding the knot back up into place. Her perfume. "You want to look your best, now, don't you? For the *board*?"

Angel pivoted on her miniskirted bottom, uncrossed her legs, and slid off Bird's desk.

"Time to do battle with Dragon Lady." She winked. "Wish Momma luck."

"Good luck," Bird croaked.

"Maybe I'll stop by the Military-Industrial Duplex later and tell you how it went," she said. "Barry's off on an overnight field trip."

"Oh?" Bird said. "Really? Gosh. What fun."

"The Aberdeen Proving Ground. He's *so* excited."

"The Aberdeen Test Center? Where the army..."

"Tests all the latest toys. Yes. Barry *adores* artillery. They're going to let him fire the M1 Abrams tank. Isn't Momma clever? He couldn't sleep last night he was so excited. Had to give him a whole pill."

"Well," Bird said, "that'll certainly make for a great show-and-tell at school."

"See you later. I'll bring you one of Dragon Lady's claws."

Off she clicked, heels on marble.

BIRD WAITED SEVERAL MINUTES, then raced from the war room, out the back freight entrance, and hoofed it to the nearest pay phone. It occurred to him that he might be the only human being in Washington, D.C., who still used pay phones—other than spies and drug dealers and other pillars of the community.

"Birdman?" Chick Devlin said heartily. "How's it hanging?"

"Houston, we have a problem."

He explained about Tierney of the *Times*.

"Reporters," Chick snorted. "Where's the patriotism? Vultures. Well, feed him whatever you need to, but keep him away from us. They're not asking about Taurus or anything, are they?"

"No," Bird said. "Not yet anyway. But they *are* asking about Pan-Pacific Solutions."

"Well, we built in enough cutaways between us and Pan-Pacific. By the time our money travels from Alabama to D.C., it's been washed so many times the numbers are coming off the bills."

"I know, but remember Watergate and 'Follow the money'?"

"Well, Birdman, the name on the door is Pan-Pacific *Solutions.* I've got every confidence in you. I gotta go. I got three kraut physicists waiting on me, and you know how cranky *they* get. Keep me posted. Keep our good name out of the papers, now. We'll talk."

Bird cradled the greasy receiver. A homeless man elbowed him aside, reaching for the coin-return slot. *Ah, the glamour of the clandestine life.*

ANGEL HADN'T HAD to do much heavy lifting. Chris Matthews was sputtering with indignation. He'd been giving it to Winnie Chang hard about Beijing's refusal to let the dying Dalai Lama return to his native Lhasa.

"How can a guy with a *brain tumor* pose a public-health problem?" Matthews demanded. "Do you really expect the world to swallow an explanation so obviously, transparently *mendacious?*"

"If you would give me a chance to explain—"

Matthews grinned. "Explain. Go ahead."

"This is not such a simple issue as it would appear," Winnie said. She looked stunning tonight: pearl earrings, Hermès scarf, sparkly eyes, cheekbones, and her never-flagging smile, behind which her mind was working furiously.

The truth was that Winnie was appalled by Beijing's handling of the crisis. They could be so self-defeatingly *stubborn* sometimes! But surely they could have come up with something better than this. She'd conveyed her own recommendations, but she had no way of knowing whether Minister Lo had passed them on. It was clear, though, what message the party leadership was seeking to convey to the world: *We don't care what you think.* And this occasioned some thinking on Winnie's part.

It was a good life she lived here in Washington. She played tennis with the president. All doors were open to her. She had girlfriends who ran corporations, with whom she went on "girl weekends" aboard private planes to expensive spas in Arizona for networking and herbal scrubs.

But Minister Lo had made it clear: At the end of the year, she would return to Beijing. "I'm promoting you," he told her. "I have great things in store for you."

Winnie suspected what, among other "great things," Minister Lo had in mind for her and recoiled at the thought. It was this prospect of having to leave her gilded life in Washington behind that made her susceptible to the (so far, Platonic) advances of Barney Strecker.

Meanwhile she was left to cope with this impossible situation of Beijing's own making.

On the way into the studio today, Winnie had found herself musing on a line from Sun-tzu: "The difficulty of tactical maneuvering consists in turning the devious into the direct, and misfortune into gain." She also thought about the American bureaucratic mantra: "It is easier to ask forgiveness than permission."

"Chris," Winnie said, "may I say that I do not think that the government in Beijing has made itself one hundred percent clear with this statement? I wonder, perhaps, if there has been some error in translation."

"Lost in translation? You're saying this is a mistranslation?"

"I do not think that Beijing intended to say that His Holiness's brain tumor—for which all people everywhere have such sympathy—I don't think they mean to say that it is contagious. This would be a ridiculous assertion, truly. Silly."

"Yeah? Okay? So?"

"No, I think what they are saying—but not so clearly—is that there are some elements in Tibet who have long been opposed to China's nation-building efforts—"

"Nation-building? In Tibet? Come on. Nation-*crushing* is more like it."

"Let me continue, please, Chris. That these elements might use the occasion of his return to foment turmoil and unrest. And whatever one's views are on the Tibet question, this surely *does* pose a public-health problem. If you have people dying in the streets because of riots and unrest, is that not—a public-health problem?"

"It's stretching it. But you're being more honest about it than Beijing."

"I can tell you that I have made some phone calls."

"Oh oh, here it comes. Look out. The Big *Spin*!"

"Chris"—she smiled—"behave, now. I spoke today with someone in the Ministry of Health in Beijing. Because I myself personally want to comprehend this situation. And do you know, it appears that there *is* a medical problem with his returning to Lhasa."

"This is going to be good. Okay, hit me."

Winnie look a little breath as she stepped off the cliff into the void.

"His Holiness is afflicted, as we all know, with a severe tumor in the brain and lungs. A pheochromocytoma." Winnie had practiced saying the word in front of the mirror. "Perhaps not so many people are aware that these tumors, in their final stages, are extremely sensitive to altitude."

"Altitude? Wow. You're not...you *are* serious!"

"Chris, let me explain. You see, Lhasa, the capital of the autonomous region—"

"Can we stop calling it that?" Matthews said. "Come on. *Tibet.* Try saying it. Tibet."

"If you look at any world map, you will see that it is called the autonomous—"

"Okay, okay, we'll do geography class after the break. Go on. So...tumor, altitude."

"Lhasa is nearly three thousand five hundred *meters* high. This is over ten thousand feet, Chris. His Holiness has been living all these years at much lower altitudes. In Dharamsala, India, where he makes his residence, it is only seventeen hundred meters high. Five thousand feet. Now he is in Cleveland, Ohio, which is nearly sea level.

There are many medical authorities who will tell you that to expose a person with a terminal brain tumor to such extreme altitude might prove fatal. So China is now in this impossible situation, because if they let him back, that will kill him, and then everyone will say, 'Aha, you see, that was their plan all along!' "

Matthews paused for several seconds—an eternity in Chris Matthews time. "I . . ." His face creased into a hundred smiles. "I have to say, that's really good. Winnie Chang, I like you. I think you're terrific. Even if you *are* a Chinese agent. And if you are, boy did you earn your paycheck today."

He turned to Angel. "Angel Templeton, what do you make of that?"

Angel said, "I thought you'd never ask."

"I'm asking!"

"Well, Chris, I'll say this much: Ms. Chang is at least being a little more creative than her Orwellian bosses back in Beijing. But—hello?—does anyone on this planet truly think that Beijing's big concern here is His Holiness's *health*?" Angel burst out laughing. "Because if that *is* what they're worried about, happily, there's a solution—hyperbaric chamber. If His Holiness is put in a hyperbaric chamber, then there's no change in pressure."

"Hyperbaric chamber," Matthews said. "You mean like one of those things Michael *Jackson* used to sleep in? With his pet *chimpanzee*?"

"I'd prefer, Chris, not to use the words *His Holiness the Dalai Lama* and *Michael Jackson* and *his pet chimpanzee* in the same sentence, but okay. Depressurizing chambers. What they put divers and pilots in. I'm sure NASA would be more than happy to lend the Chinese one."

"That's great. I like that. Don't go away. You're watching *Hardball*."

CHAPTER 19

WHAT WONDERFUL FRIENDS WE HAVE

The dream was back now, every night.
President Fa dreaded the moment when he could no longer keep his eyes open, only to wake in terror, his bed linen twisted into knots.

He was chain-smoking. He'd lost fifteen pounds, and Fa was not a large person to begin with. He looked at food—any food—with revulsion. Madam Fa was at her wit's end. She confided to her closest friends that the president was "not himself." In desperation she turned to the faithful Gang, who had served her husband so loyally for over two decades now, but he would only say, "Our dear Comrade President Fa is under severe pressure." Being the leader of Great China was an honor, to be sure, but a heavy burden. Not to worry, he told her—all will be well. But she'd known Gang long enough to know that there must be something else.

Gang himself, busy enough under normal circumstances, was truly exhausted. There was the regular business of state, and now on top of that the ongoing Lotus crisis. And on top of *that* he was now having to handle the most delicate secret communications with Admiral Zhang in San Diego, USA. Zhang—Agent Mankind Is

Red—had established contact with Beluga. A most perilous undertaking. Gang felt that his every move was under observation by Minister Lo's security apparatus. And so much depended on the operation.

As for Lo—his attitude toward President Fa now bordered on outright contempt. As global reaction continued to harden against China for its refusal to allow the Dalai Lama to return to Tibet, the meetings of the Standing Committee had grown alternately stormy and chill.

Comrade President Fa presided over these with an increasingly haggard mien. This did not go unnoticed by the other members, especially Minister Lo and General Han. Fa could barely stay awake.

Gang, listening in on the meetings through earphones, was dismayed—no, disgusted, truly—by those committee members who had initially favored the president's audacious solution and who now, sensing the changed wind, carried on as though they had always been on the side of the Lo-Han cabal. Disgraceful. A deplorable spectacle. And Lo, playing his part so coolly: *What an opportunity we missed, Comrades. If only we had acted when we had the chance.* Contemptible man!

But Gang's thoughts were less for President Fa's weakening political position than for his suffering master, who stood—or tottered and slumped—at the center of the hurricane.

Gang had procured, through the most discreet channels—namely, his college-attending daughter—sleeping pills and stay-awake pills. These he had begun to administer to the president without his knowledge. As a result the president was sleeping a bit better now and he was *much* more awake during the day. But certain effects had begun to manifest themselves. These were in evidence during the Standing Committee meeting on the day after the incident involving the television show in America, when China's top trade representative, Comrade Chang, went off-message and created a sensation.

It was generally known within the Standing Committee that Comrade Chang, ostensibly an employee of the International Liaison Department, was in fact an agent of the Two Bureau (foreign affairs) at MSS; moreover that she reported directly to Minister Lo, who had recruited and trained her.

What a tumult she had caused!

Seldom had Gang listened in on a Standing Committee meeting with such intensity and apprehension. Collating the president's briefing book the evening before, assembling the papers submitted by the various departments and ministries, Gang had noted that there was nothing—nothing at all—about the incident. Curious.

As presidential assistant, Gang had uncensored Internet access, and consequently well knew that Comrade Chang's television appearance had released a swarm of hornets. Headlines everywhere. All this he relayed to his drowsy President Fa.

Gang pressed him. "You must focus on the Chang matter, Comrade President! Here is your opportunity to put Minister Lo on the defensive!"

"Yes, yes," Fa said, as if not really hearing.

Gang decided to take bold action. He put not one but two stay-awake tablets into the president's tea that morning before the meeting.

Now, as Gang listened in, it was clear that the stay-awake pills had taken effect. Indeed, nearly forty-five minutes into the meeting, the president had scarcely stopped talking. None of the other members had been able to get in a word so far.

The president had expressed himself on a vast range of matters, from the mudslides in Anhui province to the jamming of the Voice of America and the BBC, even discussing the question of whether the new leader of North Korea—to Gang's mind a deeply deranged individual—should be permitted to enter China through Dandong in daylight or whether it was better to continue with the protocol of only letting him come and go like a rat in the dark.

Listening to the president prattle on about these less pressing matters, Gang mentally prodded him, *Chang, Comrade President. Introduce the Chang matter!*

Through his earphones Gang distinctly heard two committee members murmuring about the president's strange loquacity. *Oh, dear.*

Then—

"Comrade Minister Xe," Fa said. Gang heard him flipping through his briefing book so briskly it sounded like a deck of cards being shuffled. "Tell us about the latest public reactions in America with respect to the Lotus."

Minister Xe rambled on in his usual monotone. As minister of the Department of Propaganda and Thought Work, Xe Lu Pi had the appropriate talent for saying as little as possible in the maximum number of words. There was nothing of interest to report, he said. The usual anti-China gangsterist elements were doing the predictable things. The department was working hand in hand with Comrade Minister Lo's excellent and supportive Ministry for State Security.

Gang grimaced. *What a toad, Xe Lu Pi.*

On he droned, until Fa cut him off with a machine-gun burst of words.

"Yes, yes, good, good. But now what about *this*—"

Suddenly President Fa began to cough most violently. Gang winced. Another nicotine-wrought bronchospasm. It went on for an embarrassing duration, accompanied by bringings-up of phlegm and the necessity of a handkerchief.

"Are you...*well*, Comrade?" some member inquired.

"*Harrrgh*...You must excuse me, Comrades. A cold. *Harr-arghhhhh*—"

"Steward. Water. Water for the president. Quickly!"

Gang heard the sound of water being gulped. A wiping of lips, a clearing of throat.

"Pardon me, pardon me, Comrades. Don't worry. It is not catching. Must be the altitude!"

Gang thought, *Oh, no, Comrade President.*

"Tell me, Xe, tell me about Comrade Chang's statement on American television, of course."

Gang listened. Silence. Shuffling of paper. A nervous cough. At length Fa said, "Well, she seems to have caused quite a stir. Yes, quite a stir. Altitude. Well, I know all about *that*, as you are aware, Comrades." He laughed. "Don't sit near me when *I'm* giving a speech in Lhasa. Eh? Ha ho!"

Awkward laughter.

"Strange that you did not include mention of this in your briefing, Comrade."

Another pause. How Gang wished he were in the room to watch Minister Xe squirm. To see the look on Lo's face.

"It didn't seem worth…" Xe temporized. "There is so much media attention. What is important is—"

"But surely *this* was worth including with the rest?"

Pause.

"Forgive me. I did not wish to overwhelm Comrade President with every detail. But turning to—"

"That is considerate. I must say. Very considerate. I thank you. So then, is this now our official position? That we are acting from humanitarian impulses? Because of the…altitude?"

Another long and awkward pause. The rattle of teacups.

At length Xe said, "No, Comrade President. I believe that Comrade Chang was…" Xe looked over pleadingly at Lo. "Sometimes these television appearances can take an unexpected direction. I'm sure she did not mean to give the impression that…she gave."

Gang smiled. *He's covering for Lo. Lo—hiding behind Xe's skirts, are we?*

"Yes," Fa said with animation. "Yes, I can imagine how such a thing could happen. But whatever impression she sought to give, she has given *this* impression. She is the face of China there. Perhaps Comrade Ambassador Ding should take a more active role?"

"I wouldn't be too concerned," Xe pressed. "Our official position is articulated through the organs of state. Xinhua—"

"Comrade Minister Lo," Fa interjected in a companionable, cheerful tone. "Comrade Chang—she's yours, really, isn't she?"

"Mine?" Lo said. "Depends what you mean." Laughter. A bit *too* energetic, Gang thought.

Fa said, this time less cheerfully, "Come, come, Lo. I meant she's Two Bureau. We surely have no secrets here."

Good, Comrade President! Gang mentally cheered. Through his earphones came the voice of Minister Lo, like the rumble of an animal in its lair stirring to confront a trespasser.

"I am dealing with this matter, Comrade President. Personally. Be assured of this."

Silence.

"Yes, yes. Well, good. Good," Fa chittered on like a cricket. "I'm certainly aware of the need for discretion, yes. Oh, yes. You can't have enough of that. No. Still, I should like to hear a *little* more about this incident. As I'm sure other members would. When official state policy suddenly turns and spins in a new direction, on a television program, like the needle of a compass—*whish, whish, whishhhhh...*"

Gang thought, *No, Comrade, please. No sound effects!*

"...*whishhhh!* Oh!" he said. "I am making myself dizzy!"

Strained titters.

"Was this in Chang's brief, to say what she said?"

"No," Lo said.

"Oh?" Fa said.

"She was improvising. Without authority. This is not the way we—"

"Improvising!" Fa said with a gooselike honk. "Yes. Women love to improvise. My wife is *always* improvising."

Nervous laughter.

Again Gang heard the zippery flip of Fa's briefing-book pages.

"These headlines," Fa said. "'China Offers Novel Explanation for Lama Ban'... 'China Humanitarian Mask a Tight Fit'... 'China Dalai Position: From Thin Ice to Thin Air.' By the way, what is this 'hyperbaric chamber'? I did not understand this. And who is Michael Jackson? Does he *truly* sleep with monkeys?"

Gang held his breath as these details were explained to the president of the People's Republic of China.

"*Ah*," Fa said. "Him. Yes, yes. I remember. Did he not wear a glove made of metal?"

This detail was confirmed for the president.

"Well, well," Fa said. "I must say, Comrade Lo..." He paused, then said, "I *congratulate* you warmly on your Comrade Chang!"

Long silence.

"How...so, Comrade?" Lo ventured cautiously.

"She is creative! I like that. Yes. By introducing this new element, she has taken away some of the pressure. This is clever. From my reading of this, the Americans may not believe her, but they *like* her. It says here that she has been invited to be the guest hostess of the American national humorous show, *Saturday Night Liver.* 'Liver'? This is a strange name. Is this a comical term?"

Gang bit his lip as this, too, was explained to the president.

"Ah." Fa laughed self-deprecatingly. "Forgive me, Comrades. Between my eyes and my English, I do not know which is worse. I'll be needing a cane before long." He paused, then spoke soberly. "Well, Comrades, let us review. Harsh things are being said against our great country. I am being burned in effigy in, let's see...how many...seventeen world capitals? Surely this is a record. Not that I mind. No, no. It is my job to go up in flames. But I wish the effigies were better *looking*. Look at this one. Comrade Fin, am I truly so homely as this?"

"No, Comrade President. You are much more handsome."

Nervous laughter.

Fa continued. "Comrade Foreign Minister Wu. The United Nations. How does it go there?"

Foreign Minister Wu Fen cleared his throat. "Quite well. Very well. Zimbabwe, North Korea, Cuba, Venezuela, the Congo, Sudan, Yemen, Syria, Iran have all made strong statements on our behalf."

"Good. Good," Fa said. "What wonderful friends we have. But now tell me about these resolutions being introduced in the American Congress. Dear me. These senators in—hmm—Alabama, South Carolina, Georgia, Tennessee . . . yes, the South—they are vehement in their statements. They want to cut off sales of American wheat. We do need wheat."

"Posturing, Comrade President," said Minister Wu. "Cheap politics. These bills that have been introduced have no chance of becoming law. None. The senators from the wheat-producing states are forceful in their opposition. If I may speak in confidence, I have this on the authority of the American secretary of commerce himself. Believe me, he and I have been in regular communication. He assures me that he is most embarrassed about this. What's more, if such bills were to pass—though they will not—the American president will veto them."

"I am pleased to hear this, Wu. Well done. Well done. Now, this computer company in Texas—a large one, I see—are they really going to move their assembly plant out of Guangdong to . . . Vietnam? Vietnam! How quickly things change. Thirty-five years ago, they were at each other's throats. Now it's 'Kampai, kampai! Let's do business!' What did Lenin say? 'The capitalists will argue among themselves for the privilege of selling us the rope with which to hang them.' I *like* Lenin."

"It's only more posturing, Comrade President. More empty threats. When they look at the costs involved, they'll change their minds. However, it is true," Wu sniffed, "that the Vietnamese are acting toward us with their usual hostility."

"*Dogs,*" said General Han.

Gang reflected that General Han's hatred of the Vietnamese was exceeded only by his hatred of the Taiwanese, Tibetans, Americans, Russians, Indians, Japanese, and—who else? Ah, yes, Bhutanese. Han despised the Bhutanese.

Lo spoke up. "Comrade President, all this is so much farting in a bamboo forest. Yes, it makes a noise," Lo said, "but let's keep our heads clear—"

"And hold our noses?" Fa said. "Ha!"

"My point, Comrade, is that the wind will die down."

"Yes, yes, Comrade, I'm sure you're right."

More shuffling of briefing papers.

"Now, here," Fa said, "is a headline to strike terror into our hearts. Brace yourselves, Comrades: 'Motion Picture Association to Vote on Oscar Ban for Chinese Films.' I confess to you, Comrades, that I had been secretly hoping to be nominated Best Communist in a Leading Role."

Gang bit his lip, but there came a burst of laughter that sounded genuine.

"You certainly have my vote, Comrade," the foreign minister said. "Might we discuss your forthcoming visit to the United States?"

"Yes, please," Fa said. "Imagine how much I am now looking forward to that. What effigies *that* will inspire."

"I spoke with the American secretary of state yesterday. She extended the warmest personal wishes."

"I am very glad of that. I trust you reciprocated?"

"Oh, yes."

"Did you tell her—Naughty lady—no more hidden microphones in my limousine?"

Gang groaned.

"She..." The foreign minister soldiered on. "She respectfully suggested that under the present circumstances perhaps it would be prudent if your visit were postponed. We could always give as a reason some urgent—"

"But I was looking forward to it," Fa said. "I have long wanted to visit Disney World."

"The entire country is Disney World," Lo said, to much laughter.

The foreign minister added nervously, "She stressed a concern for your security. America is... America. Their own presidents have to ride around in armored cars."

"It is thoughtful of her to care so."

"The American government has been... I am tempted to say admirably restrained in its public comments. They have taken no official position on the Lotus matter."

"What about their vice president?" General Han grumbled. "Did you not see what *he* said?"

Foreign Minister Wu said, "The vice president's tongue is several time zones ahead of his brain. This is understood by everyone. No one pays any attention to his utterings. No, Comrades, let us at least give them due credit. And their administration is under considerable pressure by anti-China elements."

Gang heard the metallic *snick* of Fa's cigarette lighter.

"Well, yes," Fa said, "this has put them in a difficult position. One almost feels sympathy for them." He quickly added in a jovial tone, "Don't worry, Lo—I said *almost*." Laughter. He said, "So, Comrades, did we do the correct thing, not allowing him back?"

General Han spoke. "With all respect, Comrade, what's the point in bringing that up now?"

"'The past is the cause of the present,'" Fa said. "'And the present will be the cause of the future.' Abraham Lincoln." He added, "He was the American president during their Civil War, 1861 to 1865."

"Thank you," Han said. "I *was* aware."

"So," Fa said, "do we just continue to ride out the fartstorm, as Comrade Lo has proposed? These matters can take unexpected turns."

"What choice do we have?" said Deputy Minister Lin. "If we were to back down now—"

"Oh, *please*, Comrades, let us have no talk of that," Lo said with impatience. "Do you want full-scale war in the autonomous region? You heard my report. Even the American CIA is trying to restrain these bastards."

"By the way, Comrade," Fa said, "might I have a copy of that? It was most interesting."

Silence.

Lo said, in a tone that struck Gang as forcedly casual, "Of course, but you are acquainted with the contents. It is highly sensitive."

"Yes," Fa said pleasantly, "I'm certainly aware of that. But I think you can trust the president and general secretary with it. As you say, it is a troubling document. For this reason I should like to study it. Closely. Have your man bring it to my Comrade Gang. Today, if you would."

Silence. Gang felt the seconds ticking by.

At length Lo said, "Of course. As to the more urgent matter, may I share a proposition with the committee? A solution?"

Fa said warily, "Yes. Of course."

"Time is of the essence," Lo began.

TWENTY MINUTES LATER President Fa returned to his office, pale, sweaty, and limp. He nearly collapsed into Gang's waiting arms. Gang led him to an armchair, took off his shoes, went to the bathroom, and came back to apply a cold towel to his forehead.

"You heard?" said Fa, stretched diagonally across the Soviet-era armchair, his eyes hidden beneath the wet towel.

"Yes. All of it."

"I know I may be losing my mind, Gang. But now I am wondering if the others have already lost theirs."

"You were most forceful. Surely Minister Lo wouldn't proceed without—"

"The problem, Gang, is that I am no longer certain that I am in control of the situation." Fa lifted the towel, turned it to the cooler side, and reapplied it to his warm, overworked forehead. He said, "If I were a philosopher, I should draw some consolation from that. But I'm a Communist, so the only consolation I can draw is that ultimately we are all only servants of the party."

Gang was silent. Then he said, "Is the party *always* correct?"

"Well, the party can never be wrong. Can it?"

"It's your head, Comrade, not the party's."

"I suppose. And right now it is throbbing with such intensity that I should almost wish it to be disconnected from the rest of me."

CHAPTER 20

MAY I BE CANDID HERE?

"Mr. Mc-En-*tire?*"

"Yes..." *What was her name?* "...Mary...Lou?"

"Mr. Tierney is here? Mr. Luke Tierney, from the *New York Times?*"

"Thank you. Please, show him in."

Mary Lou, assuming that was her name, ushered Mr. Tierney of the *Times* into Bird's sunny, spacious corner office with its view of the Pentagon in the distance.

It was a hastily rented and even more hastily decorated space in Crystal City, a nondescript conurbation of high-rise glass. Bird had not stinted on the decor, reasoning that a well-financed "foundation" such as Pan-Pacific Solutions ought, really, to look the part.

There were Warhol reproductions on the walls, Japanese and Chinese scrolls of misty mountains and tiny Buddhas meditating in front of their caves. A Barcelona chair. Terra-cotta horses (fake) and slender faux-jade geishas. Large, soothing color shots—the photographic equivalent of elevator music—depicting appropriate Pacific-coast scenes: cliffs, kelp, sea lions, cannery rows. In the waiting room, soothing background music of the kind heard in New Age

Asian-themed spas: flute, dripping water, the flap of crane wings, hoot of owl. On the way to Bird's office, behind a wall of glass, a conference room with a large table of bird's-eye maple (very tasteful) where serious and expensive men and women might sit six times a year to discuss large thoughts.

The whole space occupied a quarter floor of the building. At the moment it was occupied by eighteen souls in suits, ties, white shirts, and sober footwear, all of them with strict orders to act busy, even a bit hurried, and under no circumstances to say anything to Mr. Tierney of the *Times* other than "Morning" or "Running late for that conference call" or "Palo Alto called again about the PowerPoint." A simple enough script, really, for Bird's Potemkin on the Potomac.

Necessity being the brother of invention, Bird had turned to Bewks in his hour of need.

After listening to Bird's proposal, Bewks said, "Big brother, you know I want to help, but that's really not the kind of living history we do."

"Bewks. Listen to me. You are the only person who can help me. I need you to do this for me."

"Half of these boys haven't had their weekly bath yet. They're fine people, believe me, but they're *basic*."

"Then take them to a car wash and run them through. And they need to shave."

"Shave?" Bewks laughed. "Good luck with that."

"They need to look like office workers, Bewks. Not the Confederate army."

"The boys take pride in their facial hair. It's part of the authenticity. Took me months to get my hair Custer-shaped."

"I've got news for you and the boys. Hair grows back. Now, I'm offering good money. I don't want to see beards, mustaches, or soul-patches. And I darn well sure don't want to see you walking past cubicles looking like George Armstrong Custer."

"I'll talk to them, but I'm not making any promises."

"Bewks. Listen to me. Think of this as a ship. If it goes down, I go down. If I go down, you go down. This nineteenth-century fantasy world of yours that I finance? *Glug, glug, glug.* Upkeep? *Glug.* Mother? *Glug.* I'm not asking you to restage the chariot race in *Ben-Hur* or the Sermon on the Mount. All I need is for your people to look like they actually live in the twenty-first century. For one hour. Two, tops. I need them in normal, boring clothes. The kind that people who work for a living actually wear. I need them not to smell. I need them not to pick their noses or hawk a gob of chewing tobacco into a wastebasket when Mr. Tierney walks by. It would be nice, also, if they did not let out the rebel yell when he arrives. I am not asking for miracles. In return, everyone gets a nice set of boring office clothes, which they can keep. Everyone gets a haircut. A barbershop shave if that's what it'll take. And everyone gets two hundred dollars, cash. Which is probably more than most of them make in a month, from what I've seen."

"That's true enough," Bewks said.

"And most of all, I need them to shut up. When Mary Lou or Mary Lee or whatever her name is trolls Mr. Tierney through the office—*no conversation.* If he tries to speak to anyone, say, 'Oops, there goes my cell phone.' We are reenacting a single hour in the life of a normal, boring office. With me?"

"Mr. Tierney, welcome. Please, sit. Care for some coffee?"

"No thank you."

"Mary...Lou, would you kindly hold the calls?"

"Yes, *sir*, Mr. Mc-en-tire, I shore will."

"Thank you."

"My pleasure, sir!" Mary Lou closed the door with a bang that caused Mr. Tierney to start.

"She's from the South." Bird smiled. "As you may have guessed.

So Angel Templeton tells me you're doing a story on the ICC. Interesting place."

Bird realized within a few minutes that he was in very deep doo-doo. Tierney of the *Times* wasted no time on persiflage; no, it was straight for the old jugular. He'd done his homework. There was little, if anything, "out there" on Pan-Pacific Solutions. Indeed, he said, "It's almost as if it doesn't really exist."

"Well"—Bird smiled once more—"the board does like to keep a low profile."

The board of Pan-Pacific, he stressed, consisted of discreet, high-worth, West Coast persons, patriotic, bound together by a concern for national security and America's continued role as global peace-keeper.

All this Tierney of the *Times* listened to with the unconvinced, almost amused expression of a detective who, wearying of an improbable alibi, decides it is time to produce the murder weapon. He also had the annoying ability, Bird saw, of being able to take notes in shorthand while keeping his eyes fixed on Bird, as Bird tried to weave his grand tapestry of falsehood. Bird saw that it was useless. There was handwriting on the wall, and it said, *Forget it. It's over, and you lost.*

"You were with Groepping-Sprunt for seven and a half years," Tierney said. "Why'd you leave?"

"Oh, you know. To every season, turn, turn, turn? Thought it was time for a fresh challenge. New opportunity."

"I see. And one week later you incorporated"—he glanced around the office—"all this?"

"Yes." Bird said. "I'm not one to let moss grow under my feet. Ha."

"And yet it's not a 501(c)(3). Why didn't you incorporate as a nonprofit foundation? That's unusual, to say the least."

"The board members are very patriotic. They actually like to pay taxes."

In fact, Groepping's lawyers had insisted, so there'd be no need for public filings and/or problems with the IRS. Pan-Pacific Solutions might be a front, but it was at least a legal one.

Tierney put down his notepad. "Mr. McIntyre, may I be candid?"

"By all means. Candor is . . . so candid. I'm all for it."

"Not to sound rude, but frankly I'm having a difficult time believing all this. Actually, any of it."

"Really? Well, that's disappointing."

"I've done some research into your funding. It took some piecing together, but it all basically originates at Groepping-Sprunt. There were a number of cutaways, but if you want, I can show you the various—"

Bird held up a hand. "No, that won't be necessary." Bird took a deep breath. "Did you at least like the decor?"

Tierney glanced around. "All this—for me?"

"Not bad for forty-eight hours, huh? Did you like the Warhols? They're not real. Still."

"Mr. McIntyre," Tierney said, putting his notepad on the desk, "now let me be candid. I don't particularly care about Pan-Pacific."

"You don't?"

"To put it bluntly, another sleazy Washington lobby story is no longer front-page news."

"Well," Bird said, "I don't know about 'sleazy,' but if you say so."

"My interest is Groepping-Sprunt."

"Ah."

"Specifically, a project they're developing for the Pentagon."

"Keeping America safe by keeping America strong. It's on the letterhead. Under the eagle."

"What can you tell me about Project Taurus?"

Bird shifted in his chair. "Taurus? Taurus. Well, I must say, I'm impressed. That's a highly—*highly*—classified program."

"Yes."

Bird leaned forward. "Mr. Tierney, shall we talk turkey?"

"I'd rather talk Taurus."

"Okay, but being a sleazy Washington lobbyist, let me put it to you: What's in it for me?"

"Well, I *could* write a story about your Potemkin foundation here. And all the nice touches and Warhols. Or I could write about Taurus. And I'd rather write about that."

"I'd rather you write about Taurus myself. But I'm somewhat reluctant to sign my own death warrant."

"Are you saying it's that sensitive?"

"You have no idea, sir. No idea."

"I wouldn't necessarily have to use your name. But that would depend on what you tell me."

"Mr. Tierney." Bird leaned back in his chair. "What do you know about muons?"

CHAPTER 21

THIS SKYSCRAPER OF PREVARICATION

Y ou told him *what?*" Chick Devlin spluttered.

Bird felt it was only fair to alert Chick to the visit from Tierney of the *Times* and the load of—taurine excreta that Bird had fed him in return for not writing about Pan-Pacific Solutions. Not that he thought there was any point in mentioning *that* part of it to Chick.

"God in heaven." Chick groaned. "Birdman. What have you done?"

"Chick. He already knew. Had to tell him something. Figured we might as well try to control the story, right?"

"Muons," Chick muttered. "Muons? How in hell did *muons* ever enter into this?"

"Well, as a matter of fact, I kind of improvised there. When Angel asked me about Taurus, I told her it was about muons."

"What? Why?"

"Thought it might throw her off the scent."

"Where did you come up with muons?"

"It's from a book. One of mine, actually."

"You telling me this is in some *book?*"

"Yes."

"But if it's in a book, how long is it going to take the reporter to find that out?"

"Not to worry," Bird said brightly. "The book hasn't been published yet. I'm holding on to it for now."

"So all I have to worry about is my phone ringing from a reporter wanting to know about our top-secret *muon* project? Thank you. You've put me in the tenth circle of hell."

"There are only nine, technically."

"What am I supposed to tell him?"

"That you can't talk about it. And that's nothing but the truth, right? It's classified. Want me to draw up some talking points for you?"

"No! I'm having chest pains, Bird."

"I really think there's a way to capitalize on the muon scenario."

Here Bird had a definite agenda: self-preservation, the purest of all motives. If Tierney of the *Times* discovered that he had been lied to—lied to massively—Bird would certainly end up the subject of "yet another Washington sleazy-lobby story," regardless of what page it appeared on.

He said to Chick, "Look, whatever Taurus really is, you want it to remain secret, right?"

"Of course I do!" Chick said.

"Then feed him muons as a decoy."

Silence.

"I don't know," Chick said warily. "That kind of thing can turn around and bite you on the ass."

"Here's the headline: 'Defense Aerospace Giant Groepping-Sprunt Said to Be Developing Top-Secret Program to...'" Bird's voice trailed off.

"I'm listening."

"'Top Secret Program to...'"

"I'm still listening, Bird."

"'Neutralize Chinese Communications Grid.'" *Why not?*

There was a long silence. Chick finally said, "All right, Bird, how did you find out about that?"

Well, well.

"As a matter of fact, I didn't," Bird said, for once truthfully. "So that's it? Taurus, like in the constellation. V-shaped network of satellites that—"

"Bird, I'm not going to *talk* about it. Leave it. Jesus."

"Well," Bird said, "I couldn't be more proud of the old home team. This'll give Beijing a case of the turkey-trots. Woo-wee."

"I can't have you going around town crowing about this like some bent rooster."

"I'm not going to tell anyone. Am I not permitted to have a moment of pride in our company?"

"Let's think this through. This Tierney. What do we do?"

"Take his phone call. You might compliment him on his last Pulitzer. He got it for..." Bird recalled that it was for an exposé of a company whose CEO ended up going to jail. "...just tell him congratulations. You know writers. They love a little stroking. Sound like you're a tad nervous—"

"*That* won't be hard."

"Tell him you really didn't want to take his call but that I told you you had to. Remember that part. It's sort of key."

"Yeah, yeah. What then?"

"Soon as he mentions Taurus, make a little gasping sort of noise and say, 'Oh, Lordy, I can't talk about *that!*' And when he says 'muon,' don't say a thing for ten seconds. Do the full count. *One-one-thousand, two-one-thousand.* Then tell him, 'Sir, I'm afraid I cannot discuss that.' Then—hang up."

"I don't know, Bird. I'm an engineer."

"Don't sell yourself short. I've seen you tell some beautiful lies. You can do this. A hundred years from now, they'll be writing ballads about you. Chick Devlin, father of the muon bomb. *Oh, gather* round, children, and you shall hear... of a man named Devlin, a great pioneer—"

"Quit!"

"Hey, be happy. You told me it looks like you're going to get your funding, right? You *should* be happy. When word of this hits the street, Groepping's stockholders are going to be *very* happy."

"I'll have to put some people in the picture about this. But maybe, as a decoy it's not half bad."

"There you go," Bird said.

"This muon book. I'm assuming you won't publish it."

"Well, that's hardly fair, Chick."

"Bird."

"I worked hard on this book. This could be my masterpiece. My *Moby-Dick.*"

"You try my patience, Bird. Honest to God you do."

"Once the *Times* exposes your big muon project, it won't matter if it's in my novel. Hell, I'll probably get creamed by the critics for lack of imagination. I'm the one taking all the downside here."

"You could talk the devil out of his pitchfork. Meantime you keep that novel in a safe-deposit box."

"Frankly, Chick, a little gratitude wouldn't be entirely out of order here."

"Gratitude?"

"Here I whip you up a fine, foamy froth of anti–China sentiment and, as a bonus, a billion dollars' worth of free publicity. And all you can do is whine. Forgive me. Forgive me for hitting a home run for the team. With bases loaded."

"Stop feeling sorry for yourself. I said you did good. Wasn't *saying* otherwise. But this thing's gotten more complicated than the specs for our R2-20 phased-array radar. I'm still not sure I understand it. Is your blond Angel of death in on this skyscraper of prevarication you've erected?"

"No, no. She's having way too much fun giving Beijing fits. I tremble to think that that woman actually once worked at the White House and the Pentagon. God forbid she should ever get her pretty little manicured fingers anywhere *near* a Launch button."

"You keep me posted."

"Roger that, Commander. McIntyre out."

Bird hung up. He let out a long sigh of relief. He considered his astounding good luck in having correctly guessed what Taurus was. *State-of-the-art stuff. Good old Groepping.* No wonder Chick wouldn't tell him anything about it. More importantly, he had managed to extract his roasting chestnuts from a very hot fire.

CHAPTER 22

THIS JUST IN FROM ZHONGNANHAI

"Y ou talk to the Big Guy about my little proposal?"
Barney Strecker and National Security Director Rogers P.
Fancock were speaking over the secure line between CIA and the
White House.

"By 'Big Guy' do you mean the president of the United States of
America?"

"No. Fatty Arbuckle. Come on, Rog, we're up against the clock
here."

"Strictly, and I mean strictly *entre nous*?"

"Did you think I had you on speaker? Yes, *entre nous*."

Fancock relived the moment. The way the sun slanted through
the windows in the Oval Office. The faint scent of honeysuckle that
wafted through the open French doors from the Rose Garden. The
president's dachshunds, Ajax and Achilles, curled up on the sofa.

"It would be accurate," Fancock said to Barney, "to say that the
Big Guy did not leap into the air like a trout to the fly. In fact, it
would be accurate to say that smoke issued from his ears and the
ground trembled beneath his feet. He expressed the keenest curiosity as to the identity of the public servant who had put forth this—he

used the word *medieval*—proposal, as well as the desire to terminate said person's employment in government. As for that, you needn't worry. Fortune was smiling on us, inasmuch as my main agenda walking in was to inform the Big Guy that even as we were speaking so pleasantly about your little brainstorm, two *Jianghu II*–class Chinese naval frigates were steaming with what might be called indecent haste toward a U.S. Navy communications ship. *Communications* as in *spy ship* in the East China Sea. Nothing like the prospect of a naval confrontation on the high seas when you're trying to distract the most powerful man on earth from having your friend's head mounted on a spike. Rather clever timing on my part, I might add. You know my rule: never enter the Oval Office without an exit strategy. In so many words, Barn, you owe me."

"Well, that's a shame, is all I can say."

"Shame?" Fancock said dryly. "That you didn't get the go-ahead to finish off the Dalai Lama? Or shame that the United States and the People's Republic of China may soon be initiating World War III? Speaking of which, I dare not tarry. My presence seems to be desired in the Situation Room. What fun this weekend promises."

"Looks like Beijing is trying to change the subject."

"Yes, that would be my evaluation as well."

"It's also obvious, Rog, if you don't mind my saying so, that we wouldn't *have* a naval incident brewing in the East China Sea if this Dalai Lama thing had gone away."

"Barn. I tried. I ran it up the flagpole. The commander in chief did not salute. He gave it the finger. All right? I have to go."

"Okay, but before you sashay over to the Sit Room, you want to hear the latest from our Zhongnanhai desk?"

"Only if it's epic. Barn, there are two PLN fast frigates bearing down on—"

"They're going to do him."

"They? Do what? To whom?"

"MSS. Chinese security. They're going to take out the Dalai Lama." Strecker added, in a tone that struck Fancock as inappropriately merry, "Great minds think alike, huh?"

"What are you telling me, Barn?"

"I'll give it to you straight up. The Chinese are going to take the life—or what's left of it—of the Right Reverend Tenzin Gyatso, aka the Dalai Lama. In Cleveland. Ohio. That's in the Midwest, where you eastern elite types don't go on account of there's no French restaurants."

Fancock sat frozen. "Is this—do we *know* this? For a fact?"

"Yes, Rog."

Fancock felt his heart pounding. "Have you called Doug Richardson at Treasury? His Holiness is already under Secret Service protection, but in light of—"

"No," Barney said. "You're the first name on my speed dial. I thought you and I might want to have a little tête-à-tête before we went pressing any other buttons. Strictly *entre nous*."

"Oh, no, Barn. No. No, no, no."

"Hear me out. Just hear me out. MSS, these people are— whatever else you think—they're pros. Frankly, I sometimes wish some of own people had their skill sets."

"Barney!"

"Listen, Rog. It's not like a dozen ninjas are going to rappel down the outside of the hospital and get into a firefight with the Secret Service. Hell, the Chinese have been at this sort of thing since Our Lord was walking the earth in sandals, sticking it to the Philistines. We probably won't even see 'em coming. Or going. You remember Clint Eastwood in that movie *Million Dollar Baby*? The scene at the end where he—"

"No, I don't. And I'm going to hang up now. I'm calling Doug Richardson."

"*Rogers*. Steady, old bean. Don't go doing something you're going to regret. Think it through. That's what you used to tell us in Exit Strategies. You go alerting the Secret Service, what's *that* going to accomplish?"

"Other than saving the Dalai Lama's life?"

"Fine. Fine. You put them on high alert. And what happens when they *catch* the guy? *Then* what? 'U.S. Foils Attempt by China to Kill Dalai Lama. Killer Held at Guantánamo.' *That'll* calm things down nicely. Hope you got your talking points ready."

Fancock confronted the fact that his choices were now reduced to the odious and the unpalatable.

"Can you stop them?" Fancock said.

"Stop them? Rog, I'm the one who *suggested* this in the first place."

A knock on the door. Bletchin's face, all shiny and eager, no doubt panting for permission to get Dr. Kissinger on the line.

"I'm sorry to interrupt, sir. You're needed in the Situation Room. Right away."

Why—*why*—had Fancock gone back into government? Here it was a Friday in June. He could have been sailing on his yacht, *Ophelia*, on a gentle reach down Nantucket Sound, wind off the quarter, bare feet on sun-warm teak deck, cutting a neat wake through green water, sipping Pimm's Cup, Dorothy beside him, knitting, listening to Mozart, trying to decide what sauce to serve with the lobster tonight. Instead... *this.*

CHAPTER 23

More Than I Could Have Hoped For

I've got an ear-ly birth-day gift," Angel said in singsong to Bird as she approached his station in the ICC war room on little cat's feet.

Given the kittenish vibrations Bird had been picking up lately, he thought it prudent to respond cautiously, in case "birthday" turned out to mean "naked."

To his relief, Angel had not stopped by the Military-Industrial Duplex the other night after her slugfest on *Hardball* with Winnie Chang.

"Birthday?" he said. "Not until September, actually."

"Guess what? I just had a call from a friend at the Pentagon. There's something cooking in the East China Sea. Something big."

"Oh?"

"Um-hm."

"We're not at war or anything, are we?"

"Not yet. But things could get very, very in-ter-est-ing." She turned to go.

"Wait."

"Got to make some calls. You don't think I'm going to wait to hear this on CNN, do you?"

"Is it . . . serious?"

"Let's hope."

"Oh, Ange, you make me nervous when you talk like that."

"Back in a jiff."

She returned a half hour later, pink-faced and flushed, looking as though she'd gone for a two-mile run in the park.

"Oh, Bird," she said. "We did it. We really did it. When we first started on this project, I thought maybe we'd nudge public opinion along a bit. But this is *so* much more than I could have hoped for. Two Chinese fast frigates—*Jianghu II* class—are on an intercept course for one of our ships."

"Oh, no. What kind of ship?"

"A surveillance vessel! The *Rumsfeld*. Spy ship! Antisubmarine. Loaded to the gills with the very latest."

"This is . . . good?"

"Good? We may be on the verge of the biggest high-seas showdown since the *Pueblo*. Yes, this is good. Why are you frowning?"

"I don't know," Bird said. "Maybe I'm a few drinks behind."

"You might show a *little* enthusiasm." She turned and left, high heels, high dudgeon.

She stopped short of the door. "I forgot to ask—how did it go with Mr. Tierney?"

"I threw him a red herring. How did your session go with the other two Torquemadas of the *Times*?"

A shadow played across Angel's face. "I suppose it's a compliment when the *Times* puts three reporters on you. But it feels a bit like a gang bang."

"Problem?" Bird said.

"We'll find out when the story appears. They seemed impressed by ICC. They didn't connect us with the Indian newspaper. So that was good. But I could really, really do without all the questions about former boyfriends."

"Yeah," Bird said. "That can't be much fun."

"So I've had a few relationships. What does that have to do with *anything*? With my work at ICC? If I were a guy, would the *Times* be asking, 'So is it true you were involved with so-and-so and so-and-so and so-and-so?' Is *any* of that in any way relevant to my work on national-security issues?"

She was hurting.

"Take it as a compliment," Bird said. "Your friend Dr. Kissinger had lots of girlfriends when he was a bachelor, and it added to his luster." Bird felt brotherly, suddenly. "Hey, it's part of your legend—Angel Templeton, policy she-warrior. Enjoy it."

But Angel wasn't enjoying. In fact, her face was starting to crumple. She looked on the verge of tears.

"You okay, kiddo?"

"They asked me..."

"What?"

"*Silo.*"

"Aw," Bird said. "That wasn't nice of them."

"It just...hurts, you know?"

"I know it does, Ange."

Looking back, Bird could not recall with total clarity the series of steps—getting up out of the chair, going over to Angel, putting his arms around her, and everything that followed. Maybe it fell into the "it all happened so fast" category. But happen it did, and however hard he tried to morally triangulate his way back out from where he had gone, he knew that this was an infraction of a very different order from the boozy night in Seoul with the woman from the helicopter company.

He was lying on the leather couch in her office. Her head and its attendant abundance of blond tresses rested on his chest: a Botticelli Venus not yet risen on the clamshell. Angel was deep asleep.

Bird regarded his bare feet protruding from under the edge of the fur throw. He wiggled his toes in playful counterpoint to the foreboding he felt forming over him like a rime of black frost.

It was cold in the room from the air-conditioning. His feet were chilly. The ironic thought occurred to him that in the process of trying to comfort Angel over the word *silo* he had managed to fall, headfirst and headlong into it.

CHAPTER 24

If This Were a Novel

There was this to be said for insomnia, President Fa reflected as he hurriedly dressed: When the emergency phone call came at two-thirty in the morning, you were already awake.

Gang briefed him as they made their way to the secure conference room beneath Zhongnanhai. The two frigates were twenty-five miles from the American vessel and closing fast. The American ship, named for a pugnacious former U.S. defense secretary, was maintaining its course as if all were normal.

But all was not normal. The Americans had retasked a carrier battle group. Fighter-interceptors and surveillance planes were launching off the deck of the *George H. W. Bush*. People's Central Air Command was also launching planes. The skies above the East China Sea were becoming dangerously busy.

"Bush...Rumsfeld," Fa muttered to Gang as they hurried along. "Bush. I have had six meals with him. Four dinners. Two lunches. No, three lunches. Seven meals. A gentle person. Very pleasant. Courteous. Rumsfeld I experienced just once. That was enough. Very different from Bush. In college Rumsfeld was on the wrestling team. It's important to remember such details, Gang."

They walked through corridors humming with activity despite the hour. It did not escape Fa's notice that his escort of bodyguards was twice its usual number, but then he remembered that this was normal procedure at times of "national emergency."

National emergency, Fa thought with a scowl. *Yes, and who decided that we should* have *a national emergency? On top of the one we were* already *having?*

"Technically," Gang said, as if reading Fa's mind, "the order came from Admiral Pang in Fuzhou. But"—he made a little scoffing noise—"I suppose we know who it really came from."

"Pang? Pah. Pang wouldn't *urinate* without permission from Han. No, I do not care to speak with Admiral Pang in Fuzhou. General Han I very much desire to speak with."

"General Han is not in Beijing, Comrade."

"Why?"

"I am informed that he departed for Wusong earlier this evening."

"Oh, this is not right, Gang. Not right. No."

"I am informed that the defense minister felt it was imperative to supervise the operation personally, at People's Naval Command Shanghai."

"Personally?" Fa growled. "Yes, well, if you're going to start a war, you might as well be there to enjoy it."

"On the positive side," Gang said, "this way you don't have to be in the same room with him."

Fa burst through the doors of the conference room with such alacrity that the four assembled members of the Standing Committee started in their chairs and another spilled his coffee. They rose in greeting.

"Where is Minister Lo?" Fa barked.

"He is not present, Comrade President."

"I can see that. I asked where is he?"

"In Lhasa, Comrade President. Monitoring the situation."

Fa thought, *So neither the minister of defense nor the minister of state security is present. And my security detail is twice normal size. If this were a novel, one of those so-called thrillers of the vulgar kind, this would be the scene where the leader realizes that a coup is under way.*

"Well," Fa said, "let us hope that the altitude in Lhasa is agreeing with him."

The chief of staff of the People's Liberation Army, General Men, began to brief the president. Fa cut him off after a few words.

"Thank you, but the only general I wish to hear from is General Han. Get him on the phone."

"With respect, Comrade President, General Han is occupied supervising the—"

"None of that. Get him on the phone. *Now.*"

General Men, sensing that his future depended on brisk compliance with this order, scuttled out of the room like an alarmed crab.

The Standing Committee members exchanged looks. *Cool Limpidity is very forceful this morning.*

Fa, watching them, thought, *So which of you scoundrels is in on this?* He smiled at them. "Good morning, Comrades."

"Good morning, Comrade President," they said in unison, like students.

General Men returned. "I have General Han for you, Comrade President. Would you like privacy?"

"Privacy? We're Communists. Don't you know we don't believe in privacy? Put him over the speaker."

"This is General Han," came the voice.

"And this is President and General Secretary Fa Mengyao. What is going on?"

"An American spy vessel is interfering with a sensitive exercise involving three of our nuclear submarines."

"What's unusual about that? It's what navies do to each other when they're not actually *at* war."

"No, Comrade President. I'm afraid this time they have gone too far. They have deployed destructive electronic countermeasures that have damaged our equipment. We must respond."

"Respond? And the orders issued to our ships—what is the precise wording?"

"Interdict and harass."

"I am not a military man, as you so often point out. Would you please define for me the term *interdict and harass*? Harass? Does that include firing on the Americans? Ramming them? Boarding? Sinking?"

"Harass means harass, Comrade. The objective is to compel them to break off their surveillance. As you yourself say, this is how it goes—a game of cat and mouse. Frankly, Comrade, your agitation surprises me. But then, as you yourself point out, you are not a military man."

"No, I'm not. So tell me then what words I should use when countermanding an order given by the minister of defense? I should like to issue such an order. Immediately."

Silence.

"Well, General?"

"I am here, Comrade, at my post."

"Stand down, General. Rescind the order. Do we understand each other?"

"We understand each other perfectly, Comrade."

"Then I will say good night to you."

General Han did not reciprocate the salutation.

THEY SAT ON STOOLS in the presidential bathroom, whiskeys in hand, faucets and shower nozzles opened, toilets flushing.

"It appears, Gang, that I am to have nightmares every night whether or *not* I'm asleep."

"I thought you handled the situation well," Gang said.

Gang was not a flatterer. Fa allowed himself satisfaction at this rare compliment.

"He'll come back at you for this. He won't stand for being humiliated in front of his staff."

"For a moment, Gang, I thought something was...under way."

They drank, listening to the sound of the faucets and shower. Somewhat different from the tranquil *drip-drip* of the fountain in the carp pond.

"He was looking for another Hainan," Gang observed.

On 1 April 2001, a Chinese jet interceptor, attempting to interdict and harass an American surveillance plane, collided with it. The Chinese pilot was killed. The wounded American plane was forced into an emergency landing on Hainan Island. The crew was detained. Prevarications, denunciations, remonstrations, explanations, reparations—the predictable trajectory of rhetoric and posturing. But a deeper damage was done: By the end, America, until then held in general esteem by most Chinese, now stood reviled. However multitudinous, vast, and varied, China always united if it felt threatened from outside. The circumstances were irrelevant. A Chinese pilot had been killed by the American military. This could be neither forgiven nor forgotten. Conveniently, from the point of view of the Department of Propaganda, the episode took place when the memory of Tiananmen Square was still fresh.

"Yes," Fa said, draining his glass. He wanted another scotch but thought it best to have his wits about him tomorrow. Gang was right—Han would not take his humiliation quietly. There would be fallout, radioactive snowflakes.

"So reckless," Fa said. "It was a different time in 2001. Now? In this climate, with all the world furious with us over the Lotus? You can push the Americans so far. Saddam Hussein learned that. It's one thing if there's an accident in the air, two planes colliding. But going after them on the high seas?" He was silent for a moment. "I wished

Admiral Zhang had been with me tonight in that room. With him beside me, I always felt confident. Well, Lo saw to *that*."

"I had a communication from Zhang. I was going to tell you earlier, but with everything going on. He's in hospital, in San Diego."

Fa frowned. "Is he . . . ?"

"He's all right. He took that pill that mimics renal failure."

"Yes, of course. I forgot."

"He has determined it will be necessary for him to remain in America. Easier to coordinate things with Beluga."

"And Operation Flourishing Vine—is it flourishing?"

"Preparations are nearly complete. Another few days. He was adamant that he will not give Beluga the signal to proceed without first getting your express order."

"Somewhat different from General Han!" Fa smiled. He stared forlornly at the ice cubes in his empty glass. "Did he give you an impression of confidence?"

"As you yourself said, this is not without risks."

" 'Hold out baits to entice the enemy. Feign disorder, and crush him.' "

"What would Sun-tzu make of our modern technology?"

"Oh," Fa said, "I think he would find that nothing essential had changed. Well, old friend, let's get some sleep."

"Do you want a pill?"

"What I would like, Gang, is to drink that entire bottle of whiskey. No, no pills tonight. Tonight? Look at the hour. It's today, already. I feel *old*, Gang."

Fa slept. For the first time in weeks, the nightmare did not come.

CHAPTER 25

Now Then, Jangpom

I t had been the weekend from hell. It was Sunday noon now, and Rogers Fancock had slept maybe five hours since Friday morning.

He'd declined Bletchin's offer to have a cot brought into his office. He felt it was undignified, sleeping on cots. And it was just the kind of detail that those incontinent numbskulls in the White House press office would leak in order to demonstrate how "serious" was the situation. Creating a spate of breathless stories about "the crisis atmosphere at the White House." *Not since the Cuban Missile Crisis . . .* Precisely the wrong way to handle it.

Instead he catnapped on the davenport. Dorothy sent in sandwiches—cucumber, pimiento, bacon, and peanut butter—along with thermoses of drinkable coffee, clean shirts, undershorts, and socks.

What in hell was Beijing thinking? First Strecker says he has actionable intelligence that the Chinese are going to try to kill the Dalai Lama. Then they go and deploy two frigates with every indication of hostile intent. And just as they're coming over the horizon, guns hot, suddenly it's all engines full stop.

Admiral Doggett said it was a test to see if the *Rumsfeld* would break off the exercise. Fancock chortled over the idea of a ship by that name "breaking off" anything except for the enemy's head. Not that there was anything amusing about dozens of U.S. and Chinese fighters circling overhead, hissing at each other like high-tech geese. The Chinese were still fuming over Hainan, which had been their own goddamned fault to begin with. Fancock had long since stopped bringing up the incident in meetings with the Chinese. What point was there? Rather insecure, the Chinese—and quick to perceive insult. Fancock called it PCSD: "post-colonial stress disorder."

But what *were* they thinking, with this *Rumsfeld* stunt? He mused on Barney's report about the power struggle going on at Zhongnanhai between Fa and the generals. Perhaps Fa had overruled the military and aborted the attack on the *Rumsfeld*. That would explain the sudden stand-down. But there was no knowing for sure.

Barney hadn't called back for hours now, which made Fancock uneasy. In his last call, he'd said he was in San Diego. Wouldn't say any more, even over the secure line. San Diego. Meanwhile the president was in a filthy mood, still in a lather over Fancock's refusal to vouchsafe the name of the Mephistopheles who had proposed putting His Holiness to sleep like some aged cocker spaniel.

Why is Bletchin taking so damned long getting—

"Sir?"

"Yes, Bletchin," Fancock said, horizontal upon the davenport, eyes remaining closed.

"I have His Holiness's secretary on the line."

"Ah. *Finally.*"

Fancock rose stiffly and shuffled over toward his desk. He had on an unbuttoned shirt, boxers, and knee socks, and yet there was still something formidable about him.

He sat. Took a deep breath, picked up the phone. His finger hovered above the button. "Bletchin, what's his *name?*"

"Jangpom Gadso Plingdam Renzimwangmo—"

Fancock scribbled. "*Enough*, Bletchin." He yawned. "What is the correct form of address?"

"They appear to incline toward informality, sir."

Fancock waved him away. He took another breath and punched the button on his phone.

"This is Rogers Fancock, director of national security at the White House in Washington. Do I have the honor of speaking with the Reverend—with the Honorable Jangpom Gadso?...Ah. Splendid. Splendid. And a good morning to you, sir. On behalf of the president of the United States, may I convey his most sincere and respectful wishes to His Holiness and to yourself? And his deepest regret about the news with regard to His Holiness's medical condition. We are all— He is? Ah. Well, I couldn't be more pleased to hear that...Yes...Yes, that's a wonderful way of looking at it. His Holiness is truly one of the most remarkable men of our time. Of all time. An inspiration. Um. Yes, to us all. Um. How's the food there, by the way? Hospital food can be pretty darned grim...Really? Well, I'm glad to hear that. And His Holiness's spirits?...No, I meant his *mood*...Yes? Wonderful, wonderful. Could use a bit of serenity myself. Yes. Now then, Jangpom...By all means, of course. It's actually *Rogers*—with an *s* at the end...Yes, it does sound rather like a last name, doesn't it? Used to get teased about it at school...I? Harvard, actually. Cambridge, but it's right next to Boston. Yes, in Massachusetts. Yes, Bunker Hill. How's that? Beacon Hill? Just down the road, really...Yes, lots of hills in old Massachusetts. Ha ha. Of course, nothing like the hills in *your* part of the world. No, I haven't. I've always wanted to go, but something always came up and...I hear it's just dazzling. Um. Now then, Jungpom, let me explain why I'm calling. Might I ask, is His Holiness feeling up to travel?...I see. I see...No, of course. He's been through the meat grinder, poor fellow. Well, the reason I'm asking is, the president and I were thinking that a change of scenery might be just the ticket. Lift his spirits.

Nothing against Cleveland, but you couldn't really call the views there, you know, sweeping or panoramic...Yes, wonderful doctors. Oh, some of the very best. Of course, No, Boston's got top doctors... Well here's what we had in mind. There's a wonderful place in the mountains...No, I'm afraid not. I assure you, Jangpom, we're trying our utmost best to get Beijing to turn around on that but they just— Yes, *very* stubborn. Now, Jong...Sorry...Jansang...No, you're pronouncing it perfectly...Rogers. That's it. Your English is wonderful. Couldn't be more impressed...No, I'm all in favor of prayers, but— Me? Episcopalian. But getting back to the reason I'm calling, what we had in mind was to move His Holiness to a lovely, quiet place in the mountains. Rather *like* Tibet. Certainly as close as we come to it here. Colorado. Um-hm. The Rocky Mountains. Not the Himalayas, but pretty gosh darned majestic, really...Um-hm. As it happens, our government has a first rate facility. Cheyenne Mountain...Yes, after the Indian tribe...Um-hm...No, no, it's not an Indian reservation. It's a facility. Been around forever. NORAD. It's an acronym. To be honest, I can never remember what it stands for, but it's right up there in the mountains, and you can't get more secure than that. His Holiness would have complete privacy. Um. So if you'd propose that to him, that would be just the ticket. Meantime why don't I get things teed up at my end so we can move quickly... Yes, well, not to sound gloomy, but under the circumstances I thought perhaps sooner rather than— So you'll— He's sleeping?... Um. Yes, of course. The medication. Jangpom, I don't mean to sound pushy, but would it be possible to nudge him awake just long enough to run our idea by him? He doesn't need to be awake for the move...I see. I see. All right...Yes, I'll be standing by. And, Jongpam, could I ask you to keep this just between ourselves? We don't want an entire circus...Of *course* the entourage can accompany him. Bring as many lamas as you'd like. There's lots of room for...Yes, I absolutely will give the president your regards...*And* your prayers, yes. And I'm sure I speak for him when I say he sends his prayers...

The president? Methodist, I believe, but he's very ecumenical, you know. Goes to all sorts of churches, synagogues . . . Sorry? Hold on, I want to write that down. Make sure I . . . Yes, go ahead . . . *Om. Man. E. Pad. Me. Hum.* Got it. And that would mean? . . . Jewel . . . Yes . . . Yes . . . Well, I think that's a lovely sentiment. Truly . . . lovely. Yes, I will pass it along to him. All right then, Jimjong, it's been wonderful talking with you. Good-bye . . . Yes, God bless you, too."

CHAPTER 26

OH, RANDOLPH!

I hope this isn't going to make things awkward between us!" Angel shouted from her office bathroom while reassembling herself.

Bird sat on the sofa of sin, mind swirling, drinking vodka.

"Oh, *God!*"

"What?" Bird said apprehensively. It had only been an hour. Surely she couldn't be pregnant already?

"My lips!"

"What's wrong with them?"

"They're chewed raw! You're an *animal!*"

"Sorry," he said.

"I don't mind. I'm a carnivore myself." Angel's head appeared from behind the bathroom door. "You don't have *herpes* or anything, do you?"

"No, Angel. I don't have herpes."

Her head disappeared again. "I usually ask before. But you were so *impetuous.*"

Bird took a large swig of vodka. "Angel, could we talk?"

"There are *so* many more things I'd rather do with you than talk, mister."

Bird poured himself another drink. He called out, "I'm not like this, you know."

"Like what?" It sounded as though she was applying lipstick.

"I mean, I don't go around forcing myself on women."

Angel emerged from the bathroom, her toilette complete. "Are we feeling guilty?"

"I've only done this once."

"Once?" Angel snorted. "I got the impression Minci was frigid—but once, in eight years of marriage? That must be some kind of record."

"Her name is Myndi. I meant—being unfaithful."

"The great circle of life. Lust, remorse, lust, remorse. Take it from a pro: Concentrate on the lust. It's *so* much more rewarding. Pour me one, would you?" She picked up the remote control and flicked on the TV.

"I thought we were going to talk," Bird said.

"I just want to hear about the East China Sea."

"Angel, I think it would be best if we didn't do this again."

"Didn't you enjoy it? That's weird. Nothing on CNN. Let's try Fox."

"No, it was amazing. Really. I..."

"Me, too. I haven't had an orgasm like that since Bush 43's first term. God I miss him."

She was sitting next to him on the sofa of sin, her thigh against his. He smelled her perfume.

"Nothing on Fox either. That *is* interesting."

"I don't want to hurt your feelings, but I am married."

"Darling," Angel said, "trust Momma. It's *all* going to be fine." . She reached over with her hand and began to walk her fingers up his leg. "'The itsy-bitsy *spider* fell down the water*spout*.' Barry loves it when I do that."

"Uh, maybe not do that."

"Where did she get the name, Myndi? Lord & Taylor?"

"Angel, could you not talk about my wife that way."

"Teas-ing. Does she have a sister named Muffy?"

"Angel."

"So where do you think *Myndi* is right now?"

"How should I know?"

"No further questions, Your Honor."

"She's training. She made the team, you know."

"Yes, you said. I was so relieved. It was like this enormous *weight* being taken off me. I'd been so worried."

"That's not very nice."

"Darling, when did I ever claim I was nice? What about that trainer of hers you're always blowing on about?"

"Sam? Why?"

"You are aware of the statistics?"

"What statistics?"

"Incidence of extramarital intercourse between equestriennes and their trainers. They did this huge study. I think I read it in *Forbes*. Something like over seventy percent. Or eighty."

"*Angel.*"

"Google if you don't believe me. Didn't it ever strike you as curious that wealthy men with younger, trophy wives hire gay trainers for them?"

"I'm not wealthy, and she and I are the same age, so I wasn't really focused on that. And where did you *learn* all this?"

"Sweetheart," Angel said, "do you think I've been in a convent all these years?"

"No. Hardly."

"Did I strike a nerve? Need novocaine? I actually do know people in Virginia and Maryland. There are these agencies that specialize in gay trainers. Apparently the best ones are English. Big surprise, there. So your Sam, is he gay?"

"I haven't asked. I don't think so. No."

"Is he good-looking?"

"Angel. I don't *know*. I suppose. He doesn't look like the Elephant Man or anything. Listen, just because in a moment of weakness I—"

"Is that what it was?"

"You have no reason—or right—to imply that Myndi and Sam are—"

"Doing the woolly deed?" Angel took Bird's glass out of his hand and put it on the table. "Darling, I couldn't care less what those two are doing in the hayloft. I just don't want *you* to end up being the chump." She was twirling a strand of his hair in her finger. "As for your moment of weakness, I don't remember you being particularly...weak."

Her skirt rode up, revealing a lacy fringe of thigh-high stocking.

"Well, well." Angel smiled. "And what do we have here?"

And so began Moment of Weakness, Part 2.

"Oh, Bird. Bird. *Bird*."

She pulled away from him.

"Darling," she said, breathing heavily. "Do you think we might come up with a different *nom d'amour* for you?"

Bird, also breathing heavily at this point, said, "Is something wrong with my name?"

"No, darling," she said, tracing a line across his lips with a fingernail. "It's a *sweet* name. But I like to...*express* myself when I'm in the arms of Eros. And shrieking 'Oh, Bird, oh, Bird, oh, Bird' doesn't...It just sounds a little..."

"All right," Bird said, impatient to get back to business, "call me Walter if you want."

"Walter? Um. Sounds...Cronkite-y."

Bird lay back on the sofa. "Then call me Ishmael. Whatever."

Angel sidled up against him. "Do you know what I'd *like* to call you?"

"No idea."

"*Randolph.*"

Bird stared. "Why would you want to call me Randolph?"

"I don't know. I've always thought it was such a hot name." She was playing with his earlobe now. "Only when we're doing it. I wouldn't call you that in front of the staff."

"Good idea. It could only confuse them."

"Do you like it?"

"I don't really have an opinion on it. But if it makes you happy . . ."

"Let's take it out for a spin, shall we?"

Back to business. Within moments Bird heard, "Mmm. *Oh. Yes, darling. Oh. Ohhhh. Yes, Randolph, yes!*"

SEVERAL PLEASANT if perplexing hours later, the defense lobbyist formerly known as Bird was in the passenger seat of a cab on the way back across the Potomac to the Military-Industrial Duplex.

Angel was certainly a more complex package than he had imagined. *Randolph?* God knows where that came from. What other surprises lurked ahead? Would he soon be dressing up as General Patton? And yet Bird felt more relaxed and pleasant than he had in a long time.

The message light was blinking. Twelve new ones. He was about to hit the Play button, and then thought no. Whatever the world wanted from him, it could wait until tomorrow.

He took a long, hot shower and soaped off the sin.

He was walking back to the kitchen when the phone rang. It was after 1:00 a.m. He felt the little barbed hook of guilt. *No, don't pick up.* He wasn't confident that his mendacity was up to the job. He would need to practice. He knew this much: after eight years of marriage a wife possessed better sonar than a submarine. One *pinggg* and you were dead in the water.

He glanced at the caller ID. Whew. He picked up.

"Randolph speaking," he said.

"You need to come back here."

Seven times and she wanted more? The woman was insatiable.

"Baby, I'm limp. I need my sleep."

"Turn on the TV. Be here in an hour." Angel hung up.

Bird picked up the remote control and clicked On.

A news correspondent was talking, but Bird's eyes went to the bottom of the screen:

DALAI LAMA DIES IN CLEVELAND

Bird heard the flow of words coming from the TV reporter but was unable to process them. The hospital was behind him. A crowd had gathered. The people held candles. The correspondent kept chattering, but Bird didn't want words. Wasn't interested in words. He pressed the Mute button and watched.

He stood in front of the TV, towel around his waist. The Washington Mall lay before him, everything very still. The only motion was the correspondent's lips and the candles flickering in the distance behind him. Bird felt a sadness descending on him that he couldn't explain. The man whose death had just been announced had been just a piece in a cynical game of chess. So he was at a loss to understand why he felt so bereft, standing there, stock-still, frozen in a private moment of silence.

The Dalai Lama's face came on the screen, the dates of his birth and death beneath. He was smiling, as though he were about to tell a slightly naughty joke.

Bird felt an inexplicable but profound sense of loss that he had never met the Dalai Lama. He was pleased that the TV people had selected this particular photograph, a favorite of Bird's. It was so eloquent of the Dalai Lama's humanity—a man who could laugh after everything he had been through—escaping assassination, fleeing his native soil, watching it fall to invaders and occupiers—all the hardships, sorrows, and deprivations, yet still somehow "a fellow of infinite jest." Bird remembered a line from one of the hundreds of articles he had read: "He giggles a lot."

What a good epitaph it was. And so the great soul was gone out of the world now and had taken his giggles with him. Bird felt the tears trickling down his cheeks. *Whoa*, he thought, *where are these coming from?*

CHAPTER 27

The Fog Machine of War

O nly at the most trying of times did Rogers P. Fancock utter
four-letter words—and then only mentally, to himself.

This delicacy of manner he had inherited, along with a substantial sum of money, from his father, Hancock P. Fancock. By way of compensation, Fancock indulged in frequent usage of nonscatological, blasphemous expostulations.

But now, Monday morning, 2:00 a.m., as the weekend from hell was segueing into what looked to be a week from hell, the s——, f——, and even the truly vulgar c—— words were cropping up in Fancock's mind.

Where the f—— was Strecker, goddamn it? And why wasn't he answering his f——ing cell phone?

"What *is* it, Bletchin?"

"Sorry, sir, but it's Mr. Strecker on the secure line, and I know you've been trying to reach him."

"Thank *God*," Fancock muttered, reaching for the phone. "Goddamn it, Barney, I've been calling you for hours. Where in blazes have you been? Why haven't you—"

"Rog. Rog. Trust me. I've been busier'n a one-legged Cajun in an ass-kicking contest."

"No, no homey metaphors just now, thank you. Are you in Cleveland? *Tell* me you're in Cleveland."

Barney whispered. "San Diego. But *shhh* about that."

"San Diego? But what about *Cleveland?*"

"Rog, calm down. Don't worry. My peeps are in Cleveland. They got the situation covered. Meanwhile, did I hear that you were trying to get him moved to *NORAD?*" Barney laughed. "Who in hell came up with that?"

"I'd rather not say."

"The Big Guy? God *save* the United States of America."

"When I told the president that I was in receipt of actionable intelligence that the Chinese were going to try to kill him, he went...Suffice to say he was adamant that we move him to a secure federal facility. And since it didn't seem quite right to put him in a supermax prison or Guantánamo..." Fancock sighed. "I ran it past His Holiness's person, Jingjam. But His Holiness was asleep. They were going to ask him when he woke up. I gather he never did. Wake up, that is. Well, at least he went in his sleep, God rest him. Barn, tell me that he died of natural causes. Please tell me that. Barn?"

"Well," Barney said in what struck Fancock as an inappropriately frisky tone, "we won't know that until we get the autopsy, will we?"

"Oh, Barn. I haven't slept since last week. I'm an old man. I don't have the energy to drag this out of you with hooks. The TV says he slipped away quietly, peacefully. Tell me this is true."

"He had cancer, Rog. Tumors on the brain like birdshot. Something like that would tend to have a deleterious effect on your life expectancy."

"Why are you talking in this elliptical fashion?"

"You recall teaching a seminar on exit strategies?"

"What on earth does that have to do with this?"

"This is all about exit strategy, Obi Wan. That chapter in your book? 'Tactical Ambiguity,' about how to use chaos and confusion as a cloak? You had that real nice term for it, 'The Fog Machine of War.' Well, we're going to generate us a little *fog* in Cleveland, Ohio."

"Now hold on, Barney. Steady on. Things are getting sticky. Admiral Doggett called an hour ago. The PLA is mobilizing ground forces in Tibet. And the Taiwan Strait looks like Broadway on Saturday night."

"Then all the more reason for fog. Remember Rumsfeld's maxim? 'If you can't solve a problem, make it bigger'?"

"Yes, I remember that one. We're not using that playbook."

"Rog—do I have the papal blessing?"

Fancock listened to the ticking of the grandfather clock in his office.

"Rog? You there? I know you're tired, but don't fall asleep on me. I'm waiting for my execute order."

"The Big Guy is very nervous about all this, Barn."

"He damn well should be," Barney said. "He's the President of the United States of America. Are you telling me he's curled up in a fetal position under his desk in the Oval Office, with his thumb in his mouth?"

"It's not *quite* that bad, but he does have reservations."

"Reservations." Barney snorted. "You got a copy of Shakespeare in your office there?"

"Of course. Why?"

"Find the 'Once more unto the breach' speech from *Henry the Fifth* and go in there and read it to him. That'll put the lead back in his pencil."

Fancock sighed. "Very well, Barn. You have authorization to proceed."

"Thank you. We'll get this right for you, Rog. Don't you worry. You were always such a tough grader. *Still* can't believe you gave me a B on my thesis."

"I'm hoping for an A on this one, Barn."

"You and me both, Professor. Failure is not an option." Barney laughed. "Actually, failure is always an option. But here goes nothing."

"That's so reassuring."

CHAPTER 28

You Really Are a Thoroughgoing
Bastard, Aren't You?

President Fa entered. The Politburo Standing Committee neither stood nor nodded in greeting. It was chilly inside the
room, and it wasn't the air-conditioning. But then Fa hadn't been
expecting a show of solidarity or collegiality—no, not this morning.
The ever-vigilant Gang had given him all the latest intelligence and
gossip. Fa teased him, "You are my *éminence jaune.*"

So here was where things stood: On his return from Lhasa, Minister Lo had gone directly to the Guowuyuan, the State Council,
rather than to the Standing Committee, to make his report on the
situation in the Tibetan Autonomous Region. This was not strictly
insubordinate, but there was a strong whiff of impertinence to it.

Gang had further learned that Lo had preemptively lobbied the
State Council against permitting the Lotus's body to be brought
back to the land of his ancestors for stupa burial. Indeed, Lo had told
the council that MSS agents within the Tibetan's circle were "issu-
ing instructions to their people back home to prepare for traditional
holy war."

Gang and Fa found the phraseology (*holy war*) revealing—almost
amusing. Both of them were well familiar with Tibetan Buddhist

terminology, and neither could recall ever coming upon the phrase *holy war.* No, this was the coinage of another, very different, religion. In his zeal and haste, Minister Lo appeared to have done some cutting and pasting.

As for that other mischief-maker, General Han: Immediately following his humiliation over the thwarted naval incident, he had convened an emergency plenary meeting of the Central Military Committee. Han had expressed to his generals and admirals that he had the "gravest reservations" about President Fa's handling of the incident. Moreover, he had wondered—out loud—whether the leadership was "up to the great tasks before us." Having openly questioned the president's judgment, he proceeded—without even consulting Zhongnanhai—to raise the Readiness Status of all PLA forces in Chengdu Military Region (Tibet) from Level 3 to Level 2. While this was formally within his authority at a time of "national emergency," it would have been polite, to say the least, for him to inform China's president and general secretary of the Chinese Communist Party.

"At least in Tibet he can't use ships," Gang observed.

"I wouldn't put it past him to try," Fa said.

He did not look well, Fa. The dream was back; again his bed was a trapdoor into a basement of horrors. He'd lost more weight. Gang couldn't bring himself to tell Fa about the cruel jibe making the rounds of the Central Committee's secretariat: *Perhaps President Fa also has a pheochromocytoma!* Gang fumed. *Very amusing! And in which ministry did this clever jest originate? Let me guess.* There was a subdirectorate at MSS whose task was to come up with this sort of thing; typically, however, the target of ridicule was not the president of the country.

Gang and Madam Fa did what they could to stop the president's caloric hemorrhaging, plying him with American-style "milk shakes" and "junk food." Gang quietly dispatched people to McDonald's and Burger King and KFC and those other temples of American cardiovascular worship. They brought back soggy, grease-soaked bags of revolting, life-annihilating foods; revolting, perhaps, but gobbling it down himself, Gang admitted, quite delicious. He became a regular sharer in these presidential force-feeding repasts, in the process gaining ten pounds. His suits were beginning to pinch.

"Look at us, Comrade," Gang said to Fa one night as they passed in front of a mirror in the Great Hall of the People on their way into a banquet in honor of a delegation from Iran that had come to buy missiles with which to threaten American ships in the Persian Gulf.

Fa and Gang winced at their reflections—the one gaunt, the other inflated like a balloon—and hurried down the corridor to toast the warm relations between Beijing and Tehran. Between Gang's inhalation of American carbohydrates and Fa's chain-smoking and pill-taking, the leadership of China could not be said to be in robust condition.

"Good morning, Comrades," Fa began.

The response was sullen and perfunctory. It was not a morning for smiles.

The state news agency Xinhua had issued a frosty two-paragraph bulletin acknowledging the passing of the "self-proclaimed Buddha reincarnation Tenzin Gyatso in Ohio, USA." It reasserted China's authority over the "management of living Buddha reincarnation." (Translation: We'll be picking the next Dalai Lama, thanks very much.) And in case there was any doubt in anyone's mind as to whether the remains would be returning to Lhasa for stupa burial: "The recent declaration of the Sanitary Subcommittee of the Central Directorate for the TAR with respect to the matter of repatriation remains in effect." (Translation: Not a Chinaman's chance.)

Xinhua had issued the statement on the authority of the deputy minister for Propaganda and Thought Work. Zhongnanhai had not been asked to approve the wording. This went beyond casual negligence. Fa bristled but remembered Admiral Zhang's admonition: Pick your own ground for battle, not the enemy's.

"I spoke this morning with the American president," Fa began.

The announcement caught the committee by surprise. All eyes turned to Fa, then caromed around the table like billiard balls. Fa tracked the glances as clues to who had been in cabal with whom.

"Ah? Who initiated the call?" Lo asked. He added with a smirk, "If I may ask."

"You *have* asked. And since you do, I will tell you that it was *he* who requested the call. But"—Fa smiled—"I don't suppose I need to tell you, Lo, what he was calling about. Since undoubtedly you were listening in."

Gang, hearing this through his headphones, tensed. *Oh, Comrade, be careful, please.*

The room went quiet. Then Fa said heartily, "But you would be a poor minister of security if you *didn't* listen in, wouldn't you? Eh?"

Nervous laughter. Lo smiled.

"Well, Comrades," Fa went on, "you will not be surprised to hear that the president was not calling about our disagreement over our steel exports. No..." Fa's voice trailed off. Gang had given him half a stay-awake pill—*after* he'd spoken with the American president. "...It was the issue of the Lotus's remains. Speaking of which, I see from Xinhua this morning that the issue has apparently *already* been settled. Well, I like to keep up with the news. Yes, yes. One wants to be informed. Especially when one is theoretically in charge."

A darting of averting eyeballs.

Lo leaped in. "I trust, Comrade, that you told the American president that this is our business, and none of his."

Gang thought, *Comrade Minister Lo is animated this morning. Did he have a stay-awake pill, too?*

"I did not use those exact words," Fa said. "But then a president and general secretary does not have the luxury of bluntness. Now that you bring up the subject, however, you make me think how refreshing it would be to look someone right in the eye—as I am you, now, here—and say, 'You really are a thoroughgoing bastard, aren't you?'"

The room froze. Gang held his breath.

"Imagine being able to say *that!*" Fa laughed. "How liberating that would be! Don't you agree, Comrade?"

Lo, caught off balance, stared coldly, jaw muscles working. He recovered, and now he laughed as well, perhaps a bit too energetically. "Yes, Comrade. Yes, I see exactly what you are saying. It would be agreeable indeed to tell the American president what a real bastard he is."

Great laughter.

"Perhaps," Fa said, "after my duties as servant of the people and the party are concluded, I will spend my retirement going around telling people what I truly think of them. Yes, that is something I could look forward to. But I might end up seeming like one of those people who have that condition where you can't control yourself and shout, 'You look like a chicken!' Or 'Hey, why don't you lick my balls?'"

Awkward laughter.

"However," Fa said, "as long as I continue to hold these positions of great responsibility, I must comport myself appropriately. And now I will tell you all candidly that the American president expressed deep concern. His manner was correct and respectful. Our conversation was cordial. He made no request or petition on behalf of the Tibetan. But he said that the matter has troubling *shi.* He said, 'This business could take on a life of its own.' Those were his exact words."

"There you have it, Comrades," General Han said. "The so-called most powerful man on earth, trembling like a girl!"

Nervous laughter.

Fa continued. "I discerned no trembling, Comrade. He told me that he will make every effort not to take sides in this business."

"'Every effort'?" Lo laughed. "Well, Comrades, then we have

nothing to worry about, do we? The most powerful man in the world will make 'every effort'! How can he fail?"

Laughter.

"He pointed out to me," Fa continued once the laughter had subsided, "that his power, unlike our own, is limited. He expects that there will be mischief in their Congress. You know what a hive of bees that can be. Well," he said, taking a piece of paper from his leather portfolio, "why don't I read you the statement that he will make this afternoon, at the White House?"

Fa looked up from the paper and said with an air of bemusement, "I'll spare you the flower petals they sprinkled over the top of it. He goes on for a bit about what a sweet old man was the Lotus. I don't suppose you want to hear *that*. Here's the meat of it: 'The United States earnestly hopes that the interested parties will resolve this matter in an atmosphere of calmness, dignity, and mutual respect worthy of His Late Holiness, the Dalai Lama.'"

"Oh, fuck *that*," General Han said.

"Well," Fa said, leaning back in his chair, "so much for dignity."

Han seethed. "The Americans have been stirring this shitpot all along! Spreading lies about how we tried to poison the old dog! And now they put on this mask of piety, like some old woman in a temple, lighting incense sticks, mewling, 'Oh, oh, let us all be *respectful* to one another. As *he* was.' I say fuck the American president. Fuck them all."

Gang heard murmurs of assent, the soft thumping of palms on the table. Though afraid for his president, he could not help but be amused by General Han's mimickry of a squeaky-voiced old woman in a temple. Had he practiced this? *Oh, to put it on YouTube.*

When the murmuring had died down, Fa said calmly, "Are you proposing to fuck all Americans, General? That will take some time. There are over three hundred million of them now."

"Don't play the fool with me, Comrade!" Han shot back. "You're in no position to."

The room went quiet.

So, Gang thought, *now it's out in the open: You are weak, and we have no confidence in you.*

Lo put his hand on Han's forearm. "Easy now, Comrade General. Our dear Comrade President Fa was only attempting to be witty. And that is not something that comes naturally to him. But let's at least give him credit for trying."

Laughter.

"I thank you for the compliment," Fa said. "You are correct, as always. Wit is a mountaintop beyond my reach. But as to the general's point—and I am most interested in this—are you saying that we now know for a certain *fact* that the poisoning accusations were a propaganda operation by the Americans?"

"It is... Yes, Comrade President," Lo said, "This can now be confirmed. CIA."

Gang caught the hesitancy. Fa caught it, too.

"Well, Comrade," Fa said gravely, "if that is the case, then our good General Han is absolutely correct. We must look with disdain on these silky lies of theirs. Yes. But in diplomacy, as we all know, the wise thing is to allow the enemy to believe that he has deceived you. Surely Sun-tzu has something in his book about that," Fa added with a chuckle. "So, Comrades, we are *not* deceived. But let us all frankly admit that this business is going to be unpleasant. In the days ahead, we will hear harsh things said about our beloved China. Harsh things. I think they will run out of straw, making so many effigies of me. But as our general minister of defense would say, 'Fuck them all.'"

Gang heard the tension go out of the room, the laughter, and breathed.

BACK IN THE PRESIDENTIAL bathroom, faucets and showers flowing, Fa and Gang sat pensively. Gang silently gorged on french fries from a McDonald's bag. Fa smoked. It was too early for whiskey. Too bad. Fa would have liked a whiskey.

"You caught the lie about the CIA?" Fa said, breaking the silence.

"Um," Gang said, wiping french fry grease from his lips. "Yes. And wouldn't you know that I still haven't received the so-called transcript of that supposed conversation between the lama and CIA agent Mike. I've asked them for it three times."

"What excuse do they give?"

"They're 'looking for it.' It seems to have been misplaced."

They sat awhile longer in silence, listening to the rush of water.

"All right then," Fa said. "It's time. Tell Mankind Is Red to start watering the vine."

Gang located a remaining french fry and ate it, nodding.

"Let's hope—" Fa interrupted himself and smiled. "Do you know, Gang, I almost said, 'Let's *pray*'? Funny. Let us *hope* that the vine flourishes. Because if it does not, we will wither along with it."

Gang grinned. "In that case then, perhaps we should pray."

Fa smiled. "Why don't you find us a good Tibetan prayer?" He stood and began to shut off the faucets. "But when we say this prayer, we shall have to turn these up very loudly. Can't you see Lo's face as he listens to us *chanting*?"

And at this the two men laughed.

CHAPTER 29

PINGGG

Friday night at Upkeep, and Bird and Myndi were in the kitchen attending to the quiet ritual of chopping things for dinner.

"Oh, my gosh," Bird suddenly declared in mid-carrot-chop, "I never asked you how the *EQ* shoot went."

"No, you didn't."

"I'm sorry, baby. That was so insensitive of me. With all this stuff going on...But that's no excuse."

Myndi looked at him.

"So? How did it go?"

"They were disappointed that you weren't here," she said, staring back down at her shallots.

"I'm sorry. What can I say?"

"Not much, frankly, at this point. It doesn't matter." (Translation: It matters.)

"Babe, you're the star of this show. I'm just...But okay, I take ownership of my assholeness in this regard. Absolutely." Pause. "Other than that did it go okay?"

"I guess."

"You sound kind of down."

"I'm fine."

"Well, I can't wait to see how it turns out. I bet it's going to be fabulous. What outfits did you wear?"

"I must have changed seven or eight times. They sent two stylists."

"Two? Wow." Bird could not think of anything more reaffirming to add. He leaned over and gave her a husbandly peck on the cheek. "Bet you looked like a million bucks. When's it come out?"

Myndi went on chopping. "Well, Walter, the name of the magazine is *EQ*, which stands for *Equestrian Quarterly*, so I would imagine next quarter."

"Babe. You sound depressed. Is everything okay?"

Myndi put down her knife. "All this fuss and feathers about the Dalai Lama and where to bury him. I know you've been in some bunker somewhere, but maybe you've *heard* something about it?"

"Yes, I...oh, so he finally died, did he? Poor old thing. Well, I guess he must have died if they're trying to figure out where to bury him."

"Yes, Walter, he died. And the Tibetans are having a thing because China won't let them bury him in Lhasa. Who cares?"

"Well, I imagine they'll sort it all out. But is this what's got you down?"

"The Tang Cup, Walter."

"Yes?"

"It's six weeks away."

"That's great. Are you excited?"

"I *was* excited."

" 'Was'?"

"Walter, this idiotic lama business could screw everything up for me. The *EQ* reporter told me that the U.S. might not send a team if things deteriorate."

Bird tried to conjure words of empathy and indignation, but they bounced on his tongue like a fumbled football.

"Oh, dear," Bird finally managed.

"Oh, Walter," Myndi said, biting her lip. "I've worked so *hard* for this."

"I know you have, darling," Bird said. He felt as if he were hallucinating. "But I'm sure it'll blow over. These things always do."

Myndi went back to her chopping. "Have you seen the TV? There are *mobs* in front of the Chinese embassy in Washington."

"Really? No, I've been in the bunker. Mobs, huh? Guess I'll avoid Connecticut Avenue and Kalorama."

"And that *actor*, Branford Dane. Spare me Hollywood Buddhists."

"Is he in a new movie or something?"

"You can't turn on the TV without seeing him. Who is *he* to issue demands to the Chinese government? I don't even like his movies. It's just a way of getting his name out there. Actors. I *despise* them."

"Yes." Bird nodded. "Hard to imagine Clark Gable or Gary Cooper doing that sort of thing. How's Harry?"

"Harry?" Myndi said. She stopped chopping. "Fine. Why?"

"I've been thinking. I've been kind of judgmental. And not very nice. About him wanting to help you out with the financing."

Myndi looked at him strangely. "I don't really know what to say to that, Walter. You weren't just 'not very nice.' You were totally rude. *Beyond* rude."

Bird thought, *So here are the wages of sin: having to apologize to the cuckolded wife for not liking her asshole rich friend. With whom she may or may not be sleeping. You made your bed, pal. Suck it up: sheets, mattress, and pillow.*

"Yes," Bird said. "I now realize that. And I'm sorry."

"That scene at the club," she said, "when you got hammered and carried on about that horrible movie. I've never been so embarrassed."

"Yes," Bird said. "Well, I certainly feel rotten about it, too. Do you think if I dropped Harry an e-mail...?"

Myndi put down her knife and looked at him. "Walter, why are you...What's *with* you all of a sudden?"

Pinggg.

"Walter?"

"Yes, Myn?"

"Have you been going to AA?"

Bird smiled sheepishly. Bit his lower lip. Nodded. "I guess there's no keeping secrets from you, is there, darling? Yes. Yes, I have."

"Oh, Walter. Thank you."

"Turns out there's a regular meeting right around the corner from my office on K. So I can pop in almost anytime."

"Walter. You don't know how glad that makes me."

Bird shrugged.

"No. Listen to me. I'm *proud* of you."

"Well, it was you, darling, who suggested it in the first place. So you should really be proud of yourself."

"Walter?" she said, suddenly in a very different tone.

"Yes, darling?"

"If you're going to AA meetings, why are you drinking an old-fashioned?"

Aaaa-oooo-gah! Aaaaa-oooo-gah! Dive! Dive!

"Oh, *this?*"

"Yes, Walter. *That.*"

"They said it was all right to have one or two. On the weekend. But absolutely no driving. And no references to *Equus*. Ha ha."

"They told you that, at AA?"

"Um-hm."

"That it's all right to drink on weekends?"

"In moderation. But no operating heavy machinery."

"I've never heard of AA advocating anything like that."

"Well," Bird said, "maybe I was reading between the lines. Want me to do the chicken?"

"Walter, talk to me. You're going to AA and you're drinking bourbon. This is not processing for me."

"Speaking of processing, where's the Cuisinart?"

"Walter!"

"Aw, baby, come on, it's not like I'm a falling-down drunk."

"You were that night at the club."

"Okay, aside from that one night at the club. One of the things I learned at AA is that I'm what they call a high-functioning alcoholic. And high-earning!" He grinned. "This project I've been working on? I think we're going to have a very nice Christmas this year. How about we go away? St. Barts? Virgin Islands? Someplace where you could wear one of those thongy things?"

"I just don't know about you, Walter. Sometimes I think I do, and then you go and do something and I feel I'm back to square one."

Bird wondered if this, too, was something for which he should apologize. *Why not?*

"I take ownership of that," he said manfully. "Yes. I will try to be more figure-outable from here on. Where are you going?"

"Upstairs."

"What about dinner?"

"I'm not hungry."

Should he apologize for this, too?

No. Enough with the prostration. But should he take this opportunity to fix himself another old-fashioned? Yes!

An hour later he was in the den watching footage of angry crowds burning effigies outside various Chinese embassies around the world when Myndi entered the room.

"Hi," he said.

"I didn't mean to be a bitch. Sorry."

"Oh, no big deal. Come sit."

She sat on the arm of his chair. She looked at the drink in Bird's hand. "Is that your first drink, Walter?"

"Myn. Cease-fire."

She shook her head in the manner of a wife inured to disappointment. "Can we at least watch something other than *that*?"

"Absolutely." Bird channel-surfed. Several clicks later, Angel's face came on the screen, a most unwelcome development. He pressed the Channel Up button quickly, but Myndi said, "No, go back."

"I thought you didn't like her."

"I hate her. But she's funny, in an awful sort of way."

Bird channeled back down. The remote felt like a hand grenade with the pin pulled.

"Actually, Chris," Angel was saying, "there's a whole *range* of things the U.S. government can do to put pressure on Beijing over this."

"Like what?"

"Student visas. There's an area where we can exert great pressure on Beijing. You do know that the Chinese are complete snobs when it comes to American education. Just the other day, the chairman of the China Development Bank announced—he actually announced it—that from now on they were only going to give internships to Chinese with degrees from Harvard or MIT." Angel snorted majestically. "*There's* Chinese Communism for you." She laughed. "Hear that sound? That's Chairman Mao rotating in his grave. Another area where we can put pressure on them? Sports."

Myndi said, "I *so* hate her."

CHAPTER 30

HOW MANY HELLS HAVE
WE BEEN THROUGH TOGETHER?

C aught you on *Hardball* Friday," Bird said.
"Mm."

It was late Monday night. They were snuggled in bed. Angel was having her very first sleepover at the Military-Industrial Duplex. Her son, Barry, was off at his first sleepaway camp, where, Bird mused, the counselors probably read to the kids at bedtime from the works of Ayn Rand.

It was going on midnight, after many pleasant hours of what the late President Nixon used to call "fornicating." The bedroom air had been serially rent with cries and moans of *"Oh, Randolph!"* Bird's curiosity over the provenance of this bizarre sobriquet was fast approaching the point of need-to-know. But for the moment there was a more pressing matter. He waited until Angel's system was awash in endorphins.

"Ange," he said, "I was wondering..."

"Mm?"

"Would you do me a favor?"

"Mm." Angel brushed a tangle of blond hair from her face so she could see him.

"Could you lay off the bit about how the U.S. ought to cancel sports events?"

"Why?" Her voice was dreamy with aftersex.

"No special reason. Just for me?"

Angel did the fingernail thing across his lips. "But, darling, you always get so cross with me when I advocate nuclear war. What's the big deal with scrubbing a few soccer matches?"

"Oh, I don't know. Just seems kind of unfair to take it out on the athletes. Not their fault. And all that training they do."

"War is hell, darling," Angel purred. "Is there more champagne for Momma?"

Bird toddled off naked and returned with two glasses full of expensive French bubbles. He slipped back under the duvet. He sat for a moment, paralyzed by the trigonometry requisite for simultaneous mendacity with wife and lover. This was a higher—or lower—math than he had heretofore attempted.

"Okay," he said, flummoxed. "Truth time."

"Um," Angel said, "not sure I like the sound of *that*."

"Remember I told you about Myndi making the U.S. team?"

"Um. Yes. And how *proud* of her you were."

"Ange. Come on. Remember the Tang Cup? The horse thing, in Xi'an? Xi'an, *China*?"

"Uh-huh."

"It's in six weeks."

"How time flies."

"Myndi's completely freaking out that it's going to get canceled, because of all this."

"Um. That *would* be a tragedy."

"*Ange.*"

"Yes, darling?"

"If it gets canceled...if my name comes out in connection with all this...to say nothing of coming out in connection with you..."

"What's that supposed to mean?"

"Hello? She's my wife."

Angel was doodling on his chest with a fingernail. "It must be wonderful"—she smiled—"being so happily married."

"All I'm asking is just not to screw up my marriage."

Angel began to laugh.

"What?" Bird said.

"'Please don't screw up my marriage'? Did you really just say that to me? In your bed? After three hours of epic sex?"

"Fair enough. Let me rephrase . . ."

"No." Angel put a finger to his lips. "It's perfect. Leave it."

Bird lay there cursing himself. As his lips parted to improvise some apology, hers closed in on them. His relief was as acute as the pleasure. Apparently he was forgiven. Soon the air was rent with cries of "Randolph!" No, this was not the time to ask. Let it go. Sometime after one o'clock, Eros did the handoff to Morpheus.

Bird woke, thirsty. Looked at the clock—4:33 a.m. How precise, our digital age. No longer can we say, *It must have been sometime after four, anyway.*

He reached over for Angel, but her side of the bed was empty. There was a faint light coming from the kitchen. He rose and padded in.

She was at the counter, laptop open before her, bathing her in weird bluish light. She had on one of his shirts, unbuttoned. She looked so lovely. Was that *his* laptop?

"Whatcha doing?" He yawned.

"Reading."

"It's late. Come back to bed. Randolph is lonely."

No answer.

"Any news?" he said.

He went over and stood behind her. Peered at the screen. It didn't look like a website. He blinked, wiped sleep gunk from his eyes.

With a grunt of stifled pain, Turk tightened the tourniquet around his thigh. Through gritted teeth, he said to Gomez, "The timer's set for 0130 hours. When those muons start activating, everything within five miles of here is going to be Sayonara City. Take the men and get out of here."

"Major!" Gomez shouted above the bom-bom-bom *of the Kalashnikovs, bullets zipping past their heads. "We can carry you!"*

"That's an order, soldier!" Turk looked into Gomez's dark Latino irises. "Ramon—how many hells have we been through together, you and me?"

"Too many, Major," returned the dolorous reply.

Turk winked. "Then what's one more?"

Gomez felt the lump rise in his throat like a mole burrowing toward the surface. His eyes flooded with lava-hot tears.

"Get out of here," Turk commanded. "Go on."

Gomez nodded. He began to crawl toward the edge of the bomb crater, where Mac and Dex and Slug huddled, lobbing grenades at their attackers.

"Ramon!" Turk called out.

"Yes, Major?"

"Tell Betty that I . . . tell her . . . tell that bitch she's a sorry-ass excuse for a warrant officer." He grinned. "You tell her that."

A smile crept across Gomez's blood-splattered face. His right hand slowly rose to his forehead as he saluted the man he called "Major," perhaps for the last time.

"Bird," Angel said, "what *is* this?"

Bird reached over and folded the lid of the laptop shut. "Reading other people's laptops? Ange, really."

"I wasn't *prying*. I woke up. It was lying here on the counter. I was going to check and see if there were any developments. *This* was on the screen. I didn't go rummaging through your hard drive. Is this your . . . novel?"

"No. It's a memo to my accountant about my taxes. Yes it's my novel."

"This muon thing, that's set to go off at 0130 hours?"

Oops. "What about it?"

"Did you get that from Project Taurus?"

"Well, sort of."

"But it's top secret."

"Extremely top secret."

"And you're putting it in a novel? Is Chick Devlin going to be happy about this? Never mind Chick. Is the U.S. government going to be happy about this?"

"I'm not going to publish it until...after."

"After what?"

"The *Times* story. By your Mr. Tierney. The one you sicced on me."

Angel frowned. "What does *he* know about Taurus?"

"He was going to expose Pan-Pacific Solutions. Which wouldn't have done me any good. Or you. Or your institute for perpetual war. So I tossed him a red herring. Taurus. He was more interested in that than another sleazy Washington lobbyist story."

"Red herring? Bird. You fed him a two-thousand-pound tuna."

"I called Chick. To give him a heads-up."

"And was he thrilled when you told him that you'd blown his top-secret project—to a newspaper reporter?"

"Initially? No, I wouldn't describe him as the happiest camper in Missile Gap, Alabama. But when great minds get together, great things result. With a little luck, everyone'll come out a winner."

Angel shook her head. "You're riding the tiger. No, you're holding onto its tail. Better not let go."

Bird yearned to tell Angel that the muons were *his* invention; that any day now, the *Times* would be informing the world that the United States was working on a spectacular new weapon that he—novelist Walter Bird McIntyre—had himself devised. But a cautionary voice whispered, *Um, no.*

"So," he said, "what did you think?"

"Think about what?" Angel seemed a little dazed. Well, it was late. Indeed, there was the dawn's first light rising blue and orange behind the Capitol Building.

"Of the novel."

"Oh. Action-packed."

"You liked it?"

"Um-hm."

"You can see that I'm going for a more literary style than your typical techno-thriller."

Angel stared at Bird. "Yes," she said, "I got that." Her eyes were darting about like guppies in a fish tank.

"Curious how it's going to turn out?"

Angel nodded. "Uh-huh."

"What I'm thinking is that Turk should—"

"Darling, why don't you *not* tell me? So's not to spoil the surprise."

"Okay. Truth is, I don't know yet how it's going to end myself. But being as how I'm taking it in a literary direction, I'm tempted to go tragic."

"Right."

"Remember the ending in *For Whom the Bells Toll*? Robert Jordan and Maria at the bridge? Robert telling her to go on ahead, he'll be right along? And of course he's mortally wounded. He's not going anywhere. Good stuff."

"Um," Angel said.

"The only thing is, it's kind of a downer."

"Yes, tragedy tends to be down."

"When you spend all this time creating characters, you get close to them. It's like they're real. It's not easy just to blow them all up."

"Yes, I imagine that must be hard."

Bird grinned. "I'm thinking of changing his name."

"Whose?"

240

"Turk. To Randolph."

A look of alarm came over Angel. "Oh. No. No. Please don't do that."

"I thought you liked the name?"

"I do. Darling, it's sweet of you. But Tork is a much better name for him."

"*Turk.*"

"Turk." She smiled. "I love the way he just keeps going, with all those wounds." Angel yawned. "I hope he makes it home, but if you decide he needs to die, I'm sure it will be very moving. And the woman, Brenda—"

"Betty."

"She's great. Can't wait to see how it ends." Angel looked out at the lightening sky and groaned. "Tell me that's not the sunrise. I always feel like *such* a vampire."

"Oh? Are you often awake at this hour?"

Angel got up, gave him a businesslike peck on the cheek. "Bit early for trick questions, darling." She padded off to the bedroom. "Momma must skedaddle. Back to her *coffin.*"

CHAPTER 31

ΠOT OΠE WORD OF TRUTH
IΠ THE EΠTIRE THIΠG

Rogers P. Fancock glowered at the headline. On top of everything—*this*?

**U.S. SAID TO BE DEVELOPING SUPERWEAPON;
"MUON DEVICE" USES SUBATOMIC PARTICLES,
CAUSING STEEL AND ARMOR "TO EVAPORATE"**

**Project Taurus Called a "Preemption Platform"
to Counter "Alarming" Chinese Military Buildup**

Fancock read, lips pursing, his mood darkening with each paragraph. Bletchin stood by nervously as his chief read.

"Bletchin. Get me Admiral Doggett on the secure line. No, on second thought, why bother with the secure line anymore? What secrets do we have *left* at this point? Get me a megaphone. I'll bellow at him across the goddamned Potomac River."

"Sir?"

"Just *get* him, Bletchin. Any line will do."

A few minutes later, the chairman of the Joint Chiefs of Staff came on the secure line.

"Yes, Dave," Fancock said, "I *am* calling about the *Times* story. Rather thought you might have called me first. Well, yes, I imagine you are busy. It's a busy time for all of us, isn't it? Just have one quick question for you: What the *hell*? I was under the impression, which is to say, I'd been told, straight out, that Taurus was highly, highly classified. It is? Then why am I reading about muons melting Chinese naval vessels, in the *New York Times*?...Uh-huh...Uh-huh. And whose brainstorm was—...Devlin? I *understand* it's Groepping's project, Dave. But inasmuch as we're footing the goddamned bill, where does Chick *Devlin* get off concocting his own damned cover story? Things are tense enough right now without the Chinese thinking we're cooking up some kind of death ray to melt their ships. You're darn tooting right I'm upset." Fancock sighed. "I'll try to figure something out this end. The president's not at all pleased about this...No, Dave, I'm not suggesting that we scrap Taurus. If anything, we probably ought to get the goddamn thing launched and online, asap. At this point we may need to knock out their goddamn grid sooner rather than later. Keep me posted."

Fancock was rereading the odious article for the third time and lining up his ducks when Bletchin's voice piped up over the intercom.

"Sir, it's Ambassador Ding."

"Oh, *God*," Fancock groaned.

"It's him personally, sir, on the line. He's insisting that he speak with you. I tried to put him off, but—"

"Thank you, Bletchin. Now my happiness is complete."

Fancock took a deep breath and stabbed the blinking button.

"Ding, old friend," he said, "how *very* good to hear your voice...Aha...Uh-huh...Indeed I did see it. I was *just* about to give you a call...Well, that makes two of us. Three, including the president...Of *course* I deny it. Not one word of truth in the entire article...Uh-huh...Ding...Ding...*Ding.* Please. Hear me out. Hear me out...Well, I'm sorry that's how they're reacting in Beijing, but—...I appreciate that President Fa is doing his best to keep a lid on things. I'm doing a bit of tamping down myself here, you know...Ding. Steady hand on the tiller..."

A few minutes later, Fancock was in the Oval Office. The president looked tired. Everyone did. Even Ajax and Achilles, the presidential dachshunds, appeared exhausted, asleep, as usual, on the couch.

The president glanced up and went back to his paperwork. "Yes, Rog?"

Deep breath. "I thought you'd like to know that our little deception plan to protect Taurus appears to have succeeded." Fancock explained about the *Times* story and the muons, leaving out only the essential details.

The president sat back in his chair and frowned. "Was I briefed on this?"

To lie or not to lie? This is the question.

"I don't like to load you down with a lot of extraneous stuff when you have so much on your plate. If my right ear looks a bit chewed on, it's because Ambassador Ding had it for breakfast. I told him the story was nonsense, so he'll conclude that it's word-for-word accurate. I don't mind having the Chinese think we're working on something that could cause the rivets on their naval vessels to evaporate. I'd rather they think *that* than know what it actually does. As Churchill said, 'In wartime, truth is so precious that she should always be attended by a bodyguard of lies.' Doggett says Beijing's cranking up a major naval exercise in the Taiwan Strait. Let's hope that General Han reads the *New York Times.* It might give him pause to think we've got something on the shelf that could turn his surface ships into submarines in less than ten seconds."

The president considered. "What do I tell Fa when we talk

again? We seem to have become regular phone buddies. What if *he* asks me about our muon weapon?"

"He's a gentleman," Fancock said. "Gentlemen do not ask each other about their weapons systems."

"Rog."

"Sir, we are doing everything we can to help President Fa. You don't owe him any apologies at this point."

"Might be easier at this point if he just defected," the president said.

The Oval Office door clicked shut behind him. Fancock let out a sigh of relief. How many lies had he just told? He wasn't sure he wanted to know. What worried him was how good he had gotten at telling them. But didn't presidents, like the truth, need a bodyguard of lies?

CHAPTER 32

DRAGON GREATNESS

G eneral Han was in a state.

"The American president—your great friend—did *he* have anything to say about this?" He waved the *Times* article. "Did he? Well?"

Fa decided to let him go on a bit more.

Han continued. "No? Nothing, eh? Nothing about how they are working to *destroy* us?"

When he could stand it no longer, Fa gently said, "No, General, strange as it may seem, the American president did not share with me the details of his latest top-secret military program. Normally, it's the first thing he brings up."

Han's eyes flashed. "Again and again they provoke us—and what do you do? Yawn!" He slammed his palm on the table.

"Would you like a gavel?" Fa said. "It might be easier on your hand."

Han grunted. "No! Give me a hammer and I'd know what to do with it!" He threw himself back into his chair. "This is intolerable!"

"Comrade General," Fa said, "I think we have spent enough time on your indignation. Let us move on."

Han was about to launch a fresh salvo when Lo put a restraining hand on his forearm.

"Shall we discuss," Minister Lo said, "the incident at our embassy in Copenhagen yesterday?"

Foreign Minister Wu said, "I have sent a strongly worded protest to the Danish foreign minister."

"Yes," Fa said, "it was unfortunate. I was not aware the Danes felt so passionately about the Lotus. But we can't have hooligans breaking into our embassies and spray-painting our ambassadors. How *is* Ambassador Xin?"

"More shaken up than hurt. We sent a plane. He's on his way back. And the Danish ambassador is on *his* way back to Copenhagen."

"Maybe we should have spray-painted *him* before sending him home. Give Xin my regards. Tell him that he conducted himself with dignity."

"Xin will survive," Lo said. "Dip him in turpentine."

Fa said, "Comrade Minister Lo, I trust that none of this unpleasantness is being reported in our media?"

"No, of course not."

"Our firewall is in good working order?"

"Some slippage, nothing serious."

"You are the guardian of China's pride, Lo. How sad it would be if our people saw what was going on in the world. Seeing their country treated with such disrespect."

"We are vigilant, Comrade President."

"I have no doubt. All right then, General, why don't you tell us about this ... exercise of yours?"

The room darkened. General Han narrated his PowerPoint presentation. When the room lights came back up, there was a blinking of eyes and a nervous silence.

"Well, Comrade General," Fa said, "the scale of this, it's certainly impressive."

"Half measures are for the halfhearted."

And the half-brained. Fa said, "Operation Longwei. Dragon Greatness?"

General Han smiled. "Does the name not sit well with Comrade President?"

"No, I like it. It's an apt name for a display of such immensity. Something like this you couldn't call 'Dragon Good-Enoughness.' Or 'Dragon Adequateness.' No. May I ask—do you have in mind to inform the governments of Nepal, Bhutan, and India that we will be dropping tens of thousands of paratroops along their borders? As well as sealing those borders? Or did you have in mind the element of surprise?"

"They will receive some advance notification."

"Ah. Good. Wouldn't want them to start panicking, would we? And Seoul—do you have in mind to tell the South Koreans about the mine laying in the Yellow Sea?"

"They're dummy mines," Han said. "As I made very clear in my presentation."

"So you did, yes. But they won't know that they're dummies, will they? I suppose it's part of the game for them to find that out on their own. Give them a feeling of accomplishment."

"Without the Americans?" Han said. "The Koreans couldn't *piss* without the Americans holding their cocks."

Laughter.

Listening in, Gang wondered if the president, too, should start making profane jokes. The committee members seemed to enjoy them so.

"I was coming to the Americans," Fa said. "Or, as you would put it, 'To my dear friends the Americans.' So are we going to give *them* some warning of all this? Or is it to be a big surprise for them as well?"

"Like Pearl Harbor!" said one of the ministers to hearty laughter.

"If Comrade President will recall from the presentation," Han said, "a key element in Longwei's strategic objective is to determine just what the American response would be in the event of an actual operation. If we tell them what we're going to do, we won't be able to know what their actual response would be. It's not so complicated, really."

"Ah. Yes. The Heisenberg principle."

Han stared.

Lo came to Han's rescue. "This is exactly what the general intends. As the Heisenberg principle states, the observed body reacts differently if it is aware that it is being observed."

Han nodded knowingly. "Maybe we'll learn something about their muon capability."

Minister Fu Yin said, "I think General Han's plan is truly excellent. Whatever else is accomplished, it will certainly get everyone's mind off the Dung Lotus."

Murmurs, nods.

"Then we're all agreed?" Han asked.

"No," Fa said. He spoke so quietly that the others had to lean in to hear him. "I am not for this. This dragon may have greatness, but I greatly fear that it could end up devouring its own tail."

"Perhaps 'greatness' is a concept too elusive for Comrade President." General Han smiled.

"Oh, is this really *wise*, Comrade President?" Gang asked.

"I am not doing it because I believe it *not* to be wise, Gang."

"If Han and Lo find out, and you know they will, aren't you just handing them a sword?"

"Dial, Gang."

Gang began to press the buttons on his cell phone, the special one. He paused. "Will you be able to hear? With all this water going?"

"*Yes*, Gang."

Gang dialed.

"Yes. Hello. Is Dr. Kissinger available, please? It is the president of the People's Republic of China who wishes to converse with him."

"YES, BLETCHIN?"

Bletchin looked oddly exhilarated. A surfeit of caffeine?

"Sir," he whispered reverentially. "It's Dr. *Kissinger.*"

"Oh?" Fancock sat up. "Oh. Well then." He reached for the phone. Bletchin turned to leave.

"Bletchin? Sit down. Listen in."

"*Thank* you, sir."

Might as well—he'd only go listen in on his phone.

Fancock picked up. "Henry?...How *very* good to hear your voice. Where are you?...Mumbai? Good God. No rest for the wicked, eh?...Yes, well, it is a bit of a mess, but we're doing what we can to stay on course...*Une belle ordure?* Yes, that's about right... De Gaulle? No, I never got to know him. We just missed...Oh? Really? Fa himself?...When?...Great Dragon?...Dragon *Greatness.* Mm. Don't much like the sound of that...Well, that's comforting to know, but he's going to have to do *something* by way of a response. He's catching hell from the right *and* left. You saw that Penelope Kent—dreadful woman—called him a 'wimp' yesterday in front of ten thousand Tea Partiers...Oh, believe me, I hope she *does* run. If we're really in the endgame of the American experiment, why not elect her president and get it over with in one fell swoop?...Henry, he can't just sit on his hands...Believe me, I, *too,* wish they'd just bury him and move on, but they're absolutely convinced the Chinese are going to cave...I've *told* them. They can put him in the Fancock family plot at Mount Auburn...What's that? Arlington? Well, yes, that *is* a thought, I must say, Henry, that's rather elegant. Yes. Oh, I certainly will. I'll present it to him right away. All right, well thank you. Thank you. Stay out of trouble in Mumbai. Love to Nancy. Dorothy sends hers. Good-bye."

Fancock cradled the phone.

"That, Bletchin, is one of the truly great minds of our time."

"Oh, *yes*, sir."

"Not a word of this, Bletchin. Not a whisper."

"No sir. But you are going to bring it to the president?"

"Yes, of course. But first get me whatsisname. And while I'm on with him, call Doggett and have him get onto the commandant at Arlington. Find out if there's any impediment. And Bletchin?"

"Sir?"

"Tell them there had better goddamn well *not* be any impediment. I don't want to hear that we can't bury the Dalai Lama at Arlington National Cemetery because he didn't serve in the goddamn U.S. military."

"I'll make that very clear, sir."

"Now get me whosis."

"Yes, sir."

"Bletchin?"

"Sir?"

"What the hell is his name?"

"Jangpom, sir. Jangpom Gadso. He's the seventh reincarnation of—"

"Never *mind*, Bletchin. Just get him."

CHAPTER 33

War Is Hell

B ird was in the kitchen, his fingers barely able to keep pace with his brain, banging away at the final chapter of the novel. Even now he couldn't decide whether Turk should live or die.

Bouncing Betty O'Toole circled above the desperate, sanguinary scene at the controls of the death-dealing AC-130 gunship, low on fuel, low on ammo, but the needle on her heart gauge still pointed to "FULL."

Bird paused. Great stuff. Where did sentences like that come from? No, don't ask. Keep going.

"Turk! Turk! Do you read me? Come in, Turk! Damn you, Turk, come in!"

"Walter? *Walter?* Walter, pick *up* if you're there!"
Bird's fingers paused. Myndi's voice on the answering machine. Why had he turned it back on?
"Walter! Pick up the phone!"

What time is it? He sat up. A jolt of pain shot through his neck. How long had he been at it?

He looked at the kitchen wall clock. Eleven-something. God bless analog clocks—they still told time the old-fashioned way. Eleven-*something*. But eleven-something p.m. or a.m.? That was the question.

There was light beneath the curtains. *Light. Morning? Jeez.* When did he sit down to work? Six p.m. Six p.m...yesterday. Whoa, he *had* been at it a long time.

"Walter! Are you *there*? *Please*, please pick up the *phone!*"

Was that...sobbing? *Uh-oh.*

"Myn? You okay?"

"No!"

"Are you...hurt?"

"Yes!"

"Oh, jeez. Oh, jeez. Okay. Stay calm. It's going to be okay. Can you get to a phone, baby? Can you dial 911?"

"Walter—I'm *on* the stupid phone!"

Fair point. Good point.

"What happened? Did you—"

"Walter, we've been *canceled*." Sob.

"Canceled?"

"The Tang Cup!" Sob. "Sam just called. He heard over the radio. Because of the Chinese navy boat and that idiot Taiwanese shrimp boat." Sob.

"What boat?"

"Walter, where you been? On *Mars*?"

Bird scratched his head. "No, just crashing on this...presentation. What's going on?"

"All because of this *stupid* Dalai Lama business..." Sob.

"What—"

"And this *stupid* Chinese navy exercise!"

"I heard something about that. What happened?"

"Some Chinese navy boat sank some Taiwanese shrimp boat, and it's turned into this huge *thing*. The Chinese say the Taiwanese started it. Is that supposed to mean they attacked them with *shrimp*? The Taiwanese say the Chinese rammed them. The TV has satellite footage of the Chinese boat ramming them. Anyway, everyone's in a stink now. All because a bunch of stupid monks are refusing to bury the Dalai Lama. Since when is Buddhism about starting *wars*?"

"It's a complicated situation," Bird ventured. "But what about the Tang Cup?"

"They announced it this morning, from the White House. And they're postponing President Fu's U.S. visit."

"I think his name is Fa."

"I don't *care* what his name is! They're suspending other things. Trade shows. Student exchanges. Museum exhibits. Sport events. But the Tang Cup! Oh, Walter."

Bird massaged his temples. His mind was six thousand miles away in Iran, in a bomb crater in the middle of a desperate firefight.

Empathy. Make empathy.

"Well, babe, war *is* hell."

From the sound of renewed sobbing, Bird gathered that his attempt to assuage Myndi's grief had not been a success.

Do-over. Switch gears. Laugh—make her laugh. You can do it!

"Look on the bright side. Now you don't have to get all those shots!"

Silence.

"Didn't you tell me you needed a lot of shots? You know how you hate shots. Myn? Babe? You there?"

No, she was not.

He got up to go to the refrigerator. *Water. Must have water.* He started at his reflection in the mirror. *Ooh.* Unshaven, unkempt, hollow-eyed, and bleary, an untidy version of himself: the Gen-X Mr. Hyde.

Bird suddenly felt tired. *Rest. Must . . . rest.* He would take a short nap, shower, have coffee, then get up and finish the novel. Finish . . . his Armaggedon Quartet! As for Turk's fate, he would let his unconscious decide, as he slept, whether Turk should live or die. He shuffled off to bed like a mental patient.

He woke. Looked at the digital clock. It read 9:07—*p.m.* He felt as though an undertaker had embalmed him as he slept. He could barely move. He lay there deciding what to do next when he remembered the call from Myndi.

He managed to get out of bed and shuffle to the kitchen and call her. Apparently his apology had been adequate, for she mounted no strong protest when he told her that he'd be home by midnight.

He phoned Angel from the car.

"Where the hell have you *been*? I called you twenty times. I *hate* it when you turn off your cell!"

"Explain later."

"Get your ass over here on the double, mister. It's *happening.* The Chinese rammed a Taiwanese shrimp boat. Fa's visit is off. The Security Council is meeting! *Yess.*"

"They scratched the Tang Cup."

"The what? Oh, please, who gives a shit?"

"Ange. She's in tears."

"Well, tell her to put on her big-girl panties and suck it up."

"That's not very nice."

"Darling. The world is going up in flames. And we lit the match! So her horse meet got scrubbed. Tell her war is hell."

"I did. Look, I've got to go. I'm in the car. These roads . . ."

"Where are you going?"

"Home. To console my wife. She may be drinking cleaning fluid for all I know."

"What about me?"

"You don't sound suicidal. You sound thrilled."

"I thought you might want to share this extraordinary, historical moment with me. I'm in the war room. *Our* war room, darling. The electricity is— God, you can practically reach out and feel the history. Oh, by the way, the *Washington Post* called. They're doing a *huge* story on us."

"Us?"

"The institute. Me. And you, if you'd stop with this ridiculous wallflower act. For heaven's sake, Bird, take a bow. They'll be talking about us a hundred years from now."

"A hundred years from now, no problem. Now? Major problem."

Silence. "Fine. Run home to Miffy. Give her a lump of sugar for me."

"Her name is Myndi."

"I'll make a note of it," Angel said, and hung up.

Bird was about to press the End Call button when—

CHAPTER 34

PLEASE, SIR, MAY I HAVE MORE?

W alter? Walter? *Dar-ling?* Wakey-wakey."
"Mm."

Bird opened his eyes to a blurry non sequitur of bright light and strange, metronomic noises. *Beep...beep...beep...beep.* He felt as though he were underwater. And yet it was pleasant. Very pleasant. His eyelids closed.

"Walter. Oh, Wal-ter."

Familiar, that voice. Was it coming from TV? Really familiar. Was it that woman on the morning show?

"Walter. Wakey."

He felt a patting on his hand. He opened his eyes again. He peered. Blinked. Focused.

Myndi? What was she doing at the Military-Industrial Duplex? She never came there. *Uh-oh. Angel.* He looked around the room. No, not Military-Industrial Duplex. Where, then?

"Dar-ling?"

"Myn?"

"How are you feeling?"

"Unh."

"You're in the hospital."

Hospital? Why hospital? Don't remember being sick.

Yes, definitely Myn. She was standing by his bed, patting his hand. There was a tube going into his wrist. *Tube? Not good.*

"You had an accident, darling. You hit a deer. With your car."

Deer. Um. Yes. Talking on phone, then ... this bang.

"You've been talking," Myndi said. "Going on for hours. Who's Turk?"

He heard a faint click, and suddenly the most delicious surge of warmth and happiness went through him, like liquid sunshine. Goodness it was wonderful. It should always be this wonderful. *Um. Oh, yes—morphine. Please, sir, may I have more? Yes, Oliver Copperfield.*

Bird's eyes suddenly blinked open. He looked at Myndi with alarm. "Turk! Did he get out? Did he make it?"

"I haven't the faintest idea," Myndi said. "I don't know any Turk. Is he Turkish? You've been going on about Turk and someone named Bouncing Betty. Who's she?"

"Betty." Bird smiled dreamily. "Amazing ... ta-tas."

"What?"

"When she's on parade and she sticks her chest out, it sort of bursts out her uniform. The guys love it. Not Turk, though. Oh, no. Turk is by the book."

"Walter," Myndi said, "I won't be angry, I promise. But were you at a topless bar or someplace like that?"

"No, no." Bird laughed. "No, Betty's not *topless*. Top *soldier*. Oh, tough, but heart of gold. Betty's the only one for Turk."

"I can't listen to any more of this. Walter, listen to me—the *police* are here."

"Police? That's nice."

"They want to speak to you. Why don't I tell them you're in no condition?"

"Why police?"

"Walter, you were in an *accident*. A serious accident. You're lucky you weren't killed."

Lucky? Three hundred pounds of meat, fur, and hoof coming through the windshield at sixty miles an hour? This a definition of lucky?

"They say you hadn't been drinking."

"Oh, a drink. Yes. Old-fashioned. Make it a double."

"And some reporter from the *Post* has been trying to reach you. He keeps leaving messages. He won't say what it's about."

"Nooooo comment," Bird chortled.

"Why is a reporter from the *Post* calling you? I thought your work was secret?"

"Nooooo comment. My zips are lipped."

"Well, you might tell *me*. I'm your wife. Supposedly."

Myn. Please stop talking. Just want to feel this wonderful, excellent feeling. I've got a won-der-ful feeeeel-inggggg . . .

"Walter, do you work for the government? Are you some kind of agent or something? Do you work for the CIA?"

"If I tell you," Bird burbled, "both our lives would be in danger."

He began to hum the opening theme music to the James Bond movies.

"Turk, is *he* some kind of . . . ? You were talking about some mission. A bomb with a timer or something. Oh, never mind. I'll be outside. Fending off the *police*."

Bird smiled as the next warm wave bore him higher and higher. He could see fishes in the waves, beautiful, many-colored fishes, backlit by the sun. Like an aquarium and stained glass, all in one.

CHAPTER 35

HAVE A VALIUM

W hat kind of message is China trying to send, sinking Taiwanese shrimp boats?" Chris Matthews said. "What's *that*
about?"

"Message?" Angel said. "Two words, first starts with *f* and the
second with *y*. I could say them out loud, but we'd get fined by the
FCC. It's perfectly clear—"

"As Nixon used to say."

"As Nixon used to say. China is sending a four-part message.
One: You think we care what the world thinks? Guess again. Imagine one point three billion hands, each with the third finger raised."

"Flipping us off? A sea of birds. What else?"

"Two: Burial in Tibet? Not gonna happen. Three: They're
totally pissed off—oops!" Angel slapped her hand. "Well, maybe the
FCC isn't watching."

"Yeah they are. The FCC watches *Hardball*. They *love* us!"

"Beijing's totally furious about all these demonstrations going on
around the world. Demonstrations, I would add, of heartfelt, genuine, and justified indignation—"

"Hold on. Are you calling what they did to the Chinese ambassador in Denmark 'heartfelt'? They *spray-painted* him orange. Saffron!"

"I know. Who *knew* the Danes cared? I say good for them. But I don't think China's going to be buying a lot of aquavit or Lego in the near future. Look, Chris, whatever else this Operation Dragon Greatness—don't you *love* the name?—is, it's a wake-up call. We simply can't go on gutting our defense budgets this way. Not with dragons stomping about like enormous, malignant centipedes. Millipedes. Gigapedes."

"What about this so-called *muon* device we're supposedly working on, according to the *Times*? Muons? Sounds scary. By the way, there's Luke Tierney's next Pulitzer. Fabulous reporter. We had him on the show. So Project Taurus, what's with that?"

"Well, Chris, I'm not *in* government at the moment, so all I know about it is what I read in the *Times*. But I'll say this: I sure as heck hope we *are* working on something like that. Obviously this is no time to be letting down our guard. Look at England during the thirties. You end up with Hitler."

Matthews turned to his other guest. "Winnie Chang. Thanks for coming on."

"Thank you for having me on, Chris."

Myndi said to Bird, "Notice how she's toned down the China-doll thing? No silk or pearls. Looks like she just walked out of Ann Taylor. Even the hair. Subtle."

She and Bird were in the den at Upkeep, watching with dinner on trays. It was three days since the accident. Now, his brain clear of the wonderful but fuzzy-making morphine, Bird realized that yes, he had been "lucky." The car was a total insurance loss. But God bless German engineering. And thank you, inventor of air bags, whoever you are.

His neck was in a brace, and his left elbow felt as though lava were being injected into it. The Percocets helped some. Nurse Myndi insisted on custody of the bottle and would dole them out only one every four hours. *And no, Walter, you may not wash them down with an old-fashioned.*

"Observant of you," he said. "She does look somewhat... Westernized tonight. The chicken is good, babe."

"It's the club recipe. You add canned mushroom soup. I use the low-sodium. The high-sodium tastes better, but I don't like that sting-y feeling it leaves in your mouth."

"So give us the view from Beijing," Matthews was saying. "Why is China sinking Taiwanese shrimp boats?"

"Well, Chris," Winnie Chang said, "first let us put this episode in context, shall we? It is a well-known fact that the regime in Taiwan uses vessels disguised as shrimp boats to spy on China's coastal defenses."

"Aw, come *on*." Matthews grinned. "This wasn't a *spy* boat. You saw the footage."

"Let's wait to see what the investigation will reveal, Chris. There may be more to this than meets the eye. But look at the incredible abuse that China has been getting around the world. Acts of terrorism against its diplomats."

"Okay, so they painted one of your ambassadors. Terrorism? Really?"

"Chris, he was physically attacked."

"Okay. Fair enough. I'm sure *he* thought it was terrorism."

"And let us not forget that this outrage took place in the same country where they produce disrespectful, blasphemous cartoons about the prophet Muhammad."

"Whoa! Hold on. Are you saying *China*, one of the most *atheist* countries on earth, is offended by cartoons of the prophet Muhammad? Nah. You don't really want to go there, do you?"

Winnie smiled. "We can debate that some other time, Chris. But you know as well as I do that many of these so-called spontaneous demonstrations are being orchestrated, and even funded, by agents of provocation. I would not be surprised if Ms. Templeton's Institute for Never-Ending War was behind some of this. She must be *so* pleased by this heightened tension between our two countries.

"Honey," Angel said in her best Bette Davis tone, "it's *your* people who are beating the drums and doing the war dance. Not the USA. Chill. Have a Valium. In fact, take the whole bottle."

"It is so interesting, Chris, that Ms. Templeton is talking about *pills*, because from what I am hearing, there is now developing evidence that it was in fact she and another person at her war institute who first planted this outrageous lie about China trying to kill the Dalai Lama."

"Are you all right?" Myndi said.

"*Chicken*," Bird gasped. "Swallowed... wrong way."

"Do you want me to hit you?"

"No!"

"Evidence?" Chris Matthews said. "You mean real evidence? We never saw Ms. Templeton's."

"Don't take my word for it. After all, according to Ms. Templeton, I am an insidious Chinese secret agent or some kind of dragon woman. But there is a story in tomorrow's *Washington Post* that will have much to say about all this. And I think everyone will be most interested to read it."

Myndi said, "Did you ever call that *Post* reporter back? Walter? Are you all right? You're pale."

"Myn, can I have one of the pills?"

"No, Walter. I told you. Not until ten o'clock."

"Babe, I need one now. Trust me. I'm in pain."

As indeed he was.

Matthews turned to Angel. "Angel Templeton, what do you know about this *Post* story?"

For a moment Angel's expression reminded Bird of the deer's, right before impact.

"I...know they're working on a story. About...the work we do at ICC on...you know, foreign issues...international...matters and such. Beyond that I...can't really say."

"Oooh," Myndi said with glee, "*she* looks nervous."

CHAPTER 36

Ought to Be Hanged, the Pair of Them

Rogers P. Fancock was only halfway through the *Post* story but
already so incensed that he had to continue reading while
standing.

> *Phone records obtained by the* Post *show a series of calls to the* Delhi
> Beast *from Templeton's private phone at the Institute for Continu-*
> *ing Conflict the day before the newspaper first reported that Chinese*
> *security agents had allegedly poisoned the Dalai Lama in Rome.*

So after all it was these two scoundrels, Templeton and this
McIntyre person? Outrageous!

Fancock scanned the remaining paragraphs in the hope of learn-
ing that the two had broken some federal law; better yet, that they
had already been arrested by the FBI and frog-marched to the nearest federal detention center. Alas, there was nothing on that score.
Well, rest assured Rogers P. Fancock would be taking it up *personally*
with the attorney general.

He was still fuming when he looked up and saw he was not alone.
Bletchin had crept in on little cat's feet.

"*What*, Bletchin?"

"It's Mr. Strecker, sir," Bletchin whispered. "On the secure line. I wouldn't have disturbed you, but I know you've been trying to reach him."

"Oh, indeed I have. I most certainly have," Fancock grumbled, reaching for the phone. Bletchin beat a hasty retreat.

"Well, if it isn't the invisible man."

"Rog. Did you forget to take your nerve tonic this morning?"

"Oh, no. No, no, none of that. None of that. Where in Hades have you been? I've been sending up flares. As long as you are on the government payroll, you may not go on disappearing at critical moments. Damn it, Barney, there's a chain of command. You are down here, and *I* am—"

"Rog, you're going to give yourself another hiatal hernia. Now, I got a pot full of honey for you. You want some, or do you want to go on ranting about the chain of command?"

"Honey?" Fancock snorted. "All right, start spooning. And it better be tasty. Did you see this story in the *Post*? About this Templeton creature and her accomplice, someone named McIntyre? Ought to be hanged, the pair of them. Together. From the same gallows."

Was Barney laughing?

"Yeah," Barney chortled. "I saw that."

Damn it, the man was *amused*.

"All right, Barney. What the hell's going on?"

"Explain later. Meantime—"

"No, no. Explain now."

"Okay, but real quick—hell, we've known about those two rascals from the get-go. That Indian newspaper they used to shovel their hoo-ha? We've been using it for years for this kind of thing. I bet more'n half their newsroom is on our payroll."

"You *knew* about this? Why in God's name didn't you do something about it?"

"Well, I was kind of enjoying the show. It crossed my mind they might be in the employ of one of our *other* sixteen intelligence agencies. But it turns out they're just freelancing. McIntyre, as you know from the article, works for Groepping-Sprunt. So he was laboring on behalf of our wonderful military-industrial complex. The lady may actually have been operating from principle, if you'd call it that."

"I'll digest that in the fullness of time," Fancock said. "But why didn't you *tell* me about this?"

"Because, Rog, I don't have ten free hours in my day to talk you into leaving well enough alone. Much as I esteem you, you do take a bit of hand-holding, you know." Barney chuckled. "But isn't that always the way of it? The protégé becomes the mentor, and the mentor develops acid reflux."

"Goddamn it, Barn. They tried to start a *war*."

"Tried? You seen the TV lately? I'd say they got us off to a fine start. Course, this whole thing did take on a life of its own. Still, you got to give them credit."

"Credit? They ought to be—"

"Rog, it's not their fault the Dalai Lama got cancer, is it? They were only trying to gin up a little anti-China mojo. As if *we* don't every so often? Let's not get too self-righteous just because they didn't have an executive order. They just happened to get lucky—real lucky—with their timing."

Fancock sighed. "How did the *Post* get this story?"

Barney chuckled. "Well, let's just say that reporter had a real good source."

Fancock paused. "You? *You* burned them? I thought you admired them?"

"Oh, I do like them. But they're not on my payroll. I don't owe them a damn thing. And I had an opportunity I couldn't pass up, to do a favor for my new best friend. About whom I am just crazy. In fact, I think I may just be in love, Rog. Imagine that, at my age. I'm speaking Platonically, of course. I'm too old for the other kind, plus Harriet would shoot me, and she is good with a gun. Never teach your wife about firearms, Rog. *Big* mistake, but it's too late now."

"Who's your 'new best friend'?"

"Her name is Winnie. Don't you love the name? Winnie."

"Winnie? Winnie *Chang*?"

"She an acquaintance of yours? I know she does get around."

"Of course I know her!" Fancock said hotly. "Everyone knows her. She's a major Washington hostess. Runs the Co-Dependency Council."

"Oh, she's a peach. Educated, bright, funny. And that *skin*. But then I've always been partial to Asian girls. Well, as you can see, I'm just plain nuts about her."

"Barn, she plays tennis with the president."

"My. She *does* get around. Does she let him win? I'll bet she does. Minx."

"Barn, you're not...romantically involved?"

"I do love you Boston WASPs. You just can't bring yourself to say, 'Barn, you banging this lady?' No, Rog. We are going to make music together, Ms. Chang and I, but of the purest professional kind. And you're a dirty old man for asking."

"Hold on. Are you telling me that you gave Templeton and McIntyre to Chang and *she* gave it to the *Post*?"

"Did you get that smart at Harvard, or did you take continuing adult-ed classes? Yes, Rog, that is exactly what happened. So now everyone knows that it *wasn't* a Chinese plot to poison the Dalai Lama. That'll take the pressure off Beijing and give our friend President Fa a little breathing space. More importantly, Miss Winnie will look good in front of her boss, Minister Lo. And he'll look good, for running such a smart agent. And that's just how we want it. He'll be patting her on the head. From what Winnie has told me, Lo would like to be patting other parts of her anatomy. Brace yourself, Rog.

Minister Lo is apparently not a gentleman. If he applies to any of your clubs up in Boston—don't let him in. People Like Us he is not." "I heard he had that reputation," Fancock said.

"Yes. Comrade Minister. Lo Guowei seems to have a real snake in his trousers. This is a bad fellow. But you don't get to be top cop in China handing out lollipops. Admiral Zhang was an exception, and he didn't last long. Do you wonder why Ms. Chang is willing to do the fox-trot with me, after all my years of gallant courting?"

"Why?"

"Lo has decided to recall her to Beijing at the end of this year. So he can *mentor* her personally. Says he's got big plans for her. She's going places. And she's got a good idea where the first stop on *that* itinerary is. So, much as I'd like to tell you that it was my dazzling good looks and irresistible charm, the fact of the matter is, Ms. Chang is willing to play with us for reasons of self-preservation. And as motives go, I have found self-preservation to be among the more dependable."

Fancock considered. "Is she . . . defecting?"

"No, no, Rog. Defection is not in the plan. *Au contraire*, as you would say. If she were to defect, what use to us would she be then? No, I'm looking forward to a long and fruitful friendship with Ms. Chang. I think she will prove to be a splendid asset. She is quite open to the prospect of receiving *two* paychecks in the future." Barney chuckled. "It would appear that her years here in our nation's capital rubbing elbows with capitalists were not entirely wasted."

CHAPTER 37

A FINGER IN MANY PIES

President Fa perused the translation of the American newspaper article before him. He had already committed it to memory, but he wanted to give the Standing Committee members enough time to absorb it. Copies had been placed before each of them.

When the last of them finished reading and looked up, Fa said wryly, "Well, Comrades, between last week's newspaper story about their muon weapon and now this, it seems we are getting better intelligence from the American media than from our own agents."

No one laughed. Standing Committee members tended to refrain from any criticism, even playful, of the minister of state security. Taunting a man who might know more about you than your own wife does is never advisable.

And yet Minister Lo smiled. Just the way that Fa, who had deliberately opened the meeting as he did, had anticipated he would.

"May I point out, Comrade President, that it was *my* agent in Washington who gave this story to the newspaper. Without her there would have been no story. And this is a very good story for China."

"You *may* point that out." Fa smiled. "And indeed it is a very good story. We stand vindicated of the vile lies. Comrades, let us warmly congratulate our Minister Lo."

There was a round of "Well done"s and a thumping of hands on the table. Lo smiled, nodded.

"And yet, Comrade," Fa said, "I confess that I am confused."

"What is confusing you, Comrade President?"

"Did you not inform us—with certainty—that this was the work of the American CIA? But from this it would seem that it was the work of these two hooligans, the woman Templeton and McIntyre."

Lo was ready for that one. "Don't be deceived, Comrade. Do you think these two are *not* CIA? Of course they're CIA. This institute of hers is CIA. It's cover."

"Oh? But then why did not the newspaper say that?"

"To protect CIA."

Fa stared. "My impression of the American media is that they are independent of the government."

"Oh, don't be fooled. The American media protect their government all the time."

"Well, perhaps you know far more about such things than I. But they often make great trouble for their government. Look what they did to poor Nixon."

"That was ages ago," Lo said dismissively. "And it was their own government that decided Nixon had to go, not their newspapers. Why? Because he had made the opening with China. And that was intolerable to the ruling class. No, Comrade, we know for certain that these two are CIA. The whole thing was an American operation from start to finish."

Fa considered. "Well, your Comrade Chang is to be congratulated. She is very capable, I must say."

Lo grinned. "She had a good teacher, from what I hear."

Laughter.

Fa added, "I hope that is one story in the American media that will somehow penetrate our great firewall."

More laughter.

"Oh," Lo said, "this is one that might slip through. We cannot stop all the stories, can we?"

More laughter. Gang thought, *What a very jolly meeting.*

Lo said, "I'm going to bring Comrade Chang back to Beijing."

"Oh?" Fa said. "Is she not more valuable to us in Washington?"

"We don't want her to get too used to the good life there. That always leads to problems. I have plans for her advancement. And there are still one or two things she has to learn if she is going to the top. This talk we're hearing more and more from the women, about how there are not enough of them in the higher echelons of the party? Well, Comrades, let no one say that the Ministry of State Security is not in the vanguard of gender egalitarianism."

Hearty laughter.

"This is quite accurate, Comrade," Fa said. "Your ministry's promotion rate for females increased by three point seven percent last year."

"Comrade President is a master of statistics," Lo said. "Sometimes I think he missed his true calling."

Laughter. Gang thought, *Somewhat inappropriate.*

"Oh, there's no doubt," Fa said. "I should have been an accountant. But the party had other plans for me. I am impressed by your Comrade Chang, however. She seems to have a finger in many pies."

"Yes." Lo grinned. He turned to the others. "I wouldn't mind having a finger in *her* pie."

Watching Lo smirk, Fa thought of the incident that Admiral Zhang had related to him years ago. Dear Admiral Zhang, now serving China in his capacity as Agent Mankind Is Red, from a hospital bed in San Diego, where he was continually dosing himself with some herbal potion that simulated renal dysfunction.

It was Zhang who had first noticed the talent of Comrade Trainee Chang at MSS. He had taken an interest in her—kindly and chaste, for Zhang was a devoted husband to his wife. One day, he told Fa,

Chang had come to Zhang in great distress and tears to tell him that her superior, Deputy Minister Lo, had made unwanted advances. Zhang summoned Lo and excoriated him most severely. The episode had almost certainly played a part in sharpening Lo's hatred and envy of Admiral Zhang. Now, years later, Chang was happily ensconced in the heart of the American capital, leading a very pleasant life. To leave all that and return to Beijing, to be hostage to Lo's lecherous whims? Such a prospect could hold little appeal.

"Comrade Minister Lo," Fa said, "it seems to me that if Comrade Chang is doing such an excellent job in Washington, why recall her to Beijing?"

He caught the brief flicker of rage in Lo's eyes.

"With respect, Comrade President," Lo replied, "I think I am in a better position than you to judge matters of security personnel."

"No doubt," Fa said mildly, looking down at his papers. "Nevertheless, let's leave her in place for the time being. Well then, shall we move on to the next item? The regime in Taiwan has presented us a bill. One shrimp boat. This is a considerable sum, I must say. Is this truly what a shrimp boat costs today?"

CHAPTER 38

But Tell Me About Your Week

L et me do that for you, big brother. Here you go. Suck. You suckin'?"

"Umph."

It was late afternoon. Bird and Bewks were on the front porch at Upkeep. Bird was in a rocking chair but not rocking, owing to the neck brace and his bandaged left elbow. The scene had a certain Norman Rockwell quality to it: a young man tending to his wounded brother.

"It's blocked," Bird said grumpily.

"Let's have a look-see." Bewks removed the straw, examined it, blew through the mouth end, propelling a recalcitrant gob of orange pulp.

"There we go," he said. He went to reinsert the straw in Bird's mouth. Bird recoiled.

"What's the matter?"

"Do you have any...?"

"No, I do not have a sexually transmitted disease."

"Wasn't implying you did. Just if you have gingivitis or some other gum thing. My body's in bad enough shape as it is without adding gum disease."

"Well, I don't *have* gingivitis neither," Bewks said, jamming the straw back in. "Hush. I swear you're worse than Mother. I feel like a male nurse. In an asylum."

The old-fashioned tasted good. Very good. Yes, an infusion of bourbon was very welcome. Might help with the pain in the neck, and the even more insistent pain in the elbow. Myndi had taken his bottle of Percocets when she left—a punitive valedictory gesture. She'd probably flung it into the frog pond on her way out, in a swirl of furious dust.

Bewks sat beside his brother, rocking, sipping from his own strawless old-fashioned.

"I expect she'll be back," Bewks said. "Soon as she cools off. But she *was* some kind of hot on her way out of here."

"Do you see that sun over there?" Bird said. "Big shiny thing in the sky over the mountains? I'll make you a prediction. That sun will be extinct before Myndi, as you put it, 'cools off.'"

"Well"—Bewks gave a philosophical shrug—"I guess what's done is done."

"Bewks, could you stop with the bromides?"

"Only trying to cheer you up."

"Well you can do better than 'What's done is done,'" Bird muttered. "For God's sake."

"No need to get snooty."

"I'm not. Just don't want to be told 'What's done is done.' And don't tell me 'Maybe it's all for the best' or anything on that general theme."

"You know, if you're going to be like this, you can make your own supper. And I'd like to see you try, too, with that arm and that Watusi neck brace."

"I apologize." Bird sighed.

"I accept your apology."

"Could I have more booze, please?"

Bewks held up the glass.

"Thank you," Bird said. "Was that polite enough for you?"

"You got stuff on your chin. Want me to wipe it for you?"

"No. Drooling fits with my frame of mind just now."

Bird glanced over at the *Post* story folded open on Bewks's lap.

"What are you, memorizing that thing? It's three days now."

"Just want to familiarize myself with the various details. In case it comes up."

"Oh, it will."

"I want to be able to discuss it intelligently. Got to hand it to you—she is one fine-looking filly."

The story included a large photograph of Angel, probably an outtake from one of her sexed-up book jackets: hybrid foreign-policy intellectual and lap dancer. Myndi had especially admired the photo, declaring as she stormed up the stairs to pack that Angel looked like a "complete whore."

"Bewks." Bird sighed. "Did you intend that as a compliment?"

"She *is* kinda scrum-diddly-umptious."

"Could we please not talk about her right now? Show a little mercy, Bewks."

"We are tetchy this evening, aren't we?"

"Tetchy? Why would I be tetchy? My career is in the dumpster. Chinese agents may be on their way here to assassinate me. The FBI may be on *its* way. I'm sure by now they've found some law we broke. My elbow feels like a Doberman is using it as a chewy toy. And there was something else, what *was* it? Oh, right—my wife left me. And took my pain pills. Why would I be feeling tetchy?"

"I can get you pills, big brother. One of the boys in the regiment, Delmer Fitts, he's..." Bewks chuckled. "He's got more OxyContin than God. Don't know where he gets it and don't *want* to know. It does make the boys a trifle nervous, seeing how he's corporal gunner of one of our six-pounders."

"Six-pounder?"

"Cannon. Model 1841. Splendid piece of artillery, but optimally speaking, you want someone with a clear head operating a piece like that. Not someone with a head full of Oxy. But it's his cannon, so we're kind of stuck with the arrangement. Anyway, if you need some pills, hey, say the word."

Bird was strangely touched. "Thank you, brother, but maybe this isn't the ideal time to become addicted to hillbilly heroin. I do appreciate the offer, though. Just keep the old-fashioned pipeline flowing."

"So were you and her—"

"'You and *she.*'"

"Were you and *she* making the beast with two backs?"

"Bewks."

"You sort of get the impression from this article that you were."

"Yes, that was Myn's takeaway, too," Bird said. "Can't imagine why she'd have drawn such an inference."

According to an eyewitness who insisted on anonymity, Templeton and McIntyre recently spent the night together at McIntyre's condo in Rosslyn, which he calls his "Military-Industrial Duplex." According to this witness, Templeton was seen leaving the condo dressed in evening clothes as the sun was coming up.

Bird wondered who the eyewitness could be. That cranky retiree woman in 14F, the one Bird had—ever so politely—asked if she might ask her yappy Pomeranian not to start barking at five in the morning?

"If it's the Chinese you're worried about," Bewks said, "don't. They want a piece of you, they're going to have to come through the Fifty-sixth Virginia Volunteers. And the Fifty-sixth is ready to engage." He smiled. "The boys are right eager to help out there. It's not every day you get to go up against the People's Liberation Army."

Bizarre as Bird found the idea of being protected from Chinese hit teams by people dressed as Confederate soldiers, there was a certain poignancy to it. As they sat on the porch sipping bourbon, six of the boys from the Fifty-sixth had established a picket line at the end of the driveway, where they stood, bayonets fixed, squirting chewing tobacco at the feet of the assembled reporters and cameramen, daring them to take just one step onto McIntyre land.

"I appreciate that, Bewks," Bird said. "It's a comfort to me."

"The boys would relish the opportunity."

"It would make for unusual living history," Bird conceded. "But I expect if and when the enemy comes, it won't take the form of a frontal infantry assault. More likely some little-bitty guy in black shimmying down the chimney and tippy-toeing up and poking me in the back with a poison-tipped needle. Poison." Bird laughed. "Wouldn't there be some symmetry to *that*?"

"Any Chinese comes wigglin' out of that chimney is going to find himself staring down both barrels of my twelve-gauge. And it ain't loaded with birdshot."

"Could I have some more booze, please, Bewks?"

"Course, big brother. Here you go."

Bird snorkeled another pipette of old-fashioned and let his mind stroll through the field out front. The sun was low now, at a slant, turning everything blue and gold. Dragonflies hovered and buzzed like tiny helicopters. Bird had always thought dragonflies the most orderly and businesslike of the insect species. Bumblebees never seemed to be able to make up their minds which flower to imbibe from. But dragonflies went right to it. And their hovering was so precise. Well, God bless bourbon.

Bird wondered, and not with idle curiosity, how Beijing was reacting to the lurid revelations. They must be pleased at being vindicated of poisoning. Were Bird's and Angel's names coming up in various offices? Would there be retaliation of some kind? Legal action? Or might the response be more subtle? Bribe Peckfuss to put anthrax in Upkeep's well water? Snip the brake cables on Bird's car? But no worries there—he didn't have a car anymore!

Maybe the *deer* was working for the Chinese? Assassin deer. Why not? Hadn't the U.S. Navy trained dolphins to plant mines?

Deer. *Might use that in the novel.* Yes, he must get back to the novel now that he had all this free time.

Angel. He wondered, what paranoid fantasies were running through *that* pretty blond head? Had she "gone to the mattresses" in the Sicilian Mafia fashion? Was she bunkered in the "panic room" at the ICC, Burka and his clinking myrmidons standing guard? Or had she fled with young Barry? What fun for young Barry—his first hands-on experience of "extremism in the pursuit of liberty." Had they taken refuge at some proverbial "undisclosed location"?

Thus was Bird mentally perambulating with his bourbon-numbed brain when from inside the house came the ringing of the phone, for the—what—hundredth time today?

"Bewks, if you insist on answering that thing, just say 'No comment' and hang up. There is no one, including Elvis Presley risen from the dead, that I desire to speak with right now."

"Big brother," Bewks said, getting out of his rocker, "I've said 'No comment' so many times this week that I'm starting to say it in my sleep. I just need to see if it's one of the boys calling in to report."

He returned a moment later with the phone and a querulous frown. "It's *her*," he whispered.

"Myndi?"

"No, your other significant other."

Bird sighed. Honestly. What was Angel thinking, calling here? Not that it mattered at this point.

"Hello, Angel."

"Where the *hell* have you been?"

Bird marveled at the tone of annoyance, as if she were mad because he'd taken too long for lunch.

"I wasn't going to call you at your house," Angel said, "but your cell's voice mail is full. Why haven't you called me? What have you been doing all this time? It's been almost a *week*."

"I went deer hunting."

"Deer? It's summer. Deer aren't in season."

"Well, that depends what you're using. Gun or bow, then yes, they're not in season. But a car? Then you can hunt year-round. Would you care for a haunch of venison? Take two. My freezer runneth over."

"Oh. Are you okay?"

"Define 'okay.' Metaphysically? So-so. Physically, my elbow appears to be shattered and I'm wearing a neck brace on account of the displaced disk."

"Oh, baby. Ouchy."

"Ouchy? No, more like *Ahhhhhhhhh! Ahhhhhhhhh! AHHHHH-HHHH!* But here I am going on about me. How are *you*? Isn't it wonderful that the entire world knows our secret now and can share in our joy?"

"Darling, the entire world was going to find out about us sooner or later."

Stunning. Insouciance of this order you didn't encounter every day. She was skipping—hopscotching, like a carefree schoolgirl—over the fact that their machinations *and* his extramarital affair had been proclaimed throughout the land—the world!—in a leading newspaper.

"If it's any consolation," Angel said, "a friend of mine who lives out there in horse world called me. I gather Muffy's shacked up with Mr. Flying Stables. I assume you knew. That's why I figured it was safe to call you at home."

Consolation? Had Angel actually said *"consolation"*?

"C-c-con..."

"Oh, God," Angel said, *"please* tell me this hasn't left you with a speech impediment."

"Nnn..."

"Oh, great."

"No!" Bird said, bursting through the verbal dam. "I do not have a *speech impediment!*"

"That's a relief. For a moment there I imagined myself twiddling my thumbs waiting for you to get through 'P-p-please p-p-pass the p-p-potatoes.'"

"Your empathy is truly overwhelming."

"Empathy?" Angel said. "Would you like to hear about *my* week?"

"By all means. Did it include hooves coming through the windshield at sixty miles an hour? And being walked out on by your spouse?"

"Honey, I'll trade you what I've been through for all four hooves *and* the antlers. Fucking reporters. Honestly. They're all just swine in the end. That bastard made it sound like it was going to be a puff piece. Puff? Ha! Puff the Magic *Dragon.* This has been the week from hell."

"Gee, that's terrible. And it's been so peaceful out here. Well, there was the excitement of Myndi punching me in the stomach and then leaving. Otherwise, not much to report. My brother, bless his heart, has the Fifty-sixth Virginia Volunteers standing by in case the PLA shows up. Oh, and the Fifty-sixth has artillery. A six-pounder! Of course, the guy in charge of the cannon is whacked on OxyContin. But as we all know, you go to war with the army you have, not the army you want. Yes, sir, we are ready for anything here at Fort Randolph."

"Randolph," Angel said, suddenly all cuddly. "Momma *misses* Randolph. Can Momma come out and play? I'll bring Barry. He loves the country."

For the third time in this conversation, Bird felt as though he'd been slapped across the face with a dead haddock.

"You want to come here? With Barry?"

"Well, it's not like Muffy's going to mind, is she?"

A *fourth* smack of haddock! This was no mere insouciance. No. This was surely something more…clinical. Something that ended in "-opathy," or "-cism." He must go online later and research. Yes.

"Darling," she said, a term of endearment that Bird was not actually in the mood for at the moment, "I really could use some R&R. It's been a circus here. I'm beat. I can't even go to the ladies' room without doing an interview. Oh, my God, I forgot to tell you—*60 Minutes* is doing a segment on us. They really, really want you to participate."

"You're giving…interviews?"

"Darling. You're supposed to be the big PR genius. Yes, I'm giving interviews. When the sun is shining, make hay! I've been spinning like a top. My head is about to come off. I'm taking the position that of *course* we gave the story to the Indian paper. But that they called us first. I'm saying we had solid evidence but couldn't reveal it because we had to protect our sources. I know that's slicing the bullshit a bit thinly, but at this point who cares? The center of gravity has moved on. Now everyone's furious at Beijing, not just because of Saffron Man but also the Taiwanese shrimp boat. By the way, Saffron Man must be getting a bit…ripe by now. It's been ten days. Everyone's waiting for the final autopsy report, not that that matters much anymore. Oh, my God, did you hear? It came out this morning—the White House offered to plant him at Arlington National Cemetery! And—get this—the Tibetans nixed it on the grounds that it was too military! Do you love it? Have you really not been following any of this? You do have television in Virginia, don't you? Oh, my God, did I mention? I've had *three* offers for my own show!"

Bird thought, *Maybe some form of Asperger's?*

"There's so much I want to discuss with you. I've still got TV trucks parked outside the ICC. It's actually getting annoying."

"You used to love TV trucks."

"I'm loving them less now. Have you got media there?"

"Yes. But that's the nice part of living in the country and having a long driveway. The Fifty-sixth are manning the gate, pointing flintlock rifles at them."

"Muskets," Bewks said. "Enfields."

"Sorry, Angel. Muskets, not rifles. That must be making for interesting photo ops. Maybe it will bring about a paradigm shift in celebrity paparazzi protection. You rent yourself a Civil War regiment and bivouac them at the end of the driveway. Might have to pay extra for the six-pounder."

"Can I come and bring Barry? He's a little freaked out by what Momma's going through."

"Nice as that might be," Bird said, "I don't think so just now. We pride ourselves on our hospitality out here in Rappahannock County but I'd just as soon Myndi—wherever she is—not turn on her TV and see you pulling up at the gate. With Barry."

"Bird," Angel said, "Muffy has left the building. Okay? She has moved in with Mr. Flying Stables. Deal with it."

"It's *Myndi*. With a *y*. You might want to practice saying it. For when you're deposed by her divorce attorneys."

"Darling." Angel laughed. "I've been through so many of those I could do it in my sleep."

"Well, that makes me feel all the more special. But the answer is no. You may not come here."

Silence.

"Fine. If it makes you happy to be out there with a bunch of *morons* dressed up as Civil War soldiers, wallowing in self-pity, go for it. Far be it from me to intrude on your bliss."

"Angel," Bird said, "the Fifty-sixth Volunteers are not quote/unquote morons. They are my brother's friends and boon companions. And they may be the only thing standing between me and the Chinese dragon."

"Who's she calling 'morons'?" Bewks spoke up. "Did she just call us morons?"

"She didn't mean you personally. You weren't calling my brother a moron, were you?"

"Not specifically. It was more of a generic statement."

"She says she wasn't talking about you. It was a generic statement."

"Yeah? Well, you tell Ms. *Templeton* she can kiss my generic—"

Angel said, "I'm gathering this isn't a good time."

"A good time? No, I wouldn't call it that."

"I'll let you deal with Jeb Stuart. But will you give Randolph a message from me?"

Bird sighed. "In the event I run into Randolph, yes, I'll give him a message."

"Will you tell him Momma misses him?"

"I'll tell him." Bird handed the phone back to Bewks. "Well, that was enjoyable."

"Who the hell is Randolph?" Bewks said. "Is he a pleasanter individual than *her*?"

"She."

Bird and Bewks had shared many a confidence over the years, but right now Bird was not in the mood to explain about Angel's bizarre boudoir nomenclature.

"He's some...oh, God knows *who* Randolph is. Bewks, we are dealing with a complex human psyche here. And I'm not a hundred percent sure about 'human.' Her name is Angel, but I'm beginning to think she may have been sent here by the Dark Lord himself, in the vanguard of the apocalypse."

Bewks considered this weighty statement. "Well, big brother, it's your neck and your pecker."

"Fix us another couple of these things, would you, Bewks?"

LATER, AFTER DINNER and another tender bedtime moment upstairs with Mother shrieking at them about the colony of ferrets that had supposedly taken up residence in her bed, the brothers returned to the front porch. The night was moonless, full of stars.

Bird had soothed Bewks's wounded pride over Angel's "morons" remark by sharing with him the strange business of Randolph. Bewks found the revelation amusing but also troubling. His analysis was that Randolph must be some prior lover of extraordinary sexual ability who might turn out to be "even more of a nutjob than her."

"She."

"What if *he* shows up, armed and jealous?"

"Well, I doubt he'd get past the Fifty-sixth."

"The Fifty-sixth Virginia *Morons*?"

The brothers laughed. They watched the sky and soon were at the old game they'd played as boys, lying side by side in meadows at night, seeing who could spot the most passing satellites.

"Got another," Bewks said. "That makes three for me and none for you." He chuckled. "And *you* working for a company that makes them."

The idea came to Bird, in all its elegant simplicity.

"Bewks. For a moron, you're a genius."

"Don't know about that," Bewks said, "but I bow to no man in the field of satellite spotting. *Whup*—got another one. Four for me. None for you. I believe you may be losing your touch, big brother."

CHAPTER 39

A Thing of Rare Beauty

M y, my, my," Chick Devlin said into the phone with an air of apprehension, "if it isn't Mr. Radioactive. I was beginning to wonder when you'd check in."

"I've been at a disclosed location."

"Yeah, I caught a glimpse of it on the TV. Who are those people pointing bayonets at the media?"

"Too complicated to explain."

"Well, guess it's about time someone pointed bayonets at those bastards. You, uh, holding up?"

"I've got something for you. Something hot."

"Oh, hold on, old buddy. You're just a tad toxic right now. To be honest, when I saw it was you calling, I wasn't a hundred percent sure I was going to pick up."

"Really? And why would that be? Old *buddy*."

"That article in the *Post* didn't exactly bathe our company in reflected glory. There are folks in the building here think we ought to—"

"Cut me loose?"

"Well, put a bit of sunlight between us, anyway. Till things calm down."

"Let's review, shall we?" Bird said. "You tasked me with whipping up anti-China sentiment. Would you agree that the whole world is in a veritable lather of anti-Chineseness?"

"I'll stipulate that, yeah."

"And now you're telling me the company needs to put a little 'sunlight' between it and old Bird?"

"Oh, come on now, Bird—"

"No, Chick," Bird said, "we are well past the point of 'Oh, come on now, Bird.' We passed that mile marker light-years ago."

"You did a hell of a job. And you will be compensated. Don't you worry about that."

"Were you thinking thirty pieces of silver?"

"No need to get insulting."

"Sorry. Must be the meds."

"If we gave out decorations, you'd be up for a Silver Star with V device. But be reasonable. As CEO of this company, I'm the custodian, the steward of Groepping's good name."

"Steward? Oh, I like that," Bird said. "Okay, then, you being the steward, would you be the go-to person?"

"For what?"

"Well"—Bird chuckled—"if you think Groepping's 'good name' needs a little buffing up now, just you wait until my memoirs are published."

"Your memoirs?"

"Yes. Oh, it's been quite a week, Chick. It started out with a bang. A real one. I had this collision with a deer a few days ago. You know how people who've been through traumatic experiences—hospital, prison, foxholes, what have you—sometimes, after they emerge from their dark night of the soul, they have these...epiphanies? Sometimes they take the form of getting religion. Sometimes losing religion. Affects different people in different ways. Anyway, *my* epiphany took the form of wanting to share with the world just what a skunk I've been. Now you might say, 'But, Bird, old buddy, that newspaper article has already *told* the world what a rascal you are.' But then I would say to you, 'Oh no, Chick, it didn't nearly explain what a scoundrel I am.' However, the general public's appetite has, to be sure, been whetted to hear more. This is America. The people demand to know more about their scoundrels. And being Americans, they're willing to pay top dollar. How do I know this? Well, I'll tell you. My phone has been ringing off the hook. Publishers. New York–type publishers, the real deal. Waving fistfuls of cash. Do I love this country? I *do*! And is it not ironic? Here I've been trying to sell these folks my novels for years—couldn't even get them on the phone. Now they're elbowing one another in the ribs trying to be the first to have lunch with me. Still there?"

"I'm here," Chick said.

"Want to hear the working title? *Bull in the China Shop*. Do you like that? I *love* it. Did you get the bull reference? Taurus? Bull? Is that clever or what?"

Chick groaned.

"Here's the subtitle: *The True Inside Story Behind Project Taurus and My Sorry-Ass Role in It All.* I know it's long, but doesn't it draw you in? Make you want to hear more? It is self-derogatory, but I'm going for a confessional tone. Like *The Confessions of St. Augustine?* Well, that might be putting it a bit grandiosely. But the revelations speak for themselves. Let me read you an excerpt. It's from the scene—one of my favorites, but there are *so* many—where I'm standing in your office, the very one you're sitting in right now, and you're telling me to go foment you some China bashing in order to grease your weapons system through the Congress and Pentagon. Listen:

"Bird, we need to educate the American people as to the true nature of the threat we face. If we can do that, then those limp dicks and fainting hearts and imbeciles in the United States Congress—God love *them*—will follow."

Bird chuckled. "Won't those limp dicks and fainting hearts and imbeciles in the U.S. Congress—the ones you work with on a continuing basis—think that's a dilly? Want to hear the part about the muons?"

"Bird—"

"I tell you, Chick, I feel a complete fool. A gold-plated fool. All these years I've been staying up nights writing novels till my fingertips go numb. And now I find out that writing nonfiction is so much easier. You don't have to invent anything, see. The words have been flowing like water. I'll be e-mailing you chapters as I write them. So you can check your quotes."

"All right, Birdman," Chick said. "I'm sweating blood here. What's it going to cost me?"

"Oh, Chick. I was so hoping you wouldn't say something like that. How long have we known each other? Do you really think this is about blackmail? I find that sad. But then I found it sad that you began this conversation by intimating that you were going to toss your old buddy under the bus. How did we ever arrive at this sorry juncture?"

Silence.

"And now," Bird said, "you can relax, old buddy. All that stuff I just told you right now about publishers and my memoir? It's all bull. Not that publishers haven't been calling. Oh, they have, believe me. But I have no plans to put pen to paper. As of now, at least. So shall we start over?"

"I'm flailing, Birdman. I'm pissing down both legs. What do you want from me? Put me out of my misery. Anything!"

"I would like my old job back."

Silence.

"Bird." Chick sighed. "How on God's green earth is that going to look? My board of directors would have my ass for supper."

"And a fine supper it'll make, your ass being so cute from all those hours on the StairMaster. But I think you may be wrong there. Walk with me, Chick, walk with me out of the valley of darkness and into the sunshine. I confidently predict to you that the board will not only be delighted to have old Bird back but will instruct you to double my salary. There might even be a bonus in there for you, old buddy. As I mentioned at the beginning of our little chin wag, I have something for you. A thing of rare beauty. Of such blinding brilliance that I have to put on sunglasses just to think about it."

"All right," Chick said, "but let me turn on some background music. Chopin's Funeral March, something along those lines."

"Music? If it's music you want, you got Handel's *Messiah* there on your iPod? Put it on the 'Hallelujah Chorus.' And crank up the volume loud enough to wake the possums. Okay, old buddy, here's the deal..."

CHAPTER 40

I'm Going to Make You a Star

R ogers P. Fancock, director of national security, sat at his desk in
the White House, mentally composing a letter of resignation.

Dear Mr. President, it is with the keenest reluctance that I . . .

No.

*Dear Mr. President, when you asked me to take on the great
responsibility of . . .*

No. For God's sake, Fancock, he's an old friend.
Whatever the wording, the fact was that the good ship *Fancock*
had finally gone up on the shoals of desolation. He was just too goddamned old for this.

Of course he couldn't resign now, in the midst of the crisis. But
when the situation resolved—*if* it ever resolved—he was going to walk
in there and tell the president that the time had come to hand the baton
to . . . anyone, really. At this point Rogers P. Fancock did not care.

As for the president, his mood these days ranged from dismal (on a good one) to foul (on a bad one). The sinking of the Taiwanese shrimp boat had caused such a furor that he had no choice but to approve the sale to Taiwan of seventy-five F-22 fighter planes and four Aegis-outfitted destroyers—*four*! This was especially painful, as he'd spent the previous two years making every effort *not* to sell more arms to Taiwan. Now what choice did he have? Even the leaders of his own party had started asking—out loud—if he was showing enough "spine" in dealing with the People's Republic. At times he felt that the only one who really sympathized with his predicament was...the president of *China*, for God's sake. They were spending so much time on the phone to each other, holding each other's hand and moaning about the hard-liners—it was beginning to resemble a high-level support group or AA meeting.

Now, as a result of the Taiwan arms sale, Fa informed him that the Central Bank of China was making noises about sitting out the next auction of U.S. Treasury bills. The stock market was doing quadruple-front-flip triple gainers off the high board, gas prices were spiking at the pump, people were being laid off everywhere. But there was some good news, at least: Gold was at an all-time high! Yay! So if things got really bad, people could buy groceries with twenty-dollar gold pieces or coupons from their gold stock certificates.

"Rog," the president said in dolorous tones, "we need to get this goddamn thing *behind* us."

Which left the unhappy Fancock to relate, in sepulchral tones, that he had just that moment gotten off the phone with the Dalai Lama's people, who were declining the kind offer of burial in Arlington National Cemetery. With all due respect, His Holiness preferred not to rest in a necropolis of soldiers. They were still, against all logic, holding out hope of burial in Lhasa.

And now *no* country wanted the Dalai Lama's body, for fear of triggering China's wrath. India, where His Holiness had resided all these years, had formally demurred, citing some obscure provision in *its* health code about repatriation of non-Hindu remains.

Outrageous! But not everyone was refusing. No—Taiwan was *eager* to have the honor! They were offering to build him a funeral monument "that would be visible from the mainland." Wonderful. And won't that just solve everything?

"*What*, Bletchin?"

"Mr. Strecker, sir, on the secure line."

"Very well."

"Sir, are you feeling...all right?"

"Why, Bletchin?"

"You look a bit tired."

"I am, Bletchin. And years from now, when you're sitting in this chair, you, too, will know the meaning of true weariness. But thank you for asking. Hello, Barney."

"You sound kind of beat. You all right?"

"I'm taking it one day at a time. What fresh hell do you have for me today? Dorothy Parker said that. I'm going to have it put on a sign over my door."

"I got something'll put a big smile on that Brahmin face of yours. You remember me telling you about my new best friend?"

"Yes."

"She and I have had the most beautiful meeting of minds. I just love working with this lady. Wish we'd gotten together before. The music we could have made. But never mind all that. Rog, the three of us—you, me, and Ms. Chang—are going to put on a performance. And you, my friend, you got the lead part! I'm going to make you a star. How about that? You didn't even have to sleep with the producer. Rehearsals start tomorrow morning. Tell your dogsbody Bletchin to carve out some quality time on your schedule for me. I'm catching an Uncle Sam red-eye. Be there first thing in the morning."

"Should I bother to ask where you are at the moment?"

"San Diego. With my other new best friend. You remember him?"

"Yes. That's nice. It's hard to make new friends—at my age anyway. I'll see you tomorrow."

Fancock was wondering what this was about, but he was too tired to worry about it.

"*Yes*, Bletchin?"

"Sir, it's a Mr. Charles Devlin calling for you? He says he's the CEO of Groepping-Sprunt, the aerospace giant."

"I *know* who he is, Bletchin. Why is he calling?"

"He declined to tell me, but he insisted that you would want to take the call."

"They all say that. Oh, very well. But in five minutes come back in and announce in a loud voice that the president wants to see me right away."

"Yes, sir."

"Mr. Devlin. Rogers Fancock. How can I help you?"

Bletchin entered five minutes later and said in a loud voice, "Sir, the president is asking for you."

Fancock made a cross face and waved him off.

Bletchin retreated, feeling somewhat brusquely used. But whatever it was had put some color back in the chief's face. He'd been looking so gray lately.

Twenty minutes later Fancock buzzed Bletchin back in. The chief looked pink and animated.

"Bletchin, get me that damn monk, Jigpong. And don't let them tell you he can't come to the phone because he's *praying*, the way they did the last time."

"Yes, sir."

"Bletchin."

"Sir?"

Fancock sighed. "What *is* his name? I wrote it down somewhere, but I can't find it."

"Jangpom, sir. Jangpom Gad—"

"Got it. Quickly, man. Quickly."

"Sir, I have His Reverence on line one for you."

"Well done, Bletchin. Your Reverence? Rogers Fancock here, at the White House…Yes, and good afternoon to you, sir. I trust you and the other reverences are holding up?…Excellent. I'm calling with what I think is very positive news…Yes. I think we have a solution to our situation. In fact, I dare to think you'll find it not only dignified but also rather exciting…Well, the idea is for you to proceed with your rituals. Stupa, I believe it's called, if I'm not mistaken?…Yes. The wrapping and anointing and all the rest…Oh, I'm a big believer myself in tradition. Where I come from we…well, never mind that. But now once all that's taken care of, His Holiness would be placed inside a… satellite…Satellite…Yes…Sputnik? Well, yes, but that was a very long time ago. The ones now are ever so much more advanced… Why a satellite? Well, I'll tell you why. And this is the part that I think makes this such an elegant solution. You see, the satellite would be launched and go up there into the, you know, upper atmosphere and then take up geosynchronous orbit over—…Geosynchronous? Ah, how to explain…Essentially, the satellite would—I don't know if *hover* is quite the right word, but it would be positioned directly above Lhasa…Um-hm. Exactly. Directly above. Smack dab above the Potala Palace. I hope I'm pronouncing that correctly…Good…Yes, I understand that's where many of the previous dalai lamas are resting. So His Holiness would be up there looking down on them, and they'd be down there looking up at him. I find that…a lovely thought…How do they do it? Golly, Your Reverence, don't ask *me* to explain. I'm no physicist. But I assure you they can. Oh, yes. Our scientists are… well, of course I'm biased, aren't I, but I'll put our scientists up against anyone's. Mm…Mm…Um-hm…Really? That's just wonderful, sir. I couldn't be more pleased. So you'll put it to the other reverences?… Marvelous. Marvelous. And you'll let me know straightaway? I can't thank you enough…Sorry?…Well, they're not cheap, but—…Oh, no. No, no, no, sir, we wouldn't dream of billing you for it. It would be an honor. A great honor. A gesture of our country's respect and esteem for His Holiness…Oh, you're very welcome. Very welcome indeed…Yes, and a very good day to *you*, sir."

CHAPTER 41

Beware of Americans Bearing Lotus

F a had readily agreed with *his* new best friend, the American
president, that it was indeed an "elegant solution." General
Han viewed things otherwise, with characteristic asperity.

The minister of defense had been rattling on for ten minutes,
fulminating about the "Trojan horse" the treacherous Americans
had devised. Fa wondered if Han had ever read *The Iliad*. He rather
suspected not.

"And, Comrades, is it necessary to point out *who* is the manufacturer of this thing? This so-called *satellite*? Groepping-Sprunt! The
same company that is at work on their muon weapon!"

Fa conceded that this *was* an inconvenient detail. But the American president had explained, with convincing sincerity, that Groepping was in fact a maker of satellites and, moreover, had one "on the
shelf, ready to go."

"Comrade General, I have been in regular contact with the
American president—"

"Oh, yes." Han smiled. "We know—don't we, Comrades?—
how much you enjoy talking to *him*. Did he send warm greetings to
the rest of us? We're starting to get jealous!"

Laughter.

No, Fa told himself, *don't.*

"As I was saying," he pressed on, "I have been in close communication. And I am persuaded that he wants to resolve this situation as much as we do. Meanwhile our goods are piling up on the docks in Shanghai. Stacks of containers, getting higher and higher. Do we want them to become as high as our skyscrapers? Surely not."

"You worry about exports," Han said. "Let *me* worry about the security of China."

Murmurs.

"I assure you, Comrade General," Fa replied, "China's security is my utmost concern."

"Is it? Well, if you say so, then I am glad to hear it." Han looked about the room. "Comrades, I am not a man of words. I am not the clever speaker that Comrade President Fa is. I'm a simple man."

Fa suppressed a groan. *Here it comes: the peasant-warrior speech. The moving anecdote about how Hua Guofeng personally pinned on him the Red Star Meritorious Honor Medal for killing all those North Vietnamese "dogs."*

"But there is nothing simple about my love of our country."

Murmurs.

Fa thought, *Wait. I have heard that before. From an American politician... who stole it from a British politician! Wasn't there some big fuss over it? No, don't say anything. You can have a laugh about it later, with Gang, in the bathroom. Where you spend most of your time these days.* Meanwhile General Han's verbal tank clanked on.

"And I believe with this red peasant heart"—he patted his chest—"that beats in my breast for China that this is a trick by the Americans. A trick we must not allow, Comrades!"

Murmurs.

Fa said, as gently as he could manage, "Comrade General, even if we all agreed that this was the case—which I with my red peasant *brain* remain convinced that it is not—even if we all agreed, what can we do about it? Are you suggesting that I phone the American president and say, 'No, sorry, we can't allow this.' They do not *need* our permission. He is only extending us the courtesy of informing us of their plan."

"I'll tell you, Comrade," Han shot back, "what you can tell him. Tell him if they proceed with this plan to position this *insulting* object above Chinese soil—and surely we do not need to discuss whether the Tibetan Autonomous Region is Chinese soil—"

Murmurs. *Oh, yes, General, we're with you there.*

"—that China will consider this a violation of its airspace!"

"Airspace?" Fa said. "Two hundred and forty-five miles above Chinese soil? That's very thin airspace. There are already numerous satellites in our 'airspace,' if you're going to call it that."

"Then perhaps, Comrade, it is time that China asserted its legitimate rights." General Han turned to the others. "The heavens above, Comrades, are they not ours, as much as the earth below?"

"WELL," GANG SAID TO the accompaniment of what he and Fa now called the Symphony of the Faucets, "you did what you could. Perhaps if the satellite were made by some other company..."

"Certainly that did not help. But really, Gang, I nearly gagged when he launched into that peasant-warrior bit. Still it was smart of the old boy to drag the Trojan horse into the room. It was stupid of me not to have anticipated that." Fa laughed. "Beware of Americans bearing Lotus! What a durable metaphor, that Greek horse. Nearly three thousand years now. Not as old as China, but... Well, no sense in shedding tears. There's enough water in here as it is. If I were chairman of the Central Military Commission, I could overrule him. But if I tried to now, who can say how that would go."

Fa held out his glass to Gang, who held up his. "Now it is up to the vine. Either it must flourish"—*clink*—"or we must perish."

Gang mused. "If you said that in English, it would rhyme."

CHAPTER 42

MARVELOUS SKIN

D o you know, Barn, I feel a bit nervous," Fancock said, "as if I were going out on a date."

"You are," Barney said, "and with a dazzling lady. I feel like I'm sending my teenage boy off to the prom again. You got your lines in your head?"

"Yes. I've been rehearsing. I was in the bathroom this morning going over them, and Dorothy came in and heard me. Didn't know *what* to make of it."

"The maître d's palm has been greased. He'll put you in the corner table, nice and cozy. The reservation's under the name 'Plymouth.' I thought you'd like that."

"*Very* thoughtful."

"There'll be a young couple at a table at two o'clock to yours. Newlywed types, smooching, taking pictures of each other on their big night out in Washington, D.C. They're mine."

"Will the Chinese have people there?"

"Oh, yes," Barney said. "That's why we had you call your date at her office to invite her out. MSS listens in on all her calls. But just to make sure everything would look on the up-and-up, she made sure to call MSS after you called. To report the contact. So they'll have the restaurant wired seven ways from Sunday. As, indeed, will we." Barney laughed. "There are going to be more microphones at the Old Angler's Inn than in a recording studio. And you'll be going out live."

Fancock considered. "Well, now I *am* nervous."

"You'll be fine. But don't overdo it. This isn't *Hamlet.* Just be your pompous old Boston self and you'll kill. And remember—don't go into any detail about what's *in* the envelope that you're slipping her."

"You told me that already. Twice."

"Just slide it on over to her. You might do a little arching of the eyebrow. That ought to be easy enough for you. Say something brief, like, 'I must tell you, Ms. Chang, we are sorely disappointed. This is *not* the way great nations behave.' All huffy like."

"I do not sound like that."

"Funny, I thought it was pitch-perfect. All right, time you hit the road. You going to be okay driving?"

"Barney. I *can* drive."

"Just figured you might be a little rusty, being chauffeur-driven everywhere these days."

"I'm perfectly capable, thank you."

"Okay, then. Now, remember, your country's counting on you."

"That's what they told us before lowering us over the side at Inchon. Well, let's hope this is less messy."

"Rog?"

"Yes?"

"No footsie under the table, now."

"I'll try to control myself."

THREE HOURS LATER Fancock was back in his office with Barney, drinking eighteen-year-old scotch.

"She *is* lovely, I must say. Marvelous skin."

"Down, boy. Told you."

Barney took a digital recorder out of his pocket and put it on the coffee table in front of them. "Care to review your performance?"

"Not the entire performance."

"Greatest hits, then."

I appreciate your willingness to meet with me.

I am happy to help. This is a difficult time for both our countries. Normally I would have taken this to Ambassador Ding, for whom I have the greatest respect. But because of the extreme sensitivity of this material, to say nothing of its potential volatility, I thought this matter might be better handled outside normal channels.

I understand. This was also done during the Cuban Missile Crisis.

Yes. And with good result. Which I am very much hoping for here. Though I must say, Ms. Chang, my government is very disappointed. Gravely disappointed. I'm not here to lecture. But this is not how great nations conduct themselves.

Barney clicked Off.

"Nice, Rog. 'Gravely disappointed.' You sound like a boarding-school headmaster."

"I've had experience of that species."

Play:

When you examine the contents of this envelope, you'll appreciate why I did not take this to Ambassador Ding.

Why?

Ambassador Ding operates out of your embassy. It would be difficult if not impossible for him to keep this information from being seen by your security services, the MSS.

I would not know about such matters. I am a trade representative, as you know, Mr. Plymouth.

Stop.

"She was flirting with you. Flirting! I think she likes you, Rog." Play:

Yes, whatever the case, I'm hoping that you will contrive a way to get this information into the right hands, Ms. Chang. Much depends on this. Our hope—our very earnest hope—is that this was not authorized by your government. If it was... well, let's just hope it wasn't.

"Were your people able to identify which ones were the Chinese agents?"

"Oh, hell yeah. That table at eleven o'clock to yours? The two women, non-Asian, mid-thirties, business suits, bangs, ponytail. The one with bangs had on those eyeglasses supposed to make you look like a Dutch architect?"

"I missed them."

"That was the point. You were supposed to."

"So what now?"

"Well"—Strecker looked at his wristwatch—"right about now your very lovely date is at an MSS safe house in Bethesda transmitting the contents of that envelope you gave her via encrypted satellite transmission to MSS headquarters back in Beijing. Don't you wish it was still called Peking? Had a nice ring to it, though it did always make me think of ducks. It's eleven p.m. here, so noon tomorrow there. I'd give it no more than an hour to reach Comrade Minister Lo's desk. At which point he is going to have a very large bowel movement in his britches."

Fancock winced. "Barn, really."

"Sorry," Barney said. "At which point he is going to *shit* his britches."

Fancock winced anew. "Your hope is he'll delay taking it to Zhongnanhai and the Standing Committee?"

"The longer, the better. He'll spot this right off for what it is, but he'll want to get all his ducks lined up. I would if it was me."

"When do you post the photograph?"

"Weren't those lovebirds at the other table just darling? Imagine how excited they must have been to turn around and see Rogers P. Fancock, director of national security at the White House, in the flesh, along with that Chinese woman who's always on TV. Let's say they wake up around nine tomorrow morning. Post it on Facebook with a note saying, 'Look who was sitting next to us at the Old Angler's Inn last night! Anyone know who the Chinese lady is? She looks familiar.'

"Facebook being Facebook, they'll get a ton of replies—from their friends—saying, 'It's that Chang lady, the trade representative who's always on TV.' And when the lovebirds see that, they'll say, 'Heavens to Betsy, we've *got* to send this to the newspaper back home!' So they will, and the *Pittsburgh Post-Gazette* will go, 'Hey, neat little scoop,' and post it on their website. So let's say it's now ten a.m. here, eleven p.m. in Beijing. Now, a photo of Rogers P. Fancock and Winnie Chang having themselves a cozy dinner—I imagine that would go viral pretty fast, wouldn't you? So say another hour... and it'll be brought to the attention of Ambassador Ding. You know how ambassadors hate it when they think they're being left out of the loop? So let's say it's going on midnight in Beijing and Ding is on the blower to the Foreign Ministry screaming, 'What the hell is going on here? Why is the NSC director meeting with Chang?'

"With any luck, Comrade Lo will still be sitting on the so-called evidence. Which means he will have kept the information to himself now for about twelve hours without alerting party higher-ups. And now *his* phone will be ringing, telling him to hustle his fat butt over to Zhongnanhai and explain what the hell's going on."

Barney paused. "At least that's the desired scenario. You never know how these things are going to pan out. But I got a good feeling about this. Course, that could be from this fine whiskey of yours. Did that come over on the *Mayflower*, too? Or did you send it on ahead with the servants?"

AMBASSADOR DING TELEPHONED Foreign Minister Wu Fen at 1:00 p.m. Washington time, 2:00 a.m. in Beijing. Foreign Minister Wu deemed the matter serious enough for him to put a call through to the president at Zhongnanhai.

President Fa pretended to have been asleep. He listened to what the foreign minister said, hung up, and instructed Gang to summon an emergency meeting of the Standing Committee for seven o'clock in the morning. The precise reason for the meeting was not given. By 7:00 a.m., Comrade Lo would have been in sole possession for almost twenty hours now of the information that Fancock had passed along to Chang.

CHAPTER 43

An Obvious Fake

Minister Lo sat more upright in his chair than usual. Fa and the other members of the Standing Committee listened in silence to his version of events. When Lo had finished, Fa said nothing for almost a minute, as if trying to process the gravity of the situation.

"You say, Comrade, that you received this report from Comrade Chang at noon?"

"Yes."

"And yet you did not notify me or the committee?"

"As I explained, Comrade, I thought it was imperative first to analyze the material before bringing it to you and the Standing Committee."

Fa stared. "But as of last night, when I received the call from Foreign Minister Wu, you *still* had not reported the matter."

"As I *keep* saying, Comrade," Lo said with a trace of impatience, "I was still making my investigation. It would not have—"

"Indeed, so you do keep saying. But not reporting something of this gravity, for almost . . . twenty hours? This seems to me an inexplicable delay."

Lo affected nonchalance. "Comrade, the only 'gravity' here is the effrontery of the Americans, trying to lay this on our doorstep."

Fa stared at the file before him. He said, "I should like to view the hospital footage again, please."

A large monitor on the wall displayed the seven-minute, forty-six-second footage. Secret Service and Tibetan security agents stood outside the hospital room's door. A man wearing a white doctor's gown and ID badge approached. The agents inspected his ID badge. He nodded at them and entered the room. Six minutes later he emerged from the room. Though it was not visible to the naked eye, closer examination of the footage would reveal that the man's right earlobe was misshapen and that he was missing the fourth finger on his right hand.

"Now, this autopsy report—" Fa began to say.

Lo interrupted. "An obvious fake. Why would it take twelve days to determine whether he had been poisoned? Someone of *his* importance."

Fa read the paper in front of him. "According to this, the initial toxicology screen came back with possible false positives indicative of drugs. Specifically, cocaine. So they..." Fa read aloud, "'reran the tox screen, on a different medium'—the fluid in his eye. Which would account for the delay. It doesn't matter that he was famous. Science can only move at its own pace, peasant or prince."

Fa continued reading: "'Large hemorrhage transformation of left hemisphere in distribution of anterior cerebral artery'— stroke—'aqueous humor positive for barbiturates, cocaine, and ben-zodiazepine.'"

He looked up from the paper. "This is too technical for my understanding. But the conclusion clearly is that he was poisoned."

"Why would *we* poison him?"

Fa looked at Lo. "Comrade, as the entire committee is well aware, you *yourself* proposed this course of action to me one month ago."

"But the situation was different then!" Lo said, his voice rising. "Does it not strike anyone here as convenient that this so-called assassination is known only to us and to Director of National

Security Fancock? And of course your good friend the American president. Eh?"

"Take care, Comrade. You're in no position to hurl insults."

"Don't you see that it is *we* who are being insulted?" Lo was shouting now.

Fa returned to the paper before him. "As to how it has remained secret. According to this, when the final autopsy report was made, the hospital alerted the FBI. The FBI impounded it and the security-camera footage and sent their report to their attorney general. He took it directly to the president. The president and Director Fancock decided upon the present course of action. But rather than go to Ambassador Ding, Fancock gave it to your Comrade Chang, thinking she would be able to get it to us, thereby circumventing MSS. But being a good MSS agent, she delivered it immediately—to you. Where it remained. Until Ambassador Ding was alerted to Fancock and Chang's clandestine meeting because some tourist happened to snap their picture."

"Comrade, I will tell you one final time: I felt it my duty to study the matter before presenting it here. It's a trick, don't you see? It's obvious. Only a fool would fall for this! A fool like *you*!"

Fa stared at Lo and said in a calm voice, "You seem upset, Comrade. Well, I hope I am not a fool. But I freely concede that I am not capable of deciding whether this evidence is real or trumped up. It seems to me that the only course is to have a full investigation." He looked around the table. "Do you agree with my assessment, Comrades?"

"Investigation?" Lo said. "Only *MSS* has the competence to investigate such a matter as this!"

"No. We must follow correct party discipline and procedure. Such a matter must be referred to the Central Commission for Discipline Inspection. They are, after all, the 'Custodian of the Integrity of the Party.'"

Fa turned to the committee members. "Comrades, what do you say?"

Everyone except Lo and Han nodded.

"Very well, then. I suggest this be done with all urgency."

Foreign Minister Wu said, "What should I tell Ambassador Ding?"

"Nothing. *No one* outside this room should hear anything of this." Fa sighed pensively. "I will have to make some acknowledgment, at least, to the Americans that we are in receipt of what they have presented. But I shall state most clearly that we are in no way accepting it at face value. I shall say we are conducting our own investigation. Does this meet with your approval, Comrades?"

AN HOUR LATER Fa and Gang sat with their whiskeys, listening to the Symphony of the Faucets.

"Comrade Deputy Inspector Zen will take personal charge of the CCDI investigation?" Fa said.

Gang nodded. "This was the arrangement made by Admiral Zhang."

"But is it not known? About Lo and Zen's granddaughter?"

"Grandniece. No, it was all 'taken care of.' At the time, Zen was only a junior functionary. Lo was chief of Four Bureau. Zen feared that Lo would retaliate and only make matters worse. So he did nothing. After the girl was released from hospital, she was sent abroad. She's in Germany. Married. It's all ancient history, swept under the carpet. But not to Comrade Zen. I imagine he will conduct the investigation with zeal. As for Lo, per standard CCDI procedure, he will not be privy to the identity of the official conducting the investigation. Any interrogations will be performed by Zen's deputy. Rigorously, I should imagine."

"Yes," Fa said. "Well, after all, this is not how great nations conduct themselves, is it?"

"No, certainly."

Fa unscrewed the cap on the bottle. "Another?"

"Why not?"

CHAPTER 44

Bling-Bling, Boom-Boom

The explosion rattled the bedroom windows. Angel jerked upright in bed. "What the hell was *that*?"

Bird looked up dreamily from the picture book on his lap. "Hmm?"

"That *sound*. Tell me you didn't hear that."

"Oh, that? The boys, I imagine. Gettysburg is next week, and they're determined to beat the North this time." Bird went back to his book.

"It sounds like a war zone," Angel said.

"Then you ought to feel right at home."

"Barry is out there with them."

"Yes, hanging out with soldiers and firing cannons. Sounds like kid heaven to me. This book is really . . . amazing."

"Did you take another of those pills? You seem out of it."

"No," Bird said.

"This *isn't* what I had in mind by a quiet weekend in the country."

"You wanted to come. And here you are. Be in the now."

Bird couldn't take his eyes off the photographs in the book. Potala Palace, perched magnificently atop a cliff pedestal, Himalayan peaks...it looked like a stepping-stone to the heavens. A stairway to heaven. *That sounds familiar...oh, yes, Led Zeppelin.* What a sensation it must be to stand there in that rarefied air, to walk in the footsteps of the monks and lamas. Bird chuckled to himself. *Oh, no, my friend, there will be no tourist visa to Tibet for Bird McIntyre!* He was suddenly filled with immense sadness at the thought.

He sighed and turned the page. Yes, this was what he was looking for: stupas, the domed tombs of the lamas. *Whoa, look at this one.*

"Angel."

"What?" Angel said sullenly, not looking up from her book, a biography of General Curtis LeMay.

"Look at this one." He pointed. "This is the stupa of the thirteenth Dalai Lama. It's made from over half a ton of gold!"

"Who knew lamas were so into bling?" Angel sniffed.

"Oh, I doubt that the lamas themselves cared. It's more a Tibetan way of honoring their holy men. Look. They also built him a devotional pagoda. Made from over two hundred thousand pearls."

"He must have been *really* holy."

Another explosion shook the bedroom windows.

Angel threw down her book. "Bird—*do* something!"

"I'm sure if you asked them to stop, they would."

"I'm not going out there. They hate me. It was so nice of your brother to tell them all that I called them morons. They look at me like I'm—"

"The devil? No." Bird smiled. "How could you be the devil? Your name is Angel."

"Bird, you sound like a complete zombie. Are you sure you didn't take any of those pills?"

"Haven't taken one in two days. But you know, it's odd. I almost feel as though I *had* taken one. I feel this sort of...It's hard to describe. Contentment."

"I'm *so* glad."

"Look at this one." Bird pointed to a page. "It's made entirely from sandalwood and covered with eighty-two hundred pounds of gold. Whoa. That's *four* tons of gold! But this one only has eighteen thousand six hundred and eighty pearls. Hardly enough for a decent necklace." Bird giggled.

"These lamas," Angel said, "make the Renaissance popes look like Depression Okies. What a bunch of frauds."

"Oh, you shouldn't speak that way. Your name is Angel. Be angelic."

"Gold, pearls. Didn't Buddha drink out of a wooden bowl? How do you get from a wooden bowl to tombs that look like they were decorated by Tiffany?"

"Someone's in a good mood this morning."

"I just have a low threshold of tolerance when it comes to religious hypocrisy. They're all the same. They start with some lunatic raving in a desert—but at least they're poor lunatics. And some of them even have one or two good ideas, like 'an eye for an eye.'"

"An eye for an eye?" Bird laughed. "*That's* your idea of a sound religious precept? What about 'Blessed are the poor' or 'Love thy neighbor'?"

"OxyContin of the masses. They're all the same. The lunatic gets things rolling, and within a hundred years you've got priests, mullahs, rabbis, whatevers, making rules about who gets into heaven, who gets burned at the stake, and who gets his hand chopped off. Meanwhile the priesthood is building itself gold tombs. With pearl inlay. And now you're taking it to the next level—providing him with a two-hundred-million-dollar satellite stupa. They ought to call him Dalai the Fourteenth—the Sun Lama. And make you an honorary lama."

Bird thought, *Satellite . . . stupa . . . stupa satellite . . .*

"The launch," he said. "Don't forget—that's an additional forty-five mil."

"I can't believe Chick Devlin isn't gagging on the cost."

"Oh, no," Bird said. "Chick is a *very* happy man. Look at

all the publicity Groepping is getting. It's not every day we war-mongering defense contractors get this kind of press. No, Chick's over the moon. He's asked me to come up with a name for it. That's why I'm reading this book. For inspiration. And it *is* inspiring…" Bird's voice trailed off dreamily. "I really wish I'd met him. He was such an amazing person. So gentle. And all the things he'd been through."

"Maybe you'll hook up with him in the next life. As reincarnated *pandas*. Bling–Bling and Boom–Boom."

"You sound so cynical, Angel. Are you unhappy?"

"If you're starting to fall for this crap, I'd say you're not cynical enough."

"Yes, I suppose it might seem that way to you. But since the accident I've had this strange urge to let things go. Live and let live. Forgive. For instance"—Bird smiled—"I know it was you who told the *Post* reporter that you spent that night with me at the Military-Industrial Duplex. But as you can see, I didn't get mad. I didn't even mention it until now. I'm *not* mad."

Angel looked at Bird uncomfortably. "What are you talking about? Why would *I* blow you to a reporter?"

Bird smiled. "So that Myndi would walk out on me and leave you a clear field. But she almost certainly would have left me anyway, once she learned I had been working overtime with you to undermine international equestrian events. How ironic is that? I'm not being judgmental, but it wasn't very nice of you to sabotage my marriage." He laughed. "Listen to me! 'Not being judgmental.' Of course I am! And I went to bed with you in the first place, so I'm hardly in a position to point fingers at you. Karma. You just can't outrun it, can you? What I can't figure out is why I feel so…happy. Oh, well. Why question it?"

"It wasn't me," Angel said huffily, avoiding eye contact.

"Of course it was, darling. Remember I walked you to the

basement garage, down the elevator right next to my door? And you got into your car—your car with the tinted windows. So no one could have seen you leave. I probably would have figured it out sooner, except for my little head-on with the deer. Poor deer. I hope it didn't suffer."

Angel exploded. "The *deer*? One minute you're accusing me of sabotaging your marriage, the next you're whimpering about some deer? Screw the deer! For that matter, screw you!"

"That's a bit harsh, darling, but I forgive you unconditionally." Bird giggled. "Sorry. I know that must sound awfully condescending."

"You know," Angel said, "this is just not working for me. I don't know if it was the accident with the deer or this screwball religion, but you've changed. You're *weird*."

"I certainly hope so. I'm only just beginning to realize what an awful person I was."

"You were a lot more *interesting*."

Bird considered. "You may very well be right. That's always the challenge, isn't it? Not becoming a bore." He laughed again. "One person's inner peace is someone else's deadly dinner partner."

There was another explosion, followed by a whistling sound and a jarring metal *clang*. From outside came a sound of distant cheering and yipping—the rebel yell.

"All right. That does it. What the hell was *that*?"

"Bewks found this industrial boiler at the scrap yard. That boy. He towed it into the field by the woods. He and the boys use it for target practice. They like the noise their minié balls make when they hit it. Sounds like they're using it for artillery practice. Well, hurrah for the Fifty-sixth."

"That's it. I'm getting Barry." Angel jumped out of bed and angrily pulled on leggings and a shirt. She stormed from the room.

"Tell the boys well done for me," Bird said after her.

He just couldn't take his eyes off the lush, mesmerizing pages. It was then that the name came to him: StupaSat-14. A good and worthy name, a dignified blend of the theological and the technological. Yes. He must thank Angel for prompting him to it.

Angel. He felt a rush of elation and serenity. And sympathy. *Poor Angel*, he thought. *Such an unhappy vortex of anger and negative energy.* Sitting next to her in the bed, Bird had sensed waves pulsing out of her, dark vibrations. It didn't seem right, when he felt so at peace, even with cannonballs flying. He laughed. *The boys. Rascals.*

Bird turned the pages. He became aware of a voice. It sounded... foreign. He looked up to see who it was.

But there was no one.

He returned to the book and again heard the strange voice. Looked up. No one.

He realized then that the voice was coming from him. But what was it saying?

Om mani padme hum. Yes, of course—that mantra. Odd that he remembered it. Odder still that it sounded as though it were being uttered by someone other than himself. He vaguely remembered coming across it during his crash tutorial in Tibetan Buddhism. It was the mantra of... Chenrezig, Lord of Love, Tibetan bodhisattva of compassion. Strange. At the time Bird had thought it sounded quaint, silly. Oops, there it was again!

Om mani padme hum.

The syllables were pleasing.

Om mani padme hum.

He said it aloud, over and over. It felt as though he were giving himself a mind massage. The phrase made him smile. His vocal cords were vibrating like organ pipes. It tickled!

Om mani padme...

"What the *hell* are you doing now?"

"...hum?"

Angel stood in the doorway, hands on hips: a blond, scowling goddess.

"Were you *chanting?*" she demanded. "Were you actually chanting? Oh. My. God. Please tell me you weren't *chanting.*"

"But I was. Try it. It feels wonderful. Repeat after me: *Om mani—*"

"No!" Angel covered her ears with her hands. "No, no, no, *no!* I am not in the mood for *chanting!*"

"It might relax you, darling. You seem a bit tightly wound. You could try saying 'Randolph' over and over, but I'm not sure it would have the same effect. By the way, since we're coming clean with each other, could I ask—who *is* Randolph?"

A steely look of triumph came into Angel's eyes.

"It's the name I use for my vibrator."

Bird weighed this information. He nodded thoughtfully. "I'd guessed Randolph Churchill or Randolph Scott. Well"—he smiled—"I hope I measured up."

"Do you know what those Cro-Magnons you call 'the boys' are doing? Aside from firing cannons at boilers? Teaching my eight-year-old to skin a possum."

"Oh, dear."

"Yes, oh, dear. And he's covered in possum uck. He and his charming new friends are going to cook it. Where's the recipe from? *Martha Stewart's Deliverance Cookbook?*"

Bird felt a wave of very dark energy, as though his soul were being Tasered. He thought, *Interesting. Now, where is this coming from?* The answer came to him straightaway: revulsion at the thought of a living being turned into food for other beings. Suddenly the prospect of eating flesh was repugnant to him. Funny. And he'd always loved cheeseburgers.

"They make possum stew," Bird said. "It's part of the living history. They're very much into authenticity. I suppose it would hardly make much sense to dress up in 1860s uniforms and then order in pizzas and Big Macs, would it?" He smiled. "Bewks says it's not half bad, so long as you put in a lot of Tabasco sauce."

"It's disgusting," Angel said. "And probably riddled with rabies. I told Barry to come inside with me, and he wouldn't. Do you think any of them tried to help? No. They just stood there. Sniggering."

"I wouldn't take it personally. It's just their way."

"It was humiliating! And now I come back to the bedroom and you're *chanting*. What's that about? Are *you* trying to achieve some kind of authenticity? God, this is a nightmare."

"You know, darling, this mantra you find so annoying comes down to us through the centuries, all the way from Avalokiteshvara."

"Spare me."

"There's no exactly literal translation for it." Bird said. "And of course we Westerners *must* have our literal translations! At the heart of it is the idea—if it could be called an 'idea'—that if we take *mani* as our refuge, Chenrezig will never forsake us..."

Angel was staring wide-eyed.

"...and spontaneous devotion will arise in our minds and the Great Vehicle will be effortlessly realized." Bird winked at her. "Pretty neat, huh?"

Angel sat on the edge of the bed.

"Bird," she said, "please tell Momma that you just made all that up. It's from your novel, isn't it? That's it. It's from the novel."

"Oh, no." Bird shook his head and smiled. "I could never come up with something as deep or pure as that." He laughed. "Funny. Along with this weird serenity I've been feeling is the realization of how truly crappy my novels are. I should be sad or even angry, having wasted all that time and energy on them. But realizing that they suck feels so...liberating." Bird was waving his hands in the air joyously, like a man finally released from prison. "Why do I feel so darn *happy*?"

Angel stared.

"But getting back to the mantra," he went on, "the commentary on Avalokiteshvara is from Dilgo Khyentse Rinpoche. Wow. Where *is* this all coming from? I'm not questioning it. *Rinpoche* means 'priceless jewel.' And no, Miss I Hate Religion." Bird laughed. "Not gold or pearls. It's another word for 'lama' or 'teacher.'"

Angel looked about the room, as if sending out a silent 911 to spirit-world EMTs to come and rescue her from her maniac lover.

None came. She said, "I'm going now, Bird."

Bird smiled and nodded. "Yes. *Yes.*"

"Is that all you have to say to me? After everything?"

"You get it, Angel! You get it!"

"Get...what?"

"That we all have to go our own way—in order to arrive at the same place!" Bird held up his hands in a triumphant *ta-da!*

"O-kay," Angel said in an anodyne voice as she gathered her things and tossed them into her bag. "Momma's leaving now. Lea-ving. Lea-ving. Leaving *now.* Good-...bye."

A few minutes later as Bird was reading about the custom of sprinkling flakes of gold and saffron on the funeral shrouds of the dalai lamas, he became aware of shouting.

"Barry! Barry! Get in the car! I said now, young man! No, leave the bayonet!"

There was a commotion of ignition: a roar of exhaust, a revving of pistons, a sudden, violent displacement of gravel.

Then...silence. Laughter.

Silence. Lovely silence.

Bird wondered, *Is silence the sound of eternity?*

Yes!

CHAPTER 45

Lot of Body Parts
in That Sentence

CHINA THREATENS "DIRE CONSEQUENCES" IF U.S. PROCEEDS WITH PLAN TO STATION DALAI LAMA SATELLITE IN ORBIT OVER TIBET. The president stared balefully at the headline on his desk. "I thought you told me we had this under control."

"I told you that we were working *toward* getting it under control," Fancock replied.

"Convenient preposition, Rog."

"Patience, sir, patience. There are phases to this operation. Phases. Like the moon."

"All right. Trade you prepositions. When do we get to being *over* the moon?"

"From my point of view, sir, yesterday would not be soon enough."

"The launch is set for Wednesday, Rog. Today is Friday."

"So it is. And another blissful weekend of government service looms. Rest assured, sir, that Wednesday is the yin and yang, the omphalos, the telos, the ne plus ultra and sine qua non of my existence. Never have I looked on a Wednesday with such intense longing."

"What the hell is *that* supposed to mean?" the president said in a loud voice.

"It means, *sir*"—Fancock's voice rising with the president's—"that on Thursday either I will be standing here before you dancing a jig, even at the risk of looking ridiculous, or they'll find my lifeless body hanging from a rafter in the Indian Treaty Room."

The president stared. "Why the Indian Treaty Room?"

"High ceilings. Longer drop from the balcony. Cleaner snap."

"Fa called me again yesterday."

"Yes, I read the transcript. As is my practice whenever you speak with world leaders."

"And what was your takeaway?"

"That President Fa, too, yearns with all his heart for Wednesday to be in his rearview mirror. Sir, let us at least acknowledge—"

"For God's sake, Rog, don't tippy-toe with me."

"—that President Fa has more at stake here than you do. One way or the other, Thursday will find you sitting behind that desk, president of the United States. Thursday could find President Fa in a rather different situation. For him this is, well, life or death. So to speak."

The president considered. "I did pick up some tension in his voice. These reports about his weight loss and erratic behavior... We sure he's dealing off a full deck?"

"Oh, I earnestly pray so, sir. If not... well, I'd really prefer not to think about that."

"High stakes here, Rog."

"I am well aware of that."

"Shouldn't have let you talk me into this in the first place."

Fancock stared. *Oh, no you don't.* "Is that so? Well, *I* should never have let *you* talk me into taking this *job* in the first place."

The two men glowered at each other.

"Oh, stand down, Rog." It was said gently.

"I don't like being fitted for a coffin. If it comes to that, I'm prepared to walk the plank. It's not my style to pass the buck. You ought to know that by now."

"I do. But if Fa can't restrain his generals... Damn it, Rog, what if they shoot the thing down? Then what? By the way, why are we calling it 'StupaSat-14'?"

"Stupa is the name for Tibetan Buddhist tombs. And he was the fourteenth Dalai Lama. It was Chick Devlin's suggestion. I don't really care what it's called, frankly."

"But what if Han blasts it out of the sky?"

"Then," Fancock sighed, "we would have to respond."

"And then they'll respond."

"And indeed we will re-re-respond. And there you have the history of civilization in a nutshell."

"Christ, Rog. The sky'll look like the August Perseid shower. Shooting stars everywhere."

"Not a consummation devoutly to be wished, sir."

"Rog, could you not talk that way just now?"

"Sorry, sir. The encumbrance of a classical education. Look, let's stay with the playbook. Even if we wanted to beat retreat at this point, it's too late. Surely you owe it to your friend President Fa, whose neck is the one on the line, not to go wobbly in the knees."

"Lot of body parts in that sentence, Rog."

"Starting Thursday, I will endeavor to be more orderly in my metaphors. Assuming I'm not dangling from a beam in the Indian Treaty Room."

"Get out of here, Rog."

"Oh, gladly, sir. Gladly."

"Sir?"

"What, Bletchin?"

"Mr. Strecker on the secure."

"Speak to me, Barney."

"Just got the word. The jury has reached a verdict in *People v. Lo Guowei.*"

"When are they coming in?"

"Tomorrow."

"Damn it, Barn. We're up against the clock."

"What am I now, sergeant-at-arms of the Politburo Standing Committee? How about a pat on the back, here? 'Splendidly done, Barney.' 'Why, thank you, Rogers. It *was* rah-ther clever of old Barn, was it not?' 'Yes, and really, old bean, you must come for tea the next time you and the memsahib are on Bea-con Hill.'"

Fancock sighed. "Splendid job, Barney. Can we skip the rest? We're running out of *time.*"

"In other words, 'Thanks, Barn, but what have you done for me in the last five minutes?'"

"Barn, there's no *time* for stroking bruised egos!"

Silence.

"I apologize," Fancock said.

"That's some improvement."

"All I seem to do these days is apologize. If it makes you feel any better, five minutes ago I was in the Oval, apologizing to the Big Guy."

"We're moving Phase Two up. Sort of merging with Phase One."

"Thank God."

"You can thank God if you want. I know how you Episcopalians like to write thank-you notes. But Agents Mankind Is Red and Beluga have been breaking a little more testicle sweat than the Almighty has."

"Strange bedfellows, Barn. A former head of Chinese State Security and a Russian émigré Internet billionaire working together, one from a San Diego hospital bed, to penetrate through the Great Firewall of China."

"It's all about motivation, Rog. Zhang's as patriotic as the next

Chinese Commie, but Fa's been like a son to him. The chance to protect him *and* neutralize the guy who screwed him out of the top job at MSS—two birds in that bush. For Lev Melnikov, it's a tri-fecta: Lo messed up EPIC's China operations. This is the payback hack. Then there's the technical challenge, which, being a nerd, how could he resist? And never overlook the good old money factor. This thing works, I imagine EPIC will be back in business in the Middle Kingdom."

"If this thing works, I will bestow kisses on any part of their anatomies they so designate."

"I'll be sure to pass that along. I don't doubt they would both cherish having their derrieres osculated upon by the great Rogers P. Fancock. How's Dot doing?"

Barney Strecker was the only human being on the planet whom Dorothy Fancock allowed to call her "Dot."

"Giving me what-for about that photo. Apparently it's Topic A among the Georgetown ladies."

"Better be careful. Might get yourself a reputation as a dirty old man. All right. Start saying those Episcopalian prayers. I will be in touch."

"Please, do be."

THE FIRST ITEM APPEARED on the People's Liberation Army website, eight.one.nineteentwentyseven.cn.

Confidence in the leadership at the highest level is said to be dimin-ishing with rapidity. Many of our esteemed military commanders are beginning openly to question whether Fa Mengyao is up to the chal-lenge of leading China through the current crisis, brought about by the illegitimate Formosa regime's blatant and provocative spying on our coastal defenses by a so-called shrimp boat.

The second item went up on the website of the army newspaper, howgloriousisthesoundoftanks.cn. It questioned Fa's "erratic handling" of the Tibetan crisis and reported that the president had "tried to talk the members of the Standing Committee, including our beloved General Han, into allowing the stinking corpse of the self-proclaimed 'Buddha' to be given burial on Chinese soil. Fortunately for China, others in the chamber successfully protested against this capitulatory and dangerous gesture."

The third item, appearing on the PLA website redisthecolorofvictory.cn, was in a more satirical mode. It called attention to the president's "unaccountable weight loss," "haggard appearance," and "bizarre behavior." It closed with "Perhaps Fa Mengyao also has a pheochromocytoma in his brain. If this is the case, he should immediately depart China (quickly, please!) and go to Cleveland, Ohio, USA. Maybe the doctors there have improved!"

The fourth item, which went up on the military website theworldtrembleswhenourgeneralssneeze.cn, struck a minatory note:

Our great General Han is said to be "stomach-sick" at Fa Mengyao's continuing licking of the American boot and his craven willingness to allow the Americans and their fellow-traveling criminal Tibetan elements to colonize China's airspace. Fortunately, he is resolved to take action if the Americans proceed with their ill-advised provocative scheme.

There were a half dozen more similar items, appearing within twenty minutes of one another.

Strecker had a bet with Lev Melnikov that no item would remain online for more than five minutes. He lost. One stayed up for eight before being taken down.

CHAPTER 46

A Most Villainous Hack

President Fa glanced around the table. Never had the faces of
the members of the Politburo Standing Committee looked so
grim. The atmosphere of embarrassment was suffocating.

General Han stammered, "Comrade President, I...I..."

Fa held up a hand. "Comrade General, we have other business
to conduct first. Then we shall discuss"—he sighed heavily—"*your*
matter."

"They did not originate from within—"

"*General.*" Fa spoke so sharply that the members sitting nearest
him flinched. "Later."

Fa studied the folder before him. He began:

"This is the report of the investigation by the Central Commission for Discipline Inspection into whether our security organs
played a role in the apparent assassination of the Lotus in America.
For reasons that will not be necessary to explain, no duplicate copies
of this will be made. You may study this copy in this room, after our
meeting is concluded. In the meantime let me tell you what it says.

"'Item 1. Comrade Agent Chang followed correct MSS procedure by alerting MSS Beijing to the contact made by Director

Fancock. The meeting at the restaurant was at all times under surveillance by MSS–Washington.

"'Item 2. Autopsy report.'" Fa drew a breath. "The document appears genuine."

The room stirred.

"'Death was caused by intracerebral bleed secondary to hypertensive emergency. Metastatic pheochromocytoma. Cocaine intoxication proximate to the time of death. A copy of the full autopsy is attached to this report.

"'Item 3. Hospital security camera footage. Examination could detect no tampering, erasures, or insertions. Digital time stamp is intact and time-stamp encoding is consistent with chronology of Lotus expiration.

"'Item 4. Identity of individual seen entering and leaving Lotus's hospital room. Enhancement of film reveals certain physical characteristics (misshapen right earlobe and missing fourth digit on right hand). Examination of MSS Thirteen Bureau operatives produced positive identification.'" Fa looked up and said, "His actual name has been redacted." He continued to read: "'Identity confirmed MSS Bureau Thirteen operative code name TACONITE. American national. Chemical specialist. Twenty-three eliminations, North America and Canada. Present whereabouts TACONITE unknown.'"

Fa sighed.

"'Item 5. MSS encrypted text message to TACONITE. Decrypt of text phone message sent to TACONITE from MSS HQ three days prior to Lotus expiration reads: "Proceed Cleveland. Implement OP WHITEOUT. Fullest authority." Signed'"—Fa took off his glasses, leaned back in his chair, and rubbed his temples. He'd rehearsed the gesture with Gang—"'NIU. Ox. Operational code name MSS Lo Guowei.

"'Item 6—'"

"Save your breath, Comrade," Lo said. "And spare me having to listen to any more of this shit."

He lit a cigarette, inhaled, looked around the table slowly, from one member to another. "And you, Comrades. What about you? Are you all part of this shadow-puppet show? Eh?"

No one spoke. Most averted their eyes.

"What about you, Wu?" Lo said. "Did you throw in with our dear Comrade President because of what I know about your bank accounts in Zurich and Monaco? Eh?"

Fa thought, *Well, well. Tree is shaken and hidden birds fly out.*

Wu paled. "That's not so."

"Oh? In that case you won't have anything to worry about if the CCDI—Custodian of Party Integrity!—takes a look into it. What about you, Xe? Still sucking off that fourteen-year-old boy in Hangchow? Eh? Still trying to stick your limp little—"

"Lo!" Fa commanded. The room froze. *"Enough."*

Lo glared, his facial muscles twitching.

"You are dismissed," Fa said.

Lo stood. He stubbed his cigarette out on the table's polished wooden surface. "All of you. You will look back on this day and curse your mothers' wombs."

The door opened. Three CCDI agents were waiting to take Lo into custody.

The door closed. Fa let the air settle a moment. Comrade Ministers Wu and Xe looked as though they might be physically ill. Fa said to them gently, "Comrades, no one here is on trial. But if you need to be excused..."

Both Wu and Xe shook their heads.

"Very well, then," Fa said, "let us proceed with the next matter. General Han. Can you explain to us these...items that have been appearing on your websites?"

Han seemed more rattled than before, unnerved by the rapid takedown of his fellow cabal member Lo.

He protested vehemently that the "despicable items" were the result of "a villainous hack" clearly orchestrated by the Americans.

His technical people were vigorously investigating. More time was needed, but they would get to the bottom of it. Meanwhile each of the offending items had been speedily removed, within minutes—"seconds, even"—of appearing. All PLA website staff had been "taken into custody" and "were being interrogated with utmost rigor."

Fa flinched inwardly. He'd not anticipated this. "Do you mean, General, that they are being tortured?"

Han shrugged. "Does Comrade President truly think that I would not proceed with *all* necessary measures to find the snakes and rats at the bottom of this well? Rest assured, Comrade, this was an act of sabotage against China's national security itself!"

Fa said quietly, "You will release these people, General. Immediately. I will not have our fine military people subjected to that."

"They'll be released when I am satisfied of their innocence."

"*Now*, General."

Han went on, blaming the Americans, urging immediate cyber-retaliation, reiterating his indignation and fury, but he was a man giving a speech on the deck of a sinking ship.

Fa let him go on. When Han had finally exhausted himself, a mortified silence again descended on the room.

At length Fa said, "Let us follow procedure, Comrades. This matter too should be referred to the CCDI." He affected a look of corporate disappointment and shame. "I must say, we seem to be giving the commission much work to do these days."

Han objected that the CCDI had no military jurisdiction, but by now the water was up to his waist, and it was cold. A few moments later, he was gone from the room, for the last time.

FA SAT IN HIS USUAL SEAT, the toilet. Gang on a stool, opposite. They sipped their whiskeys to the accompaniment of the symphony.

Fa looked around the bathroom. "We won't have to have our

talks in here anymore, now. Do you know, Gang, I think I shall almost miss it."

"I won't miss having to pee every five minutes. All this rushing water. But it is tranquil, in its own way." Gang smiled. "The president of the People's Republic of China. General Secretary of the Communist Party. One of the most powerful men on earth. Hanging about in bathrooms. Let's hope *that* doesn't end up on a PLA website."

Fa considered. "That would be unfortunate."

The two men laughed and clinked glasses.

CHAPTER 47

How Are the Admiral's Kidneys Doing?

"Barney? Is that you, you rascal?"

Rogers P. Fancock sounded quite upbeat.

"You sound like you been sucking on helium, Rog. Don't fly away, now."

"Yes, I *am* feeling rather light, now that you mention it."

"Well, keep holding on to something. Can't have you floating off into the big blue. Not with all those satellites going by."

"Yes, it's going to be a little bit more crowded up there, isn't it? Tell me, are you with our friends?"

"I am. The Gang of Three is all here. Admiral Zhang sends his compliments. And Lev sends his regards. I owe him ten dollars. Can I bill that to the government?"

"Oh, I don't know," Fancock said, "I'd have to run that by Treasury. And we run a pretty tight ship, you know."

"Well, Lev being a Russian oligarch billionaire, maybe he'll cut me some slack. Let me pay him in installments."

Fancock thought he heard Melnikov's accented voice in the background pointing out that he was a naturalized American citizen.

Barney said to Fancock, "Says he's a naturalized American. But

I'd like to take a close look at his papers. Another ten bucks says they're forged."

"How are the admiral's kidneys doing?" Fancock asked.

"Better since he stopped taking that stuff that was spiking his creatinine levels."

"Good. Good. Well, the Big Guy had a *very* good phone call this morning with President Fa. President Fa said that he was mortified—mortified beyond *words*—by the unfortunate revelations about Minister Lo. He hopes the president will accept his word that Lo acted *entirely* on his own. Further, he very much hoped that we might see a way to keeping the revelations from ever becoming public. Of course I told him that the president said that would rather depend on whether China dropped its objection to the satellite. In that event, our president would incline to call it a day, dispose of the evidence and move on. By the way, did you hear the news that General Han resigned as defense minister? Health. Maybe *his* kidneys are failing. Anyway, it came over the news fifteen minutes ago—China is dropping its objections to the satellite."

"Big of them," Barney said.

Fancock laughed. "Of course, being China, they did it with a maximum of face-saving. The announcement came from some underdeputy of a department no one here's heard of before. It called the satellite a quote 'Practical solution to the dilemma of lama disposal.' Don't you love that? *Lama disposal!* Never miss a trick, the Chinese. Just when you're ready to give them a hug, they revert to form. Well, clarifies things anyway.

"You'll like this, too. They used the occasion to announce the identity of the fifteenth Dalai Lama. It appears that the new Dalai Lama is a twelve-year-old *Chinese* lad—living in Beijing! How convenient is that? Talk about an 'elegant solution'! And what do you know, his mum and dad are *both* loyal party members. What a coincidence, eh? Apparently mum and dad are a bit nonplussed by it all but they're—I'm quoting here—'willing to permit their son to be the living Buddha reincarnation so long as his comportment is consistent with party standards and doctrine.' Reminds me of what the lady said about Oscar Wilde and his gentleman friends. 'My dear, I don't care what they do so long as they don't do it in the street and frighten the horses.' The lad told Xinhua he wants to pursue a career in metallurgy—metallurgy!—once he's completed his military service. A very modern lama, I'd say. How do you suppose all this is going down in Lhasa? I wonder. I imagine now we'll have not one but two dalai lamas. Like the Avignon popes. Imagine my joy... Hold on, Barn. What *is* it Bletchin?...Yes, yes, tell him I'll be right there...Barn? Got to run. The Big Guy is calling."

Barney said, "Did you have that boy come in and pretend the president wants you just so you can get off the phone? I call that sad, Rog. After all I've done. I call that almost tragic."

"Well, you'll just have to wonder, won't you?" Fancock chuckled. "Maybe he wants to give me the Medal of Freedom. I'll admit—and only to you—I've always rather wanted one of those."

"That's fine, but if I was you, I'd keep my eye out for more incriminating photographs of you having cozy suppers in dark restaurants with beautiful women one-third your age."

"That *would* put me permanently in the soup with Dorothy. Well, toodle-oo, old friend."

"Toodle-oo?"

"Barn?"

"I'm still here, Rog."

"Well done, my boy. Damn well done."

"See? It's not that hard, telling someone you love him."

"Um. Can't promise I'll get used to it."

Look, the Crickets Are Dancing!

Bird and Bewks stood bathed in the orange glow of the flames, an unlikely pair: one in sandals and saffron robe, the other in the uniform of a colonel of Confederate cavalry.

Mother and Belle had been safely evacuated. Mother was now trying to bite the EMTs and being restrained by the pregnant Belle. The volunteer fire department had done what it could, but the conflagration, so spectacularly ignited, had spread quickly and voraciously, from the old pump house adjoining Upkeep. It had been a rainless summer. Upkeep's century-and-a-half-old wood was dry as tinder. And this time there were no devoted slaves to put out the blaze.

"Sorry about this," Bewks said. "Peckfuss. I can't believe he moved his damn meth lab into the pump house. No wonder he took off out of here like a scalded dog."

"I'm just glad he wasn't in the shed at the time."

"That's more understanding than I'm inclined to view the situation with."

Bird was smiling, holding his hands out toward the heat, as if to warm them. "Possessions," he said. "What a splendid fire they make!"

"Is that one of your Buddha deals? Not caring when someone burns down your house?"

Bird considered. "I have a lot of reading to do. I don't know if Chenrezig specifically teaches us to forgive those who fire cannonballs into meth labs next to our houses. But I guess the general drift is to live and let live."

"If it's any consolation, I'm sure Delmer Fitts is going to feel terrible about this. Once the Oxy wears off."

"Tell him it's no big thing. But he might want to correct his aim to the left a click or two."

"That's nice of you, big brother, but I don't think Delmer will be handling artillery for the Fifty-sixth in the future."

They watched the house crackle and burn.

"Look at the crickets in the firelight," Bird said. "They're dancing!"

"Looks more to me like they're trying to get the hell away from the fire. You didn't take any of those pills, did you?"

"Oh, no. My pain is over."

"Is it like being born again, only instead of Jesus it's this Chenzigger individual?"

Bird smiled. "That's such a complicated question, Bewks."

"You don't have to answer. Whatever it is, you seem pretty chill."

"Chill?" Bird held his hands out again toward the flaming house. "No, I'm warm."

Bewks gave him a look of concern. "You're not going to walk into the fire or anything, are you? I know Buddhist monks have a propensity to immolate themselves on occasion."

"Wow," Bird said. "It's so weird you should say that. I was *just* about to run into the fire!"

Bewks looked at him.

Bird grinned.

"Don't do that, big brother. Right now I'm not sure I'd put

anything past you, what with this transition you appear to be going through."

They watched the fire.

"It does seem a waste," Bird said.

"I know. Honest, I feel horrible about this. Soon as I'm done smacking Delmer unconscious, I'm going to find Peckfuss and—"

"No, not that. I was only thinking what an amazing living history of the burning of Atlanta you could have done with this. Your own *Gone with the Wind*! What a backdrop this would make!"

Bewks stared at his brother.

Suddenly Bird said, "No!"

"No what?" Bewks said with concern.

"It's perfect as it is! Why do we always say, 'Oh, it could be better'? When it's already perfect?"

"Not sure I have an answer to that, big brother. But I will mull on it."

"Look. The crickets!" Bird put his hand on his brother's shoulder. "See? They *are* dancing. Thank you, Bewks. Thank you for allowing me to share this moment with you."

Bewks didn't really know what to say to that, so he said, "You're welcome, big brother."

APPRECIATIONS
AND APOLOGIAS

Thank you, my very dear Mr. Karp, now at Simon & Schuster. A heartfelt *"Om mani padme hum"* to Living Karp Reincarnation Cary Goldstein at Twelve. Blessings and incense upon Dorothea Halliday and her team. Thank you once again, Amanda "Binky" Urban. My daughter, Caitlin, gave her old da precocious advice, as did beloved longtime (and long-suffering) first responders Lucy Buckley and John Tierney. Dr. Hege Mostad and the doctors of the LSHTM's DTM&H class of 2011. I plundered and pillaged like a Mongol in Richard McGregor's *The Party: The Secret World of China's Communist Rulers*; Andrew J. Nathan and Bruce Gilley's *China's New Rulers: The Secret Files*; Evan Osnos's fine reporting in the *New Yorker*; and, not least, in Henry Kissinger's magisterial Sino-summa, *On China*. My admiration for Terry Southern and Stanley Kubrick will be obvious from certain passages; and yes, I know it's *For Whom the Bell Tolls* (see page 240).

A number of actual people appear here under their own names, most conspicuously His Holiness the Dalai Lama, my good "taciturn" friend Chris Matthews, and, offstage, the aforementioned magisterial author of *On China*. Neither they nor any of the other real-life personages herein should be held accountable for my liberties. This *is* a novel, after all.

Finally, another large Milk-Bone to the Faithful Hound Jake, who kept the perimeter secure and barked, especially when no one was there.

Summer Solstice, 2011
Stamford, Connecticut

ABOUT THE AUTHOR

Christopher Buckley is the author of fifteen books, among them *Losing Mum and Pup: A Memoir* and *Thank You for Smoking*, which was made into a movie in 2005. He first visited China in 1974 as a guest of the government. He did not eat any puppies, but, out of politeness to his hosts, managed to choke down numerous sea slugs, the memory of which still makes him shudder. A spontaneous attempt to present Chairman Mao with a jar of American peanut butter resulted in his nearly being gunned down by unamused palace guards. He lives in Connecticut with his wife, Katy, and yellow Labrador retriever, Jake, who no longer retrieves, preferring things to be brought to him.

ABOUT TWELVE

TWELVE

TWELVE was established in August 2005 with the objective of publishing no more than twelve books each year. We strive to publish the singular book, by authors who have a unique perspective and compelling authority. Works that explain our culture; that illuminate, inspire, provoke, and entertain. We seek to establish communities of conversation surrounding our books. Talented authors deserve attention not only from publishers, but from readers as well. To sell the book is only the beginning of our mission. To build avid audiences of readers who are enriched by these works—that is our ultimate purpose.

For more information about forthcoming TWELVE books, please go to www.twelvebooks.com.